The Peacock Summer

The Peacock Summer

HANNAH RICHELL

ORION

First published in Great Britain in 2018 by Orion Books,
an imprint of The Orion Publishing Group Ltd
Carmelite House, 50 Victoria Embankment
London EC4Y 0DZ

An Hachette UK Company

1 3 5 7 9 10 8 6 4 2

A CIP catalogue record for this book is
available from the British Library.

ISBN (Hardback) 978 1 4091 5221 7
ISBN (Export Trade Paperback) 978 1 4091 5222 4

Typeset by Born Group

Printed and bound in Great Britain by Clays Ltd, Elcograf S.p.A.

www.orionbooks.co.uk

For Jess

PART ONE

'The hope I dreamed of was a dream,
Was but a dream; and now I wake,
Exceeding comfortless, and worn, and old,
For a dream's sake.'

Christina Rossetti

It does not take much to remain unseen in a house like this. A soft tread, a downcast eye, knowledge of the creaking stairs and loose floorboards that betray my presence. And the inhabitants, of course, so busy with their own lives – their troubles – their desires – so busy with themselves they do not notice the ones like me bearing witness from the shadows.

But I see them. I see it all. The things I am supposed to see – and the things that I am not. I see the flare of a cigarette lighter in a dark room, and the lipstick marks on a glass. I see the indentations on a pillow, the bloodstains on the sheets. I see furtive looks – trembling hands – clenched fists – tear-stained handkerchiefs.

It's all there – the secrets of their lives – if you will only look.

Because a house like this has eyes.

I am the eyes of the house . . . and I am always watching.

CHAPTER 1

She wakes a little after midnight, too hot and with the sheets tangled round her legs. Something insistent has pulled her from her dreams, tugged her from a fitful sleep. Lying in bed, the house stretching vast and silent around her, she tries to think what it could be. Rustlings. Whisperings.

She waits for it to come to her: the room. It is the room of trees. The sound of the wind moving through their branches, the trembling of the leaves. The trees are calling to her, singing their night song.

Ignoring the protestations of her old joints, she slides out of bed and retrieves the ornate brass key from its secret place, heading barefoot into the dark corridor, following the curved staircase down into the entrance hall, her feet feeling carefully for each step, her fingers trailing the dusty banisters.

A draught blows under the front door, its cool breath moving over her too-hot skin, sending a stray brown leaf scuttling across the tiles. She drags the heavy tapestry to one side and unlocks the door behind, following the winding corridor until she stands outside the room that has called her. She steadies herself against the doorframe, before stepping over the threshold.

She isn't entirely sure if she is awake or asleep as she walks ghost-like in her white nightdress among the trees, the musky scent of the place wrapping itself around her,

her hands running over smooth, grey bark, her fingers tracing knots and whorls as familiar to her now as old friends. Overhead, the canopy hangs dense and rich. In the darkness she imagines she can see its opulent flashes of blue and green and gold. And the eyes – those ever-present eyes – watching her as she goes.

Tiredness comes, as it does so frequently these days. She sits, allowing it to claim her. It is so easy to drift away. It is so tempting to leave the present and wander through chambers of the past – to return to familiar faces, cherished moments and memories. She meanders the corridors of her mind, only jerking awake at a piercing scream – high-pitched, like the shriek of a peacock, or a woman in pain.

Real or remembered she isn't sure, but the darkness looms all around her, thick and cloying. An acrid scent hangs heavy in the air. Her nightdress clings to her sweat-soaked body. She does not feel like herself. She does not feel well. It's not real, she thinks. None of it is real. But gone are the trees, the shimmering leaves, the watchful eyes. All lost in a thick cloud of soot and smoke. She presses a hand to her forehead. She is so hot – burning up – and the smoke – the black, smothering smoke – rolls ever closer.

She drops to the floor, afraid and disorientated, crawling on her hands and knees. Is it real or imagined, the voice she can hear calling to her through darkness? 'Lillian. Lillian, can you hear me?'

Her mouth opens to answer but no sound comes. Instead, smoke rushes in, filling her lungs, stealing her voice and her breath. The trees crackle and hiss. Orange embers rain down. 'I'm here,' she says. 'I can hear you.' But the words are lost and so is she, cast into suffocating darkness.

CHAPTER 2

It's 3 a.m. when Maggie stumbles out of the nightclub with two girls and a tall man with a snake tattoo curling up his forearm. The comparative quietness of the street outside and the cool air on her skin are a welcome shock after the heat and noise of the pounding drum and bass inside the warehouse. Maggie adjusts the fabric bag on her shoulder and turns to her newfound friends. 'How about a little adventure?'

'What exactly did you have in mind?' asks the man. Tim. Jim. She doesn't remember exactly.

'Follow me.' She leads him up the alley towards the glittering lights of Oxford Street, the girls tripping and laughing, arm in arm, as they trail behind. They pass a late-night kebab shop and a window display of Barbie-pink mannequins dressed in fetish gear. Outside a Seven-Eleven a homeless man sits with his head bowed, a ripped cardboard sign on the pavement in front of him and a brown Kelpie curled at his feet. Maggie spots the yellow light of a taxi drifting towards the city centre and sticks out her hand. She clambers into the back with the man, the girls jostling for the front seat. 'Clovelly beach, please,' she says and the driver, catching her eye in the mirror, nods and pulls a U-turn, heading out of the city towards the Eastern suburbs.

'The beach?' the man beside her asks, his warm hand sliding up her inner thigh. 'We *could* just go back to mine?'

He smiles, dimples forming in his cheeks, but she shakes her head. 'I want to see the ocean.'

'Is that someone's mobile?' asks the girl beside them.

Maggie listens. From the depths of her bag she hears a faint beeping – a phone that hasn't rung in such a long time she's almost forgotten what it sounds like. She lets it ring out, concentrating instead on the yellow lights of Bondi Junction sliding past the car window and the insistent pressure of the man's hand on her leg.

The taxi drops them in the car park beyond the surf club. Maggie slips off her shoes and leads them onto the rocky headland jutting out into the Pacific, the flat stone cold beneath her bare feet, the taste of salt in the air. She can feel the man following close at her heels but the girls are a short distance away, stumbling and laughing in the darkness. The sound of the waves below is a roar in her ears. She trips once but her companion catches her easily and holds her steady. His hands are rough and thick-fingered – a workman's hands. 'Where are you from?' he asks, sparking up a cigarette, passing it to her as they navigate the uneven platform.

She takes a drag before passing it back. 'England.'

'I guessed that much from your accent. Where in England?'

'You won't have heard of it.'

'Try me.'

'It's just a village. A speck on a map.'

'Called . . . ?'

'Cloud Green.'

He shakes his head. 'Nah. Never heard of it.'

'You're a long way from home,' says one of the girls, catching them up.

'As far as I can get.'

She finds a spot, as good as any, drops her bag then moves out across the ledge until she is at the very edge, looking down at the black water. It surges below her, just a hint of white foam glinting in the darkness.

'Is she all right?' she hears one of them ask.

She holds her arms wide and allows the air to hold her in place.

'Come back,' says the man with a nervous laugh; but she closes her eyes and trusts herself to the wind, the ocean rushing below. She feels like a bird – a gull – hovering on the breeze. She remains there until, scoured by the salty air, she turns and picks her way back across the rock to the group.

They sit and share a spliff, and Maggie, shivering a little now, wraps her arms around her knees. The man slings his arm over her shoulder, a cigarette dangling loosely from his hand. The girls get bored and peel away, back towards the lights of the car park, but Maggie stays put, staring out at the dark, roiling sea.

'So, what are we doing here?' he asks.

Maggie shrugs. 'I like the sea. It helps me forget myself. Besides, I wasn't ready to go back to the hostel. One of my roommates snores like a pig.'

'Fair enough . . . it's getting cold, though.' He grinds out his cigarette butt on the rocks then leans in to kiss her, the taste of tobacco and beer on his breath. 'I'd better warm you up.' His hands pull at the straps of her top, pulling them down over her shoulders, exposing her skin to the cool air. She leans back, his mouth on hers, his hands pulling at the zip on her skirt. She turns her head to the ocean, where the faintest glimmer of light sits on the horizon. She's not ready to face the morning. Instead, she closes her eyes and tries to forget everything but the sound of the waves crashing onto the rocks below and the sensation of this stranger moving on top of her, pinning her to the rock. With her eyes shut tight, and the sound of the water moving below, it could almost feel as though she's drowning.

When she wakes he is gone – it's just her and a couple of curious seagulls standing a few feet away, eyeing her with suspicion. Her shoulders are stiff and there are grains of sand stuck to the side of her cheek where she has slept with her face pressed against the rock. A procession of runners has begun to stream along the coastal path, the slap of their trainers a steady drum beat. In the car park behind her, two women in brightly coloured activewear stretch and chat. Their laughter pierces the morning. The sight of Sydneysiders going about their early-morning exercise makes her feel grubby and unwholesome. Maggie reaches for her bag, thankful her new friends didn't think to relieve her of her stuff. If she hurries, she might have time for a shower at the hostel before her shift at the cafe.

Walking back towards the car park, the faint ringing of her mobile rises up again from the depths of her bag. She pulls the phone out and studies the screen: WITHHELD NUMBER. It's tempting to let it ring off again, but at the very last moment curiosity gets the better of her. 'Hello,' she says, her voice a dry rasp.

'Is that— Oberon?' The line crackles. The woman's voice sounds very English and very far away. 'Hello . . . Maggie Oberon?'

'Yes,' she says. 'That's me.' Maggie swallows. Her tongue is dry and heavy in her mouth and the first trace of her hangover is beginning to beat in her temples.

'Oh, thank goodness. My name is Kath— Davies. I'm calling from— hospital in Buckinghamshire— I've been try–' The line crackles again with static. Maggie closes her eyes. Somewhere out over the water a seagull shrieks. '— track you down. Maggie, are you there?'

'Yes,' she says. 'I'm here. Sorry, the connection is terrible.'

'I'm calling about Lillian. Lillian Oberon.'

Maggie keeps her eyes squeezed shut. 'Is she – is she . . .'

'—Are you her next—'

' . . . OK?'

'— of kin?'

Their voices criss-cross confusingly over each other.

'I'm her granddaughter. Is she OK?'

'Can you hear me, Maggie? This is a dreadful line.'

'I can hear you. Tell me,' she urges, even as her words bounce back at her from twelve thousand miles away. 'Tell me . . . what's happened to Lillian?'

Heathrow is a grubby wash of people, luggage, diesel fumes, crying babies, tears and exclamations. In the early-morning crush of the international arrivals hall faces peer expectantly, pressed up against the railings. It's hard not to feel self-conscious – on show – as she walks through the waiting crowds. Two little girls wave a hand-painted WELCOME HOME DADDY banner, while their mother dances from one foot to the other impatiently behind them. A woman in a black burka embraces a tall, weeping man. An elderly lady sits slumped in her wheelchair as her family converse animatedly over her head. There is no one waiting for Maggie.

She didn't sleep at all on the long flight from Sydney to London, but something about the juddering motion of the Heathrow Express soon has Maggie dozing in her seat, her head slumped chin-to-chest, and so unaware of the world around her that it's a shock when a station guard shakes her shoulder and tells her that she's arrived in Paddington. Bleary-eyed, she navigates the Underground to Marylebone, buys a bunch of red tulips from a flower stall in the station concourse, then collapses into the corner of yet another train carriage. It creeps its way out of London's grey urban sprawl until it hits the open countryside and begins to gather pace.

After the heat and light of the past few months, it's strangely comforting to be back in this landscape of muted browns and greys and greens. She'd found much to like about Australia: the endless blue of the sky, the red dirt, the pale, peeling gum trees with their shimmering green leaves. She'd grown to relish the early-morning shrieks of the lorikeets outside the hostel windows, the cicadas singing to a noisy crescendo in the hottest part of the day, the small glasses of ice-cold beer served in the pubs, the scent of coffee wafting out of cafes, the sting of sun and saltwater on her shoulders. She'd embraced each difference as physical proof of the distance she'd put between herself and her home – between her and the site of her wrongs. But for all the miles she has travelled, all the experiences she's weathered and all the people she's met, deep down she's not sure she's any different from the person she was when she first left England almost a year ago.

The general medical ward is relatively easy to find amid the labyrinthine corridors of the hospital, although the unmistakable scent of boiled vegetables and bleach makes her jetlagged head spin. She takes shallow breaths all the way to the nurses' station, then gives her name to the matron and asks if she can leave her rucksack with them.

'Here we are,' says the nurse, leading her to the very last bed on the ward. 'It looks as though Mrs Oberon's having a little rest, but you're welcome to sit with her. The medication makes her very drowsy.'

Maggie regards her grandmother from the foot of her bed, shocked at her appearance. Her face is pale and slack-jawed in sleep, a trace of blue veins just visible below the surface of her skin, her lips dry and flaking, a white bandage on her right temple and a cannula taped to the back of her hand. Her thin white hair, usually pinned neatly in place, falls limply around her shoulders.

'Would you like me to put those in a vase for you?' the nurse asks, nodding at the tulips in her arms.

'Thank you.' She pulls up a plastic chair, settling herself onto its creaking frame beside the bed. Lillian frowns and murmurs in her sleep. Watching her, Maggie feels a deep ache rise up.

'Gran, it's me, it's Maggie.' She reaches for her hand as Lillian's eyes flutter open and fix momentarily on her face. 'It's Maggie,' she says again. Her grandmother stares a moment longer before her gaze slides away towards the window. 'How are you feeling? Can I get you anything?' Still Lillian doesn't answer. 'Would you like a drink?' She's not sure if the slight movement of her grandmother's head is acquiescence, but needing to feel helpful, she pours water from the plastic jug, finds a button to raise the bed slightly then brings the cup to her grandmother's lips. Lillian takes a couple of obliging sips before resting her head back on the pillows. 'I came as soon as I heard.'

Maggie leans back in the chair, perplexed by Lillian's silence. Earlier, on the train, she'd imagined how it might be, sitting there at her grandmother's bedside holding her hand and offering words of comfort, but this isn't the woman she left nearly twelve months ago and Maggie feels scared at how diminished she looks. The scent of bleach and the sounds of the ward stir a memory in Maggie's mind; the sour taste of unripe cherries on her tongue, the snap of a rotten tree branch, the sharp ache of a broken arm. Back then, it had been Lillian who had scooped her up from the orchard and driven her to this very hospital. Lillian who had sat at her bedside on the children's ward and coaxed her through the procedure as she'd had her arm set in plaster. It was Lillian who had told her how brave she was and who had been offered the first signature on the clean, white cast. Always Lillian. Always there.

Staring at her grandmother's frighteningly pale face, Maggie can't help but feel shame that this is how she has repaid her – living a hedonistic life on the other side of the world in Lillian's own moment of need. And now that she's here, she sits useless at her bedside, uncertain what to do or how to help. She owes this woman so much more.

A couple arrive on the ward with a large fruit basket for the grey-haired lady in the bed opposite. They smile at Maggie before pulling the curtain around the other bed; Maggie hears their low murmurs of greeting followed by laughter. She glances back to Lillian, whose gaze remains fixed steadfastly on the ceiling.

'She told me I was being watched.'

Startled at the sound of Lillian's voice, she leans in a little closer. 'What was that, Gran?'

'She warned me. I didn't believe her . . . but he was watching, all the time.'

Maggie stares in confusion, unsure if she's misheard. 'Sorry, Gran, *who* was watching you?'

'There are eyes in that house.'

Lillian isn't looking at her but staring instead at the foot of her bed. Maggie follows her grandmother's gaze but there is no one there. Her skin prickles.

Lillian's head turns slowly back to Maggie and her gaze refocuses.

'I got all your letters,' tries Maggie. 'I loved reading them. Sorry I wasn't the greatest pen pal.'

Lillian reaches out and grips Maggie's hand with her own, her skin surprisingly cool and soft. 'Take me home,' she says, her voice low and urgent. 'Promise me you'll take me home.'

Maggie squeezes her grandmother's hand. 'I promise, Gran. As soon as you're feeling better.'

'Nowhere but Cloudesley. Do you understand?'

14

Maggie nods.

'Promise me.'

'Yes, I promise. As soon as you're well enough.'

Lillian nods and lies back against her pillows, closing her eyes.

Maggie stays a while longer. Outside the window another identical hospital wing looms across the car park. Maggie wonders what stories are unfolding in that building: babies being born, loved ones being lost; lives shifting on their axes. Down on the asphalt she sees two cars vie for the same parking space. Maggie watches as one driver gets out of her car and storms across to the other, gesticulating angrily. Emotions run high in a place like this, where everything boils down to life and death. I promise I'll take you home, she thinks. She's stuffed up so many things in the past twelve months, but this, surely, is one thing she *can* get right.

The taxi drops her at the house at dusk, the violet sky darkening like a bruise as it turns through the open wrought-iron gates. Stone peacocks, speckled with lichen and perched like sentries atop the gateposts, glower at her as she passes. Tall beech trees crowd the twisting drive on either side, their leafy boughs blocking out the sky. The effect, in the failing light, is of a forbidding tunnel curving away into darkness.

She'd held the anxiety of her return in check, like a small, coiled spring buried somewhere deep in her gut as the taxi had navigated the country lanes of the Chiltern Hills, winding up through villages of brick-and-flint cottages, past hedgerows rustling with life and rippling fields of young wheat. Her driver had been blessedly mute, just the low hum of the radio to break the silence. Every so often a 'Stop HS2' protest poster had appeared stuck to a house window or nailed to a fence. At the sign for the village of Cloud Green, she'd sunk a little lower in her seat, averting her gaze as she'd passed the Old Swan pub on the village green, keen to keep news of her return under wraps for as long as possible. Less than a mile on, past the old Saxon church with its tilted gravestones littering the churchyard like rotting teeth, and they'd turned through the familiar metal gates.

Potholes are scattered at intervals along the drive. The taxi judders and bumps past bristling banks of nettles and cow parsley. A magpie flutters from a low tree branch, gliding ahead of the car before soaring up into the dark canopy above. They carry on until the trees eventually begin to thin and the dusky purple sky reappears, stretching over an unkempt lawn spotted with clover and daisies until finally, there in the distance, stands Cloudesley, an old manor house of brick and flint, with its arched stone entrance, grand, gabled roofline, and chimneys twisting skywards.

The taxi driver lets out a long, low whistle. 'Home?' he asks.

She nods. Home.

'Not a bad place to grow up.'

She nods again. 'Yeah, not a bad place.'

She had never thought to ask how the house had got its name, presuming, as a child, that it had something to do with its position, perched atop a hill like the crowning decoration on a huge cake, or grazing the sky like a large cloud. To her, it had always just been Cloudesley.

There was no denying it had been a solitary sort of childhood, tucked away in the heart of rural Buckinghamshire, living with her grandparents in the old house, with its twisting corridors and draughty rooms; but her points of reference mostly had been the characters she sought from the dusty books in the library, and when compared to some of her companions – Mary Lennox, David Copperfield, Jane Eyre – it hadn't seemed so very strange. It was only as she grew older, when she'd returned from boarding school, or later, hanging out with the Mortimer boys, that she'd come to see the house through others' eyes, and begun to realise how unusual an upbringing it had been.

She asks the taxi driver to drop her at the rear of the house. As her car door slams, a flock of rooks take flight from the branches of a tall beech tree, their raucous cries fading into the sky. She stands for a moment, gazing up at the towering facade with its blackened windows and creeper scrambling unchecked across the exterior. The house looks shuttered – no visible signs of life – and Maggie can't help the slight shiver that runs down her spine. Strange, she thinks, how you often have to leave a place, before you can truly see it. The driver hefts her rucksack out of the boot of the car and she watches as his tail lights disappear up the drive.

Inside the back entrance, a long flag-stoned corridor stretches away before her. To her right is the scullery, a small utility room that would have once been a flower room, and a door leading down into the cellar; to her left is the kitchen. Ahead looms a wood-panelled staircase, a steep set of steps winding into the upper reaches of the house, once used by the staff. The scent that assaults her is achingly familiar: a heady mix of damp stone, lilac, polished wood and a fragrance reminiscent of the cold, white ash left in an old grate. 'Hello?' she calls out, making for the only light spilling from the open kitchen door.

Radio 4 plays softly on the Roberts radio in the corner of the kitchen. Jane Barrett hasn't heard her and Maggie takes the moment to observe the reassuring familiarity of the scene in front of her. The scrubbed oak table and the pots of herbs and geraniums growing on the windowsill, the old willow-pattern china standing on the dresser, a jug filled with peonies spilling petals onto the floor.

Maggie clears her throat and watches as Jane spins around, her face transforming from surprise to delight. 'Maggie! I didn't hear you arrive.'

Jane dries her hands on her apron and meets Maggie in the centre of the room. 'Oh, my dear,' she says, drawing back to hold her at arm's length, 'not even that tan can hide the fact you're all skin and bone. Let's get you some tea. I'll put the kettle on.'

She doesn't give her a chance to answer, but bustles around, filling the kettle, pulling out cups and saucers and a tin of loose-leaf tea. 'Can I help?' Maggie feels redundant in the face of Jane's activity. 'Let me do something.'

'No, no, sit down.'

Maggie relents, exhaustion settling over her as she seats herself at the oak table in the centre of the room, watching as Jane lays a tea tray.

'I waited specially,' says Jane, retrieving the milk from the fridge. 'Didn't want to leave before I'd seen you. You went straight to the hospital? How was she?'

Maggie thinks of Lillian lying pinned beneath the white hospital sheet and her desperate plea: *take me home*. 'She seems very tired and confused. But the doctor I spoke to said she is doing well. The kidney infection is under control and she's responding to the new medication.'

Jane shakes her head. 'She gave me quite a fright, finding her lying in the hall like that in her nightdress. I dread to think how long she had been there.'

Maggie nods. 'I'm glad it was one of your mornings.'

'I've been making it my business to pop in a little more frequently in recent months.'

Not for the first time does Maggie silently thank her lucky stars that she had the good sense to hire Jane, a local woman from the village, to check on Lillian a few times each week. For a year now, Jane has been helping Lillian with a little shopping and cooking. She's a cheery, uncomplicated sort, the kind of no-nonsense person you'd want at your side in a crisis.

Jane pulls out a chair and sits opposite Maggie, pushing a plate of biscuits toward her pointedly. 'I hope you don't feel I'm speaking out of turn, but I've been worried about your granny. This house . . . it's too much for her on her own. How she copes with all those stairs I don't know. But she won't hear a word about it. Stubborn as a mule.'

'She certainly is.'

'Sometimes I arrive in the morning and find things have been moved. Vases and the like, disappearing. Dirty footprints trodden through the house. I suspect that wasn't the first night she's spent wandering about, though Lord only knows why.'

'How odd.'

'That's not all. The other day she asked me when Charles would be returning from London. I think she had really forgotten.' Jane gives Maggie a meaningful look over her mug of tea. 'Then she asked me to get Albie's room ready for a visit, though I'm certain he hasn't phoned in months. She keeps losing things, too. Her spectacles . . . a pair of slippers . . . last week it was a key. She seemed quite beside herself about it, though when I pressed her a few minutes later, she'd gone blank. She's been increasingly confused these past weeks. Agitated. Repetitive.' Jane pauses.

'I had no idea.' Maggie thinks of the correspondence she has exchanged with her grandmother, brief but cheerful letters Lillian had written to her with news from the village and repetitive questions about life in Australia, questions Maggie had never seemed to have the right answers for. She'd replied as best she could, waxing lyrical about the weather and the beaches, while editing out the gorier details of the grimy hostels she had stayed in, the disappointing cafe where she'd found waitressing work, and the random men she'd found momentary distraction with. It seems, perhaps, that she isn't the only one who has been hiding truths; maybe they had both been masking the reality of their solitary lives. A wave of guilt washes over her. She should have guessed all was not well. No, more than that; she never should have left in the first place. She owed Lillian so much more.

'If it's any comfort,' Maggie offers, clutching at a straw, 'the doctor I spoke to seemed very upbeat. He thought they might release her at the end of the week.'

Jane tuts. 'Release her? Back here?'

'Yes.' Maggie thinks for a moment of her promise to her grandmother. 'I suppose they might consider transitioning her to a care home, but the doctor implied that if she had people around her here then there was no reason she shouldn't come home.'

Jane rolls her eyes. 'Well, that might be fine for some patients; but I'll bet most of them aren't eighty-six years old and living in a house like this. If you ask me, they just want the bed back. All these cuts . . .' She shakes her head.

'Yes. Perhaps. Though with me here now, and you helping out, and Mr Blackmore of course . . .'

'Oh no, dear. Didn't you know?' Jane leans forward in her chair. 'Mr Blackmore retired at the end of last year. It all got a bit too much for him.'

Another omission from Lillian's correspondence; well that explains a few things, thinks Maggie, remembering the state of the lawn and the vines scaling the house.

'Your grandmother did hire a new groundsman to help about the place – a little gardening and some general handy-man jobs, you know . . .' Jane trails off, suddenly looking uncomfortable.

'That's good, isn't it?

'Yes. It is,' says Jane firmly. 'I thought she might have told you. I have to say, I wasn't entirely sure what you'd think.'

'As long as they don't mind a little hard work and can put up with Gran's demands, it can only be a good thing.'

Jane looks as if she might say something else, then seems to change her mind. 'Yes,' she says firmly. 'That's exactly what I thought.'

Maggie reaches for Jane's hand and gives it a squeeze, her resolve growing. 'I don't want you to worry. You've been such a great help, but I'm back now. I'll do whatever it takes to help Lillian and bring her home.'

'Well, it will certainly be a weight off my mind to know you're here with her.'

Maggie shrugs. 'I'd put money on the fact that you and Lillian will be the only people pleased to see me back in Cloud Green.'

'Now, now, we'll have no self-pity in this kitchen,' says Jane, reaching for the tray and gathering the cups and saucers. 'I'm sure you'll find any fuss died down a while ago. You know what village life is like: a hotbed of gossip for five minutes, but the flames that fan rumours soon burn themselves out.'

Maggie eyes her doubtfully as the woman continues.

'We've seen upsets in Cloud Green before and I'm sure we'll see them again. You mark my words. Most people will have far better things to talk about than what happened, you'll see. Besides, it's really none of anyone's business, is it?'

Maggie nods but she isn't convinced; for all her talk, Jane isn't quite able to meet her eye. They both know *exactly* what life in a small English village can be like.

Maggie's feelings of unease only grow as the sound of Jane's car fades away down the drive. The house stands eerily silent. Wanting to reacquaint herself with the old place, she moves through the ground floor, following the twisting, wood-panelled corridors, opening doors and switching on lights, gazing upon each room in turn before plunging it back into darkness.

In the dining room, the draught created by opening the door makes the dusty chandelier jangle overhead but the rest of the room has an abandoned air. The shutters are closed and the walnut chairs, the long, polished table and sideboard stand draped in ghostly sheets. Her grandfather's eclectic tapestries and painted African masks still hang upon the panelled walls beside a collection of mounted horns and antlers, while the porcelain dinner service and crystal wine glasses stand redundant in a huge glass cabinet.

It's a similar scene in the library: the bookshelves jammed to the rafters with leather-bound volumes, the tall ladder still resting against them, but the armchairs are now covered in white sheets and the Persian rugs have been rolled up and left propped against a wall. Over on the hearth Maggie notices a once-prized collection of carved ivories covered in a thick layer of dust. Two of the window-panes are cracked and tendrils of ivy creep into the room between the rotting window-frame and the wall. The air smells musty and dank, fetid like a greenhouse.

On into the morning room and it's an even worse story: shuttered windows, faded Chinese wallpaper, and abandoned clutter and ornaments. Several buckets stand dotted at ominous intervals beneath the ceiling rose, most of them half-filled with grey water, stains spreading around them on the carpet. When she looks up, she sees the watermarks leaking across the ceiling and a large zigzag crack scarring one wall.

Her grandfather's study is intact, its walls lined with Charles's entomological collections – beetles and butterflies pinned to boards in box frames – but so dusty and the air so still it feels like a vault that hasn't been opened in decades.

With each new room, Maggie's spirits sink a little lower. In the year she has been away, the house seems to have fallen in on itself; wandering its rooms and corridors feels a little like venturing through a museum only to find many of its exhibits damaged or closed for restoration.

Other than the kitchen, the only room that maintains any semblance of order and activity is the drawing room, still in regular use as evidenced by the presence of her grand-mother's favourite shawl, a pair of reading glasses and a crossword lying beside her armchair. On the wall opposite, Maggie sees the painting she gave Lillian for her eightieth birthday, a crude, colourful abstract she'd completed during a more experimental phase at art college. Looking around, it makes Maggie sad to realise what a small and intimate radius Lillian's life has shrunk to in this huge, echoing house.

Sick of the cloying stillness, Maggie moves across to the window and unlocks the catch, throwing it open to the night air. A welcome gust blows into the room, lifting a pile of papers off the writing desk and sending them tumbling to the floor.

Maggie retrieves the one nearest her feet: an outstanding electricity bill, FINAL DEMAND printed in red across the top. She drops to her hands and knees and gathers the rest of the papers. They are all bills, dozens of them – gas, water, roofing work, the unpaid invoice of a plumber, several of Jane's own invoices – all of them overdue. Maggie stares at them in dismay. She gathers up the papers and takes them with her. It's becoming all too clear that it's not just Lillian's health that is a concern, but also the state of the vast, decaying house.

Eventually, she comes to the grand entrance hall. She flicks a light switch and hears an ominous fizzing sound overhead. The French chandelier flickers then shorts with a loud bang. She turns on one of the beaded lamps on the console instead, brushing off the cobwebs hanging from its shade, looking around as the dim light throws eerie shadows up into the gallery where rows of gilt-framed paintings hang upon the wall, their occupants gazing down at her with blank eyes. She can see loose tiles lifting here and there across the gritty chequered floor, another bucket waiting for the next downpour, mouse droppings strewn in the corners and a carpet winding up the grand curved staircase so worn and full of holes it could only be deemed a safety hazard. Hardly a home fit for an elderly patient recuperating from a serious illness. For the first time she wonders about her rash promise to Lillian: she has given her word that she will bring her home, but is this really the right place for her to recover?

She runs a hand over the huge, faded tapestry hanging across the wall – then turns to climb the curved staircase to her own room. Halfway up she stops and listens. There is no scrabble of dog paws on the tiled floor, no shuffle of newspaper pages from the library, no distant murmur from her grandmother's radio. There is nothing; not even the glug of water moving through old pipes. This house, that has witnessed so much throughout the years – dinner parties and laughter, conversation and arguments, dancing and music – a house that has seen so much life, had so many people pass through its doors, stands utterly silent. It is unnerving to be its only occupant. What echoes would she hear – what stirrings from the past – if she only knew what to listen for?

Her eyes fall upon the grandfather clock in the hall and she turns and heads back down the stairs, blowing dust from its wooden case before opening the cabinet to wind it the way Lillian once showed her. She watches with a certain satisfaction as the pendulum begins to sway, a steady tick rising up out of the old clock like a resuscitated heart beating in a chest. One small thing corrected.

She doesn't want to think yet of all the other wrongs she still needs to set right.

CHAPTER 3

Lillian sits at the dressing table in her bedroom, counting the chimes of the grandfather clock as they echo through the house. Half an hour before their guests will begin to arrive. A crystal tumbler of whisky and ice sits on the table in front of her, bleeding a white ring onto the polished wood. Lillian takes a sip and squints at her reflection in the mirror, studying for lines at the corners of her eyes, lifting her chin, tilting it first this way then that, smoothing her fingers gently across her throat. *Mrs Charles Oberon*, she says quietly. She barely recognises herself. Twenty-six years old and she feels ancient and exhausted. Tonight will require a little extra effort.

She brushes her fair hair and pins it up into a neat twist. The ice cubes clink and slide in the tumbler as she drinks. Outside, a blackbird perched on the wisteria beyond her open window lifts its voice in full-throated song, as if to accompany the instruments being tuned by the jazz band down on the terrace below. All around her, Cloudesley seems to hum with activity. There is the scrape of a ladder moving across the terrace as a man hangs the last of the Chinese lanterns. A trolley rattles across flagstones, glass-ware and bottles clinking. She hears the muffled giggles of two maids passing her bedroom door, extra staff drafted in for the occasion. There has been no shortage of work in the run up to the evening. The chandeliers have been cleaned, flowers cut and arranged, the furniture dusted, rugs rolled back, cutlery polished and counted, the champagne chilled and the extravagant ice sculptures Charles has insisted upon delivered and set in pride of place in the dining room. Even the peacocks seem to understand the importance of the evening, patrolling the lawns like jewelled sentries. The house is all bustle and action; only she, it seems, is a fixed point, redundant amid the maelstrom.

Ignoring the shaking of her hand, she brushes blusher onto her cheeks and paints her lips scarlet before pursing them in the mirror. The colour helps to disguise her pallor. She lifts her glass once more and discovers it is empty.

Her dress is laid out on the bed, a long but simple halter-neck gown in jade green silk. She steps into it, the fabric moving like water around her legs. It's only as she turns back to the mirror that she notices Charles standing silently at the door. 'Oh!' she says. 'You startled me.'

He smiles at her reflection. 'Can't I watch my beautiful wife getting dressed?'

Lillian gives him a faint smile, holding the dress to her chest. He looks handsome in his black tuxedo, his thick russet-coloured hair slick with pomade, the sheen almost masking the distinct shock of white at his parting. 'Glad to see you're putting your best foot forward, dear. Well done.' His eyes drop to the empty tumbler on the table in front of her. 'Feeling better?'

She nods, fumbling with the fabric ties.

'Allow me,' he says, moving to tie the halter at the nape of her neck, his fingers fastening the line of covered buttons running down her spine before taking a step back to admire her. 'Perfect . . .' he says, '. . . almost.'

Charles pulls a black velvet box from his jacket and snaps it open to reveal an impressive pearl choker, four strands deep, fastened by a glittering diamond and emerald clasp. He holds it out to her. 'Should do the job,' he says, glancing at her throat.

The necklace is, of course, exactly what's needed. 'It's beautiful,' she says.

She allows him to fasten the choker, the cold pearls pulling taut against the hollow of her neck, before his hands come to rest on her shoulders and his face leans in to hers – so close she can smell the lingering traces of Pears soap and sandalwood on his skin. She forces herself to meet his gaze in the mirror. 'There,' he says, '*now* you're perfect.'

'Thank you.' Her heart beats like a drum in her chest, their eyes locked until Charles steps away, adjusting the cufflinks at his wrists. 'It's turning into a beautiful evening.'

She releases the breath she has been holding and reaches for an earring, raising it to her lobe before discarding it. 'Yes. Clever you for picking tonight.'

Charles rubs his hands together briskly. 'Well, on with the show.' He is almost at the door when he turns back to her, narrowing his eyes a little. 'Just do your best, my dear. It's not too much to ask, is it?'

As soon as he's gone, she lifts a hand to the pearls around her throat. They press cold and tight against her skin but there is no question of her not wearing them. She pushes her shoulders back, lifts her chin and regards herself for a long moment in the mirror. Before she even knows what she is doing, she reaches for the empty glass tumbler on her dressing table and sends it sailing across the room. It shatters against the wall, splintering into a hundred deadly shards, the small act of destruction releasing a little of the pent-up emotion caught in her throat. *On with the show*, she thinks, adjusting the necklace one final time before leaving the room.

*

She is on her third glass of champagne when she finds herself cornered in the dining room by a man talking too loudly at her, his wife standing silently at his side. Lillian can't take her eyes off the canapé crumbs jostling in the bristles of his moustache.

'I've been coming to Charles's May Day Ball for as long as I can remember,' he announces with distinct pride, 'but I don't think I've ever seen Cloudesley look quite as lovely as it does tonight. Wouldn't you agree, Barbara?' He nudges the dark-haired woman beside him and she murmurs her assent.

Lillian knows he is someone important; one of Charles's business associates, though his name escapes her. Hugh Somebody-or-other. Charles's friends all look the same to her – a parade of stout, greying men – even more so tonight in their uniform black tie. 'Thank you,' she says, knowing it is her role to take the credit, though she has had little to do with the evening's preparations, other than instructing the staff and ensuring Charles's requests were followed to the letter.

'Of course, you Oberons know how to throw a party,' he continues. 'Do you recall the year Charles brought out that contortionist? My word! The poses she got into up on the bar made the mind boggle.' He nudges Lillian. 'Do *you* remember, my dear?'

She doesn't know the particular party the man is referring to – presumably it took place before her time, when the first Mrs Oberon helped to arrange Charles's soirées – but she smiles politely.

'I've always loved coming here,' the man continues. 'Everywhere you look there's something wonderful to admire. That husband of yours does have extraordinary taste.'

'Yes,' murmurs Lillian, glancing around at the huge pedestal arrangements of roses and peonies, the flickering

28

silver candelabra and the peacock ice sculptures now melting slowly in the unusually warm May air. 'He does.'

'We heard you hadn't been well. Are you feeling better, dear?' It's the wife, peering beady-eyed at her over a champagne glass.

'Yes, thank you.'

'There has been a nasty influenza going around. You can't be too careful. I'm sure Charles is very . . . cautious . . . after poor Evelyn. He must want to keep you wrapped up in cotton wool.'

'Oh yes,' says Lillian with a small laugh, 'he is very careful.' She can't help her quick glance at the portrait of the late Mrs Oberon, hanging over the fireplace, her narrow shoulders swathed in pink satin, her pale, round face and hazel eyes gazing out over the proceedings with a look of serene acceptance.

Feeling a tug at her dress, Lillian looks down and sees Albie standing at her side. 'Hello.' The boy's face is white with tiredness, his amber eyes wide like saucers.

'I'm bored,' he whispers.

She bends down and puts her mouth to his ear. 'I'll tell you a secret. Me too.'

'Will you play with me?'

She smiles at him. 'I wish I could. Tell you what . . . go and find me something beautiful . . . a feather . . . a flower.'

He smiles and nods in understanding. It is their little game, a treasure hunt, where the only rule is that whatever he finds must be from the natural world. Nothing artificial or man-made. He darts through the open doors onto the terrace and is gone.

'Such a shame,' says Barbara in an affected tone. 'He must miss his mother terribly.'

A waiter materialises with a tray of devils-on-horseback and the couple fall upon them with gusto. Lillian watches the shiny, pink meat disappearing into the man's gaping mouth. She has no appetite and only half-listens as the conversation moves on around her, her eyes drifting back to the portrait of Evelyn Oberon. Was this how it was for her, she wonders? Did she relish these evenings of Charles's? Was she the life and soul of the party, or did she bear them, like her, with stoic resolve?

Ignoring the bluster of the man still ranting at her side, her ears attune to the rising babble coming from the terrace. She hears the jazz music, the popping of champagne corks, the exclamations of old friends greeting each other and exchanging news and jokes and innuendo. Judging by the crescendo, they are reaching that point in the evening when inhibitions fade with the setting sun. A laughing woman clutching a bottle of champagne balances precariously on the edge of the oriental fountain, the train of her evening dress trailing through the water as her companions encourage her on her perilous circle around the wall. Couples dance beneath the Chinese lanterns like moths drawn to the light. All is movement and dizzying colour.

Beads of sweat prickle on her back. She puts a hand to her temple and feels her pulse beating beneath her fingers. 'Will you excuse me?' she says to no one in particular. 'I think I need a little air.'

She leaves through the open French doors and makes for a spot at the far end of the terrace, where the balustrade is cast almost in darkness. It is a relief to escape to the shadows and lean against the cool stone, gazing out into the torch-lit gardens. The black silhouette of a peacock flutters up into a tree, retreating to its nest for the night. High above her head the stars seem to fizz and dance in the sky. She attempts to run a finger beneath the pearl choker round her neck and wishes she could take the damn thing off.

'Are you feeling all right, Madam?'

She turns to find Bentham standing behind her, hands clasped at his back, his solemn, unblinking gaze fixed, as usual, just a fraction from her face; looking but not looking. 'Yes, I'm fine, thank you.'

'Mr Oberon thought you might need—'

'I'm fine,' she says again, more firmly, and the butler gives a stiff nod.

'Of course.'

Lillian softens slightly. 'Aren't you ever off duty, Bentham? You should relax a little.' She waves her glass at him.

Bentham shakes his head, his eyes still not quite meeting hers. 'It's an important night for Mister Oberon. All hands to the pump.'

'Yes, quite. Silly me.' She turns and looks out over the gardens. 'We must all do our duty,' she adds with a sigh.

He nods and Lillian listens to him walk away, that distinct, stiff-legged gait as he moves across the terrace. Grateful to be alone again, she turns and leans over the balustrade, gazing out across the lawn to where a group of guests cavort in the shadows, the men's white dress shirts and their drunken whoops giving them away in the darkness. They're either playing croquet or chasing the last of the peacocks up into the trees. Perhaps both.

Lillian presses her hips against the cool stone and closes her eyes. Is any of this real, she wonders? Could she open her eyes and find herself back in Lucinda's draughty house, rearranging the books in her library? Or sitting with her sister, Helena, on the stone bench overlooking her steep, winding garden? Or waking as a child in her bed in their old family home in Pimlico, to the sound of her parents moving in the house below? Could all of this be some surreal dream? She feels so lightly tethered to the world.

'It's a little early to be falling asleep,' says a voice, soft and low, at her side.

Startled, she spins to face the man who seems to have materialised from nowhere.

'By all accounts,' he adds, 'there are still hours of this to get through.'

She doesn't recognise him. In the near-darkness his face is smooth like sculpted marble and his eyes shine almost black; his expression is hard to read — playful, perhaps — but it's his choice of words that intrigues her most. 'You're not enjoying yourself?' she asks.

The man shrugs and pulls a cigarette case from his tuxedo pocket. She accepts with a small nod of thanks and leans in to the flame he offers from his silver lighter. 'I'm not much of a one for parties,' he says simply and without apology. 'All the small talk, the social grandstanding. I'm not very good at it.'

'Then if you don't mind me asking, why are you here?'

'Turn down an invitation from Charles Oberon? I didn't know such a thing was possible.' The man smiles, his teeth glinting white in the shadows. 'Besides, it arrived with the most intriguing note.' He clamps his own cigarette between his lips as he reaches into his jacket pocket again and pulls out a stiff cream card, offering it to Lillian. In the dim light of the lanterns swaying overhead she reads the words scrawled in a corner of the invitation in her husband's looping handwriting.

Do hope you'll come. Bring a chum, if you like.
I have a proposition for you. We'll discuss.
C. O.

It is so like Charles, she thinks. The assertive 'we'll discuss', as though the matter of the man's attendance had already been settled. 'Did you?' she asks, handing the invitation back.

'Did I what?'

'Bring a *chum*?'

'No.'

Lillian studies the man, thinking she has the measure of him. With looks like that he's bound to be a playboy. A ladies' man. She exhales smoke out over the lawns, watching it fade into the darkness.

'I heard there will be fireworks later. I thought I'd slope away after.'

'Oh yes, the fireworks. Of course.' She sighs. 'Chinese lanterns, champagne fountains, peacocks, ice sculptures . . .'

'. . . And a perfect full moon,' he finishes for her.

Lillian glances up at the night sky.

'Do you think he ordered it specially?' he asks.

'I have no doubt,' she says drily, tapping ash from her cigarette onto the terrace floor. 'So what do you think this "proposition" could be?' she asks.

'No idea. I'm still waiting for a moment with our gracious host.' Something in his wry smile offsets the intensity in his eyes. Really, he is very handsome. 'And in the meantime,' he adds, with a sideways glance, 'I have you.'

He is flirting with her; very gently, but definitely flirting and it's at that moment that Lillian realises he must have no more idea of her identity than she has of his.

A loud cheer erupts out on the lawn. The man beside her turns his back on the antics in the gardens and gazes up at the house instead, the lights blazing from the windows illuminating the side of his face.

'So, you're telling me you know nobody here?' she asks.

'Not a soul.'

'Perhaps I can help put that to rights.' She spins back to face the terrace. 'Let's see . . . The lady there – the one performing the energetic can-can across the dance floor – is Mabel Grey, the West End actress. Have you heard of her?'

The man at her side shakes his head again.

'Her friend, the blonde in the pink silk, is a celebrated fashion model – just back after a rather scandalous divorce from her American banker husband. She came out of it rather well, they say, which should please her new toy-boy lover. Over there, monopolising the cocktail shaker is Charles, of course, with his entourage. Men in high places,' she says, exhaling a long stream of cigarette smoke. 'Police. Politicians. Lawyers. High Court judges. Apparently, Anthony Eden himself might make an appearance later.'

'Goodness! The Oberons *are* connected. Hardly a night for bad behaviour then,' says the man at her side.

'Oh, you'd be surprised,' she says, glancing at him sideways before looking away, exhaling another stream of smoke out into the garden.

She really doesn't know what has come over her. She's had too much to drink. Or perhaps it's the fact that he has no idea who she is that she finds appealing. Whatever the reason, she tells herself a little light flirtation with a handsome stranger is hardly the worst thing in the world. Charles is busy with his friends and having looked about the terrace, she can see far worse behaviour taking place. Far worse.

'He seems to have the right idea,' says the man, nodding to where a young boy in a dark suit lingers near a table of drinks, reaching out to surreptitiously swipe a half-empty glass of champagne before skulking away into the garden.

'Oh dear,' she sighs.

'Charles Oberon's son?'

'Yes. That's Albie.'

'He looks like a little scamp. And where is Mrs Oberon? I haven't met her yet either.'

Lillian hesitates. Her silly subterfuge has gone on long enough.

'By all accounts,' the man continues, lowering his voice, 'she's a timid thing. Rather sickly . . . forever taking to her bed. They say Charles Oberon was still grieving the death of his first wife when he married her.'

Lillian blushes furiously, grateful for the cover of darkness. 'Well if that's what they're saying I suppose it must be true.' She clears her throat. 'So what is it that you do, Mister . . . ?' she asks, hastily changing the subject, suddenly horrified at the thought of revealing herself.

'Fincher,' he says. 'Jack Fincher. I'm an artist,' he adds, a hint of apology in his voice.

'An artist?' Lillian has not expected this reply. 'Are you any good?'

The man gives a wry smile. 'If I say "yes", you will think me horribly conceited. And if I say "no", you'll probably vanish at the earliest possible opportunity and find someone *far* more interesting to talk to.'

'You wouldn't want me to vanish?' she asks, once more surprised at her daring.

'No,' he says, holding her gaze. 'I wouldn't want you to vanish.'

There is a loud splashing sound from somewhere behind them. Raucous whoops rise up into the air, the fountain claiming its first victim of the night; but Lillian doesn't turn around. She can't seem to pull her gaze from the man standing before her. 'So are you?' she asks again, after a long moment. 'Any good?'

He shrugs. 'I've enjoyed a little success.'

'Congratulations.' Lillian toasts him with her champagne glass.

The man leans in, lowering his voice. 'My suspicion is that Charles Oberon has invited me here to undertake a family portrait. Something for the wife's birthday, perhaps?'

Lillian swallows. 'Should I assume from your tone that you don't like painting portraits?'

'There aren't many working artists who can afford to turn down a commission from a rich patron; but I prefer to paint what I feel — what inspires me. Painting portraits for the rich and privileged, so that they might hang another vanity object upon their walls . . . well, that sort of art doesn't interest me much.'

Lillian is still staring at him, surprised at the man's honesty, when a figure appears beside them. 'Aha!' says Charles, making them both start with his booming voice. 'So this is where you've been hiding,' he says, addressing Lillian. 'I see you've met Mr Fincher?'

Lillian takes a step towards her husband, her heart fluttering at Charles's sudden interruption. 'Not formally,' she says, wishing she could avoid the awkward revelation that she knows is imminent.

'In that case allow me.' He gestures at the artist. 'Meet Jack Fincher, touted by *The Times* as one of the most exciting young artists working in Britain today.'

Jack shakes Charles's outstretched hand, frowning. 'You're very kind.'

'Oh come now, there's no need for modesty. "A bold virtuoso of the new order", isn't that what the critics are calling you?' Charles doesn't seem to require an answer and carries on with the introductions. 'Mr Fincher, allow me to introduce my wife, Lillian Oberon.'

If Jack Fincher is alarmed to learn Lillian's identity he hides it well; the only sign of surprise is the high arch of one eyebrow as he takes her hand in his and says, '*Mrs* Oberon. It's a pleasure.'

A smile plays on the artist's lips. He holds her hand firmly, his fingers warm against her cool skin. At his touch, she feels the current of something pass between them and tries but fails to hold his gaze. She drops her hand.

'I'm so glad you could join us this evening,' continues Charles, his attention fixed on Fincher. 'I'm a great admirer of your work. I'm already the proud owner of one of your earlier paintings. It hangs in pride of place in my study here.' He turns to Lillian. '*Somerset Glory*. You know the one, don't you, darling?'

Lillian nods, although truthfully she has no idea which painting he is referring to. Charles is forever bringing home some new object or curiosity to display around the house and his study is not a room she frequents often.

'You trained at the Slade,' continues Charles, keen to impress his knowledge upon them both, 'then worked as a war artist.'

Jack Fincher nods, seemingly both flattered and a little embarrassed that his host should appear to know so much about him.

'I served myself,' says Charles. 'Royal Artillery.' He pauses for a moment then seems to gather himself. 'I enjoy your work, Mr Fincher. There's a playfulness to it . . . those glorious rural scenes with their hidden motifs . . . the dreamlike quality of your paintings. The trompe l'oeil. Very clever.' Charles puffs contentedly on his cigar. 'Yes, I enjoy it very much.'

Lillian stands silently at her husband's side, feeling like a spare part. She wonders if she should slip away and leave them to their conversation, but as if sensing her discomfort, Charles reaches out and takes her hand, fixing her there.

The artist clears his throat. 'Thank you. I haven't been in your charming home long but I can see you're quite a collector. Not just paintings but some . . . interesting antiques too?'

'Yes, indeed,' laughs Charles. 'Porcelain, birds, furs, insects, furniture . . .' he lets go of Lillian's hand and slings his arm around her waist, pulling her closer, '. . . women. I can't seem to help myself. I'm a fool for beauty. A family weakness. Would you believe,' continues Charles, warming to his subject, 'that my father started Oberon & Son with

37

just two thousand pounds, leasing one small shop front on Bond Street? Others laughed at his ambition to create a fanciful "bazaar" right there in the capital, but he soon proved them wrong. I can still remember the day he sat me on his knee and told me, "Charles, my boy, in this life you have to set the fashions, not follow them." He filled the shop with the weird and the wonderful – ornaments and fabrics, clothes and furnishings – and London couldn't get enough of it. My father was a self-made man, and aren't we all glad of it?' he says, looking around with obvious satisfaction at the party unfolding around them.

Lillian tunes out of Charles's soliloquy. She has heard his potted history of the late Max Oberon's business success many times before. Instead, she watches the artist as he listens to her husband. In the dim light of the swaying Chinese lanterns, it's hard to read his expression but once, as Charles's gaze drifts out across the lawn, she sees his dark eyes slide across to her and wonders if she imagines the slightest twitch of a smile pulling at the corners of his mouth.

'. . . Of course we now occupy premises five times the size. My father bought this house as his country retreat – a playground, he liked to call it.' He twirls his moustache thoughtfully between his fingers. 'We've been through some difficult times; the wars hit us hard, and my father's passing was a terrible blow. But business is bouncing back. There's an undeniable feeling of optimism, wouldn't you say? The end of rationing . . . the rebuilding of the city . . . a young queen and a new prime minister. Here we are, 1955, and finally it feels as though we're a country on the up again.'

'I only have to look around at the evening you have so generously laid on to know that you're right,' says the artist.

Charles smiles, pleased by the compliment. 'I'm glad you came, Mr Fincher,' he continues, rubbing his hands together briskly, suddenly business-like. 'You see, I've had a rather good idea and I think you might be just the man to help me with it.'

'I'm intrigued,' says Jack, turning to Lillian, as if to draw her back into the conversation; but Lillian remains silent. She has no idea what Charles is planning. This is her husband's stage.

A waiter appears with champagne. Charles thrusts fresh glasses into their hands. Lillian can see the excitement building in his face – a little boy with a secret to spill. This, she knows, is her husband at his most appealing: Charles throwing his ideas out onto the breeze like paper planes, confident they will take flight.

'My father had always intended for Cloudesley to be a home where we might store and enjoy our own private treasures,' he continues. 'And of course, what every great collection needs is the right space for display. I need a room dedicated to my most valuable artefacts, a place to show them off to their full advantage – perhaps even to the public.'

Jack is nodding politely, although Lillian can see he is confused. 'It's a good idea,' he says, 'though I'm not sure how I . . .'

'The more I thought about it,' says Charles, interrupting, 'the more I realised just how wonderful the opportunity was. I want this collection room at Cloudesley to be as beautiful as the objects themselves. And,' says Charles, pausing for dramatic effect, 'I think you're just the artist to create it for me.' Charles leans back against the stone balustrade, looking pleased with himself.

'You'd like me to paint a room here at Cloudesley?'

'Please,' says Charles, waving his cigar, 'I wouldn't insult an artist of your talent with such a suggestion. I'd call in the decorators if this were about a change of wallpaper or a new coat of paint.' Seeing Jack's confusion, he tries again. 'You're familiar, I assume, with the Elizabethan fashion for painted rooms?'

Jack nods slowly.

Charles takes a long drag on his cigar and lets the smoke drift from his half-open mouth. 'I want to give you a room here at Cloudesley and I'd like you to treat the walls, the ceiling, the entire room as your canvas. I want you to create a visual experience . . . a gilded chamber. I want a jewellery box of a room. A space fit for my finest treasures. No expense to be spared.'

Jack Fincher is shaking his head, clearly bewildered. 'And what exactly would you want this room to look like?'

'Well that, my dear chap, will be entirely up to you. You'll have free rein. Let your imagination run wild.'

Lillian can see the artist's frown but Charles ploughs on regardless. 'I thought you might like to lodge here for the summer. Treat it like a residence. I'll be your benevolent patron; isn't that what you bohemian types call it?' Charles looks around at them both, smiling, willing them to indulge him in his vision.

Lillian glances from Charles to the artist again. A whole summer with this man lodging at Cloudesley? The thought is unsettling. It feels as though the blood is moving too fast through her veins.

'The Chilterns are beautiful in the summer – quite the welcome breath of fresh air after London,' he continues.

Jack clears his throat. 'I don't know what to say . . .'

'I will pay you, of course. Generously.' He lets the last word hang in the air with pointed emphasis.

'This is all rather surprising.'

'You'll find, Mr Fincher, that I like to think a little bigger than most. But if that's not enough for you, we can always throw in a portrait or two of the good wife here? You'd like that, wouldn't you, Lillian?' says Charles, squeezing her arm. 'Something to hang in your room, perhaps, for us to enjoy when your beauty has faded?'

Lillian feels the blood rise in her cheeks and can't help glancing across at the artist. She assumes from the way he doesn't quite meet her eye that he too is remembering the dismissive manner in which he'd spoken of a portrait.

'There's no need to decide now,' Charles adds quickly. 'Enjoy the party. Lillian will open the room for you in the morning.'

Lillian glances at Charles in surprise. 'I had intended to visit Helena—'

Charles doesn't appear to hear her. 'It's a charming space over in the west wing,' he continues.

'The west wing?' asks Lillian. 'But we hardly use those rooms.'

'Exactly.'

Lillian studies Charles. 'Which room were you thinking of?'

'The old nursery,' says Charles.

Lillian continues to stare at Charles, a rush of emotion rising up from the pit of her stomach; but her husband, oblivious, remains focused on Jack. 'Just promise me you'll take a look? The room enjoys the most wonderful morning light.'

Jack nods, seemingly out of excuses. 'Of course.'

Bentham has arrived while they've been talking, hovering discreetly at Charles's shoulder. Lillian sees him lean in and speak to her husband in a low voice. Charles smiles and claps his hands together. 'Wonderful! Now, if you'll excuse me, Mr Eden has arrived and I really must go and say hello to our dashing new PM. Please,' he says, taking Lillian by the arm and beginning to guide her away from the stone balustrade, 'enjoy the party, Mr Fincher. Tonight, my home is a playground for you all.'

Lillian casts a backwards glance at the artist as Charles leads her away. Her last glimpse is of him standing in the shadows, his eyes, dark and unreadable, following her back into the fray. She turns to Charles when they are a safe distance away. 'The nursery?' she asks, the steadiness of her voice belying the ache building at the back of her throat.

'Yes,' says Charles, looking out over her head and waving a greeting at a guest by the bar. 'Doctor May has made it quite clear that we have no use for such a room anymore. You saw to that.' His fingers tighten a little on her arm.

'*I* saw to that?' she asks, aghast.

Charles smiles benignly as he increases the pressure on her arm, his fingers pinching tight enough to make her wince. 'Now, now, darling. This is hardly the time or place for a scene.'

Before she can reply, he has let her go, following Bentham through the French doors into the dining room, leaving Lillian alone in the centre of the terrace, rubbing her arm as the guests mill about her and the band plays on.

It's gone two in the morning when she eventually escapes, leaving the hardier guests swaying to the slow waltzes of the band and the most dutiful waiters offering cigars and nightcaps, gathering up empty glasses and overflowing ashtrays. Passing the open door to the library, she sees Charles sitting with a group of men sprawled in the leather armchairs, the top buttons of their shirts undone, bowties hanging limply around their necks, a bottle of port between them and a low cloud of cigar smoke hanging in a veil above their heads. They talk in loud, overlapping voices and every so often a burst of boisterous laughter erupts into the air. There is no sign of Mr Fincher. She hopes, for both their sakes, that he has made his escape into the night.

42

Upstairs, she finds Albie sprawled across his bed, still dressed in his shirt and trousers. The bedside lamp spills a pool of light onto the boy's sleeping face. She spots the folded piece of paper on the table, with 'For Lillian' written in a childish scrawl. Tucked inside is a long peacock feather. Her something beautiful.

She takes her treasure, then brushes the damp hair from Albie's forehead, her eyes tracing the familiar curve of his cheekbone, the scattered freckles across the bridge of his nose, the long sweep of his eyelashes. Her heart aches with a deep and protective love. Not her son – not her flesh and blood – but a boy she loves as fiercely as any mother could. Lying there, he looks younger than his eight years; softer and somehow more vulnerable, the little-boy rough-and-tumble erased in sleep. She knows the world he faces can be hard and cruel. 'Stay soft,' she wills him. 'Stay gentle.'

Albie, sensing her presence, stirs and half-opens his eyes. 'Lillie,' he murmurs.

She smiles and pulls the sheet over him. 'Go back to sleep,' she says and switches off the bedside lamp.

Back in the corridor a couple stagger ahead of her – one of Charles's business associates clutching a bottle of champagne in one hand and the waist of a shapely brunette – definitely not his wife – in the other. She hangs back in the doorway, watching them weave down the hall and disappear into a bedroom, their laughter muffled by the closing door. When she reaches her own room she locks the door behind her with a sigh.

The lead-paned window beside her dressing table is still open, a soft breeze billowing the pale gauze curtain and carrying with it the faint, melancholic strains of *Blue Moon*. She shrugs off her heels and dress and stands naked, allowing the night air to move over her bare skin. She closes her eyes and wraps her arms around her body; tries to imagine being held by someone, being led around a dance floor, a cheek pressed tenderly to her own. With the thought, a pale face comes unexpectedly to mind.

Her memory is hazy with champagne and the many people that have drifted before her all night, but if she concentrates she can still conjure his dark eyes and that wry smile. How foolish she had been to hide her identity and allow them to stumble into such awkward territory. And how lucky that Charles hadn't discovered the silly charade that had played out between them; two strangers enjoying a mild flirtation – for that was all it was; yet she knows Charles wouldn't have liked it.

The music ends. Silence descends. She pulls on a silk robe and slumps at her dressing table, unclasping the pearl choker from around her neck and returning it to its velvet box. She reaches for a pot of cold cream and removes her make-up, leaning in to study her reflection in the mirror. She looks pale. There are dark shadows under her eyes and when she lifts her chin, she sees the damage the choker has concealed all night: a fading ring of violet bruises encircling her throat, each one the size of a man's fingertip, imprinted on her skin.

She's still sitting there, staring at her reflection, when the scream rings out: a loud, unearthly cry breaking the silence. *Aaaaaiiiiooo. Aaaaaiiiiooo.*

Lillian shudders. Those damn peacocks. Charles's pride and joy – an ostentatious symbol of his success and, Lillian can't help thinking privately, his vanity. All part of the showmanship Charles so excels at – the staging of their *perfect* life. Of course, Charles has never seemed to mind their night calling, but no matter how many times she hears the birds' mournful cries, the sound always makes her shiver.

She pulls her robe more tightly around her body and tries to ignore the prickling sensation on her skin; but she is still hearing their screams as she slips between the sheets of her own bed and closes her eyes.

Lillian makes her way to the dining room at ten the following morning, hoping for tea and a moment of peace. Her head is dusty from too much champagne and too little sleep, but it's a lovely day and she intends to escape the house and visit Helena just as soon as she can.

By some miraculous sleight of hand, the dining room has been restored to its former incarnation. No trace of the previous night's party remains, except for Jack Fincher seated at the table in a pool of spring sunshine. He is drinking coffee and reading the morning paper, alone but for Monty, Charles's Irish wolfhound lying sprawled at his feet.

'Good morning,' she says, covering her surprise and addressing him from the open doorway. 'I hope you slept well?'

'Hello, *Mrs* Oberon,' he says, a slight emphasis on her title as he folds the newspaper and stands to greet her, that smile spreading across his face. 'Thank you, I did.' He indicates the chair opposite him. 'Will you join me?'

She doesn't move. 'I do hope Monty isn't making a nuisance of himself.'

'Not at all. He's the perfect companion.'

The dog, as if sensing he is the subject of their conversation, lifts his head off the parquet floor and eyes them both, then sinks back down again with a loud sigh.

Jack smiles. 'I've been admiring the view. I couldn't take it in last night but the aspect here is truly lovely.'

She nods, but she doesn't want to get drawn into pleasantries about the estate. She'd rather get on with the awkward task ahead. 'Charles asked me to show you the room,' she says, adjusting the silk scarf at her neck, raising her chin slightly. 'Would now suit?'

'Please,' says Jack, 'lead the way.'

They are a procession of three: Lillian in front, Jack in pursuit, and Monty loping at the rear. Lillian walks fast, her heels clicking down the corridors until they reach an arched doorway off the main entrance hall. 'We're passing into the west wing now,' says Lillian over her shoulder. 'It was a later addition to the original sixteenth-century house. All the rooms on this side look out over the arboretum.'

'We're heading to the nursery?'

'Yes.' She hesitates. 'Albie insists he's too old for such things now. He's away at school in the week. He's probably right.'

'Albie is your step-son?'

'Yes.'

Silence falls between them, only the sound of their footsteps accompanying them as they progress down the panelled corridor.

'I'm awfully sorry about last night,' Jack says finally. 'I had no idea that you were . . . well, who you *are*.'

'Please don't mention it.' She is glad she has her back to him.

'I could have kicked myself. Now that I've met you, I don't find you to be at all timid or . . .'

'Sickly?'

He groans. 'Not sickly. Not in the slightest. I sense a great . . . a great inner strength in you.'

Lillian nods but she doesn't turn around. She certainly doesn't want him to see the colour rising in her cheeks.

'Here we are,' she says, coming at last to a halt outside a heavy wooden door at the end of the corridor. She squints down at the ring of keys in her hand, trying first one, then another, her fingers fumbling at the lock.

'Third time lucky?' he suggests, and they both seem relieved when the key turns with a click.

Lillian steps back. 'After you, Mr Fincher.' She still can't quite meet his eye, but waits with her gaze slightly averted. His fingers hover momentarily over the intricately engraved doorknob before he twists it open and steps into the room.

For a moment he is lost inside the space. Lillian waits, listening to his footsteps echoing across the floor. She hears the squeak of a catch being lifted on a pair of heavy shutters then sees a large arc of sunshine appear as he pushes them back. Jack moves to open a second set of shutters then draws a pair of heavy velvet drapes hanging upon the furthest wall, revealing the third long sash window with a velvet-covered window seat built into its bay. With the light now streaming into the room, Jack turns back to regard the space.

Little has changed since Lillian last visited this room and she feels the ache of nostalgia rising up as she surveys the creamy butter-coloured walls and the high ceiling with its ornate circular glass dome at its centre. Along the wall nearest the door is a wide, stone fireplace, empty and soot-stained, while nearby are stacked several tables and chairs, as well as a bookcase holding a small collection of books. In the centre of the room is a large wooden desk. A family of jointed teddy bears, several small tin cars and soldiers as well as a faded rocking horse stand bathed in sunshine near the window seat. The most unusual feature, however, is the large curved wall that bows out into the arboretum, making the room almost feel circular in shape. She watches the artist moving about the room, the dust motes disturbed by his arrival spinning in the air. She has no idea what he is thinking.

'It's a lovely room,' he says at last, turning back to Lillian.

'It was used as a school room during the war,' she says. 'For the evacuees. I was one of them,' she adds.

'You were?'

She nods, leaning against the doorframe, watching him and awaiting his verdict. Monty, sniffing the air, leaves her side and pads across to Jack. Traitor, she thinks. 'The room was designed to look like a castle turret from the outside. The architect liked the idea of a curved nursery . . . fewer corners to be sent to, if you were naughty.'

Jack smiles. 'There's something rather poignant about it though, don't you think? These toys and books lying here unused.'

Lillian's gaze follows his to the abandoned teddy bears. 'There are so many rooms in this house. We can't possibly use them all,' she says, the words sounding a little sharper than she'd intended.

'How extraordinary,' he murmurs, 'to live in a house so large you can just lock up rooms and forget all about them.'

Lillian watches him move across to the desk, his fingers trailing across its surface, leaving tracks in the dust. She supposes he is right, though in this house, she has grown accustomed to the closed doors and private spaces; Charles's own bedroom, a private domain she only ever enters on invitation . . . his study a space that he alone occupies . . . and of course the late Mrs Oberon's rooms, closed and shuttered. Only once, in a moment of curiosity, had she dared to enter, slipping quietly behind the solid oak door, gazing around at the set of hairbrushes lying abandoned on the dressing table, the dresses hanging unworn in the wardrobe, the collection of coloured glass bottles gathering dust on a windowsill. The room had felt steeped in the deep silence of absence and she had closed the door quietly behind her with a feeling of such profound sadness that she had never entered it again. In a house like this – for a family like this – perhaps it wasn't so very strange to have ghost-rooms no one ever entered.

'Have you seen enough?' she asks, taking a tentative step towards the door; but Jack Fincher doesn't seem ready to leave.

'I've never worked on such a large scale before,' he says. 'I've painted a single mural but this would be quite different; a painting to walk inside of.'

'Charles is used to getting his way. He'll be disappointed, but I can break it to him gently.'

The keys jangle in her hand – the sound of impatience – but Jack stands in the centre of the room and closes his eyes. 'No,' he says eventually. 'You can tell your husband I'll do it. Tell Charles that I'll paint his room.'

Lillian isn't sure she's heard him correctly. She studies him, waiting for a smile that doesn't come. 'You will?'

He nods, his eyes tracking to hers. 'Yes.'

Lillian swallows and looks away. 'I see.'

Jack tilts his head. 'You don't think I should do it?'

There is a strange fluttering in her belly she doesn't quite understand. 'It doesn't matter what I think.'

He looks as if he will say something, then seems to change his mind. His hand moves to Monty's head where he combs the dog's scruffy brow and scratches gently behind his ears. 'It may take me a little while to clear my diary, but you can tell your husband to expect me by the end of the month.'

It's not the artist's fault, she tells herself. She mustn't blame him for Charles's plan, but she can't seem to quell the unease rising in the pit of her stomach.

Jack takes a step towards the door then hesitates, as if reluctant to leave. 'I can do something good in here,' he says quietly, before turning and moving past her, heading back into the corridor, the huge wolfhound trotting at his heels.

Lillian locks the door behind them, and then, in a fit of defeat, detaches the key from the ring and holds it out to him on the flat of her palm. 'Here,' she says. 'I suppose this is yours now.'

They stand close, the dark wood-panelled walls closing in around them, casting a strange and intimate air, his eyes

49

fixed on hers. She shifts, uncomfortable under such close scrutiny, but somehow unable to look away and when he does eventually take the key from her hand, his fingers brush her palm, like a feather moving over her skin. The sensation startles her out of her stillness. She spins on her heel and walks away down the corridor towards the main house, leaving Jack and the dog trailing in her wake.

'Mrs Oberon,' he calls after her. 'Wait! Mrs Oberon.'

She doesn't stop. She doesn't want him to see the tears welling in her eyes; and she doesn't understand why it should be tears that threaten to spill when what she really feels is anger; anger to have been once more so outmanoeuvred by Charles; anger to be feeling punished for something she knows is not her fault.

CHAPTER 4

'Mrs Oberon!' The man's voice is calling her from down a long, dark corridor. Lillian screws her eyes shut and tries to ignore him.

'Mrs Oberon. Can you hear me? Will you open your eyes for me?' The voice is insistent.

It takes a huge effort to prise open her eyes, and when she does, she is momentarily blinded by white strip-lights overhead. Blinking to focus, she finds herself lying in the white hospital room with the beeping machines and the curtain drawn round her bed. A tube is taped to the back of her hand, through which clear liquid snakes from a plastic lung hanging on a nearby stand.

A man is leaning over her. 'Mrs Oberon, I'm Doctor Ahmed. I've come to check on you. How are you feeling today?'

He has a nice face, young and handsome with dark brown eyes.

The doctor moves to the end of the bed and consults the charts on a clipboard. 'It's good news, Mrs Oberon. Your fever has come down. Carry on like this and we could be looking at discharging you in a couple more days.'

'I have to go home,' she says, her voice a dry rasp. 'I have to go back to Cloudesley.' Beside the bed, she notices a vase of drooping red tulips; petals, curled and browning, are scattered across the table top. How long has she been here? Time has lost its form.

Home. She closes her eyes and thinks of a swaying meadow, dappled sunlight falling through green branches, walking among tall, leafy trees. She thinks of long, tapered feathers with eyes the colour of emeralds and sapphires. 'I need to go back.'

'Well, you just keep doing what you're doing,' says the doctor, scribbling onto the clipboard, 'and we'll have you out of here in no time.'

CHAPTER 5

'We're in a world of trouble, Harry. I don't know what to do.'

Maggie has called Harry Granger from the phone in Charles's study, hoping that her grandparents' lawyer might have some inside knowledge to impart. 'The house is in a terrible state – barely fit for habitation – and there are bills coming out of our ears,' she tells him. 'I found a huge stack of them on Lillian's desk. None of them have been paid.'

'I'm sorry to hear that,' says Harry.

'We've got leaks all over the place. Last night's rain turned the house into Niagara Falls. I can't empty the buckets fast enough. I have no idea how I'm going to pay what is owed to Jane, let alone keep the electricity and gas running. I really need to access Lillian's bank accounts if I'm to pay them all off, and get the house fixed up to even the most basic standards, for her return.' Maggie can hear the hysterical note in her voice. She stops and takes a deep breath. 'Sorry, Harry. I'm stressing out. I want to help Lillian. I want to bring her home. But I'm going to need some money.'

'I take it Tracey Emin isn't looking anxiously over her shoulder just yet?'

Maggie sighs. She thinks of all her paints and brushes and the blank canvases she left behind last year. What does she have to show for her time since she graduated art college, other than some mediocre barista skills and a talent for taking food orders and not dropping plates on customers? Not even her time abroad has helped her press the 'reset' button. How to tell Harry that the glittering art career that had seemed so promising just a couple of years ago has stalled spectacularly, along with the rest of her life? 'I've . . . er . . . hit a bit of a creative block on that front.'

'Well, I'm still the proud owner of the Maggie Oberon original I bought for a song at your graduation show. I'm convinced it will be worth a small fortune, one day.'

Maggie can't help her dry laugh. 'While we're all waiting for that day to arrive, perhaps you know of a way I can access some of Lillian's money, to help make this place more comfortable for her?'

Harry lets out a pained sigh. 'That's what I wanted to talk to you about, Maggie. I'm afraid Lillian's investments are almost gone.'

'What?' Maggie takes a moment to let Harry's words sink in. 'But how? Where has all the money gone? Lillian must have received a significant pay-out when the business was sold?'

'I don't know about significant. Oberon & Son was in pretty bad shape at the time of the take-over. She's had to sell it off piecemeal over the years to cover various expenses. But yes, she did receive a sum.'

'So where is it?'

'Maggie, you and I both know that these old houses can become terrible financial drains if they're not managed properly. There have been expensive medical bills over the years — first your late great aunt Helena . . . then Charles, after his stroke.' Harry Granger hesitates. 'And of course your father, Albie, has needed significant . . .' he hesitates again, 'help. Debts and so on. Lillian has been very generous.'

'I see.' Maggie chews on a fingernail. She thinks of Lillian's generosity last year when Maggie herself was at her lowest ebb and feels a flash of guilt.

'I did try to warn her. I couldn't see how Lillian would be able to see out another year at Cloudesley unless something significant changed; but she didn't seem to want to accept that she might not be able to stay on in the house. She seems very . . .' he pauses, as if seeking the right words, '. . . emotionally connected to the old place. Fervently so.'

'Yes,' murmurs Maggie, remembering her grandmother's fierce insistence that she return home. 'She is.' Maggie sighs. 'I had no idea things were this bad. She never mentioned any of this. In the letters we exchanged she implied that all was well.'

Harry maintains a tactful silence for a moment before asking, 'May I speak candidly?'

'Of course.' Maggie gazes unseeing out of the wisteria-clad window.

'You know how long I've worked for your grandparents. I've grown very fond of Lillian. But I'm afraid, Maggie, that I saw this day coming. I warned your grandmother about this very scenario a while ago and I'll tell you exactly what I told her then. You will either need to find a way to maintain the house and generate an income large enough to cover its upkeep, or I'm afraid you will *have* to sell Cloudesley.'

'Sell Cloudesley?'

'Yes.' The lawyer's voice softens. 'There is an interested party. It might be something to consider, if an alternative solution can't be found. Lillian was adamant she wouldn't leave the house when I first raised it with her, but unless the situation changes – and changes fast – I can't see that she will have any other option.'

Through the thick tendrils of wisteria, Maggie notices a coil of smoke rising up over the trees in the arboretum.

Sell Cloudesley. The thought is shocking to her. She came back to help Lillian recuperate – to bring her home – not to sell the house out from under her. 'I can't. I can't do that to her. This is her home. It's where she wants to be.'

'I don't know if you remember, Maggie,' continues Harry more gently, 'but Lillian made you her Power of Attorney.'

Maggie has a vague memory of signing papers in Harry's office, though she hadn't paid much attention at the time; she hadn't liked to think of the day Lillian might require someone to act on her behalf.

'I don't know if we're quite at the point where we should activate it, but if it comes to it, we can certainly make the necessary arrangements.'

'I see.' Maggie feels a fresh wave of anxiety that Lillian should have trusted her with this responsibility; that it should be Maggie who is now expected to know what is in both her grandmother's and Cloudesley's best interests.

But Maggie *doesn't* know. And if she had to hazard a guess, surely it would be to keep the family home secure, so that Lillian might return to the place she has lived for over sixty years.

More than a little depressed at the outcome of their conversation, she ends the call and sits in a daze watching the smoke billowing in the distance. It takes her a while to register what it signifies, and to remember who will be stoking the flames. She sighs. She supposes she can't skulk around the house avoiding him forever.

She lets herself out of the French doors, taking the stone steps down to the lawn, heading past the forlorn-looking oriental fountain – moss-covered and empty bar a thin layer of green sludge and leaves – before wandering through the arched entrance into the arboretum.

When Jane had alluded to the new groundsman her grand-mother had hired, the very last person she'd imagined it could be was Will Mortimer. Yet sure enough, there he had been the next day, loping across the drive with a coiled hosepipe slung over his shoulder as she'd returned from a second hospital visit to Lillian. As she'd pulled up outside the house, he'd turned and stared, his expression utterly unreadable through the windscreen. She'd wanted to smile, should have at least waved, but the burning shame that had welled up had paralysed her and instead she'd just sat there, staring back at him, until he'd turned and disappeared round the side of the house.

Since then, Maggie has noticed traces of him about the place: a wheelbarrow of weeds standing by the overgrown borders below the terrace; the sound of leaves being raked in the old courtyard, the distant sight of him perched up a ladder in front of one of the old barns; and every day she's found reasons to avoid him.

She can't deny Will is working hard and while she has no doubt his efforts about the place are not only valuable but also, in most cases, absolutely essential, her conversation with Harry has only served to increase her worry. She knows they need to have a conversation.

She follows the scent of smoke until she comes upon him at the bottom of the arboretum near the giant Monkey Puzzle tree, shovelling last winter's debris onto a bonfire. His dark, unruly hair is a little longer than she remembers, his frame a little leaner. He is so distracted by his work he doesn't notice her until she clears her throat loudly. He stops shovelling and steps back from the fire, shaking his hair from his face and eyeing her through the rising smoke. 'You're back then?' he asks. His words sound more like a challenge than a question.

'Yes. I came home as soon as I heard about Lillian.' She forces herself to hold his gaze. 'You didn't think I'd stay away, did you?'

'After last year, I don't think any of us knew quite what you'd do.'

A damp branch spits in the fire. She is the first to drop her gaze, scuffing at the grass with the toe of her trainer, annoyed to feel the blood rising in her cheeks. 'Thanks for helping Lillian out,' she says, ignoring the barb and trying a more conciliatory approach.

He shrugs. 'I was between jobs and Lillian asked if I'd take over for a few weeks and . . . here I am. There's a lot to do,' he adds.

'Yes. I'm only just beginning to realise how much. God knows the place could do with a little TLC.' She smiles at him but he remains blank-faced, staring at her across the smoking pile with expressionless blue eyes.

'How is she doing?' he asks after a moment, adjusting the spade slightly to lean his weight on it.

'Much better. They're releasing her later today.'

'That's good. Where to?'

Maggie sighs. First Jane. Now Will. 'She's coming home, of course,' she explains patiently. 'To Cloudesley.'

'You think that's a good idea?'

'Yes, of course it's a good idea. It's the only place she wants to be.'

Will frowns. 'I don't want to speak out of turn, but I've been a little worried for her. This place . . . it's a lot to manage on her own. Surely you can see for yourself how it's starting to crumble around her?'

'But she's not on her own. She's got Jane . . . and you.' She takes a breath. 'And now she's got me, too. I'm going to look after her.'

'You are?' He shakes his head in disbelief. 'OK. Wow.' He picks up the spade again and tosses another heap of leaves onto the bonfire between them. Sparks crackle and fly into the air.

Maggie feels another surge of annoyance. 'What's that supposed to mean? *Wow?*'

He looks as though he wants to say something but then stops himself. 'Nothing.'

'No, go on. Don't hold back. Say what you were going to say.'

They face off under the trees, smoke billowing up into the air, both of them bristling with tension. She knows what he's thinking. She knows he doesn't think she can do it . . . that she doesn't have it in her to commit to this responsibility, nor the staying power to remain at Cloudesley for Lillian. But he doesn't say a word, he just holds her gaze, shifting the spade in his hands, and suddenly and somewhat unexpectedly, she finds that it's her who's speaking again, blurting the one question she knows she has no right to ask. 'How's Gus?'

Will eyes her coldly, then looks away to a space somewhere just above her head. 'He's fine. Actually, he's great.'

She nods. 'Is he back here too?'

'No. He's still in London.' With a sudden sigh Will seems to sag, resting his weight onto the spade, running a hand over his brow, his fingers leaving black soot streaks on his temple. 'What a massive fuck-up, Maggie.'

She hesitates, unsure if he's talking about Lillian's decline, or the state of Cloudesley, or what happened last year between her and Gus. Perhaps he's just giving a general character statement about Maggie. In any case, she supposes it's an accurate summation. 'Yes,' she agrees, feeling overwhelmingly exhausted, 'a massive fuck-up.'

The wind sends another gust of smoke spiralling between them. When it clears she finds Will is still staring at her with that dark, inscrutable look. Unable to look away, she feels a deep ache of longing, a sudden, desperate urge to close the gap – to walk around the fire and hug him. She wants to ask him how it came to this, how all those years of friendship could just dry up, count for nothing, go up in smoke like the dead wood and mulch burning in front of them. But Will doesn't seem to want to hang around talking about the past. He doesn't seem to want to spend a moment longer in her presence. He lifts the spade again and makes to shovel another pile of leaves onto the bonfire. 'I can't stand here chatting all day,' he says brusquely. 'Things to do.'

Maggie starts talking, before he can turn away. 'I know Gran's behind on the wages she owes you. I've spoken to Harry Granger and I'm planning to get everything sorted. You won't be out of pocket for much longer.'

Will nods but he doesn't look at her, just tosses another heap of off-cuts onto the smoking bonfire. 'OK.'

'And I'm sure Lillian would love to see you, when she's settled back in,' she adds through the billowing smoke.

'Sure.' He still won't look at her and feeling the full force of his judgement, she throws her hands up in defeat and turns to leave. There is nothing more she can say.

Trudging back through the arboretum, her mind skips over their conversation. Gus. He said Gus was fine. No. Better than fine. He said he was 'great'. She gently tests how she feels. Relieved? Disappointed? Ashamed? Yes, it's still there: that deep, burning shame she carries right at her core. The mistakes she made last year – the way she handled things – she knows she was in the wrong.

Will hadn't asked where she'd been all this time. She supposes he doesn't care enough to ask. And why should he? She let Gus down badly. Of course he is going to play the protective older brother. She just wishes she knew of a way she could make it right.

The western side of the house appears through the trees. She doesn't approach Cloudesley from this direction often and at this angle it's all jutting chimneys, crumbling stone-work and unruly vines. Closer still and she can see the boarded-up windows of the separate wing, the curved, single-storey turret room with its crenellated roof. Virtually hidden from view behind the overgrown creepers, it's the part of the house she doesn't know; the part she has never stepped inside, not in all the years she has lived there. The door leading into the west wing had never been unlocked. *Never go in there, Maggie*, her grandfather had told her in his sternest voice. *It's not safe.*

Thoughts of collapsing walls and roof beams meant she had obeyed him, for the most part. Just the one time she'd attempted entry, inspired by a childhood story, bending one of her grandmother's hair pins and twisting it hope-fully in the old lock until her grandfather had come upon her, silently wheeling up behind her and roaring so loudly she'd fallen back onto the floor, snapping the end of the pin in the lock.

'What do you think you are doing?' he had shouted in his strange, slurring voice, wheeling his chair close enough to grab her by the arm with a surprisingly strong grip. 'Get away from there!'

She had never seen him so angry, his face turning an alarming scarlet. 'I just wanted . . . I wanted to know what was inside.' She'd held her arm, rubbing at the red marks where he had held her, blinking back tears. 'I'm sorry.'

'Snooping. That's what you were doing. You mind your own business, young lady. There's nothing for you behind that door. There's nothing for anyone in there.'

The next day she'd found a heavy tapestry had been nailed across the door in the hall leading to the wing, obscuring it completely from view. Charles must have requested it be done overnight. Soon, it was as though that part of the house had never existed. She'd forced all thoughts of the abandoned rooms from her mind – preferring to forget the altercation with her grandfather – and had never attempted entry again. The house and gardens had plenty of other corners and curiosities to satisfy an inquisitive mind.

Thinking of the locked door and realising that the whole house stands empty, Maggie feels the first thrill of an idea. Who is to stop her now?

She makes for the entrance hall and stands looking at the tapestry hanging exactly as it always has over the door. Only, the more she studies it, the more she realises that something is amiss. She bends to examine the lowest corner and reaches out with her fingers. It is heavy and coated in a layer of dust, but peels away from the wall easily. 'Huh,' she says to the empty room.

She's not sure who would have prised the tacks out of the tapestry, leaving it open on two sides, or why they might have done so, but now that she's standing there alone in the hall, there seems to be no valid reason not to satisfy her curiosity. She pulls the tapestry back a little further and reveals the old wooden door behind; the same one she'd tried to prise open all those years ago.

She reaches out, feeling both a sense of daring and a tremor of fear – half-expecting to hear the booming voice of her grandfather at any moment as her hand tries the handle. It rattles beneath her fingers but will not turn. The door is still locked and she doesn't have the key.

Disappointed and perhaps a tiny bit relieved, she drops the tapestry back over the door. Her grandfather's words echo in her mind: *There's nothing for you behind that door.* He's right. She's already got more than enough on her plate – more crumbling house and maintenance than she can handle. She needs to focus on the job at hand: Lillian and the house. Mentally, she rolls up her sleeves and steels herself for what's ahead. There's just enough time to put the finishing touches to Lillian's room. She needs to stop getting distracted by Will and silly childhood memories and focus on the real issues.

CHAPTER 6

The sunlight dances in the treetops. Lillian lies in the ambulance watching the flickering patterns cast through the window high above her head. They are driving at a slow and steady pace, climbing higher and higher into the Chiltern Hills. No need for speed or sirens today; just a feeble, old lady being delivered home.

The vehicle turns sharp left and the familiar sound of gravel crunching beneath the tyres tells her that they are almost there. The driver's low whistle, when it comes, is right on cue. 'You never told us you were to the manor born, Mrs Oberon. If we'd known we'd have charged you double. Isn't that right, Tony?' The paramedics laugh and Lillian tries to smile at their joke, the muscles in her face feeling strangely stiff.

To the manor born. A charmed life. Isn't that what they've always said? She can still remember the piece that had run in *The Lady* all those years ago, the one Charles had urged her to do after they were married, accompanied by that awful photo of her standing in a stiff tweed suit by the front door, one hand resting on Monty's shaggy head. *Mistress of the Manor* had read the headline. Charles had thought it perfect. A nice profile raiser for the clientele of Oberon & Son, he'd toasted that night. 'You've come a long way from the shy little thing you were when you first came to visit.'

The ambulance slows then comes to a complete halt. The man in the passenger seat unbuckles his seatbelt and hops out. She can hear him greeting someone outside as the rear doors are opened, bringing a rush of sunshine and the fresh, clean scent of recently mown grass.

'Do you need any help?' a female voice asks. Maggie, Lillian realises and her heart gives a little leap.

'No. All part of the service, love.'

'Welcome home,' Maggie says, her face coming into view as Lillian emerges from the ambulance, propped half-upright on the stretcher bed. 'It's so nice to have you back.' The girl squeezes her hand.

Lillian blinks at her in the bright daylight, gripping her warm hand in return, not trusting herself to speak.

'Where to then, love?' the driver asks her granddaughter, as if he were wheeling a cumbersome piece of furniture into the house. Lillian tries not to mind.

They carry the stretcher bed up the front steps then in through the entrance hall. Lillian wants to protest that this is all ridiculous and she's sure she could walk if they would only let her, but the words won't seem to leave her mouth. 'Amazing place you've got here,' says one of the paramedics, staring about as they move through the hall. 'It's like the Natural History Museum.'

'Yes,' says Maggie. 'My grandfather was something of a collector. His father before him, too. A long history of hoarding.'

'I'll say,' says the other, giving a long low whistle as they pass a row of glass cases housing a collection of vases and ceramic figurines. 'What's with all the peacocks?' he asks, nodding at the dusty taxidermied bird staged on a branch over the door arch.

'Oh, my grandfather had a bit of a thing for them. He kept them on the estate, back in the day. I'm told they'd wander about the grounds causing havoc and digging up the flower beds. Isn't that right, Gran? Oh, watch your step on that rug,' she warns suddenly.

Lillian doesn't reply. She is remembering the feel of a favourite silk scarf running through her fingers and sunshine glinting on a blue car bonnet; eyes meeting in a wing-mirror and a small, shared smile. *Thank you, my dear, for your dazzling ornithological knowledge*. The words rise up and bob on the surface of her memory like corks floating on water.

'Through here,' Maggie directs, 'to the drawing room,' she adds, addressing Lillian now. 'I thought you'd be more comfortable. You won't have to worry about all those stairs . . . and you've got a telly and your radio and a lovely view of the garden.'

The paramedics lift her carefully from the stretcher then lower her into the new bed. Maggie adjusts the sheets. 'You're home now, Gran . . . at Cloudesley,' she adds, presumably to check she recognises her surroundings.

Lillian looks about. 'My gloves,' she says, to no one in particular. 'It won't do to go without my gloves.'

'You don't need gloves,' says Maggie, patting her hand. 'It's a lovely, warm day.'

The ambulance men seem to need various signatures from her granddaughter and are talking loudly about medication and physio. 'Her memory,' she hears Maggie say softly. 'It still seems a little off.'

'Yes,' says one of the men, 'nothing to worry about. Being home should help her settle. If she wants to move about a bit, that's fine but it's best if she uses the walker until she's really steady on her feet again. Any concerns or worries, call your GP. If it's an emergency, call 999.' They turn back to Lillian. 'Goodbye, Mrs Oberon,' they shout cheerfully. 'You take care of yourself.'

Lillian gives a small wave. 'Thank you,' she says, although she's not sure anyone hears her, for they are already halfway out the door, Maggie showing them back towards the entrance hall.

Lillian glances about. The bed they have put her in has been set up in one corner of the drawing room, her favourite kingfisher-blue velvet armchair shifted slightly to accommodate it. Her reading glasses lie upon a table beside a collection of framed photographs. Her eye is drawn to a black-and-white image of her and Charles on their wedding day standing outside a register office, Charles looking handsome but sombre in a dark suit, Lillian clad in a simple white lace tea dress. A young Albie stands at her side, his small hand held in hers and while Charles looks straight into the camera lens, her own smiling face is tilted to look at the little boy. She studies her younger self for a moment. So innocent – so certain of her choice to marry Charles and become a step-mother to Albie. How confident she had been that she would make everything better for them all. How impossibly naive.

The wedding photo stands beside a framed black-and-white image of a young Helena, aged about eleven or twelve, sitting on the top step to their house in Pimlico. It is the only photo she has of her sister from their London days. She wears a smart blue and white dress with a neat Peter Pan collar – a dress Lillian can still remember her mother running up late into the night on her sewing machine, a dress Lillian herself had coveted with barely disguised envy. The photograph, she knows, would have been taken by their father on the Bakelite camera he loved to mess about with.

Another silver frame houses a portrait of Charles dressed in full captain's uniform, while beside it stands a formal photograph of Albie as a young boy, contrasting markedly with the printed photo propped in front, one of him as an older man, relaxing on the prow of a yacht in dazzling sunshine, his face weathered, his eyes crinkled against the glare. The last photo is of a younger Maggie at her college graduation, Lillian standing at her side, beaming with pride. She eyes the photos for a long while before turning away.

It is good to be away from the stale, sterile air of the hospital ward, free of the stiff starched sheets and the endless muffled coughs and murmurs, beeps and buzzers. She probably doesn't need to be in bed exactly, but perhaps a little rest won't hurt. She relaxes back against the pillows and looks out towards the garden where the light is beginning to fade, the sky shifting slowly from blue to soft dusky pink. From far away comes a blackbird's warble.

'Can I get you some tea? Something to eat?' Maggie is back. 'Shall I let a little fresh air in?'

Lillian swallows the saliva building in her mouth. 'The birds,' she manages, although the words sound a little garbled.

'You'd like to hear the birds? Of course!' The girl rushes to the glass doors and pulls them open, seemingly grateful to be able to do something to make her a little more comfortable. 'They sound lovely at this time of day, don't they?'

A breeze catches the curtains, billowing them out towards the bed before they fall still. 'Albie?'

'Oh, no, not yet . . . but I'm sure he'll visit soon. Look, I've brought some things down from your bedroom.' Maggie indicates a small collection of items on the table beside the bed: a snakeskin vanity case, a bottle of perfume, a favourite pewter jug holding pink roses, and a set of engraved silver hairbrushes. 'If there's anything else you'd like, just let me know.' Another burst of the blackbird's evensong filters through the open doors. 'You're probably tired.'

Lillian is tired. The light, the perfume of the roses mingling with the scent of the cut grass, the sound of the bird trilling in the tree all stir something inside her.

'Gran? Are you OK?'

She feels her granddaughter's hand cover her own but Lillian doesn't answer.

'We'll soon have you back on your feet.'

And there it goes, her mind turning back on itself, finding the fragment of a memory and drawing it up into the light.

CHAPTER 7

Lillian is upstairs hunting for a missing white glove when the car horn blares loudly. She rummages through a drawer of undergarments and finds it at last in a tangle of silk stockings. Snatching up her handbag and a pair of sunglasses, she runs from the room, down the curved staircase and out into the brilliant summer's day.

Charles is standing with the artist, their backs to the house as they admire Charles's latest acquisition: a sleek blue Aston Martin, roof down, its walnut dash and tan leather interior gleaming in the sunshine. 'Isn't she something?' she hears Charles say. 'Just off the production line.'

Jack circles the car and emits a low whistle. 'She's a beauty.'

'Hop in. If Lillian hurries up we'll have time to take her for a little spin, though you might have to fold yourself like a paper crane to fit in the bucket seat.'

'Hello,' Lillian says, addressing both men as she draws closer, pulling on the errant glove and lowering her cat's-eye sunglasses. She notices Jack, like Charles, is dressed in cricket whites, though his appear a little too big around the waist, borrowed, perhaps, from Charles or Bentham. 'Sorry to keep you both.'

'Hello.' Jack smiles and gives her a polite nod before sliding into the back of the car.

'About time,' tuts Charles. He slams the passenger door behind Lillian then walks round to the driver's seat. 'I knew your visit to Helena would make us late.'

'I'm here, aren't I?' she says lightly. 'No Albie today?'

'No. The blasted boy refused. Said it was "boring".' Charles shakes his head with obvious exasperation. 'I had a good mind to force him anyway . . . but he must have sensed my mood because he's gone AWOL. Probably drifting about the woods as usual, grubbing around for his useless treasures.'

'I see Charles has roped you into the game?' she asks, shifting slightly in her seat to try to look at Jack, a clumsy deflection from Charles's irritable rant.

'Yes.' Jack gives her a rueful smile. 'I told him I was no good at cricket but he simply wouldn't take no for an answer. That's something I'm starting to learn about your husband,' he adds.

Charles revs the engine and they speed down the driveway, leaving Cloudesley and a spray of gravel in their wake, careening around the curved drive. Sunlight strobes through the overhanging trees. The breeze tugs at Lillian's loose hair. At this rate they'll be at the village green in no time, she thinks, hopefully with Charles's bad mood left at the house; but no sooner has she had this thought than Charles is slamming on the brakes, sending all three of them lurching forwards and Jack's knees ramming into the back of Lillian's seat. 'Damn!' Charles thumps the steering wheel with his fist.

Standing ahead of them and blocking the exit through the wrought iron gates is a peacock, its long tail feathers trailing across the dusty gravel. The bird is positioned side-on, staring at them with one haughty eye. Lillian senses Jack craning forward between the seats, angling for a better look. Charles edges the car a little closer, revving the engine, but the peacock holds its ground. It doesn't even flinch.

Lillian sees Charles considering the grass verges to either side but it's obvious to all of them that they are too high for the low chassis of the Aston Martin. 'Chop chop!' he yells, leaning heavily on the horn, but the bird simply tilts its head and gives them a nonchalant glare. 'Come on, you overblown turkey, get out of the way.'

Charles edges the car closer still, hoping to intimidate the bird into moving but it remains rooted to the spot until, with a small shiver, it counters by lifting its tail feathers and spreading them into a spectacular fan.

Lillian has grown used to seeing the birds around the estate, but the sight of its flamboyant feathers shimmering in the dappled sunlight cannot fail to amaze her still. Even Charles is silenced momentarily by the display, admitting defeat with a long, low sigh and switching off the car engine.

'So beautiful,' murmurs Jack from the back seat.

Lillian glances in the wing-mirror and finds her gaze locking with the artist's. She looks away, her eyes returning to the bird. 'And *so* stubborn,' she says. 'You watch. That peacock won't be going anywhere; not until it's good and ready.'

'Thank you, my dear,' says Charles drily, 'for your dazzling ornithological knowledge.'

He leans out of the car and flaps ineffectually at the creature but Lillian is right: the peacock isn't budging. A battle of pride, she thinks with a wry smile. 'How are you settling in, Mr Fincher?' Lillian asks, forcing herself to resist another glance in the wing-mirror. 'I hope you have everything you need?'

'Yes, thank you. Your staff have been very accommodating.'

'Good. You're very welcome to dine with us in the evenings, if you'd prefer?'

'I've been keeping rather irregular hours. I think it best I eat in the kitchen; and Mrs Hill has been very helpful, sending food up to my room on occasion.'

'Well tonight we insist,' says Charles. 'It will be a chance to celebrate victory against our arch cricketing foes.' Charles leans on the horn again, but the peacock remains exactly where it is. 'Assuming we ever make it to the blasted game.'

'Cigarette?' asks Jack, offering a slim case, first to Lillian who declines, then to Charles. 'Here,' he says, offering Charles his lighter.

'Very nice,' says Charles, studying the inscription engraved on the silver Zippo. *Boldness be my friend.*' He hands it back to Jack.

'A gift from my father,' says Jack. 'It's a quote from Shakespeare. My old man wasn't too keen on my pursuit of a career in art; he hoped I'd follow him into the cabinet-making business. Still, once he'd accepted my mind was made up, he gave me this.' Jack turns the lighter over in the palm of his hand. 'I think it was his way of telling me he accepted my decision. He told me if I was going to throw my life away on art, I should do it properly. Be bold. No half measures.'

Charles nods. 'Quite right. One never gets anywhere in life without taking a few risks.' He turns and studies Jack, a light smile playing on his lips. 'Seems to be paying off for you.'

Jack shrugs. 'I've been lucky.'

Charles scoffs. 'Hardly luck. Talent, I call it. Dare I ask how my room is coming along?'

'It's early days,' Jack says, casually deflecting Charles's enquiry.

Lillian removes her sunglasses and ties her scarf over her hair before ducking down to check her reflection. She feels a small electric current pass through her as her eyes meet Jack's again in the wing-mirror. He throws her a small smile before averting his gaze.

'He's certainly rather pleased with himself, isn't he?' says Jack, after another moment's silence, nodding his head at the peacock.

'Oh yes, a terrible show-off.' Charles takes a considered drag on his cigarette. 'But then you would be, wouldn't you,' he adds, 'looking like that.'

Lillian is reminded of something. 'Who was it who said, "the most beautiful things in the world are the most useless: peacocks and lilies, for instance"?'

'I think that was Ruskin,' says Jack.

'Ha!' laughs Charles. 'There's truth in that. Could have included women too.' Charles laughs loudly at his own joke.

'Only if you're to assume a woman's sole purpose in life is to look good,' counters Lillian.

'Well of course . . . there's looking good . . . and there's child-bearing,' adds Charles, still looking ahead at the bird.

Lillian grips the bag in her lap a little more tightly.

If the artist seated behind them is aware of the tension, he deflects artfully. 'I think Ruskin misses the point,' he says. 'Beauty is never useless. It has purpose. Look at us, sitting here. We've ceased all other activity just to pause for a moment and wonder at the sight of this bird. The extraordinary jolts us from the mundane and makes us *feel* something. It reminds us we're alive.'

'Rather like art,' says Lillian, after a moment.

Jack meets her gaze in the wing-mirror and nods. 'Yes. Art. Music. Love.'

Lillian drops her gaze, unexpected heat flooding her cheeks.

'This bloody bird is certainly making me *feel* something,' says Charles. 'And I don't mind telling you it's not generous. Anyway,' he adds with a snort, 'the difference is that unlike lilies – or peacocks, or indeed women – art doesn't age. It's static. A fine painting remains beautiful for all time. Which means that great art holds its value – indeed often growing more valuable over time. Which is why I choose to collect it, of course.

'A living creature, by comparison, cannot stay beautiful forever. Unless you can find a way to preserve it.' He gives a low laugh. 'Do you hear that, old boy?' he asks, addressing the peacock. 'If you don't move soon I think a little early "preservation" might be in order for you. I know a very good taxidermist,' he adds, turning to Jack with a wink.

Charles sends a final stream of smoke into the air and flicks his cigarette butt at the bird, only just missing. To the relief of them all, the peacock gives a last tilt of its head and struts slowly up onto the grass verge. 'Much obliged,' shouts Charles, doffing an invisible cap as it disappears into the undergrowth.

Unimpeded, they turn through the gates, heading out along the crest of Cloud Hill, Charles driving fast, accelerating around corners and putting his foot to the floor on open stretches of road, the church nothing more than a honey-coloured blur as they whizz past. Lillian grips the door handle and tries to focus on the road ahead as it dips down into the dell and on towards the village.

'Lillian hates it when I drive fast,' Charles shouts over his shoulder to Jack in the back seat. 'Though I often remind her that it's thanks to my love of speed that she met me in the first place.'

'Oh yes?'

'It was a collision of hearts, wasn't it, darling? Story for another day, old boy,' shouts Charles over his shoulder.

Instead of heading straight to the village green, Charles takes them on a whistle-stop tour of the village, pointing out local landmarks to Jack as they go, shouting snippets of information at the back seat, his words whipping away on the breeze. '. . . I tell you, there's nowhere better than the Chilterns in the summer . . . they say Oliver Cromwell hid in that house there . . . his initials scratched onto a glass window pane . . . famous soprano lives up that lane . . . the most enormous bosom . . . like the figurehead of a ship . . . that hill is the best place for winter sledging . . . come back and visit us in the snow!'

Charles is so determined to show off the village that by the time they arrive at the green, most of the players and spectators have already assembled, dotted in their cricket whites on the immaculate snooker baize pitch. 'They won't start without us,' says Charles, ever confident. 'Besides, I'm flavour of the month for finding a stand-in for Cartwright and his twisted ankle. Come on, Fincher, I'll introduce you to the other chaps.'

Lillian removes her headscarf and tucks it into her handbag, watching from beside the car as the two men walk into the fray, Charles, with his broad shoulders and thickening waist striding confidently in his cricket whites, next to the slimmer, rangier Jack.

A collision of hearts. Charles's words from the car come back to her.

The first time she'd met Charles, he'd been dressed in cricket whites. She had been cycling back to Lucinda's house after tea with a friend when he'd come careening around a sharp bend in his gleaming sports car, taking the turning far too late, forcing her up onto the verge, sending the bike sprawling out from underneath her and her flying straight into the hedgerow.

The car had screeched to a halt. 'I say,' Charles had shouted back at her, 'are you all right?' He'd got out of the car and approached the verge where she stood trembling as she dusted off her skirt. 'You really shouldn't be riding in the middle of the road like that. I could have killed you!'

She'd known who he was straight away, though she'd never met him face to face. Mr Oberon, owner of the manor house on the outskirts of the village. He'd been away fighting in the war when she'd first arrived in the village and had attended school lessons up at the house.

'I'm . . . I'm fine,' she'd told him, looking down at her ripped stockings and the nasty graze on her shin.

She's not sure if it was the ensuing silence or the sight of the blood welling on her leg, but suddenly the man's bluster had faded. 'I say, you are all right, aren't you?'

'I – I think so.' It was then that she'd seen the small, white face peering at her from the back window of the car. A little boy of no more than three or four. She'd remembered Lucinda talking about the tragedy the previous winter – the beautiful wife who'd died of pneumonia – leaving Charles Oberon a widower and a young boy motherless.

'Terribly sorry,' the man had said, seeming to soften. 'We've been celebrating our cricket win. I didn't see you coming. My fault entirely.'

'Hello,' she'd said, noticing the little boy sliding out of the car, sidling up to his father. He'd been staring, trans-fixed, at the blood trickling down her leg. 'It's all right,' she said, 'it's just a graze. Nothing to worry about.' She'd knelt down and smiled. 'What's your name?'

'Albie.'

'What a lovely name.'

'It's short for Albert.' The boy had peered at her before ducking back behind his father, holding on to his legs and making the man stumble.

'Don't cling to me like that, boy! Didn't you hear her? She said she's fine.' He'd looked at her a little oddly. 'You are fine, aren't you? You're not just saying that?'

'I am,' she'd said firmly, although she could still feel her knees trembling beneath her tweed skirt.

'Is your bicycle all right?'

'Yes.'

He'd looked at it uncertainly. 'That front wheel doesn't look too tip-top. Shall I take a look at it for you?'

'That won't be necessary.'

'At least let me give you a lift? Where are you headed?'

'Lucinda Daunt's house, in Chestnut Lane.'

'Lucinda Daunt? I didn't know the old dear was still alive! Are you a relation?'

'No. She's my guardian . . . has been ever since the war.' There had been no need to explain any further. The circumstances of the London orphans and evacuees arriving in Cloud Green were well known in the village. Lillian and Helena had been two of the luckier ones, finding a comfortable home with the kindly Lucinda Daunt and an arrangement they'd muddled through with long after the war had ended. Lillian had counted her lucky stars that they had been homed with such a kindly soul, given their situation.

Charles Oberon had nodded. 'Well, it's not far. I might be able to fit the bicycle in.' He'd looked at the twisted metal frame dubiously.

'Please, don't worry. I'm sure it's best I get straight back in the saddle. Isn't that what they say?'

'Well, yes, although I think they mean horses. Still, if you're sure . . . ?'

She had nodded and waited for them to drive away, with the last thing she'd seen of them being the little boy's pale, heart-shaped face gazing at her through the rear windscreen as they'd rounded the corner.

Still shaken, she'd picked up her bike and hobbled back to Lucinda's house, where she had recalled the encounter over dinner later that evening, turning it into a comedic episode and making light of her bruised legs and ruined bicycle.

'Well, well. Charles Oberon,' Lucinda had said, studying her thoughtfully through half-moon spectacles over her plate of ham and boiled potatoes. 'They say he's a man with a keen eye for beauty. Something of a collector. I wouldn't be surprised if he pops up in your life again someday, young lady.'

Lillian had laughed. 'I hardly think so. A man like Charles Oberon moves in very different circles.'

But Lucinda had merely tilted her head and raised her wine glass to her lips. 'We'll see.'

Charles Oberon's apology had arrived two days later in the shape of a shiny red bicycle with a woven-straw basket attached to the front, within which had sat a hand-written invitation to afternoon tea at Cloudesley.

Lucinda's crab-apple cheeks had turned quite pink with the excitement of it. 'Didn't I tell you?'

'It all seems a little . . . unnecessary,' she'd said, looking down at the letter. 'It was an accident.' She'd read through the invitation once more. 'Mr Oberon has suggested you might like to accompany me.'

This had seemed to please Lucinda no end. 'Of course. It would be only right and proper. We must reply right away.'

'But what about Helena? I can't leave her here.'

'Rubbish! I'll ask Mrs Brown next door to come and sit with her. Trust me,' she'd said, suddenly serious, 'this is important, Lillian. Do you hear me? This is life knocking at your door. Throw it open, young lady. You don't want to end up an elderly spinster like me. Don't sit here mouldering . . . no one for company but your poor, sweet sister.'

'But Helena—'

Lucinda had held up a hand. 'It's afternoon tea. I insist that you accept.'

Lillian hadn't been convinced – and if she were honest, she felt a little afraid at the thought of visiting Charles Oberon in his huge house. Certainly he was attractive, and so sure of himself in that way men of privilege and a certain age could be, but Lillian didn't feel worthy of his time or attention. She remembered how she'd felt standing at the roadside with him: foolish, diminished, a silly young girl. What on earth would they talk about? No doubt he would find her bland and disappointing. But Lucinda had been adamant: it would be rude not to accept.

From the moment they had arrived at the front door, Cloudesley had appeared nothing short of extraordinary. The sheer size of the house, its endless twisting corridors, the numerous doors hinting at untold rooms and treasures, the luxurious rugs laid across the floors, the strange and wonderful objects littering the hall as they'd followed the maid through to the drawing room, had all captivated her. As they'd sat drinking tea with Charles, she'd found it hard to focus on the ebullient man sitting before them, her eye instead drawn by the most extraordinary and wonderful sights. The carved gilded furniture with its velvet uphol-stery. The Victorian glass domes housing stuffed birds, coral and shells. The paintings lining the walls from virtually floor to ceiling. The enormous vases perched on pedestals. The furs and the fabrics. The room was a riot of colour and sensation. Lucinda's cottage on Chestnut Lane was certainly charming, but Cloudesley was an opulent palace by comparison.

She'd always known, on the days when she'd visited the house as an evacuee, sitting as a pupil at the wooden tables in the makeshift school room, that something extraordinary lay beyond. On the occasions when they'd been released from their desks and allowed to run in the arboretum, she had glimpsed through an open wooden gate to a lavish lawn bordered by extravagant topiary. But until that day, she had never been inside any of the luxurious rooms in the main house. Judging by the drawing room, she'd known then that they were more than she could have ever imagined.

'I'm so glad you could come,' he'd said, one hand resting on the head of an enormous wolfhound as he'd eyed Lillian keenly. 'I've been feeling rotten about the accident. Did you like the bike?'

'Very much. Thank you. But really there was no—'

'Oh rubbish,' Charles had said, waving away her protest. 'There was every need.'

Charles had smiled at her as he'd scratched behind the huge dog's ears and Lillian had returned his smile, relaxing a little. He seemed quite different from the blustering man she'd met on the roadside just a few days ago.

'Your home is beautiful, Mr Oberon,' Lucinda had offered graciously.

'I'll show you around, give you the grand tour, if you'd like?' Charles had looked at them both hopefully, like a small boy keen to show off his treasures.

'That would be wonderful,' Lucinda had answered for them both, before turning to Lillian and beaming up at her with a knowing look.

Moments later, the door to the drawing room had creaked open and Charles's son, dressed in a smart shirt and short trousers, had been steered into the room by a nurse. 'Here he is,' the nurse had said in a bright voice. 'Albie wanted to come and say "hello", didn't you, Albie?'

The little boy had nodded. 'I hope you are feeling better after your accident,' he'd said, his voice stiff and scripted, but heart-meltingly sweet all the same.

'I am feeling much better. Thank you, Albie. What's that you've got there?' she'd asked, pointing to the object clutched in the little boy's fist.

'It's a snail shell. I found it outside.'

Lillian had leaned in to inspect it more closely. 'It's a very fine shell, Albie. A real beauty.'

The little boy had smiled and when Lillian had looked up at Charles, she'd found him studying her keenly, with the oddest expression on his face. She had sensed that day that he was a man used to getting what he wanted. She'd simply had no idea then that what he wanted was *her*.

On the far side of the cricket pitch, villagers are spreading their picnic blankets on the grass and unfolding deck chairs, while over at a small white-painted pavilion several stout ladies in floral dresses fuss over cake tins and tea urns. Lillian is not in any rush to join them. Now that she's here she's reluctant to get drawn in to the gossip and village politics, the petty squabbles and subtle one-upmanship between the other wives.

The umpire, a chubby, red-faced man in a wide straw hat flips a coin. The visiting team win the toss and opt to bat first. As Charles strides out onto the pitch, directing his men to their different fielding positions, Lillian sees Jack turn and look back towards the car. There is something of the lost boy about him, trudging off to do his duty. She lifts her hand in acknowledgement – then feels instantly foolish, realising he isn't looking at her at all, but probably casting an admiring glance at the car. With a deep breath, she turns towards the pavilion, steeling herself for the afternoon ahead and praying silently for a win that might help to settle Charles's volatile mood.

Up on the veranda it is all gossip and small talk. Lillian greets the group of women with the appropriate kisses and hellos. 'Lucky us,' says Barbara Palfreyman, a buxom busybody, always to be found at the centre of any village event. She grips Lillian's arm tightly. 'We don't often have the pleasure of your company, dear.'

Lillian ignores the reproach hidden in the woman's greeting. 'It's such a beautiful day. How could I resist?'

'Quite right,' pipes up Susan Cartwright, one of the prettier girls from the village. 'We should all be doing our bit for the chaps.'

Lillian catches the eye of her friend Joan, her closest ally, and shares a small smile. 'Our bit for the chaps?' Joan mutters under her breath. 'Give me strength.'

Lillian busies herself with teapots and teacups, retrieving them from a dusty cupboard and rinsing them out as she listens to the women's conversation volleying around her. There is widespread outrage over the price increase of milk at the village shop as well as thinly veiled competition over the homemade cakes and scones. She finds herself drawn back into the conversation as Susan reaches over and fingers the fabric of Lillian's summer dress. 'You are a lucky duck,' she sighs. 'Is it Dior? It looks it. Oh for a husband who owns a fancy shop in London and showers me with beautiful dresses and jewels.'

It's Joan who rescues her from Susan's gushing. 'Here, be a love would you, Lillian darling?' She steers her away from the pavilion to where a pram stands in the shade. Joan reaches inside for a plump little baby in a blue playsuit and thrusts him at her. Lillian grapples with his fat little arms and legs until he has stopped wriggling and is secure in her arms. 'Ah look at you, little Georgie-Porgie,' Joan says, grinning down at her son, 'you're going to be a real heartbreaker. You don't mind, do you?' she asks Lillian. 'Only he won't lie there for too long without wailing and I said I'd help Barbara with the cucumber sandwiches. You *know* how pedantic she gets about her crusts,' she adds in a dramatic whisper.

Lillian feels the baby's warm head pressing against her chest. She lowers her face instinctively and breathes in the scent of him. 'I don't mind in the slightest.'

Joan eyes her carefully. 'You've been rather reclusive of late. Everything all right? I heard you weren't well.'

'Just a touch of spring flu. It kept me in bed for a few days. I'm fine now.'

'How's Helena?'

Lillian nods. 'She's fine. The same, as always.'

'Well I think you're a saint.'

'I'm no saint. I'm all she has.'

Joan nods. 'Well, I wish I had a sister like you. Oh look!' she says, suddenly distracted by the baby in Lillian's arms. 'He's smiling. He likes you, Lillian. You're a natural.'

'He's beautiful,' she says, putting her face closer to the baby's.

Joan leans in closer, conspiratorial. 'Now tell me, who is that divine man you brought along with you today? I'm sure I recognise him from somewhere.'

Lillian glances out to where Jack stands on the boundary and nods. 'Jack Fincher. Perhaps you met him at the ball last month?'

Joan shrugs. 'Darling, the only thing I remember from that night was your scoundrel of a husband plying me with gin fizz. Gerald had to practically carry me home. I could have met your handsome friend and danced a horizontal rumba with him and I wouldn't remember. Fincher, you say?' she adds, lifting her sunglasses to study him again. 'Why is he here?'

'Charles has hired him to paint the nursery. He's staying with us for the summer.'

'Oh . . . but you don't mean . . .?' Joan casts a delighted glance down at Lillian's flat stomach. 'You are a sneak. I never would have guessed.'

'Oh, no.' Lillian shakes her head. 'No. I'm not expecting. He's not *decorating* the nursery. He's transforming it, at Charles's request.' She gives Joan a pointed look. 'We've missed the boat as far as babies are concerned.'

'Oh surely not! You're doing a marvellous job with Albie, of course – but there's nothing quite like that bond between a mother and her *own* child.'

Lillian nods and tries to smile. Joan could never understand how much her words might hurt.

'Besides, you're still young enough. What are you? Twenty-six? Twenty-seven? Hardly over the hill. A baby or two would help to keep you busy in that sprawling house. Plenty of room for them to run around and then you simply ship them off to boarding school the moment they get troublesome. I really do recommend it. Oh! What is it?' Seeing Lillian's frantically blinking eyes, Joan reaches out to touch her arm. 'What have I said? Is it Charles? He's not keen?' She leans in closer again. 'You do surprise me. A hot-blooded man like him . . . I'd have thought he'd be pawing at you every night.'

Lillian shrugs, still not trusting herself to speak.

'Maybe he'll change his mind? Men do, you know. They're scared of change. They're afraid of competing for your attention. But all it takes is a little feminine persuasion. A little guile.'

Lillian shakes her head. 'It's not that.'

'Nonsense. We'll get you and Georgie set up on a picnic rug at tea. One look at his beautiful wife holding this bouncing baby boy will be enough to convince him.'

'You're sweet, and George is, of course, the perfect advertisement for parenthood, but believe me—'

'Oh but you mustn't give up!'

Lillian can't bear it any longer. She cuts her off. 'I lost a baby.'

Joan's hand flies to her mouth. 'Oh my dear, I'm so sorry.'

'It wasn't flu – I – I was expecting a child and then . . .' She takes a deep breath and says the rest in a rush, desperate to have it done with. 'Well, there were some complications and afterwards, the doctor told me that I wouldn't be able to conceive again. It's been a . . . a terrible blow.'

Joan pats her hand. 'I'm sorry. I've really put my foot in it, haven't I? No wonder you've been looking so wan. I had an inkling at the ball something was up. Oh dear. Gerald's always telling me to think before I shoot my mouth off. Forget I said anything. You're a wonderful step-mother to Albie. Best thing that could've happened to that boy after losing his mother.'

Lillian nods. 'He's the only child I'll ever have. I do love him – like he's my own.'

'Of course you do. And perhaps there will be grandchildren?' Joan smiles hopefully at her and Lillian nods and holds the baby just a little bit closer.

'Go on,' Lillian says, nodding her head in the direction of the pavilion. 'Go and help Barbara. We'll be fine over here, won't we, George?' The baby gurgles obligingly.

'I'm so sorry, darling, I've been an awfully clumsy clod.'

Lillian watches Joan go, holding the baby to her cheek, feeling a painful yearning building in her like the pale grey clouds massing on the distant horizon.

The afternoon meanders at a creeping pace. The air grows still and stultifying under the gathering clouds. The home team take three slow wickets but even Lillian can see that their bowler is off pace and the visiting team's batsmen are blocking easily. She watches Charles from the pavilion, red-faced and irritable, his growing frustration evident. She knows the evening ahead will be a difficult affair if the game continues like this.

A group of young children play on the grass. Lillian watches them for a while, her eye drawn to two young girls with long corn-coloured plaits playing at the edge of the green; quite clearly sisters. Together, they perform a series of roly-polies and cartwheels and Lillian smiles to see them, the sight bringing a distinct memory of that most freeing sensation of tumbling over the ground, the feel of grass beneath hands, bare knees and dizziness.

The memory links easily to another, lying under a tree, feeling the curve of the earth's embrace solid beneath her, as she and Helena whiled away an afternoon with their father, picking buttercups and weaving long daisy chains in a blossoming London park. There had been an outing on a rowing boat, their father navigating them about the still waters of a large, green lake with impressive skill and as they'd disembarked, Helena, larking about, had lost a shoe over the side of the boat where it had sunk without a trace. All this before the war had struck and their family had been altered forever. What freedom. What joy. If only they had known then how precious those fleeting moments were – how they would have to be enough to last a lifetime.

A loud 'crack', the unmistakable sound of leather hitting wood, pulls her attention back to the match. Lillian scans the sky and spots the ball, a flash of red against the clouds hurtling out towards the boundary. Shouts of *'catch it!'* rise from the players on the field. Her gaze finds Jack, running backwards and then sideways, trying to predict the angle of the ball's descent. He lifts his arms, readying himself, but with his next backwards step he stumbles, his heel tripping on the hem of his borrowed cricket trousers. Her heart lurches as Jack begins to fall.

'Catch it!' she hears Charles roar.

Lillian squeezes her eyes shut, unable to watch, only opening them fully when the cheers of the Cloud Green fielders reach her ears. Looking again she finds Jack lying on his back, arms raised in triumph, the cricket ball gripped tightly in one hand.

Jack is helped to his feet by a teammate. Lillian sees the umpire lift one finger to declare the batsman out. Jack tosses the ball into the air then trots in to meet the fielders. As applause rises up from the bank of Cloud Green supporters, Lillian lets out a quiet sigh of relief.

At tea, everyone wants to congratulate Jack. His catch has changed the pace of the game, crumbling the opposition's batting order, and energising the Cloud Green players. They cluster round him, rattling teacups and slapping him on the back. Lillian watches from the trestle table where she helps to serve cake and sandwiches, grateful to have a job to keep her occupied. She notices how the ladies of the village are particularly attentive to Jack's presence, Susan Cartwright leading the charge with an impressive display of skirt-swishing, giggling and hair tossing.

Joan walks past and leans in, whispering so that only Lillian can hear. 'It's like watching the mating rituals of the black widow spider. They're supposed to devour their mate after copulation, aren't they?'

'Joan,' laughs Lillian. 'You're awful.'

'What?' asks Joan, all wide-eyed innocence. 'She's shameless, that girl,' she adds in a lower voice, nodding at Susan. 'Still, if I didn't have my Gerald you can bet I'd be elbowing Susan Cartwright out the way. He is rather attractive, don't you think?'

Lillian glances across at Jack again. His full lips are set in a firm line, his skin flushed from the sun, or the attentions of the crowd. 'I suppose so,' she says.

'Married?'

Lillian shakes her head. 'Apparently not.'

Joan sighs. 'You have to admit that there's something rather romantic about an artist . . . soulful . . . tortured . . . I bet he's good with his hands.' She elbows Lillian suggestively then turns to stare at her. 'Why! Lillian Oberon, I do believe you're blushing.'

Lillian turns away. 'Don't be silly,' she mutters, uncertain why Joan's joke and the sight of the women in their colourful summer dresses fluttering around Jack like a kaleidoscope of butterflies should have stirred such a strange sensation within her. 'It's this weather,' she adds.

It *is* the day, she tells herself. The heat and the stillness of the air, the clouds pressing down upon the sky, and all of Joan's ridiculous talk of mating rituals and babies. It has got her all het up and flustered. She never should have come.

'You missed a good game this afternoon,' Charles says pointedly to Albie that evening as they sit around the long mahogany dining table at Cloudesley. Charles's good mood has lasted the rest of the afternoon, his anger at Albie's absence kept at bay like the clouds that had hovered on the periphery of the Chiltern Hills all afternoon but failed to deliver their promised rain. Bentham has opened the French doors, letting a faint current of air into the room, but it is not enough to shift the atmosphere. Heat lingers in the house like an unwelcome guest, its presence heavy and oppressive.

'You don't enjoy cricket?' Jack asks Albie.

The boy shrugs. 'Not really.'

'I don't know what to do about him,' says Charles, only half-joking. 'My son is more interested in wandering aimlessly about gathering his strange objects. Bottle tops and books of matches, conkers and flints. What was it Bentham called you? *A little bower bird.*' Charles snorts.

Albie flushes red but keeps his gaze fixed on his soup bowl.

'The apple doesn't fall far from the tree,' says Lillian lightly. 'It's not hard to see where he gets the interest from.'

Charles stares at Lillian, then reaches for his wine glass and takes a large swig.

Jack clears his throat. 'I've always thought it important for a boy to have his secrets. I used to collect feathers. I kept them stashed in an old biscuit tin. A few secrets never hurt anyone.'

Albie stops stirring his soup and looks up at Jack. 'Is that why you keep the room locked?'

A large moth flutters about the flames of the silver candelabra, casting a flickering shadow onto the tapestries lining the walls.

'Oh ho!' shouts Charles. 'Albie, you've let the cat out of the bag there. You've been down to the room, have you, rattling the door? Trying to sneak a look?'

Albie blushes and sinks lower into his seat.

'I'm sorry,' Charles says, this time addressing Jack. 'The boy can be a little impertinent. Albie, you're to leave Mr Fincher alone, do you hear me? Let him work without distraction.'

Bentham arrives, a silent shadow slipping through the open doorway to refill wine glasses. Lillian places a hand over her glass. 'I'm fine, thank you.'

'We should all be more curious about the world around us, don't you think?' says Jack, addressing Albie. 'I suppose I am being rather secretive. I keep the door locked because I don't want anyone to see the room yet. It would be like attending the first rehearsal of a play or reading the earliest draft of a novel. Very disappointing.'

Lillian listens to Jack's explanation, twisting the stem of her wine glass between her fingers. Like Albie, she too has been rather intrigued by Jack Fincher's comings and goings in the west wing. First had been the plentiful deliveries of paint and turpentine, the dust sheets, scaffolding poles, lamps and ladders. Then had come the artist himself, returning to Cloudesley, as promised, at the start of the month with a small leather suitcase, a bundle of brushes rolled up in a cloth and several large sketch pads. He had asked for the guest suite he had stayed in the night of the cocktail party. He'd told them it was perfectly comfortable and that he liked its close proximity to the west wing. 'I may be keeping rather unsociable hours,' he'd warned them. 'This way I won't disturb anyone.'

Unsociable hours or not, he had certainly kept to himself since then, spending from morning until often very late at night locked inside the room. Once or twice Lillian had spotted him walking the grounds, usually after lunch, when he would step out onto the terrace, sketchbook in hand, and disappear somewhere within the gardens; but until this evening's dinner, the car ride to and from the cricket match had been the longest she'd spent in close proximity to Jack Fincher since he had returned.

'Perhaps it's vanity,' Jack continues, 'but I prefer to reveal my work when it is complete. More so than any other art form, there is an immediacy to a painting that should be respected. You'd understand that, wouldn't you, Charles?'

Charles, who has a piece of bread roll halfway to his lips, murmurs his agreement. 'I would. The big reveal.'

'It's a risk though, isn't it?' says Albie quietly.

Jack tilts his head. 'What do you mean?'

'Well, I don't think Father much likes surprises.' Albie turns to Charles. 'Do you, Father?'

Charles lets out a bark of a laugh. 'The boy does have a point. Though I doubt very much we have anything to worry about. I know Mr Fincher is going to do a very fine job.'

Far away, across the hills, a rumble of thunder carries on the warm air.

Charles dabs at his brow with his napkin before throwing it carelessly onto the table. 'Have a word with cook would you, dear,' he says, turning to Lillian. 'This is hardly the weather for soup.'

'Of course.' She pushes her own soup bowl away. 'How about a game of Mahjong after dinner?' she suggests, trying to lighten the mood. 'Albie is quite the tactician,' she explains, for Jack's benefit.

Charles shakes his head. 'I have some business to attend to. I'll be returning to London at the weekend, for a few days.'

'Mr Fincher?' she asks. 'Are you brave enough to take on our young champion?'

The artist smiles. 'Another time? I'd like to spend a few more hours in the room tonight.'

Lillian nods and tries to ignore the small flicker of disappointment. Of course he is busy. Of course it is right she keep her distance from this strange, rather intriguing man.

There is a faint crackling sound. The moth that has been fluttering about the silver candelabra falls to the table. Albie reaches for the insect, plucking it off the tablecloth and bringing it close to his face. 'Singed to a crisp,' he says, studying it with a look of intense fascination.

'That's what you get when you play with fire,' says Charles, reaching for his wine glass. 'Now there's a warning for us all.'

Another low rumble of thunder echoes across the grounds, this time a little louder. Meeting Charles's gaze across the table, Lillian can't help the shiver that runs down her spine.

CHAPTER 8

Maggie isn't sure what has woken her. At first she assumes it is the thunder, the distant rumble of a summer storm echoing over the hills. But as she lies in the dark, watching the pale fabric of her bedroom curtains ghost backwards and forwards at the open window, she hears the scuffling sound. It is coming from somewhere downstairs, the noise echoing out from the fireplace across the room.

It must be an animal – a mouse, a rat, or please God, she shudders, not a bat. The thought sends her burrowing a little deeper beneath the covers, closing her eyes and trying to halt the sudden yet persistent loop of thoughts about pest inspectors and chewed electrical wiring and spiralling maintenance costs.

After a while, the noise stops. Maggie feels sleep begin to pull her under again, when the definite but far-off sound of a door slam jolts her back to consciousness. She sits bolt upright, listening in the dark, her heart pounding. Lillian? Wandering the house?

It's eerily quiet down in the entrance hall and nothing seems out of place as Maggie sweeps the light from her phone across the front door – still locked – and over the gilt-framed paintings lining the walls. She carries on through the house, making for the drawing room. She half-expects at any moment to come across Lillian collapsed on the floor,

93

so it is a relief to open the door and find her grandmother sitting upright on the edge of her bed, illuminated in the light spilling from her bedside lamp. She looks otherworldly in her long cotton nightgown, her thin, white hair standing in a static fuzz about her head.

'Are you OK?' Maggie asks, her heart still thudding loudly in her chest.

Lillian nods slowly. 'I thought I heard a noise.'

'Yes, so did I. Just mice, I think.'

'No.' Lillian shakes her head. 'It was the peacocks. I heard them calling.'

Maggie frowns. 'No, Gran, there aren't any peacocks here. Not anymore. You must have been dreaming. Look, your covers have fallen off the bed. Let me help you.' She goes to help Lillian slide back into the bed when she hesitates. 'Your feet,' she says, touching the sole of her grandmother's foot. 'What is this?' she asks, staring at the grimy black mark left on her finger. 'Your feet are filthy. Have you been outside?'

Lillian stares at her blankly.

'Gran? Were you sleepwalking?' She waits a moment longer but Lillian just gazes over her head. 'Don't move,' she sighs. 'I'll be right back.'

In the bathroom she fills a bowl with warm water and soap and finds towels and a flannel. Peacocks. She shakes her head.

'I'm glad you're feeling well enough to be up and about a bit,' she tells her when she is back in the room, bent over one of Lillian's sooty feet, 'but you'll catch a chill, or worse, if you start wandering about at night like this.' She dips the cloth into the warm water and gently sponges the heel of Lillian's left foot. The white cloth comes away black. Maggie catches the faintest trace of a familiar scent, though she can't quite place it. Burned toast. Bonfires. Smoke.

94

'Just like Albie,' murmurs Lillian, gazing down at her.

Maggie's hand freezes. 'Me? Like Dad?'

'Yes, such a sweet boy. So caring. Things were never easy for poor Albie.'

Maggie swallows and tries not to smart at the comparison. First of all, Albie is hardly a 'boy'. And 'sweet and caring' is certainly not how she would describe her ageing father. Reckless, flighty, irresponsible and absent are words she might favour. As far as she's ever been able to tell, Albie has lived exactly the life he pleased, drifting in and out of their lives at Cloudesley with seemingly no regard for anyone but himself. 'There is one indisputable difference between him and me,' she mutters under her breath, wringing the washcloth into the bowl, 'I'm *here*.'

'Yes you are,' says Lillian, smiling benignly. 'Yes you are.'

When she has patted Lillian's feet dry, Maggie helps her back beneath the bedcovers. 'Now, no more wandering about. Shall I turn the light off?'

Lillian reaches up and touches her cheek. 'Thank you, dear. You go to bed. I shall sleep now.'

Reassured that Lillian seems a little more herself, Maggie returns to her own room. She eyes the pile of cardboard boxes stacked in one corner – eight of them – her things from the London flat returned to her by an angry Gus last year – then looks away. She isn't ready to confront that part of her life yet. Climbing into bed, she focuses instead on Lillian, mentally adding another two worries to her ever-growing list: her grandmother's unpredictable sleepwalking and now Maggie's resemblance to her flaky father. Where has Albie been these past days, while she's wrestled with the house and bringing Lillian back to Cloudesley? And perhaps more importantly, why should it still surprise or affect her so much that he remains an absent figure in their lives? That he should still be able to command such emotion in her after all these years of disappointment remains a mystery to her.

Albie had first brought her to Cloudesley when she was five years old, on a night of howling wind and rain – a stark contrast to the warmth and sunshine of the Spanish islands they had left behind. Until that night, the only life she had known was a transient one of sunshine and island hopping, on the road with her mum and dad, a colourful painted van taking them wherever they wanted to go. There had been, for a time, a white cottage overlooking an azure sweep of sea. She could still remember fragments of their life there: pale pink shells in a bucket, bonfires burning on the sand, a bouncing piggyback ride on her father's shoulders, her mother's soft laugh, falling asleep to the sound of the ocean. Life had seemed a joyous bubble of love and togetherness until the morning she woke to find Albie sitting on the end of her bed, his head in his hands.

'Gone,' he had told her. 'Your mother's gone. Run off. Following her destiny, she said. That's how much she loved us.' He had looked up at her with such fear and despair in his eyes that Maggie had felt afraid and hadn't dared ask any questions about her mother, not even when Albie told her they were packing for a long journey to England. 'We'll have our own adventures, Mags. We'll show her.'

Albie had driven them down the long, forbidding drive of tangled trees and bundled her up the steps, moving quickly to avoid the stinging rain, ringing a brass bell hanging at the huge front door. She'd had no idea who or what lay beyond. She'd never heard Albie speak of his family home or parents before. Maggie had stood there, staring at the most fantastical birds carved into the wood panels, while from somewhere deep inside the house had come the sound of a dog barking. Maggie had shrunk behind her father's legs as the door had been thrown open by an ancient-looking, grey-haired man in a wheelchair. He had peered at them both over wire-rimmed spectacles with what she now understands was a look of both surprise and irritation. One of the man's hands had rested on the collar of a huge, grey-haired dog, preventing it from bolting out of the door as it sniffed excitedly at the new arrivals.

The old man had studied her father for a moment. 'Albie,' he'd said, just his name, spoken in strange, slurred voice.

'Hello, Father.'

'The wanderer returns. To what do we owe this unexpected honour? Run out of money again?' Maggie had noticed how the left side of the old man's face did not move quite as it should when he spoke, giving him a strange, sunken look.

Albie hadn't had a chance to answer as the door had suddenly opened a little wider and a woman had appeared at the man's side. She'd looked tall and startlingly regal standing there at the top of the steps with her fine features and her pale, almost white hair swept off her face with two silver combs, dressed in a burgundy wool cardigan with a glittering brooch of a stag beetle pinned to her lapel. Maggie hadn't been able to take her eyes off her.

'Albie!' the woman had exclaimed. 'What a wonderful surprise.' She had moved to greet him, but then her glance had fallen to Maggie standing at his feet and her eyes had widened. 'Well now, who do we have here?' she'd asked, peering down at her.

'This is Maggie. My daughter.' There was something in her father's voice – an unfamiliar tone at once both belligerent and bashful. 'Maggie, say hello to your grandparents.'

The dog had started barking again and Maggie, a little frightened both by the noise and the look she'd seen the older couple exchange, had shrunk back into Albie's legs, pressing her face into the fabric of his trousers.

97

'Poor little mite,' she'd heard the woman say. 'She must be exhausted. Come in, come in. Don't just stand there in the cold. Let's get you inside.'

Maggie had trailed closely behind her father, eyeing the dog warily as it sniffed around her legs in the vast hall with a floor like a chessboard and a staircase curving up to a grand gallery.

'It's late,' the man in the wheelchair had said, the reproach in his voice obvious. 'You're staying the night?'

'Of course they're staying.' The woman had fussed around them both. 'Take the girl up to the blue room, Albie. The bed is made up.'

She remembers being carried up the stairs in her father's arms, past the startling bone-white skull and antlers of an elk mounted on the wall and a gallery of sombre portraits, eyes gazing blankly at her as they'd passed by. They had continued down a wide, carpeted corridor, then up a few raised steps until they came to a halt outside a door.

'This will be your room, Maggie,' her father had said, switching on a bedside lamp and sitting her on the huge four-poster bed. Isn't it nice? There's a bathroom next door. I'll leave the light on, just in case.' He had tucked her in beneath a heavy brocade bedspread that had made her feel like one of the pale pink hibiscus flowers she had squashed between the translucent pages of the flower press she had used with her mother, only that summer.

'It smells funny,' she'd said. 'I want to go home.'

'Home is wherever we make it, darling.' Albie had smiled, his face softening. 'I know your grandfather seems a little fierce, but Lillian is very kind. The kindest woman I know. They're both going to love you, I promise,' he'd whispered.

'I want Mama.' It was the only time she ever dared say it out loud.

Albie had stared at her. 'I know you do. But it's best you forget her. She's gone and we're better off without her, Mags. Trust me.' Then, with a kiss on her forehead, he'd tiptoed out of the room, leaving just a triangle of light to fall through the crack of the open door.

Maggie had lain utterly still, her eyes tracing the faint outline of the printed cherry blossom and the shimmering birds repeated over and over upon the silver wallpaper. There had been strange noises: clanking pipes and creaking wood. Mama. Where was she? Why would she just leave them? What had Maggie done to make her go? She knew it must be something terrible. Why didn't anyone tell her, so she could make it right and bring her back?

After a while, she'd crept out onto the landing, thinking she might use the bathroom, but the sound of raised voices echoing up the staircase had held her paralysed: her father and the white-haired woman.

'Where's her mother? Why isn't she with her?'

She'd heard her father's derisive grunt. 'Amanda? She wafted away to some ashram . . . She said she needed a little time to "find herself" . . . Said something about balancing her energy and "visualising" her future. Only it seems the future she visualised didn't include Maggie and me. She never came back – left me floundering. I've tried hard to be the parent Maggie needs, but . . . it hasn't been easy. She needs far more than I can give her. You understand.'

'You're making excuses, Albie,' she'd heard the lady say. 'You're afraid.'

'Of course I am afraid.'

'Of what?'

Her father had seemed to hesitate. 'There's too much of him in me. No one could understand . . . except you.'

'We all have our struggles, Albie; but you can choose what kind of man you want to be. Don't you see? Perhaps the girl – Maggie – is just what you need.'

'What I need is help.'

Maggie had stood transfixed in the corridor. She had never heard her father sound so plaintive. She'd had to crane to hear his next pleading words.

'It's only three months, Lillian. It's a good place. A real chance to straighten myself out. Three months and then I'll be back for her. I promise. There's no one else I'd leave her with; no one but you.'

She hadn't heard the woman's answer because at that moment the huge dog that had greeted them earlier at the front door appeared at the bottom of the staircase, gazing up at her, tongue drooling and long tail wagging. The sight of the grey-haired beast had been enough to send her scuttling back to bed, where she lay shivering, eyes squeezed shut, willing herself to sleep, unaware that by morning, her father would be long gone and she'd be left to face a startling new life at Cloudesley, with grandparents as foreign to her as the landscape she now inhabited.

She hadn't understood then, but she did now: Albie's addictions. The drinking and gambling. It was rehab he'd needed, to straighten himself out; but little could he or Lillian have known how Maggie had clung to those few overheard words. Three months, and then he'd return for her. She held the promise like a precious secret, like a beloved treasure stashed deep in her pocket.

She had learned the rules of her strange new home diligently, all the while counting down the days. Socks and shoes were compulsory about the house. Her feet, so used to roaming bare, were squashed into new black leather lace-ups that Lillian taught her how to tie, her unruly hair brushed a hundred times twice a day with a large silver hairbrush.

There was a correct, but troublesome new way to eat peas: not scooping them up with a fork or spoon, but crushing them onto the back of the fork with a knife. No running in the house. No touching any of her grandfather's precious antiques. There were certain rooms she was told she must not enter and times she must not disturb Charles. Lillian had made it very clear: Charles Oberon was a man who needed his space. He was not to be bothered by a young child. Lillian had impressed this last point on her with the most solemn of looks. 'You must understand,' she'd said, 'he can get a little . . . frustrated. It's the wheelchair . . . so hard for him. It's best for you – best for all of us – if you stay out of his way.'

Maggie had nodded solemnly and told her she understood; and, for the most part, she had complied with the strict dictates laid out by her grandmother. Only once had she forgotten, during a solitary game of marble-rolling across the tiled floor of the great entrance hall, when an errant marble had vanished down a corridor and her pursuit had led her to the door of a room she knew was for her grandfather's sole use. The door stood ajar and as Maggie bent to retrieve the small ball of coloured glass glinting beside the skirting board, she'd become aware of movement inside. Peering in, she'd seen her grandmother bending to tie one of her grandfather's shoe laces. Nothing so remarkable in that, except for the dark look she'd seen pass her grandfather's face as he'd stared down at Lillian from his chair. It was a look she could only interpret as pure, angry hatred. She'd watched, not fully understanding, as Charles had raised an arm and attempted to strike her grandmother, his fist glancing feebly off Lillian's skull. At that, her grandmother had reared up and given the old man a look. 'Come now, Charles,' she'd said, as if soothing a young child. 'There's no need for that.'

Sensing her presence, Lillian had looked from Charles to the open door, and spotting Maggie standing there gazing wide-eyed upon the scene, she had crossed the room and closed the door wordlessly, preventing Maggie from prying further.

Maggie, not exactly sure what she had just witnessed, but certain it was something not meant for her eyes, had turned and run into the garden, the errant marble still clutched tightly in her fist as she'd climbed high into the branches of a favourite tree in the arboretum, trying to banish the image of her grandfather's ugly, twisted face. Lillian had already explained, of course; it was awful to be stuck in that horrid chair . . . but more than that, Maggie suddenly understood something else: how much Lillian must love her husband to care for the cantankerous old man as she did. From that day, she had doubled her efforts to stay out of her grandfather's way; but just as her fear for her grandfather had taken root, conversely, her love for her grandmother had blossomed. Lillian was an angel, in Maggie's eyes.

She had doubled her efforts to maintain the house rules, turning it into a game of sorts, counting down the days, ensuring she met every request, knowing that if she kept to her end of the silent bargain, Lillian would be happy and Albie would return at the end of the three months.

But Albie hadn't returned. Three months had turned into four . . . then five, until, eventually, Maggie had stopped counting, barely able to remember the life she had once lived, her memories distilled to odd fragments, like the faded images from a favourite picture book. When she had finally accepted that he might never return, he had arrived with a fanfare of presents and hugs and gushing praise about how Maggie had grown and how proud he was of her.

It had been a relief to see him again. It almost felt as though life were complete, once more. They had played ball games out on the lawn and taken walks through the woods together. Maggie had started to grow accustomed to his presence about the house, waiting patiently for the day he would tell her to pack her bags and ready herself to return to their old life. But the days had slid by, and being at Cloudesley seemed to do something gradual to Albie. Slowly, his jovial moods began to falter. The brightness in his eyes dimmed and his face settled into an anxious frown. He grew snappish with Maggie and increasingly impatient with her requests for him to play with her. A new distance crept into his interactions with Lillian, no matter how hard her grandmother tried to soften him. It was as if the house itself were dragging him down, stealing his light. Maggie had worried silently about his transformation until she had woken one morning and found Albie's room empty, his suitcase gone. Her father had packed up and stolen away once more into the night and Maggie, inconsolable at the discovery, had thrown herself onto his bed and cried into his cold pillow.

It had become the pattern of their lives: Albie blowing in and out like a leaf on the wind, and the mother she had once known featuring in only the most distant echoes of memories and dreams: her voice crooning night-time lullabies, her flashing smile, beads plaited into dark hair and a red ruffled skirt that had spun round and round as she'd danced on the sand in front of a burning fire. Those were memories she knew it was not worth dwelling on. Lillian and Cloudesley, she grew to understand, were the only consistencies she could rely upon.

She lies in the same bed in the same room as that very first night at Cloudesley; only now, as a woman of twenty-six, Maggie knows the truth: the people you love leave. Or they get old and frail. Time marches on and everything fades and crumbles. Your life gets squeezed into eight cardboard boxes you can't bear to open until all you are left with are the broken-down pieces of a huge, echoing house and the ghosts that haunt your dreams.

Lying there, Maggie feels the scale of the place and her sense of responsibility to it like a heavy weight pressing down on her. She has returned to do her duty – to do right by Lillian, the one person who has never let her down – and while she'd thought she could do it, alone in the dark she feels a growing sense of panic that she is not up to the task. She is not the person she needs to be. She needs to be more like her grandmother, strong and stoic. She needs to stay and fight for her legacy; but every fibre of her being is screaming at her to flee. To run away. *To be like her parents*.

The bed is cool and clammy, the sheets imbued with a musty scent that reminds her of loneliness. She curls up into a foetal position and rubs her feet together for warmth, knowing that it will be a long time before she falls asleep. All she has to do is stay, she tells herself. *Don't be like them*. She just needs to close her eyes and wait for morning. She just has to see it through – to fulfil her promise to Lillian – one day at a time.

CHAPTER 9

Lying in Charles's four-poster bed, waiting for him to come to her, Lillian thinks about the promises she has made to her husband. To love and to cherish. For better or worse. Till death do us part.

She had said the words in good faith, hope fluttering like a bird in her chest, certain that the vows were the beginning of something wonderful and life-changing. And it has been life-changing. Lillian barely recognises the young woman she once was, or the ground she now finds herself standing upon; for her marriage to Charles is a complicated, volatile landscape. There are so many unspoken rules; so many uncertain dictates; so many fluctuating emotions to anticipate and interpret. She knows he has seen too much – lost too much. She does not, for one moment, underestimate the damage he has endured in those unspoken years away at war, followed so closely by the tragic loss of his first wife.

She only wishes she were more adept at navigating her life with him, better able to understand the man she now finds herself bound to. For each day she wakes and steps out into the marriage, she feels as though she balances precariously, never quite sure if the ground she steps on is firm or quicksand, sucking her down into one of Charles's more erratic moods.

She shifts beneath the sheets and listens for the sound of his approach. At least the pattern of their intimacy is clear to her now, established by Charles in the earliest days of their marriage. She visits his bedroom only at his request, arriving at his door on those nights at 10 p.m. sharp. The routine is always the same: she lets herself in, removes her robe in the light of the small bedside lamp then lies in this bed, staring up into the dark fabric canopy, waiting for her husband to come to her . . . to make love to her.

She supposes that what they do in the dark constitutes making love, though she has nothing else to compare it to, and no one close enough whom she can discuss it with. Joan, perhaps, is her only real confidante, but Lillian knows she couldn't bear to reveal her naivety to a worldly woman like Joan. She could only imagine her friend's gasp of shock at the questions she might ask her, and how in doing so she would expose the fractures and failures of her marriage. She loves Joan, but she's not entirely sure she trusts her – not with those darkest of secrets.

The door to Charles's bedroom opens with a familiar creak. A small shiver runs through Lillian. Wordlessly, Charles moves across the room. He undresses quickly, sliding into bed beside her and adjusting the covers so that he can manoeuvre on top of her, his face hovering just above hers. He reaches down and tugs her nightdress up around her waist.

She glances up, catching his eye, and he frowns and tilts her face to the side, so that she is no longer looking at him but staring instead at the blank white pillow beside her head.

She closes her eyes and tries to swallow back her small cry as Charles presses down upon her, his breath hot on her cheek as he moves silently, his hands holding her shoulders and pinning her in place, his fingers squeezing tightly.

In her head, she goes to another place. She closes her eyes and imagines a wide pebbled beach, a place she once visited with her parents as a child. She remembers running across the uneven stones, the ocean a cool, blank grey washing onto the shore, over and over, water moving relentlessly across rock. Back and forth. Back and forth. Charles, too, she knows goes somewhere – somewhere unreachable. She glances up and sees the glint of tears squeezing from his closed eyes, sees his contorted face, the pain written there, only ever visible in this moment of release as with a last groan he collapses down onto her.

Lillian lies very still. Slowly, she reaches up and places her arms around him. She feels him relax into her embrace and for the briefest moment he lets her hold him. Her fingers move through his hair, soothing him as if he were a child. Perhaps tonight he will allow her to stay. Perhaps tonight will be the night he doesn't wake shouting from the violent nightmares of his sleep. 'You're safe with me,' she whispers into the darkness, willing him to let go and allow her in.

At the sound of her voice, his body tenses. He pushes himself off her and rolls onto his side of the bed. 'You may go,' he says, his voice cold and Lillian, realising she has erred – said or done the wrong thing – slides out from between the sheets and pulls on her robe.

'Goodnight,' she says, but Charles doesn't answer. She lets herself out of his room and walks the long corridor back to her own empty bed, feeling a dull ache between her legs, and the sharp shard of loneliness and frustration lodged deep in the pit of her belly.

No, her marriage is not at all as she imagined it would be, but as she slides into her own bed and curls in on herself, a small ball of nothingness, she tells herself that all she has to do is fulfil her promise to Charles, one day at a time. For better or for worse.

*

Lillian is sitting at her writing desk in the drawing room the following morning, blotting ink on a letter when she feels the eyes upon her. Someone is standing in the doorway, watching her. She turns, expecting to find Charles, or perhaps Sarah, her housemaid, hovering at the entrance to the room, unsure whether to enter and dust or polish with her mistress present, but the space is empty; just an open doorframe, the creak of a floorboard, and a ghostly draught of air, moving as if stirred by someone's departure.

Lillian shakes her head. She is tired. It took her too long to fall asleep last night and her imagination, she knows, can play vivid tricks in this house. She lowers her head to the letter, then instantly lifts it again. There *is* something else. A scent; something dark and indefinable, carried on the air. Smoke, she realises. A bonfire outside, perhaps. Or Mrs Hill, cursing in the kitchen, scraping at the blackened pan of something forgotten on the hob. She dismisses the thought, her attention already returning to her task, when a fearful roar echoes down the hall. Lillian starts again. That noise. Something is terribly wrong.

She finds them in the library, Albie cowering by the marble fireplace with his hands covering his head and Charles standing over him, his face scarlet with rage, his amber eyes flashing dangerously. 'You imbecile!' Charles shouts at the boy.

'I'm sorry. I'm so sorry,' says Albie, his voice trembling. 'It was an accident.'

'What is it?' she asks. 'What's happened?'

The scent of burning is much stronger in the room, an acrid smell washing over her, catching at the back of her throat. She glances round and notices the pile of ash smouldering in the grate, the loose sheets of singed paper scattered nearby.

Charles turns to her, his fists clenched. 'I'd just asked Bentham to load up the car for my London trip when I smelled the smoke. I came in here to investigate and I found this little fool trying to set the house on fire.'

She looks from Albie to the grate, where she can now see the pile of ash is actually the burned remains of a leather-bound book, while closer to Charles, a large, black mark smoulders on the ornate Persian rug.

'I'm sorry,' Albie pleads, still crouched at his father's feet.

'What were you thinking? You could have destroyed the entire house!'

'I – I – I don't know. I found the matches. I wanted to see if I could light a fire . . . I was just . . . curious.'

Charles rolls his eyes and runs a hand through his thick russet hair. 'Good grief,' he says to no one in particular. 'It appears I'm raising a half-wit.' He moves to the mantelpiece and takes a cigar from a box, lighting it with one of the offending matches from the box Albie has used to start his inferno. He takes several long puffs on his cigar, allowing the smoke to drift from his mouth as he studies first Albie and then the burn mark on the rug.

Lillian waits, uncertain whether to intervene or remain silent as Charles assesses the damage. She decides silence is best. Her interference might only enrage him further.

'It was an accident,' says Albie again, his head still hung low. 'The pages caught so quickly. I dropped some of them and they scattered and set the rug on fire. I'm very sorry, Father. I promise it won't happen again.'

Charles studies Albie through narrowed eyes. 'Well, I'm glad to see you are remorseful. That is something.'

Albie nods and lifts his head for the first time, meeting his father's gaze. 'I am. I'm very sorry.'

Lillian lets out a small breath of air.

'But this is an irreplaceable rug,' continues Charles, 'shipped all the way from the Middle East by your late grandfather. It's one of a kind . . . incredibly valuable.'

'He's said he's sorry, Charles,' says Lillian, a twist of fear in her gut. 'I know he's caused some damage, but I don't think you'll be playing with matches again, will you, Albie?' she asks, turning to the boy.

Charles casts an irritated glance in her direction as Albie shakes his head solemnly. He seems to consider the rug for a moment longer, then he looks back to Albie. 'Step forward,' he says.

The boy's gaze darts to Lillian. She can see the fear in his eyes, the trembling of his skinny legs as he steps forward.

'Hold out your hand.'

'Charles,' says Lillian, her fear rearing up like a snake, watching as Charles pushes the boy's sleeve up to his elbow. 'He's apologised.'

'Yes, and now he will receive his punishment.'

'Charles. He's eight years old,' says Lillian, her voice rising in pitch. 'It was a mistake. What more do you expect of him?'

'I expect him to think twice about playing with matches in the future.' Charles takes the cigar from his mouth and, before Lillian has understood what he intends, he places the smoking end against the inside of Albie's bare arm.

The boy cries out in pain. Lillian lets out an anguished shriek and flies forward, pushing Charles's hand away from the boy, sending his cigar flying onto the stone hearth. 'Stop it,' she screams. 'Leave him alone.'

Charles turns to Lillian, a cold fury burning in his eyes. 'You forget, my dear, that you are not the boy's mother. Stand aside.'

Lillian is rooted to the spot. 'I won't let you hurt him. Hurt me, if you have to punish someone. But not him.'

Charles reaches for Lillian's face and holds her by the chin, squeezing her jaw so tightly that she feels the bones crunch under his fingers. She senses Albie falling back behind her. Charles tilts her face until she is looking him in the eye, his breath hot on her skin. 'Don't goad me, dear. You have no say in how I raise my son.'

She flinches, readying herself for the blow and wonders if he can sense the flare of white-hot hatred she feels for him in that moment; but then, just as suddenly as he has grabbed her, he lets her go, stalking away across the room. 'I'll be gone a week,' he says, throwing the words over his shoulder at her. 'Perhaps longer. Have the rug replaced before my return. I don't want to see it again.'

As soon as he has left the room, Lillian darts to the service bell in the corner of the room before pulling the still-whimpering boy towards her. 'Albie,' she says, 'Albie, listen to me. He's gone.'

He looks up at her through teary eyes. 'Did he hurt you?'

'No. I'm fine.'

Sarah arrives in the room, hovering in the doorway. 'Yes, Ma'am?'

'We've had a little accident,' she says. 'Please bring us some iced water and bandages, as quickly as you can.'

Sarah's eyes widen at the sight of Albie crying in Lillian's arms. 'Of course, Ma'am. Right away.'

When she has gone, Lillian draws the boy close. 'I'm so sorry, Albie.'

Albie lets out a choking sob. 'It's not your fault.' He sniffs and wipes his face with the back of his hand. 'I know he can be horrid, but he loves us.' He sniffs again. 'I think he must do, don't you? He's always sorry . . . in the end.'

'Of course he loves you,' Lillian says, holding the boy close. 'He's a . . . complicated man, but he's your father.'

Albie winces and holds his arm. Damn it, thinks Lillian. Where is Sarah?

'It doesn't hurt. Not that much.' Albie pulls away from her and looks up at her with huge eyes. The lie is easy to read on his face. He is trying to be brave. 'You mustn't leave us. We've already lost Mother. I couldn't bear to lose you, too.'

Lillian nods in understanding. He is afraid that she will judge Charles harshly and leave them both. But the truth is, she would walk through fire to protect Albie – she would throw herself in front of Charles's fists over and over to prevent this boy feeling pain. He needs her in a way that no other ever will. Holding the trembling boy in her arms, she thinks of the dark-haired woman in the portrait above the dining-room hearth. Poor Evelyn, stolen from her life – her child – too soon; and poor Albie, because Lillian herself knows the pain of losing a beloved parent.

This is what it means to be a mother. She may never bear her own children, but she will always have Albie. She will always put him first.

Lillian releases a long breath of air as she presses the boy fiercely to her chest. 'When I married your father, Albie, I made a promise to love him, for better or worse. But I also made another promise: to love you as much as a mother ever could. And I do, Albie. I love you very much and I will never leave you. You have my word.'

CHAPTER 10

It's not the fault of the man at the end of the telephone, but Maggie still lets him feel the full force of her disappointment the next morning. In her head, everything has been hanging on this one call: Cloudesley will either thrive or fall, depending on her powers of persuasion.

'But you don't understand,' Maggie says, trying to retain a degree of patience, 'the house is old. *Really* old. Built in the 1700s, or something.' She is sitting in her grandfather's study, her feet up on the desk, gazing unseeing at the mosaic of objects scattered across its surface. She reaches for a heavy crystal paperweight, turns it over in her hand absent-mindedly before returning it to the desk. 'I've had a good look on your website and it's really not that different from any of the other places your members pay to visit each year. You know, the blue-rinse brigade? All those old biddies who love flower gardens and teashops? With just a little work, they'd love it here too. I know they would.'

The man at the other end of the phone clears his throat. 'At the National Trust, we're very proud of the fact that we've expanded our membership database to become much broader than "the blue-rinse brigade" as you call it, Ms Oberon.'

'Yes, of course,' agrees Maggie, quickly. 'Families would love it here too. There's plenty of space for kids to run around and trees to climb. It's magical.'

'Yes, yes, I understand,' says the man. He sounds younger than she'd imagined, and he's not exactly unsympathetic. 'It sounds charming. And of course it's our aim as an organisation to preserve as many heritage properties as we can. Everyone who works here believes passionately in protecting our cultural history.'

Maggie nods, encouraged. 'Exactly.'

'But I'm afraid it's simply not feasible for us to support every property that comes our way,' he continues. 'We're a charity, dependent on memberships, donations and legacies for our income and we must be guided not just by our mission statement, but also by financial objectives and targets. We have very strict criteria that must be met before we'd even begin to consider a new property. Tell me,' he asks, 'have you considered a private investor? Perhaps selling the property to someone better equipped to undertake the restoration work required?'

'There is a potential buyer sniffing around, but I'm not sure restoration is quite what he has in mind. Besides, we don't want to sell,' she says, lowering her feet and leaning forwards in the chair. *Nowhere but Cloudesley*. Lillian's words echo in her ears. 'It's been the Oberon family home for over a century. We want to preserve it. I was thinking that my grandmother and I could move into one wing of the house and hand the rest over to you, to restore and open to the public. You'd never see us. We'd be like mice. I promise.'

'I'm afraid it's not that simple, Miss Oberon. Believe me, I do understand your distress—'

'But I don't think you do. If you don't help us, Cloudesley might not even be standing here in a year's time. If you'd only come and see it?'

The man sighs. 'All I can do is pass on your details to one of our regional contacts,' he concedes wearily. 'I can ask them to consider your proposal. *If* they deem it a viable property, it would move forward to our acquisitions panel and trustees.'

'Great. How soon could that happen?'

'I wouldn't feel comfortable giving you an exact time frame. There are a great many properties across the country suffering the same fate as Cloudesley, I'm afraid.'

'But are we talking weeks or months?'

'Months . . . perhaps longer.'

Maggie's heart sinks. It had seemed like such a brilliant plan when it had come to her in the middle of the night. It had felt like the most obvious way to save the crumbling house, in the light of their financial stress. Yes, it involved signing it over to a new entity and opening their home to the public, but if that's what it took to save the old place . . . She had never anticipated such a lukewarm response.

'I must advise you, Ms Oberon,' continues the voice at the end of the telephone, 'that in the case you've outlined to me, it is unlikely we would take on Cloudesley. As beautiful as your home sounds, in these matters the head must rule the heart. If the property doesn't have unique historic or cultural significance then in these financially challenging times, I don't believe it's something we would consider taking on. I wouldn't want to give you false hope. I feel your time would be far better spent seeking an alternative solution.'

Maggie puts the phone down. All around her are papers and bills spread across the desk. A rather eccentric ornament of a frog, mouth gaping in a wide 'o' gazes up at her from beside the banker's lamp. His shocked expression mirrors exactly how she feels. 'I know,' she says, dropping her head into her hands and letting out a long groan. 'Seems we can't even give the old place away.'

CHAPTER 11

Lillian wakes to the churring call of a nightjar, singing out across the garden. She hasn't been sleeping well since Charles left for London. Every time she closes her eyes she sees the red cigar burn on Albie's arm and hears his anguished cry.

Though dawn is little more than a glimmer of grey at her curtains, she pushes off the covers and slides out of bed, dressing quickly. Some mornings, in that quiet hour before dawn, before the staff has risen and the place is still cloaked in sleep, Lillian likes to move about the house. It's then that she walks Cloudesley, free and unobserved. It's then that she feels free from scrutiny and judgement – the one time she almost feels she *is* mistress of her domain, rather than the caretaker of another's.

She tries not to think too much of Evelyn, but this morning she can't seem to help her preoccupation with her. She tortures herself with thoughts about the woman whose shadow she now occupies. Did she suffer the same furious outbursts from her volatile husband, or was Charles more satisfied with life with his first wife? Charles never discusses her, but the portrait hanging in the dining room suggests a woman of grace and confidence. By comparison, Lillian can't help but feel small and ill-equipped for such a life. The fault must surely lie with her. A complicated man like Charles – so bottled-up, so full of repressed emotion – needs careful handling and she seems to be failing him – and Albie.

Why hadn't she intervened sooner in the library? Why hadn't she stepped in and saved Albie from Charles's punishment? Perhaps Evelyn is looking down upon her right now, from whatever celestial perch she might occupy, horrified at Lillian's inability to pacify her husband or protect Albie from Charles's brutal outbursts. Perhaps she doesn't deserve any of this – Charles, Albie, Cloudesley? Lillian tortures herself with thoughts of her failings as she moves through the silent house.

Down in the kitchen, Monty stirs in his basket and, sniffing the possibility of adventure, trots along at her heels, following her to the flower room where she gathers secateurs, gloves and a basket.

There is no one in the walled garden for company but the dog and a lone blackbird fluttering hopefully through the espaliered fruit trees and over the netted gooseberry bushes. The sun is still a low rose-gold blush on the horizon. Dew seeps through her silk slippers but she hardly notices. She moves quietly along the borders, breathing in the morning air, her thoughts circling endlessly back to Albie.

Since Charles's departure for London, she's felt a certain peace descend over the place, as if the house and its inhabitants have all released a collective breath in the absence of his frenetic energy. The fire-damaged rug has been rolled up and stored in a barn; Albie's ugly red burn is bandaged and hidden beneath the boy's shirtsleeve; yet the after-effects of the incident remain as silent ripples spreading through the house. Albie himself is noticeably more quiet and withdrawn, spending time on his own, walking the grounds or lying on his bed. She doesn't know how to reach him – how to make him feel safe. She's seen the artist chatting with him out in the garden, laughing and ruffling his hair as they've shared a joke. In Albie's bedroom she noticed what looked to be a hastily scrawled sketch of the boy, drawn by the artist on the back of an envelope. Albie had pinned it in pride of place on his corkboard of collected stamps and postcards. Perhaps Jack Fincher's calm presence might prove to be a balm for the boy. She can only hope.

Stopping at a damask rose bush laden with pink flowers, she cuts several stems, laying them in her basket before bending to breathe in their fragrance, sweet and pungent like Turkish delight. Further on, she trims bunches of ruffled sweet-pea blossoms, growing in spirals around tall cane pyramids.

She stays in the garden, ruminating on her frustrations and failings until the sun has risen above the brick wall of the garden. Returning to the house, she empties her basket in the flower room. Across the corridor she can hear Mrs Hill and Sarah chatting in the kitchen, accompanied by the sound of running water and pots clanking on the range. Lillian removes the thorns, trims stems and arranges the roses into a large vase for the drawing room, and the sweet peas into two smaller jugs. It's as she's appraising her efforts that the idea comes to her: she will take one arrangement to her sister, as she'd intended, but the smaller of the two she will deliver to the artist's bedroom – just a small gesture – an unspoken thank you for his kindness to Albie.

Knowing how early he starts his work for the day, she doesn't expect a reply, but she knocks on the door to the guest bedroom and waits an appropriate amount of time before pushing it open.

She had presumed that an artist would live in something of a chaotic state, but the bed is neatly made and there are just a few personal items dotted about, here and there: a pair of discarded brogues, worn but polished, lying beside the bed; a pale-blue shirt hanging on the door of the armoire; a book splayed on the bedside table. Hemingway's *A Farewell to Arms*. There's a half-finished cigarette stubbed in the ashtray beside it, as well as a comb and a pair of cufflinks. The window stands flung open to the morning sun. Jack's presence sits upon the room with the lightest touch, and yet the space feels transformed – somehow more masculine – the air now scented with the faintest trace of aftershave and leather, aromas that mingle with the jasmine drifting in through the open window.

She places the jug of flowers on the bedside table, stands back to assess its effect, then changes her mind and moves it to the small desk beneath the window, positioning the sweet peas beside a cloth bundle of paint brushes, a cigarette lighter and a large, well-thumbed book bound in red leather. It's the same book she has seen him carrying about the grounds on his lunchtime wanderings.

Something about the sight of it holds her. All those hours he has spent closeted in the old nursery and none of them any the wiser as to what he might be painting. With a quick glance back at the open door, she reaches for it and lifts the cover.

The first few pages show details of Cloudesley. She recognises a sketch of the arched stone portico; the carved peacocks decorating the front door; a gargoyle perched high on the guttering, mouth yawning wide, ready to spill rainwater. She finds a detail of the wooden gate leading to the walled kitchen garden, then a drawing of the rear of the house in its entirety, viewed from the lawn, down near the ha-ha.

She knows she is being a terrible snoop, but now that the book is in her hands, she can't seem to stop herself. She continues to leaf through the pages, scanning exquisite charcoal images of trees and leaves, peacock feathers and flowers. His eye for detail and his accuracy in rendering each subject is startling.

She is about to close the book and return it to the desk when she catches sight of a face passing on the flickering pages. She leafs her way back until she finds it again – not an entire face, but a section; an eye, the sweep of a cheekbone, the curved line of a neck observed from side-on; all illustrated as if seen in the reflection of a small, oval mirror. A car wing-mirror.

She peers at the page more closely, breath held in her chest as the moment returns to her: sitting in Charles's new car, Jack scrunched in the back and Lillian in the front, a peacock barring their path. It is exactly how he would have seen her reflected back at him in the wing-mirror.

As with the other drawings, the accuracy is remarkable. She is amazed at his ability to recall the smallest details. There is the pearl stud at her earlobe and the almost indiscernible beauty spot above her lip. Yet the more closely she studies the sketch, the more she is discomforted. It isn't just the precision of the pencil lines conjuring her on the paper – but more the expression he has captured – a certain wistfulness she hadn't known she wore so plainly. The portrait feels so intimate; almost as if he has laid her bare on the page.

She continues to leaf through the sketches and finds a second portrait. This time she is seated in the drawing room, her face turned to the window, the skirt of her dress falling in a fan to the floor. A third reveals her standing on the terrace, leaning against the balustrade, a long evening dress sweeping about her legs. The night of the party. The next page shows just her arm, identifiable by a favourite diamond bracelet dangling at the wrist. The last is of her head and shoulders, viewed from behind, the curves of her neck rising up to a twisted knot of hair. Looking at the images she isn't sure how she feels; flattered to be seen, to be deemed worthy of his time and attention, though at the same time a little uncomfortable at the intimacy of his gaze and at the thought of having been so scrutinised when she hadn't even known he was watching her.

She lays the book back on the desk and turns to leave, letting out a small gasp to find Jack standing at the open door watching her. 'Oh,' she says, the blood rushing to her cheeks. 'I was just . . .' She gestures feebly towards the jug of sweet peas. 'I thought you might like . . .' She trails off.

'They're lovely,' he says, his eyes tracking to the flowers then back to the sketchbook lying on the desk. 'I forgot my lighter.'

Neither of them move. They both know what she was doing but the apology she owes him is stuck at the back of her throat. 'Please . . .' she stutters, finding a small voice.

He raises an eyebrow.

'Please . . . forgive me,' and she rushes past him, darting down the landing to the safety of her room.

She avoids him for two days. Or perhaps he avoids her. Either way, it is a relief not to come upon him in the immediacy of her embarrassing blunder. She busies herself with menus and staffing arrangements. She spends time with Albie, playing chequers in the drawing room and ball games out on the lawn. Mostly, she tries not to remember the expression on Jack's face – that one arched eyebrow – nor think about how long he might have been standing in the doorway watching her leaf through his sketchbook.

Her luck runs out on the third day as she sits at her desk in the window of the drawing room. She is writing a short piece for the parish council magazine about the seasonal changes in the gardens at Cloudesley. The sun slants through the glass pane onto her paper while a fat bee, trapped inside, buzzes lazily at the glass. Out on the lawn the peahens peck at the grass, three scruffy brown chicks following behind. Lillian watches them for a moment then sighs and concedes defeat. She lays the fountain pen on her pad of Basildon Bond and watches the birds for a while. The grandfather clock in the entrance hall chimes midday. The morning has already slipped away.

Frustration bubbles up inside her. She knows this life of hers is steeped in privilege. Unlike many women, she has a freedom to do as she pleases. No menial tasks or housework for her. Her marriage to Charles has brought her a standard of living she never expected. So why does she feel as if she's living some alternate shadow life? Not a true, meaningful existence but one based on falsehood or illusion.

It's certainly not the life she'd imagined when she agreed to marry Charles. Back then, she'd assumed she would bear his children. She'd dared to think she might even have a role to play in his business. How naive she was. How little she understood the complicated man she shares a life with. And how frustrated she is with the bland tenor of these hours she now spends in this house. She feels the days of her life falling away, like playing cards tossed to the wind, scattered and meaningless. She is no more use than the myriad of Charles's expensive trophies cluttering the house – beautiful but pointless. Like a lily. Or a peacock. Perhaps she could write that for the parish magazine, she thinks with a wry smile. A column on the tedium of a life of privilege.

The bee falls silent. Lillian watches it slowly scale the glass pane, almost making it to the opening at the top where fresh air and freedom beckon, before it falls back down to the sill with an angry buzzing.

Watching the trapped insect, her thoughts turn with a guilty flash to Helena. She hasn't visited her in almost a week. She really must go. Experience has taught her that the longer she leaves it between visits, the more she begins to dread the occasion and the harder it will be. Her boredom certainly seems all the more awful when she thinks of her sister. It could so easily have been her – their fates exchanged with the simple toss of a die. She can't help but think were it Helena and not her sitting here in this house, her sister would be coping far more admirably. Helena would have known how to handle a man like Charles. She only has to think of Helena's quick wit, her ability for dramatic flair, the afternoons she'd push the table back against the wall and wind up their father's gramophone and dance for their mother; or the way she'd dash along the London pavements on a Saturday morning, dragging Lillian behind her, anxious not to miss a single moment of the films showing at the picture house, to know her sister would have been a more formidable match. It had been Helena's dream that she might one day be a celebrated movie star – an actress to rival Vivien Leigh or Katharine Hepburn – and with her enviable looks, the lightness of her laughter, the readiness of her smile and that fierce streak of determination running through her blood, Lillian had always known her sister would succeed.

She sighs and stares blindly at the words she has scrawled onto the paper before her. She should be living for the both of them. She owes it to Helena to make something of this life, not to sit here bemoaning her existence, watching bees bash themselves silly against windows as the days slip slowly by.

The sound of the French doors creaking open in the dining room next door interrupts her thoughts. She leans back, obscuring herself behind the brocade curtain, and watches as Jack Fincher steps out onto the terrace. He stands for a moment in the bright sunshine, lifts his hands to the sky and stretches, the fabric of his shirt pulling taut across his shoulders before he drops his arms and begins to make for the wide stone steps leading down onto the lawn. He saunters casually, one hand in his pocket, the other holding the red leather-bound sketchbook, loping in that relaxed, loose-limbed way of his. The sight of the book makes Lillian's stomach fall and she ducks a little further behind the curtain.

Jack skips down the steps then heads across the lawn, careful to skirt around the peahens and their chicks, making for the distant ha-ha and, she assumes, the meadow beyond. He stops as he reaches the drop then spins slowly back to the house.

Lillian holds her breath. She's almost certain she cannot be seen at the window, but she remains perfectly still, watching as he begins to retrace his steps up the lawn before stopping ten metres or so from the peahens. He considers them for a moment then lowers himself cross-legged onto the grass, opening his book and retrieving the pencil from behind his ear. It's the birds, she realises; he is going to sketch them.

She doesn't know how long she watches him for, but there is something rather soothing, almost hypnotic, about observing the artist at work. He is bent over the paper, lost in his task, glancing up every so often to study the birds as they strut across the lawn. Occasionally, he reaches out and brushes at the paper with his fingers.

Jack watching the birds.

Lillian watching Jack.

Is this how he observed her? she wonders, thinking back to the portraits in his sketchbook. Did he hide from view, surreptitious and furtive? The idea still unsettles her.

Drowsy in the warmth of the sun, with the bee bumbling lazily at the glass, Lillian closes her eyes. It was such a silly thing, to be found leafing through his sketchbook; hardly as though she were reading his private diary. If only she'd taken the opportunity to address her faux pas immediately, rather than dashing off, a vision of guilt. Perhaps she would have told him how good she thought they were – the vignettes of the house – the feathers and the plants. There would have been no need to mention those pictures of her. No need to let him know she'd even seen them.

The sunshine is a caress on her neck, like warm fingers trailing across her skin. She sits, eyes closed, lost in the sensation and her thoughts, when a loud *thump* rattles the windowpane beside her.

Startled, she looks up just in time to see a dark shape about the size of a gentleman's hat sliding down the outside of the glass and dropping to the terrace.

She stands and peers over the edge of the sill and sees that the crumpled object is not in fact a hat, but a large brown bird, its chest rising and falling in shallow breaths and its orange eyes wide open and unblinking. Lillian stares at it, taking in the sharp curved beak, its bright yellow talons, the chevron pattern of its chest feathers, until another movement captures her attention out on the lawn. Jack is racing across the grass, bounding up the terrace steps two at a time, his pace only slowing when he reaches the top and catches sight of her standing at the drawing-room window. She raises her hand – half greeting, half request that he stop where he is – and he seems to understand, nodding as she indicates that she will join him outside.

'It's a sparrowhawk,' she says, as she draws up beside him.

'Yes, it flew right over me chasing a dove. Looks as though the poor fellow has done some serious damage.'

They move closer and Lillian notices that its chest has stopped moving and its eyes have taken on a blank, glassy look. 'Poor thing,' she murmurs. 'I've never seen one this close before. It's beautiful.'

'Yes, though unfortunately I think he's taken his last flight.'
She looks around. 'We can't just leave it here.'

'No.' Jack thinks for a moment. 'Do you have a box?'

She knows she could ring for one of the staff to come and help, but something about the sight of the damaged bird has affected her. She doesn't want to sit by passively watching others work. She wants to do something. 'Yes,' she says. 'Wait here.'

It only takes a few minutes to run to her dressing room and retrieve an old hatbox. She shows it to Jack, who nods his approval, watching over her as she bends and carefully scoops the inanimate bird into it. She can't help flinching as it flops heavily into the box. 'I'll leave the lid open a crack, just in case . . .' she says, although they both know it's unnecessary. 'We need a suitable resting place,' she says. 'Somewhere the cats won't be able to get at it.'

Jack looks across the gardens to the wildflower meadow and woods beyond. 'I have an idea. Allow me?' he asks, reaching for the box.

Even with the camaraderie that has risen between them through their shared task, Lillian still struggles to make small talk as they head down the lawn then through the high grass of the untamed meadow where poppies and ox-eye daisies brush against Lillian's legs. Only the sound of the grass moving around them and the low drone of insects break the silence. She knows she still owes him a proper apology and though the words dance on the tip of her tongue, she can't quite bring herself to say them out loud.

At the edge of the beech trees, Jack stops to offer her his hand over the wooden stile. She hesitates, turning to glance back at Cloudesley, seeing it standing there, a jewel gleaming on the crest of the hill. If she steps into the trees she knows she will no longer be visible to anyone up at the house; she will blend like a smudge into the shadows. The thought is not unappealing as she accepts his hand and steps over the stile, dropping down into the woodland beyond.

'Any signs of life?' she asks hopefully.

Jack shakes his head.

They weave between the trees and bracken, leaves and sticks cracking beneath their feet, grey flints and white chalk jutting like shards of bone glinting through the soil. Out of the direct sunlight, the air is soft and green, as if they walk through cool water. The further they go, the thicker the insidious ivy scaling the beech tree trunks and the denser the canopy. 'You seem to know where you're going,' she says, breaking the silence.

'I walk out here, sometimes, to escape the room. The vastness of the task . . . it can overwhelm me. Plus, there's something about being out here among trees. A familiarity; like being with old friends.'

She stumbles on a thick tree root sprawling across the ground, grabbing at the hand Jack offers, then dropping it quickly.

'I've read about this,' says Jack. 'It's quite common for sparrowhawks to crash while showing off to a mate or chasing prey.'

'It is?' She looks about, realising they have left all signs of a path behind them. Just as she is about to protest that she really shouldn't go any further in her house shoes, the grey tree trunks part and Lillian finds herself stepping out into a natural clearing.

'Here we are,' says Jack.

Lillian stops and looks around, marvelling at the high, green canopy and the soft light streaming through the branches. Overhead a magpie flits through the branches of a tree, rustling leaves until it takes flight with a mournful cry, its wings beating the air. 'This is beautiful,' she says.

'Yes,' agrees Jack. 'It's like standing inside nature's own cathedral, don't you think?'

Jack removes the lid of the hatbox and gently tips the bird onto the forest floor. They both take a step back, watching hopefully, but the bird lies stiff and unmoving among the leaves.

'Oh dear. Perhaps we should bury it,' she suggests.

Jack nods but as they haven't thought to bring anything to dig with they eventually, in unspoken agreement, cover it half-heartedly with dry leaves before retreating a short distance to sit upon a fallen tree trunk, neither of them, it seems, quite ready to return to the house.

It is quiet in the clearing, though gradually Lillian's ears attune to the soft rustling of insects and birds moving through the undergrowth, the faraway tapping of a woodpecker high in a tree. Down on the ground, a bronze-coloured beetle tries to scale the side of her shoe. It slips on the smooth leather and tumbles back into the dry leaves, waggling its legs in the air.

She shifts slightly on the tree trunk then watches as Jack pulls a strand of grass from a clump growing nearby and sucks on one end, looking about at the canopy overhead. 'Wonderful light,' he murmurs. 'I wish I hadn't left my sketchbook at the house.'

She knows she must say something. But the moment stretches and she can't find the words so instead she looks about, trying to see the clearing as he might, trying to view the world through an artist's eyes. What details would he pull from this scene, what elements would he commit to memory to reproduce on paper?

A cathedral, he'd said; and she supposes there is something rather celestial and awe-inspiring about the tall, arched trees and the light streaming in golden shafts through the soft green branches, filtered as though through stained glass.

Her eyes slide to Jack's profile, her gaze lingering on the fullness of his lips and the strong angle of his jaw. He shifts slightly on the log. His hand is only centimetres from her own; his fingers long and slender – how she imagines a pianist's would look, if it weren't for the smudges of grey charcoal on his skin.

'It's so peaceful,' she says, closing her eyes, shaking the hair from her face, succumbing to the warm light falling through the trees. She allows her breathing to slow and her shoulders to relax. Soon they will turn back for the house. The world will keep spinning and this moment with the dead bird and the woods and the intriguing man at her side will be gone, relegated to hazy memory.

She isn't sure how long they sit like that, the two of them side by side, lost in their own thoughts, but it's a soft scratching sound that brings her attention back to the clearing. Opening her eyes, she looks across to where they had left the prone bird and is startled to see the hawk no longer lying beneath the leaf litter but standing upright, its head cocked, one beady orange eye peering at her with suspicion. 'Look,' she whispers, reaching for Jack's arm.

Jack follows her gaze. The bird studies them a moment then hops clumsily away through the leaves towards the base of a tree. Lillian holds her breath, watching as it half-extends one wing. It hops a few more paces but it looks off-balance; too damaged to fly; but it's as if it hears her thought and determines to prove her wrong for suddenly it stretches out both wings and, in one fluid movement, takes flight across the clearing to land in the lowest branch of a nearby tree. Lillian feels her heart beating in her chest, a heady mix of excitement and elation.

The sparrowhawk perches on the bough, its eye still fixed in their direction before it glides off the branch and sails low across the clearing in a showy swoop before soaring away through the trees and out of sight.

'Well how about that?' says Jack. 'Lazarus rises.' He turns to her and Lillian, suddenly aware that she is still gripping his sleeve, drops her hand.

'It's lucky . . . lucky we didn't bury it.' She tries to smile but all the muscles in her face seem to have frozen. Her heart thuds loudly in her chest. The moment stretches.

'I'm sorry,' she says, finding at last her long-awaited apology. 'In your room . . . the other day . . . I wasn't rifling through your belongings.' He raises one eyebrow and she finds the grace to correct herself. 'What I mean is that I didn't enter your room with the *intention* of looking at your private things. I wanted to leave the flowers. Then I saw your sketchbook and I couldn't resist. I should never have looked at your drawings. I'm sorry,' she repeats.

She's not sure what she expected in response, but it certainly isn't his hand shifting on the tree trunk and coming to rest lightly over her own. She looks down at their hands lying together on the log – and wonders if the fast pulse beating beneath her skin is as obvious to him as it is to her.

Somewhere high above their heads a finch chatters in the trees. In a move so instinctive she barely knows it's happening, she lifts her fingers and laces them through his, so that their hands sit entwined on the trunk.

A sigh leaves Jack's lips – a soft exhalation – and in that moment she is lost. There is no Cloudesley, no Charles, no ticking clocks, no past or future; there is nothing but the clearing and Jack, and their hands clasped together. When she looks up at him, his face seems closer, so close she can see the amber flecks in the slate-grey of his eyes.

It is like gravity, she thinks, as she leans in towards him, her lips meeting his. It is a force so natural – so inevitable – so like falling – or flying – that she isn't sure she could stop their kiss even if she tried.

CHAPTER 12

Maggie is running a bath for Lillian. 'How hot do you like it?' she shouts into the room where she's left her grand-mother undressing. There is no answer so she leaves the water running into the old claw-foot tub and returns to find Lillian hunched over, struggling to undo her blouse.

'Here, let me help you.' Maggie unfastens the buttons and slides the shirt from Lillian's shoulders.

How strange life is, she thinks. All those years as a child when Lillian cared for her – helped her to bathe and dress, checked and labelled the uniform in her school trunk, combed her hair for nits, rubbed salve onto cuts. All those times Lillian tested her on her spellings or made her chant her multiplication tables. The excruciating sex talk, the first box of tampons, the revolting yet magical cure she had mixed up for her first violent hangover. The weekend they sat and discussed her career options and Maggie had dared to admit for the very first time that what she really wanted to do – most of all – was go to art college and be an artist and Lillian had looked her in the eye, nodded once and said, 'Someone once told me that if you're going to throw your life away on art, you should do it properly. Be bold. No half measures.' And Maggie had understood that Lillian wasn't laughing at her, as she'd feared she might, but accepting her decision, unconditionally.

Beneath it all – the care and the advice – had been a constant and unswerving affection; and here she is now, returning the favour, helping an ailing Lillian undress and slip into a warm bath. Perhaps it is the simplest acts of devotion, she thinks, folding the shirt and laying it onto a nearby chair, that send the strongest messages of love.

Lillian, struggling with a stocking, sits herself down on a gilt chair and Maggie kneels down to help peel it off. As it slides from her leg, Maggie rests back on her heels. 'What are those marks?' she asks, her gaze fixed on the thick, raised ridges of white flesh that twist around her grandmother's calves like vines.

'They're scars.' Lillian doesn't return Maggie's stare.

'Yes, but how did you get them?'

'Oh, it happened a long time ago now.'

Maggie narrows her eyes at Lillian. 'Gran?'

'Just a silly accident. Nothing for you to worry about.'

'A silly accident? Does it hurt?'

'Not anymore.'

'But how? And how did I never notice this about you?' She thinks back to the night of her grandmother's wanderings when it was dark and her long nightdress had fallen down to her ankles, covering these awful scars.

Lillian sniffs, still not looking at Maggie. 'In my day, it wasn't the done thing to appear in public with bare legs. Stockings were more seemly. I've upheld the standard over the years.'

It's true, Maggie realises; she has never seen Lillian with bare legs, though she always assumed it was a certain sense of decorum that had driven the older lady to cover up with stockings, even in the warmer months.

'Besides,' adds Lillian, 'I don't recall any other occasion when you've had cause to help me bathe?'

'True.' Maggie rises quickly from the floor, remembering. 'Oh hell. The bath water. Hang on.'

She knows from the thin, firm line her grandmother's mouth has settled into that she isn't going to get anything else out of her on the matter, but she is still thinking of those strange twisted marks on Lillian's legs as she rushes back into the bathroom. The water in the bath is deep and warm. She turns the hot tap off easily, but the cold tap twists round and round endlessly in her hand as the water continues to gush into the bath. 'Shit.' The washer must have gone – or the thread has broken – and the bath water continues to rise.

'Is Will still here?' she asks, running back to where her grandmother sits, half-dressed.

'I think so. Yes. I heard him outside putting the mower away.'

'Quick, put this on.' She thrusts a dressing gown at Lillian and then she runs.

She finds him outside, closing up the doors to the barn. 'I need some help,' she gasps, '. . . it's the tap . . . upstairs bathroom.'

He doesn't seem to need her to explain further. He nods and runs into the house, Maggie following a little way behind.

In the bathroom Will tries the cold tap. 'It won't turn off,' says Maggie, frustrated to see him repeating her efforts. It twists round in his hand just as it did for her. Will rolls up his sleeve and pulls out the plug – of course, why hadn't she thought to do that? – before tugging at the tap again. Maggie watches as the whole thing lifts off in his hand.

'Uh-oh.' Will stares at it for a moment, a useless lump of china, as the water continues to pour into the bath. He tries to twist it back onto the metal prong, but it won't gain any purchase and suddenly there is water spraying everywhere, jets squeezing out the top of the thread like a high-pressure sprinkler. 'Fuck!'

Maggie squeals as the cold water blasts her full in the face. Will swears again and tries to twist the thread of the tap with his bare hands, water continuing to spray at crazy angles through his fists, drenching them both.

'Is everything all right in there?' Lillian's voice drifts through the open doorway.

'We need to turn the mains water supply off,' Will shouts to Maggie. 'Where's the valve?'

'I don't know!' shrieks Maggie.

Lillian appears in the doorway, a safe distance from the water spray. Her gaze takes in the drenched bathroom and the two of them soaked to the skin, water still shooting out from between Will's hands. 'The mains valve is in a box, in the flower room downstairs,' she says, her voice calm but the amused smile on her face obvious to them both.

Maggie thunders away down the stairs again, finds the valve in a wooden box in the room opposite the kitchen and turns the mains water supply off. When she arrives back in the bathroom, the fountain from the tap has stopped and Lillian is handing Will a towel from a wooden rail. All is silent except for the dripping sound of water falling from the ceiling into the draining bath.

'I thought I was the one supposed to be taking the bath?' says Lillian.

'Ha ha,' says Maggie, rolling her eyes at Will. His sodden T-shirt clings to his body. She looks down at herself, her jeans and T-shirt soaked through, her hair plastered to her face, and she can't help the bubble of laughter that rises up from her throat. Will stares at her, and then he is laughing too, both of them falling about until tears leak from their eyes.

'If only you'd asked me,' says Lillian slyly, watching them both, 'I could have told you where the mains valve was right away.'

Maggie throws a towel half-heartedly at Lillian. 'You're a devil woman, Lillian Oberon.'

Ten minutes later, with Lillian settled back downstairs in the drawing room and her own damp clothes changed, Maggie goes to the kitchen. Will is leaning against the sink, shivering slightly in his wet T-shirt. 'Here.' She throws him an old sweatshirt she has pulled from her drawers. 'It should fit. I liked them baggy back then.'

He glances at the top, which features the name and tour dates of a favourite band.

She nods. 'I got it at that Brixton gig the three of us went to.' She can't help a quick glance at his lean torso as he peels off his wet T-shirt, more muscular and brown than she ever remembers seeing him.

He pulls the sweatshirt over his head. 'Thanks.'

She holds his gaze, the smile still playing on her lips. There are droplets of water caught in his hair. One spills onto his cheek and she has to fight the urge to reach out and catch it on her fingertip. 'I think we've both earned a drink after that drama.' She goes to the fridge and opens the door. 'There are some cold beers in here. Want one?'

She pops her head up over the fridge door and meets Will's solemn gaze, but the light in his eyes from just moments ago seems to have extinguished. His mouth is set in a tight line. He shakes his head.

She doesn't know what she has said or done to make his mood change so suddenly, but it's as if a shutter has been pulled down. 'Just one? For old time's sake?' she tries gently.

'I'd best be off,' he says, his voice gruff, his eyes not quite meeting hers.

And it's then, looking at him standing there across the kitchen from her in her old sweatshirt that she fully understands how much she has missed him, how much she has lost, and how desperately she wishes she could find a way to get their friendship back on track. 'Please?' she tries.

But Will, oblivious to her rising emotion, shakes his head. 'I've got to go. Busy day tomorrow.'

Before she can say another word, he has spun on his heel and left the kitchen, the dull sound of the back door echoing back at her.

Maggie stands in the empty kitchen, wondering if she imagined that small, singular moment of connection between them, wondering if she will ever be able to break through the barriers she has put between them.

CHAPTER 13

It's Albie who suggests the game of Mahjong, coming to find her in the library where she sits reading on the velvet sofa. Lillian agrees without thinking, lifting her head from the book in her lap. 'Of course I'll play. Let me finish this page and I'll be right there.'

'Good. I'm setting it up in the drawing room. Don't be long.'

She finds him minutes later, though to her consternation, Albie isn't alone.

'Mr Fincher,' she says, greeting him with a nod. 'I didn't realise you were joining us.'

'I should be painting, but Albie here was most persuasive.'

'We can easily play with three,' says Albie, juggling the tiles in his hands. 'We just remove some of the bamboo tiles.'

'Right,' says Lillian, silently cursing her luck, moving across the room to settle herself at the card table beside Albie. 'I'm glad you know what we're doing.'

She glances up at Jack and finds he is watching her, a small smile playing on his lips. She wonders if he is at all alarmed to find himself in such close proximity to her after their shared encounter in the clearing the day before.

'You'll have to go gently with me,' he says to Albie, his eyes still on Lillian. 'This is all rather new to me.'

Lillian blushes and stares down at the wall of tiles laid out on the table before them. 'Albie is the expert. You should know that neither of us stands a chance against him.'

'I'm lost already,' he says quietly. 'My concentration is completely off today.'

Lillian swallows.

'You'll be fine,' says Albie.

Over the next hour or so, Albie runs rings around them both, dominating the game and winning his hands easily. Lillian struggles to keep her attention on the game, her thoughts frequently drifting away from the small ivory tiles stacked in front of her and sliding back to the shimmering green clearing beyond the house. Jack's close proximity has her breathless and tense. The warm timbre of his voice. The light smattering of hairs on his forearms, working their way up into the folds of his shirt sleeves. The hollow at the dip of his neck. The kiss they shared just twenty-four hours earlier playing over and over on repeat in her head.

She has kissed Jack Fincher. She, a respectable, married woman, has thrown herself at a virtual stranger. She cannot fool herself; there had been no coercion, no persuasion. She had wanted to kiss him and met him willingly in the heat of the moment. The evidence was there in the way she had gripped his hand, the way she had leaned in to him, the way she had sighed as his hands had held her face and his fingers had combed through her hair, the way her lips had parted.

She blushes as she remembers how she pressed herself close, all heat and desire, only pulling apart when the sudden crack of a twig startled them both from the moment, Lillian staring wild-eyed about the clearing and relaxing only when Jack pointed to the peacock strutting out from a leafy bank of bracken. The spell had been broken. She had stood, adjusted her skirt and smoothed her hair. 'I should . . . we should . . . I need to get back.'

She had walked several paces ahead of him as they retraced their path through the woods, feeling dazed – hot – a little dizzy – as if she'd sat for too long in the sun; and yet somehow also more alert and aware of herself, conscious of Jack's eyes following her across the meadow, of the flittering mayflies rising up from the tall grass, of the brush of her skirt moving against her legs, of the blood rushing too fast through her veins.

'Lillian,' he'd started, back on the terrace outside the French doors to the house, 'I hope—'

But she had cut him off, unable to bear whatever apologies or excuses he had been about to offer. 'Excuse me,' she'd said. 'I really must find Mrs Hill. She's expecting me.'

'I don't think you two have even tried to beat me,' says Albie with obvious dissatisfaction as he declares 'Mahjong' for a final time and reveals his winning hand.

'Sorry, Albie,' she says. 'It just wasn't going my way today. Well done.' She reaches across the table and begins to stack the tiles to pack them away, her hand accidently brushing against Jack's as he simultaneously returns his pieces to the centre of the table. She glances at him, wondering if he too felt the surge of energy pass between them.

'I'd like a rematch,' says Jack, his eyes fixed firmly on Lillian's. 'I feel sure I can only improve my performance with practice.'

'Any time you like,' says Albie eagerly.

Lillian stands so quickly she jostles the table, several tiles falling to the floor. 'I'm sorry. There's something I must see to. You'll pack away, won't you, Albie?' And with that she turns and leaves the room.

*

Standing in front of the long gilt-framed mirror in her bedroom that evening, it's as if she is seeing herself for the first time. She runs a finger over her lips, then turns slightly, scrutinising her face, marvelling at how her physical appearance can remain so unchanged when inside she feels so stirred, so altered. What is wrong with her? Why can't she stop thinking of him?

Is it visible on her face, she wonders? Is it there in her eyes, a glint of wickedness she has perhaps always known she held somewhere inside her? She stares again at her reflection, notices the flush on her cheeks and puts a hand to her forehead. No fever. This is a different kind of sickness. Madness, perhaps?

Why would he have kissed her like that? She knew so very little about him but the brushing of their hands that afternoon . . . the suggestion of a 'rematch'. Surely she hadn't imagined the meaning behind his words.

A creeping dread begins to unfurl in her gut. Perhaps this sort of behaviour is de rigueur for such a man? Jack would be accustomed to moving in very different circles from her. A bohemian artist's world might be full of casual encounters. She remembers the sight of him surrounded by adoring ladies at the cricket match. He must have women throwing themselves at him wherever he goes. Maybe she is just another conquest.

Of course she can't rule out that he might be some kind of charlatan. Or opportunist. She doesn't know him at all. What could he do with such a hold over her? What if he has more malicious intent, to use her moment of indiscretion against her – bribery or blackmail? It doesn't bear thinking about.

The very worst thing of all is that Jack will be here for weeks yet. She'd like to bury her head in the sand and pretend the kiss never happened, but she knows now, after their excruciating afternoon game, that whatever has passed between them must be addressed. And buried. Immediately. It must be recognised as the silly mistake it was. She must make it clear that it will never happen again; and she must tell him, right away.

If he is surprised to find her standing outside the door to the old nursery he hides it well.

'I have to talk to you,' she says.

He glances behind her into the corridor.

'Not here. Can I come in?' His discomfort is obvious but she presses. 'It's important.'

He looks back into the room, then nods and opens the door a little wider, standing aside to allow her to enter.

Lillian isn't sure what's she's been expecting, but it certainly isn't the perfectly blank room she enters. Looking around, she notices the old desk standing in the centre, the rows of pristine brushes and unopened tins of paint; in one corner a pile of neatly folded dust sheets and scaffolding lie beside two tall ladders; and all around are the empty cream walls – not a hint of paint to be seen, except on one small patch of wall near the fireplace where a series of jewel-coloured strokes have been daubed, like the first splashes of colour on an artist's palette.

She turns back to him, confused. 'You . . . you . . .'

'. . . haven't even started?' he finishes for her, hanging his head so that he doesn't have to meet her eye. 'Yes.'

'But why?'

He shrugs. 'It seems I can't turn inspiration on and off like a tap. I suppose you might call it a "creative block".'

Lillian stares at him, stunned. 'Does Charles know?'

Jack shakes his head. 'Why do you think I've been so adamant about keeping the door locked?'

'Oh.'

'So,' he says, 'now you know my terrible secret.'

She doesn't know what to say.

'Lillian, if this is about what happened in the woods—'

She has been thrown off course by the unexpected revelation, but Jack's change of subject jolts her back to the reason she is standing there. 'I'm a married woman, Mr Fincher,' she says, cutting him off, wanting to take control of the conversation and say the words she has rehearsed all the way to the room. 'I'm devoted to Charles and Albie. What happened yesterday was a – was a . . .' He is staring at her with those intense charcoal eyes. 'It was an indiscretion on my part. It never should have happened. I want to make it clear, in no uncertain terms, that it will not happen again.'

Jack doesn't say anything but there is something about the twitch at the corners of his mouth that suggests that he might be trying to conceal a smile.

She does sound a little prim, but the thought that he might be amused at her distress, or think her to be blowing things out of proportion angers her. 'These sorts of occurrences may be commonplace for a man of your . . . profession,' she says in her grandest voice, 'but I can assure you that I am a loyal wife.' She draws herself up. 'I can't think what came over me. It was a mistake,' she adds more forcefully, 'and not one I shall be repeating.'

She is relieved to see him nod. 'It was a mistake,' he agrees. 'A terrible mistake.'

'I'm a good wife,' she adds, trying not to feel stung at his unnecessary addition of the word 'terrible'. 'I think it would be for the best if we both pretend yesterday afternoon – in the woods – it never happened. Wouldn't you agree?'

'I would.' He takes a step closer, his eyes still locked on hers. He is no longer smiling.

'And I think we should avoid any future situations that put us in close proximity to each other.'

'Like this one?'

'Yes.'

Jack nods, still holding her eye and she tries hard to control the rise of blood to her face as a fragment of something from the woods comes back to her — the sensation of his fingers running down the curve of her collarbone, his mouth against her neck.

'Good.' She clears her throat. 'I'm glad we understand each other.'

'We do.' He takes another step towards her, so close now that she wonders if it is the breeze through the open window she can feel on her skin, or his warm breath. 'I think that is our problem, Lillian. We understand each other. You and I, we seem to share something.'

Lillian can hear her heart beating in her ribcage.

'I felt it that first moment I saw you . . . at the party.'

Lillian swallows.

'You feel it too, don't you?' he asks.

The sun, now low in the sky, filters through the trees outside in the arboretum, casting them both in a burnished glow. She knows she must go. She knows she must turn and leave the room, but something in his eyes holds her fixed to the spot.

'Tell me that it's not just me, that I'm not imagining this,' he says in a low voice.

There is a stillness in the room, as if they both await the next breath, the next word.

She swallows. 'I feel it, too.'

She isn't sure who takes the next step but it doesn't really matter; she is in his arms again and he is kissing her, pulling her close and all reason and rational thought — all the jumbled arguments she has agonised over — fly away like a flock of birds startled from the branches of a tree. Her arms are wrapped around his waist and his hands are

143

on her face and in her hair as they stumble backwards. She meets the edge of the desk, and then he is lifting her onto its surface, several brushes clattering to the floor as he presses against her.

'We mustn't,' she sighs, but already her fingers are tugging at the buttons of his shirt. She parts her legs and his hands move under her skirt, his fingertips grazing the bare skin above her silk stockings.

'Do you want me to stop?' he asks, his breath hot against her neck.

But she draws him to her again, pressing her mouth against his ear to whisper her answer. 'Don't stop. I don't want you to stop.'

PART TWO

'So fold thyself, my dearest, thou, and slip
Into my bosom and be lost in me.'

Alfred, Lord Tennyson

It's in the shadows of the night that I move most freely. The watchman, patrolling his domain, walking the corridors, moving silently from room to room. It's in the dark that I take up the mantle. I rest on their chairs, spray their cologne, taste their wine and touch their fine things. Lost in sleep, they do not know how I move through their world – how I occupy their space.

Perhaps it's innocence – blind trust – or just a naive surety of their place in this world – that makes me invisible to them. Maybe it's simple arrogance; what the hierarchy demands. Whatever the reason, they assume – blindly – that they go about their lives unseen – that their whispers slip away unheard and that their deeds pass unnoticed. But a good watchman sees it all. A good watchman notices everything.

Something moves in the darkness; the softest tread of feet moving on wooden floorboards. I fall back into the shadows and a figure hurries by, travelling with such haste they do not notice me here. They do not know that I see them tapping at the door, pushing on the door handle, sliding into the darkened room. They do not know that I stand here in the corridor, a witness to their soft sighs, the creaking bed springs, the sounds of the forbidden.

But I am here . . . I am watching . . . I am waiting.

CHAPTER 14

'Come on, you piece of junk,' Maggie murmurs, twisting the key again in the ignition, listening to the car engine turn over until with a last choked gasp, it springs to life. She presses her foot on the accelerator and revs it hard. Thank God. She's not sure she can deal with another dysfunctional thing right now.

She knows the errand is a ruse on Jane's part, but she has decided to play along, to prove to herself as much as to Jane that she isn't hiding from the world. If Jane needs butter to make pastry for her treacle tart, then butter she shall have. A short drive to the village shop, some polite small talk with Mrs Abbott behind the counter and then home again. How hard can it be?

She releases the handbrake and steers the car up the rutted drive, passing beneath the tall beech trees then out through the iron gates. Bursts of pink foxgloves and dandelions sway on the verge as she passes. Overhead, perfect white clouds dot an even blue sky. Even Maggie's lack of sleep and preoccupations with the house can't hide the beauty of the day.

Taking a bend in the lane, her heart skips a beat as she spots a familiar figure dressed in cricket whites walking a little ahead of her. She doesn't know what to do. It would be rude to barrel past him, but she doesn't know how Will might react if she stops. In the end, good manners prevail. She slams on the brakes, jerking to a halt beside him. 'Hello,' she waves. 'On your way to a match?'

'Yes.'

'Hop in, I'll give you a lift.'

He hesitates, but after a moment shakes his head. 'No thanks. I'm fine walking.'

She can't read his expression behind his sunglasses but something about his cool delivery annoys her. She didn't *have* to stop for him. 'But I'm going right past the green,' she says, the exasperation evident in her voice.

Will looks up and down the lane before throwing up his hands and opening the passenger door. 'Thanks,' he says, sliding in beside her, but she notices how he keeps his face turned to the windscreen. 'Did the plumber get the tap sorted for you?' he asks.

'Yeah, 150 quid later.'

Will winces. 'Ouch.'

'I'm glad to see you, actually,' she says, pulling away from the verge, deciding it might be best to keep their conversation strictly business. 'I've been going through Gran's paperwork.'

'Sounds fun.'

'Not really.' She pauses, wondering how much to say before deciding she might as well come right out with it. 'Being straight up, we're in a bit of financial difficulty. But I think you probably knew that already?'

'I had my suspicions.'

'Well in the short term, it would be great if you'd stick around and help us out . . . if you want to, that is?' she adds quickly. 'I'll make sure you're paid.'

He shrugs but keeps his face fixed on the road ahead.

'I'd really like it if you did,' she adds, pushing him for something more.

'Sure,' he says. 'I'm happy to see through my commitment to Lillian.'

She changes gear, taking a bend in the road just a little too fast. Will slides in his seat towards her before quickly adjusting himself.

'I've got a bit of a job keeping Cloudesley solvent and habitable for Lillian. She's absolutely determined to stay on here . . . says the only way she's leaving is in a box. But, as we both saw first hand the other night, the house is in dire need of some repairs.'

'Right.'

She's beginning to overshare, and Will's inscrutable manner is unsettling, but she can't seem to stop herself. It's either that or they sit together in awkward silence. 'I was wondering about the stables, whether we might rent them out to local riders, to raise a little capital. What do you think?'

Will shakes his head. 'They're in a bad way. You'd need to do some significant work before you could put animals in there.'

'I was afraid you were going to say that. Still,' she says, hating the forced brightness in her voice, 'it was just one idea. I'm sure there will be others.'

After another silence, Will clears his throat. 'The land is valuable. The meadow could be good for grazing livestock, if the ha-ha were repaired. You could sell it, or rent it out to a local farmer.'

Maggie nods. 'It's a good idea, but one field is never going to raise the kind of money I need to carry out the necessary work on the house. I was wondering about offering bed and breakfast . . . but really, who's going to want to come and stay here with the rooms in their current state? "Welcome to Cloudesley – please excuse the damp, the leaks, the faulty electrics and the resident mice."'

She falls silent as they pass the old stone church and carry on towards the pub at the edge of the village green. The usually sleepy lane is filled with cars. Red and white sun shades stand to attention in the pub garden. Children play on the green in the distance. 'How much money do you think we've spent in that place over the years?' she asks, nodding at the Old Swan, trying for a change of tack. 'Between the three of us I think we must have funded that fancy new dining conservatory out the back. We were in there almost every Friday night, as soon as I turned eighteen.'

Will nods, pushing his sunglasses up onto his forehead. 'Geoffrey was a stickler for the ID, wasn't he?'

'Do you remember the night Gus persuaded him to let him serve behind the bar? We had that lock-in.'

'Oh God,' groans Will. 'Don't remind me. The "cocktails" Gus made. I was so ill.'

Maggie laughs. 'Wasn't that the night you lost your key and tried to break into Damson House through the downstairs bathroom window?'

'And Dad phoned the police not realising it was us,' he finishes for her. 'Yep. Same night.'

Maggie laughs. 'Your dad's face.'

Will glances at her, the smile still written on his face, but as their eyes lock, his face seems to freeze.

'I can still picture it,' she says.

Will nods but he is looking away again, now at the green, surveying the busy scene ahead. 'Why don't you drop me here,' he says.

'I'll take you up to the pavilion. It's no trouble,' she says.

Will doesn't reply but she can see his glance at the crowds milling in the distance, the sudden tension in his jaw, and she understands. He'd rather not be seen with her. 'Oh. Of course,' she says, flushing red with the realisation. 'Here?'

He nods and lowers his sunglasses again. 'Thanks for the lift.'

'No problem.'

He slides out of the car without a backwards glance but just before she disappears around the bend in the road she glances in her rear-view mirror and sees him standing on the grass verge, exactly where she left him. It's hard to tell, but it looks as if he is staring after her. She shakes her head. Inscrutable Will.

She drives on through the village, past the community tennis courts, the allotments and the tiny redbrick primary school she'd briefly attended before boarding school, until she finds herself at the shop, a sign advertising a local ice-cream brand swinging in the breeze and the parish notice-board fluttering with adverts and notices. A poster for the annual flower show is tacked to the inside of the door — a colourful design drawn by a local school student.

Inside, Mrs Abbott is sitting behind the till, flicking through a catalogue and punching numbers into a calculator. Behind her are rows and rows of sweet jars lined on shelves, giving the place the feel of a curious, old-fashioned apothecary. 'I'll be right with you,' she calls without looking up from her sums. Maggie heads straight to the back of the store and finds the butter she needs before returning to the counter. She waits a moment, bracing herself.

'Right then,' Mrs Abbott says, lifting her head and giving Maggie a smile. Maggie watches as recognition dawns, the woman's eyes widening slightly, the smile faltering, then rushing back, brighter, more exaggerated. 'Oh, hello, love. I didn't realise . . . you're back, are you?'

'Yes,' says Maggie with a faint smile. 'I'm back.'

'Helping your grandmother up at the house?'

'Yes.'

'I was sorry to hear she'd been poorly. How is she now?'

'She's OK. Getting stronger.'

'Glad to hear it.'

There is an awkward silence. Maggie fidgets at the counter then reaches for a packet of mints. 'Just these and the butter, thanks.' She rummages in her purse. 'I see the flower show's on again soon,' she says, searching for small talk.

'Every year, like clockwork. Will you be sticking around for it?'

'Yes. I suppose so.'

Mrs Abbott nods, and then rolls her eyes with good humour. 'I swear there is more and more to do for it each year. The committee want to add an old-fashioned carousel and an inflatable Wipeout course this year, I ask you.'

'That sounds like a lot of work.'

'You're telling me! And I've still got the marquee and furniture hire to sort . . . and all the signage, not to mention the permits to chase with the local council.' She lowers her voice slightly. 'Patricia Lovell up at the vicarage wants everything "vintage" themed this year. She wants it all 1950s *Country Living* style. You know the sort of thing: pastel bunting, flowers in jam jars and mismatched teacups.' She rolls her eyes, showing Maggie exactly what she makes of *that* idea.

Maggie thinks for a moment. 'I could help with the flowers. We have masses at Cloudesley. They're just going to waste in the garden. I could arrange them in jam jars for the tea tent and deliver them on the day. How many would you need?'

Mrs Abbott looks thoughtful. 'Well, I don't know. Twenty, maybe thirty small arrangements.'

Maggie nods. 'Let me do it.'

'Are you sure, love? That's awfully nice of you and it'd be a huge weight off my mind.'

'Leave it with me,' says Maggie, feeling pleased to help. 'I'd like to contribute.'

The bell over the door rings, announcing a new customer. Maggie turns, her smile fixing awkwardly as she comes face to face with a tall woman in a blue chambray dress, her grey hair cut into a neat bob, a wicker basket slung over one arm. Maggie swallows. It's as though the air in the tiny shop has suddenly been sucked out. 'Hello, Mary,' she says.

The woman stops in the entrance. 'Maggie.'

Maggie can feel the shopkeeper's gaze flickering between them, though Mary keeps her eyes fixed on Maggie as the awkward silence deepens. 'Will told me you were back,' she says at last.

'Yes.' Maggie tries to resurrect her smile then shrugs. 'Here I am.' The words sound flippant, her nerves twisting them into something cold and brusque and she sees Mary Mortimer flinch.

The similarity between Mary and her two sons is suddenly laid bare to Maggie in a way she has never noticed before. She sees the echo of both Gus and Will in her almond-shaped eyes, the high cheekbones, the proud chin.

'I was sorry to hear about your grandmother,' Mary says, her voice still cold. 'Do pass on my regards.'

'Thank you.' She notices that Mrs Abbott has turned away and begun fiddling with her calculator again, clearly embarrassed and seeking distraction from the soap opera playing out in her store. Maggie swallows, knowing that the stage is now hers, feeling the long-awaited apology hanging over her. 'I – I wondered about coming to see you and David. I wanted to, but . . . I didn't know if I'd be welcome.'

Mary doesn't give anything away; she merely raises an eyebrow.

'I wanted to explain . . .' Maggie blunders on. 'To tell you why . . . well, you know . . . to apologise.' Mary still doesn't say a word, the only sign of any emotion the two spots of colour burning on her cheeks. 'I am *really* sorry for what happened. I never meant to hurt Gus. I'd really like it if we could find a way to put it behind—'

But Mary Mortimer has reached the limits of her patience. 'Don't, Maggie. We're way past that, don't you think?'

But now that she's started talking, Maggie can't seem to stop. 'I miss you. All of you. I wish we could go back to—'

Mary's eyes blaze with anger. 'I don't think you realise, Maggie; you don't get to wish for things to be how they were. You gave up any right to that last summer, remember?' Maggie swallows and drops her gaze. 'We considered you a part of our family. David and I, we welcomed you into our home and loved you like a daughter. But you threw it all back in our faces.'

'I'm sorry,' blurts Maggie, full of remorse. 'I never meant to hurt him. I never meant to hurt any of you.'

Mrs Abbott still has her face averted but Maggie can tell from the way her hands have fallen still over the calculator that she is transfixed by the car crash happening on the other side of her counter and can only imagine the gossip that will work its way around the village. 'Perhaps we could chat somewhere a little more private?'

But Mary lets out a sharp laugh. 'You want to spare our blushes, is that it?'

'I messed up, I know. But I only ever wanted to do the right thing. I thought it would be better in the long run . . .' Her excuses sound pathetic, even to her ears.

Mary's eyes are glittering with fury and looking at her, Maggie realises she has never seen this side of the woman before. Like a mother bear, prodded and poked, her maternal rage is a quiet yet terrifying sight. 'The *right* thing?' she spits. 'Don't make me laugh. What you did was shameful. The way you left . . . without a moment's thought for Gus or his feelings.' Maggie hangs her head but Mary isn't finished with her yet. 'Now, here you are, sauntering around Cloud Green as if you haven't a care in the world, expecting us all to forgive and forget? Twelve months.' She shakes her head. 'Is that all it takes? Is that long enough, do you think, to mend broken hearts and rebuild trust?'

'No . . . I don't expect—'

But Mary cuts her off. 'Well forgive me, Maggie, if I don't feel like throwing you a welcome-home party. You seemed a nice girl, a little lost, a little confused, but I thought you had a good heart.' She shakes her head again.

'I – I'm sorry.' Maggie stares at Mary. She doesn't know how to fix this. She doesn't know how to appease this woman's anger, how to make any of this right again. Mary is right. She is selfish. She was a coward. She can stay here muttering her apologies, but in the face of Mary's anger she knows there is nothing she can say that will undo any of the hurt she has caused this woman and her family. Her face blazing with shame, she darts past the woman and bursts out into the bright sunshine, the bell on the door jangling noisily behind her.

Unable to face the stifling atmosphere of Cloudesley, she leaves her car outside the shop and races down the lane, fiercely blinking back tears until she finds herself at the entrance into the rec. She pushes through the swing gate and heads down the grassy track weaving between the allotments, past freshly tilled plots of earth and canes heavy with tangled beans and tomatoes, hollyhocks and carrot tops bursting from the soil. She runs out of steam at the children's park at the very bottom and settles herself on one of the three empty swings dangling from the metal A-frame.

Nothing much has changed in all the years she's been coming here. The swings are still old and rusty, creaking on their chains. The metal slide winks at her in the June sunshine. Behind her the huge old tractor tyres lie sunken into the dirt as climbing equipment. Perhaps it is no accident, she realises, that she finds herself here; for it was here that she first met Gus and Will over a decade ago.

Back then, the beech trees had been a spectacular copper colour and she'd kicked her way through deep drifts of leaves to reach the park. She'd returned to Cloudesley from boarding school, for the October half-term holidays, a stroppy teenager, deep into a short-lived Goth phase, returning home with ripped tights and dyed black hair and violent purple nail varnish that had made her grandfather's eyebrows shoot skywards and Lillian's lips press into a thin line. She'd expected 'a serious talking to' but Lillian had merely directed a slight shake of her head at Charles where he sat in his wheelchair, and she'd known then that the topic of her appearance wouldn't be mentioned. Well good, she'd thought, slinking away to wander the village; it was high time they saw her as the grown-up she *almost* was. In her pocket was a pilfered packet of cigarettes and an old lighter, both of which she'd found hidden at the back of her grandfather's desk. She'd played with them, flipping them over and over in her deep coat pockets, until she'd finally found herself in the park.

She'd sparked up a cigarette and sat on one of the empty swings, scraping her boots back and forth across the muddy ground, revelling in her sad, solitary state.

The two boys had seemed to appear from thin air, quietly settling themselves into the empty swings beside her and starting to swing back and forth with quiet purpose. She'd glanced across and nodded at them and one of them – the older one – had thrown her a casual 'Hi' before returning to his task.

They'd seemed to be involved in some unspoken competition. Maggie had watched with surreptitious glances as they'd urged their swings higher and higher until the whole A-frame shuddered with their force and Maggie had found herself wondering for one thrilling moment if they mightn't pull the whole thing from the ground and send them all flying. On they went, backwards and forwards, pushing towards the sky until the slightly older boy, the one with the darker hair, had called out, 'You first,' and the boy with the freckles and the wide grin had pulled back his leg and on the arc of his forward swing, kicked one wellington boot off his foot and propelled it out into the sky. All three of them had watched it soar until it landed with a thud halfway to the hedge.

'Not bad.' The darker-haired boy had taken a couple more swings then sent his own boot arcing out, until it crash-landed on the grass beside the first boot, bouncing up off the turf and landing a foot or so ahead.

Maggie, her head still spinning from the cigarette, had listened to them arguing over who was the rightful winner. There had seemed to be some contention over whether a bounce was allowed. Was it the first spot the boot landed or its final resting place that was the measure of the kick?

While they'd bickered, she'd started to swing, pushing herself higher and higher. Gradually, she'd edged her Doc Marten boot off her heel until it balanced precariously on her toes, and then she'd pulled back her own foot and let it fly. The boy with the fairer hair had given a low whistle and they'd all watched as it hurtled through the air and fallen a metre beyond the dark-haired boy's boot. She'd restrained her celebrations to a cautious sideways glance through the curtain of her hair.

'Nice,' the younger boy had admitted, grudgingly. 'But Doc Martens are easier. They're smaller and heavier, so you had a natural advantage.' He'd eyed her. 'You don't live round here, do you?'

'Yes,' she'd said, pleased to prove them wrong. 'I live with my grandparents on the other side of the village, but I board during school term time.'

'We live in the house near the shop, the one with the red front door.'

She'd nodded. She knew the one. It had a damson tree in the garden and white shutters at the windows. She'd pulled the cigarettes from her jacket pocket. 'Want one?'

'Sure.' The taller boy had taken the packet from her, removing two and sticking one into the corner of his mouth before passing the other to his younger brother. 'I'm Will,' he'd said. 'This is Angus, my brother.'

'Gus,' the other boy had corrected.

'Maggie.' They were a little older than her. Will looked to be about fifteen or sixteen, Gus a little younger; fourteen, perhaps.

'You've got a pretty good wang.'

'Pardon?'

'A welly-wang. That's what we call it: the game,' he'd added, nodding in the direction of the scattered boots.

'Oh. Right.'

She'd passed the lighter and watched Will hold the flame to the end of Gus's cigarette, then his own. Before he'd handed it back to her he'd read the engraved inscription out loud. '*Boldness be my friend.* Cool.'

She'd nodded. She had no idea if he was taking the mickey or not.

Gus had inhaled deeply and then exhaled with a loud, spluttering cough.

Will had looked on, amused. 'Want to go again?' he'd asked, nodding at the boots. 'Prove it wasn't beginner's luck?'

Maggie had smiled at the challenge and begun to swing immediately, her grin spreading across her face as she'd flown high into the sky, the two boys goading her with gentle insults and attempts to put her off her swing.

Sitting there now, so many years later, she can almost hear the echoes of their laughter. Of course it had been lame – stupid, childish fun – but the truth was there was a lot to like about hurling boots out across a muddy field with the two boys. Will had won the second round hands down, Gus the third. He'd taken a victory lap around the swings with his T-shirt over his head.

She had left boarding school for the Christmas holidays that year with a sense of anticipation. Christmas at Cloudesley was usually a quiet affair. There was the Oberons' annual attendance at church followed by a formal lunch and the customary exchange of presents in front of a roaring fire in the drawing room, Charles slumped in his wheelchair and Lillian trying to jolly things along as much as possible in the usual absence of Albie. (Was it Ibiza that year? Or perhaps Morocco? She vaguely remembers the crackling phone call, the sound of jovial partying in the background, the shouted promises of presents in the post, which of course never materialised.) Yes, there wasn't much to look forward to; but that year, everything changed. After she'd returned home, unpacked her trunk and taken tea with Lillian and Charles in the morning room, she'd excused herself with the surprising announcement that she was 'off to see friends in the village' and ignoring Lillian's startled look, had raced outside, grabbed one of the rusting bicycles from the stables and headed straight to Damson House. It was Will who'd opened the door to her. 'Well hello there,' he'd said. 'You changed your hair?'

She'd reached up and touched her bob, now back to its natural russet hue. 'Yeah. Do you guys want to hang out for a bit? Come to the park?' She'd waited, shivering on the doorstep, trying not to look too bothered either way.

'We can't.' He'd looked slightly sheepish. 'It's a bit of a family tradition – games afternoon with the folks.'

'Oh, OK. Another time.' She'd been crestfallen.

'But you could come in, if you like? We're playing Pictionary. I'm losing. Badly.'

'Won't your parents mind?'

'Mind?' Will had looked startled. 'Course not. Come on.' He'd already turned, leaving the door open and there was nothing for her to do, it seemed, other than to close it behind her, slip off her Doc Martens and stand them next to the pile of casually discarded boots scattered around the porch before following him down the carpeted hallway.

They'd been sitting in the lounge, the Pictionary board spread across the coffee table, Gus slouched next to his mother on the couch, their father seated in an old wingback chair near the fire. 'Mum, Dad, this is Maggie. She's from the big house on the other side of the village. It's OK if she joins us, isn't it?'

Their father had leapt to his feet and shaken her hand enthusiastically. 'The more the merrier. Welcome, Maggie.'

'Hello, Mr . . .'

'Mortimer,' he'd answered. 'But please, call me David. And this is Mary, my wife.'

She'd greeted the boys' mother with a shy, 'Hello', still unsure if it truly was OK that she was there.

'Have a seat, Maggie. Would you like a cup of tea? A mince pie? They're homemade. Not the best, but Gus has managed three.' Mary Mortimer had gestured to a plate of misshapen pies on the table behind them.

'I'm fine, thank you.' She'd grinned and waved at Gus.

'Over here,' Will had said, patting a spot beside him on the rug in front of the fire. 'You're on my team.'

'Bad luck,' Gus had commiserated. 'Will's terrible at Pictionary.'

They'd picked up the game again and Maggie had quickly forgotten her nerves and joined in enthusiastically. She and Will had begun to pull ahead on the score sheet. 'You didn't say she was an artist,' said David, faux annoyance in his voice.

'I had no idea,' admits Will.

A marmalade-coloured cat had come and curled in a warm circle on her lap. 'Push her off if you don't want her,' Mary had said but Maggie shook her head. It was nice to sit there with this family, in front of the log fire as the night drew in, with their pets and their laughter and their gentle teasing. It was better than nice. It was heaven. Cycling back to Cloudesley later that evening, she'd thought about how she'd never before been anywhere that had felt so wonderfully *normal*.

Damson House had soon become her home away from home. Over the years as her friendship with the Mortimers had strengthened, she had sat around the kitchen table, threaded daisy chains upon its lawns, climbed the branches of the old damson tree, sprawled on the shabby sofa watching movies and eating ice-cream. She had washed up Sunday lunch dishes in the kitchen sink and made cups of tea in the chipped teapot. She had lain upstairs on the boys' beds watching clouds race past the window as mix tapes played on an old cassette player.

Of course as they grew older things had shifted: movies and games in the lounge at Damson House gave way to trips to the pub and house parties. Sometimes they'd stay up late playing cards and drinking cheap wine. Sometimes – but not very often – she'd take them back to Cloudesley, where they'd play croquet on the unkempt lawn, steal Charles's cigarettes and spirits from the drinks trolley, or play cards in the drawing room; but usually they were more comfortable in the warmth and cosiness of Damson House, or roaming outside, enjoying the freedom of their youth.

Then Will had met a girl. Gus and Maggie hadn't much liked her – she was beautiful but uptight and had seemed wildly mismatched with Will's relaxed nature; they'd teased him relentlessly, then nursed him through his first broken heart. Things changed, of course; they grew closer and fell out, squabbled over music and movies and whose round it was, but until Will left for university, it was always the three of them, every holiday.

Remembering how things had once been between them, Maggie can't help but feel the deep void of their absence. Will is little more than a distant stranger now, every exchange between them fraught with underlying tension. And Gus? Well, they haven't spoken since she left last summer. Had she imagined that glimmer of connection with Will, as they'd stood there in the bathroom, drenched to the skin? Had it just been wishful thinking on her part, that they might find a way to rebuild their friendship?

Maggie sighs. She should get back to the house. Jane will be waiting for the butter and she's not going to fix anything sitting here on the swing feeling sorry for herself as she reminisces about bygone days.

Leaving the park, she begins a slow trudge back to her car, her shoulders a little more hunched, her jaw a little more firmly set. She'd lived in hope that perhaps things wouldn't be as bad as she'd imagined on her return; but now she's faced the full force of Mary's anger, she knows it's unlikely the Mortimers will ever be able to forgive her for what she did. Perhaps the sooner she tries to get over them all, the better.

CHAPTER 15

The clock strikes eleven down in the entrance hall. Lillian, lying restless beneath her sheets, hears it echoing through the house. Every minute she lies there alone feels as slow and interminable as an hour.

Bentham has finished his rounds for the night: she's heard him moving through the house checking doors and window locks, bidding goodnight to the housemaid and switching off lights. Sarah has retreated to her quarters in the attic, her footsteps creaking overhead followed by the clanking of pipes and the flushing of a cistern, all familiar sounds of the house settling down for the night. As silence settles over Cloudesley, she lies in the darkness and tries to control the emotion raging within, a swirling mix of anticipation and desire, self-loathing and guilt – and fear, too. Fear that it will be tonight that Jack is caught creeping along the corridor to her room – and perhaps, even more so, fear that it will be tonight that he comes to his senses and stays away.

She shifts, hot and tangled in her silk nightdress, then goes still as somewhere beyond her bedroom door comes the sound of a creaking floorboard.

She gives an involuntary shiver and holds her breath, waiting. There is nothing but silence. Lillian sighs and shifts again under the sheet. It's just the house settling around her.

It's been two weeks since the madness of their kiss in the woodland clearing. Two weeks since she went to him in the old nursery and they made love on the desk. Two weeks since their lives collided in such an intense and unexpected way.

Whenever she is alone now, whenever she closes her eyes, she is back there in the golden light of that room, allowing him to undress her as her own fingers pull at the buttons on his shirt, move through his hair, pulling him closer.

It shocks her to think of herself in that moment; no passive, acquiescent female, but rather a woman filled with heat, driven by want and need. She blushes just to remember it; but she knows she couldn't have stopped herself even if she'd wanted to. Here she lies in the dark, counting clock chimes, waiting for her lover to come to her.

Her lover. The word seems shocking, even now. It is madness, she knows. She's told herself over and over that it is insanity – that she must put a stop to it – whatever 'it' is that she and Jack have started. She is a married woman – a wife and step-mother. She has responsibilities and a reputation to consider. But while she is not so carried away that she doesn't feel the sting of shame that comes with her infidelity, she knows she cannot deviate from the course she has set upon, not even if she wanted to.

There is another quiet creaking sound from outside her bedroom door, this time followed by the lightest tapping. She doesn't utter a word, but lies still and silent, watching from the bed as the door opens and a figure slips into her room, his form lost to the darkness as soon as the door has closed behind him. She hears footsteps moving across the floor, feels a waft of cooler air as her sheets are lifted, the slight tilt of the mattress as he slides in beside her.

'My dearest heart,' he says into her ear as he curves his body around hers and pulls her to him, his lips finding hers in the darkness.

'You smell of paint,' she says much later, curled languidly into the crook of his arm as they pass a cigarette back and forth in the darkness. 'Paint and turpentine.'

'Sorry.'

She draws his hand up to her mouth and kisses each of his fingers in turn. 'I quite like it.' They have flung open the curtains, the cooler night air and moonlight drifting across their skin, a canopy of stars just visible through the open window. His hand traces a line from her ear lobe down her neck to the outer edge of her collarbone. Lillian sighs and curls in closer to him. 'Shall I take it as a good sign?'

'Yes. It's a good sign,' he says, nuzzling her neck. 'Though I missed you today,' he says.

'You could dine with me in the evenings, now that Charles has extended his London trip.'

He shakes his head. 'I couldn't bear it. Sitting so close to you, politely pretending while Bentham pops in and out to clear plates and pour the wine. I'm afraid I'd give myself away.'

'Yes,' she says, pulling back to look into his eyes. 'This spark between us is so strong. Sometimes, I feel it might steal the oxygen from the air around us.'

'Exactly.' He smiles and leans in to kiss her on the mouth. 'Besides,' he adds, 'now that I have fixed on an idea for the room, I'm afraid to stop painting. I'm afraid to lose the momentum.'

'Well then, I'm glad. Don't come. I know how much work you have to do,' she adds, nudging him in the ribs.

Jack doesn't rise to the bait. 'He's an odd fellow, isn't he?' he says after a moment.

'Who? Charles?'

'I was thinking of Bentham.'

'Oh I don't know. He's quiet, certainly. Unreadable. Truth be told, I was a little afraid of him when I first moved here. Though he's been ever so loyal to Cloudesley. We lost a lot of staff to the war and have been operating on a skeleton outfit ever since. But Bentham's been here through it all, thick and thin. We're lucky to have him.'

'Yes, it must be hard only having a cook, a maid, a butler and a gardener to look after you.'

Lillian slaps him on the chest. 'Don't.' Then she adds, with a hint more seriousness, 'Don't laugh at us.'

'I'm sorry. I'm not laughing at you. It's all rather foreign, this life you lead.'

'I'd give it all up tomorrow . . . if I could.'

'Would you?' He turns to study her in the darkness.

'I would.'

Jack doesn't say anything. He just stubs his cigarette out in the ashtray beside the bed and wraps her more tightly in his arms.

'Do you ever wish,' she asks softly, 'that you could make the rest of the world just disappear?'

He kisses the top of her head. 'It does . . . when I'm painting . . . and when I'm with you.'

Lillian nods, but she's not entirely sure he's understood what she meant. She doesn't know how to put into words the deep longing she feels to escape the life she is bound to. The heavy constraints she feels – the weight of the promises she has made.

Somewhere out in the grounds a peacock shrieks, the sound echoing out across the garden. She feels Jack tense beside her. 'Christ,' he says, 'I'll never get used to that sound.'

She smiles and steals the cigarette from his fingers.

'So what is the news from London?' Jack asks and her smile falters at the reminder of Charles. She doesn't want to think about Charles, not with Jack lying there in her bed.

'We spoke this morning. There are problems with a delayed shipment. He's not sure he'll return in time for the village flower show.'

'Good.'

'He did ask how the room was coming along.'

'What did you tell him?'

'The truth: that you're spending your days cloistered away and that you only emerge for sleep and sustenance.'

Jack seizes her arm and nibbles the crook of her elbow. 'I suppose that makes you sustenance, does it? It's your fault, you know.'

'My fault?'

He nods. 'Ever since the sparrowhawk . . . since that day . . . you've released something in me.' He clears his throat, as if embarrassed, but he doesn't stop. 'For days I was all angst and despair, tortured by the blank walls, uncertain how to cover such a vast space. Then, after that first night together, it was there; the idea arrived, almost fully formed. It's exhilarating, and terrifying.'

'Terrifying?'

'Yes. I'm so gripped by it that I don't want to spend too much time away from the room. I'm terrified I will lose the thread of it if I don't keep going. There's a moment when you're creating, when you lose yourself in the act of it, when you know you're finally hitting the flow of the piece. That's what I'm desperate to hold on to. Though it's quite a challenge. The size of the room means I have to work a little differently. It's all an experimental process, a sort of unfolding.' He reaches out to stroke her bare shoulder. 'I've never felt so inspired, so excited by a piece's possibility.' He glances at her, that wry smile

169

of his just visible in the darkness. 'I think I may have discovered my Muse.'

'Cloudesley?'

He laughs and shakes his head. 'No, you clot. You.'

Lillian smiles. She can't think of a greater or more unexpected compliment than being called Jack's Muse. 'Can I see it?' she asks and instantly regrets the question.

He hesitates. 'Yes. But not yet.'

She rolls over onto her stomach, her hair falling across her face as she props herself up on one elbow. Jack reaches out and tucks a loose lock behind her ear and she leans her cheek into the curve of his palm. 'Then promise me one thing,' she says softly. 'Don't finish it too quickly.'

'I told Charles I would need the whole summer and that hasn't changed.'

The summer. There are still weeks ahead of them, but she knows even now that it isn't enough. It could never be enough. She is greedy for him – for all of him. The hours they are apart are torture. Her head is full of fantasies. She can't imagine him packing up his belongings and leaving her here.

'Is it like this with him?' he asks.

Lillian lies back against the pillow wondering how to explain. Should she tell him about Charles's screaming nightmares? How the war has had a private, lasting impact on her husband? How his night terrors mean they must sleep in separate bedrooms? Are there words to explain how different their intimacy is? Could she even begin to tell him how she had tried to read her husband's cues and understand his desires, but Charles only ever wanted her to lie silently, her nightdress around her waist, her head pressed into the pillows. Something perfunctory. Something to be endured. And afterwards, how he insisted she leave him, leaving her aching and feeling somehow more alone than if they had never shared the moment in the first place.

How can she explain the complexities of the man she shares her life with? She's not sure she even wants to. Somehow it feels shameful — a gross failing on her part — unable to satisfy her husband or make him happy. These are things that should be kept in the dark; not brought to light in this precious moment with Jack.

'Sorry. I shouldn't have asked that.'

'No,' she says, after a moment's pause. 'It's not like this with him.'

'Do you intend to have his children?'

Lillian closes her eyes. 'I can't. I can't have children.' She feels the loss rise up in her, then settle like a heavy stone in her stomach. Her hands move unconsciously to her belly. 'I was pregnant but there were complications. I lost the baby and I'm not able to conceive. The doctor said so.' She says it matter-of-factly, trying to disguise the ache of grief at the back of her throat. She will never hold her own baby in her arms. Never hear a child call her 'Mama'.

He pulls her close. 'I'm sorry.'

She blinks back the tears. 'I shouldn't feel sorry for myself. Fate has been kind in lots of ways. I have Albie. He is all the more precious in the face of my own loss.' She smiles in the darkness and they are both silent for a while, lost in their own thoughts until Jack speaks again.

'There's something about you, Lillian. If you don't mind me saying, it's as if you don't seem to quite fit here. Most women would revel in their status as mistress of this grand old house. Yet you seem detached from it. You glide through these rooms and corridors as if you were a visitor.'

Lillian nods. 'Yes. It's a strange role, the second wife . . . second best. I'm a disappointing Lady of the Manor, I know. A disappointing wife now, too. Barren. Unfaithful.'

Jack is quiet for a moment. 'You don't disappoint me.'

She sighs. 'Some days I wonder how it is I've ended up here. It feels like a strange dream.'

'A good dream?' he asks, after a long moment, and she hears the flat note that has crept into his voice. Is it jealousy?

She turns away from him in the darkness, hiding her face. 'No,' she says. 'Not a good dream.'

Jack waits a beat before he asks his next question. 'Do you love him?'

Lillian shrugs. 'I was twenty-one when Charles proposed. He was a widower with a young boy and this extraordinary house. I had only known him a matter of weeks, but he seemed so lonely, so in need of someone to love him. I was flattered by his attention. Charles can be very charming when he wants to be . . . very persuasive.'

'Don't I know it,' murmurs Jack.

'It's a special place to be in Charles Oberon's spotlight. And I suppose I thought I could help him. I thought he needed me. I suppose I thought that's what love was: finding your purpose and making a better life, together. But I was wrong. Charles didn't need rescuing. At least, not by me.'

'How did you meet? You mentioned you came to Cloud Green as an evacuee?'

'Yes. I was eleven years old when my sister Helena and I were sent to live with a lady in the village. Lucinda Daunt. She was a solitary type and quite elderly, but she was very kind to us, especially given Helena's condition.'

'Tell me about your sister.'

Lillian smiles. 'She was wonderful. So vibrant. So full of life. There are two years between us and from the moment I was born, she was there. A constant, effervescent presence. I drove her spare, following her around, copying her, wanting to *be* her. She could do the most precocious Shirley Temple impression, complete with terrible tap dancing.' She smiles at the memory. 'No one could make me laugh like Helena.'

'What happened to her?'

Lillian sighs. 'Our father died in France during the war and mother was desperate for Helena and I to leave London; but we refused. We didn't want to leave her, not in her grief. But we should have listened. Months later, our house in Pimlico suffered a direct hit in the Blitz. I was the only one who made it to the Anderson shelter. Mother was trapped in the house. She didn't make it out alive. And Helena was struck by shrapnel as she ran through the garden. She was only a few yards behind me. It was the most awful luck. The doctors did their best but she was . . . she was quite changed.' She glances across at Jack and sees his eyes trained intently on hers in the darkness.

'How dreadful,' he murmurs. 'Is she in a hospital?'

'No. She lives in a residential care home. Charles has been very generous. Cedar House is a good place and I can visit her as often as I like.'

'That's good of him,' says Jack, his voice gruff. He curls his arm tightly around her shoulders. 'You poor thing. To have your entire family so altered in the space of a few months.'

Lillian nods and stares up at the ceiling overhead. She's tried not to think of it for so long. She's pushed all thoughts of her parents' deaths from her mind. She's tried hard to forget her mother's warm, perfumed hugs, the soft songs sung at bedtime, falling asleep to the low buzz of her sewing machine downstairs, gentle hands brushing her hair and tying ribbons, the laughter as they splashed through puddles on grey London pavements. Her father too – barely more than a shadowy memory of a tall man, his long legs folded into an armchair, face hidden behind a rustling newspaper; humming as he dabbed shaving foam onto his stubbled chin; a man of few words but always a ready smile. And Helena . . . beautiful, vibrant Helena disappeared with one flying piece of metal buried in her skull. Lillian has closed herself off from the grief for so long it's as though she's existed in a bubble, frozen from truly feeling. Numb loneliness has become a state as natural to her as breathing. But something about lying next to this man, being so open and vulnerable, brings the emotion back to her.

She swallows the lump in her throat and steers the conversation onto safer terrain, back to Jack's original question about Charles. 'Lucinda Daunt was so kind. After the war ended, she insisted we stay. I think she was lonely, too. I worked at the local school and helped Lucinda with her library in the evenings. I read to her each night and cared for Helena as best I could. For a long time, life simply slid by. I worried about what we would do – where would we go – if something happened to Lucinda, or she should no longer want us. But I was busy – lonely, too – until I met Charles.'

'Go on.'

She shrugs. 'There's not much to say. We met by chance. An accidental encounter on a country lane; one of those moments when life could go in a myriad of directions and for whatever reason, fate delivered me to Charles . . . or him to me. He proposed just six weeks after we met.'

Closing her eyes, Lillian can vividly remember the romantic scene. Their morning drive through twisting Buckinghamshire lanes to a charming riverside village. Charles spreading a picnic blanket on the banks of the Thames. The clunk of oars moving in locks as rowing boats slid by on the water. There had been strawberries bursting with late summer sweetness and champagne poured into tall glass flutes. He had arranged it all, seen to every detail – a perfect riverside picnic – rounded off with Charles on bended knee, offering her a diamond ring dazzling like fire in the sunshine.

It had been so unexpected. She had stared down at him, baffled. Charles Oberon wanted to marry *her*? 'Albie and I, we need you. Say "yes",' he'd urged her. 'Say you'll be my wife.'

But she hadn't said yes, not straight away. Tears had sprung to her eyes. 'I cannot marry you,' she'd said. 'I cannot leave Helena.'

Charles had studied her, then smiled. 'If we join ourselves in marriage, my darling, then our lives – our families – our burdens – become each other's. I am aware that marrying me means sacrifices on your part. Albie, my son, is part and parcel of my offering to you.'

'Albie is no sacrifice,' she'd interjected quickly. 'He's wonderful.'

Charles had nodded. 'Just as you would agree to take on my challenges, a marriage between us would mean I too would shoulder the burden of yours. I will find somewhere for Helena to go. She will have the very best care. Let me help you, dear Lillian. Let me carry some of your load.'

'It seemed like the answer to all my worries,' Lillian says, opening her eyes, finding herself back in the darkness of her bedroom, Jack lying warm and still beside her. 'Truthfully, it was the first real decision I'd ever made for myself. I thought I was choosing my destiny, creating my own life – a family.

'We were married in the autumn of 1951, just a small ceremony in London, nothing fancy, it being Charles's second marriage, and I moved to Cloudesley immediately after.' She sighs. 'I've been here ever since.'

Jack gives a small laugh. 'You say that like it's a penance. A prison. And you're an old lady.'

She shivers and pulls the sheet up around her. 'I was twenty-one. I thought love was a man on bended knee holding a diamond ring. I thought love was looking into a little boy's eyes and promising to always care for him. I thought love was making sacrifices and offering kindnesses to each other's family. And it was, for a time. But it wasn't the love I had been hoping for. And a house that at first dazzles with beauty and promise can, after a while, feel quite different. Less fairy-tale castle and more gilded cage. Sometimes, it seems the promises we make to one another can start to feel less like love and more like binding chains.'

Jack lies very still in the darkness. She notices how their breathing has fallen in sync, the rise and fall of their chests perfectly attuned. 'And what happened to the fairy godmother? Lucinda?' he asks, after a while.

'She passed away six months after I was married and Helena had moved to The Cedars. She'd grown increasingly frail. I've often thought it was as though she'd been holding on until she knew we were taken care of. Such a kind woman. I miss her.'

Lillian closes her eyes. 'I'm sorry. I'm talking too much.' She is revealing things she hasn't shared with anyone before. It is a strange sensation, not least because she feels a giddy uncertainty with Jack, a teetering vulnerability that makes her heart race. Here she is revealing all of herself – even the sides that she knows are less appealing – her grief – her loneliness – and yet she cannot stop. She needs him to see her as she truly is – not the mask she wears for the rest of the world, but the soul behind it. For the first time in her life she wants to open herself up.

'I'm glad you told me. I like knowing more about you. But it's very late. I should go back to my room,' he says, shifting slightly on the bed.

Lillian reaches for his arm. 'Don't go. Not yet.'

'I don't want to leave you.'

'Stay then.'

'I can't be here in the morning. It's too risky.'

176

'I know . . . but just a little longer. Please.'

Jack sighs again but he doesn't move and Lillian relaxes a little, re-tuning to their breathing.

Is what they are doing so very wrong? Of course, ethically, morally she knows she is breaking a code . . . breaking the sacrosanct tenets of marriage. And yet, if no one finds out, are they harming anyone? Can it be wrong to feel such desire and pleasure with another person? Can it be wrong to experience such happiness?

She falls asleep with her head resting in the crook of his arm. Jack lies next to her, listening to the wind moving through the beech trees, watching the gauze curtains lifting in the breeze, gently tracing the delicate bones in her wrist as he stares up into the darkness overhead. It's after four, just before the first birds begin their dawn chorus, when he eventually leaves her and tiptoes back to his room.

CHAPTER 16

The property developer arrives at Cloudesley in a gleaming black BMW and Maggie knows from the moment she opens the door to Todd Hamilton that she isn't going to like him. There is something about his shiny grey suit, tanned skin and the efficient way he folds his sunglasses into his jacket pocket and shakes her hand, looking past her into the hall as if expecting someone more important-looking to appear, that makes her bristle.

Maggie offers him tea but he tells her in his broad Texan drawl that he'd rather get on with the business of inspecting the estate, so she leads him outside, walking him briskly about the grounds, showing him the arboretum, the meadow and the orchard beyond the kitchen garden, before leading him back through the stable yard.

He forgoes the offered tour of the house, opting instead for a coffee on the terrace, where he spreads his maps of the estate across the table and marks up points of interest with a red pen as Maggie outlines the boundaries. She notices how he circles the barns and stables with a red pen, then slashes through a large wooded area and the grey square delineating the house. She wonders what it all means. 'Harry mentioned you were looking for a site to develop a new golf club?' she asks, more to make conversation than anything.

'Yeah,' he says, leaning back in his chair. 'Could be a potential gold mine round here.'

'So you think Cloudesley might be suitable?'

'It's looking very promising. The topography is perfect. Exactly what we've been looking for.'

'My family have lived here for several generations. We are, naturally, reluctant to sell, but for the right price . . .' she trails off, still finding the whole conversation unpalatable.

The American peers more closely at the map. 'There are good travel links to London and I think I'm right in saying no other golf courses around here, not for several miles?'

Maggie nods. 'And the house?' she asks. 'You like it?'

'The house?' He dabs at his brow with one of the linen napkins Jane has supplied.

'Yes, Cloudesley. You'll turn it into a clubhouse? Or perhaps a small hotel?' Then seeing his blank look she tries again. 'Maybe a restaurant?'

He shakes his head. 'Oh no. It's lovely, sure, but it would be commercial suicide to attempt to renovate this old place.' He glances dubiously up at the rear facade of the house, as if doubting its ability to remain upright. 'It would be far more cost efficient to rebuild from scratch. I'm imagining a new manor house perched on this hill. Something grand but contemporary. All mod cons. Now wouldn't that be something?'

Maggie stares at him, barely able to conceal her horror. 'You'd bulldoze the whole place?'

'Trust me, once you start peeling back the layers of an old girl like this, it's all over.' He smiles at her, flashing a row of perfect white teeth. 'These places are nothing but trouble. I doubt you'd find many developers interested in its restoration. It's land everyone wants these days. Golf courses. Housing developments. Cutting-edge grand designs for overseas investors wanting their piece of the English countryside. That's where the real money lies.'

'I think you might find there are a few heritage restrictions around an estate like this,' she bristles.

But if he hears the irritation in her voice he doesn't register. He laughs easily. 'Oh don't worry, Miss Oberon. You'd be amazed what throwing an obscene amount of money at a problem can do.' He slurps noisily from his coffee cup then turns and looks out over the hills. 'Yes indeed, a very fine golf course. Maybe even a spa, too. Something for the ladies. First manicure on the house for you, of course, Miss Oberon,' he winks. Maggie glances down at her chewed nails and flushes an angry red. 'I'll have my lawyers get in touch with your Harry,' he continues. 'I'm sure we can come to a mutually agreeable deal.'

Maggie escorts him back through the house and shakes his hand on the doorstep. Back inside, she makes her way to Charles's study. She dials the number on the old rotary phone and waits, tapping her fingers impatiently on the paper-strewn desk. The line has barely connected when she starts speaking. 'We are not selling Cloudesley to *that* man. I don't care what we have to do, but we are not going to let him and his bulldozers have it.'

She can almost hear Harry's smile at the other end of the phone. 'Good morning, Maggie. Am I to assume you met with the charming Todd Hamilton?'

'I mean it,' she says. 'No way are we selling Cloudesley to the Hamilton Consortium.'

'Message received loud and clear. Once more unto the breach . . .'

She puts the phone down and turns to stare at the silver-framed photo on her grandfather's desk, a younger Charles standing proudly in his army uniform, a host of medals pinned to his chest. So different from the old man she knew, folded up in his wheelchair. Tell me what to do, she begs him silently. Tell me how to save all this.

It's only as her burning anger begins to fade that the realisation comes to her: perhaps this is what Harry wanted. He *knew* she'd hate Todd Hamilton and his vision for Cloudesley. Harry sent him on purpose; to show her what was at stake.

Well, she thinks, screwing up Todd Hamilton's letter of interest and tossing it into the waste-paper basket beneath her grandfather's desk, it's going to be one hell of a fight, if she's got anything to do with it.

The old shoebox rattles and clinks with promise as she pulls it out from under her bed. 'Pick a colour,' Maggie says, lifting the lid and holding it out to Lillian moments later in the drawing room. 'Go on.'

Lillian smiles and reaches for one of the small glass bottles. 'This one, I think.'

'Good choice.' Maggie takes the jar of fluorescent pink nail varnish from Lillian and gives it a shake. She helps her grandmother move to the old wingback chair near the window, the dresser of photographs beside them glinting in the sun. Her grandmother splays her fingers over an old book balanced on the armrest as Maggie sets to work. Screw you, Mr Hamilton, and your beauty spa plans.

Up close and under such intense scrutiny, Lillian's hands are quite extraordinary; thin and long-fingered with raised veins running across the backs of them in thick blue tributaries, age spots dotting the skin like faded topographical markings on an ordinance survey map. The jewelled rings she wears on her fingers seem almost welded to the clefts of her skin.

Over the last few weeks, through the necessity of physical intimacy – the dressing, the lifting, the undressing, the bathing, the dispensing of pills, the propping of pillows – all the functions of caring for her grandmother have brought about a new familiarity. She is coming to know her grand-mother's body in surprising ways. It's no longer strange to touch her – to brush her hair, to massage a cramped muscle or sponge her neck in the bath. Beside them, young Lillian watches on from her wedding-day photograph, beautiful in a simple, white lace tea dress with a wide silk sash cinching the waist. Maggie glances across at it. She looks so young and the sight of her pretty, unlined face makes Maggie feel sad and a little afraid.

'There.' Maggie sits back on her heels while Lillian holds her hands up and waggles her painted nails.

'Thank you, dear. They look very jolly.'

'Yes, they do.'

'There's something else I'd like to do. Would you help me up?'

They take the stairs slowly, one at a time, shuffling along the landing until they are at the door to Lillian's bedroom. 'Here we are,' she says, a little out of breath.

'I could have fetched whatever it is you need and saved you the trouble.'

'Thank you, but this is something I'd like to do *with* you. After all, if we're to attend the flower show, we shall both have to dress the part.'

'The flower show?' Maggie can't hide her surprise. 'You want to go?'

'I most certainly do. You've been working so hard on those flower arrangements, it would be a shame not to go along and see them.'

Maggie studies her for a moment. 'It's just a few flowers from the garden. I really haven't done that much. And it will be very hot . . . and very busy. The crowds might not be a good idea with your—'

'Oh nonsense. I should like to go. I can sit in Charles's wheelchair, if you don't mind pushing me?'

Maggie hesitates. She'd been intending to deliver the flowers early the next morning and leave before the event had begun. The thought of attending the show fills her with horror. All those people, all the whispers and gossip. But Lillian is either oblivious to Maggie's reluctance, or artfully ignoring it. 'You'll drive me, dear, won't you?' she presses.

Maggie studies her grandmother. 'Do you remember teaching me to drive?' Maggie asks, a memory suddenly rising up.

'Of course I remember.'

'I was terrible, but you were very patient.' As a teenager, it was Lillian who had taken her out into the fields and let her practise in an old Land Rover, her grandmother clinging valiantly to the dash as Maggie had bumped them over muddy ruts and through copious cowpats. And it was Lillian who had retrieved one of the most expensive bottles of vintage champagne from her grandfather's wine cellar and toasted her when she'd passed her test. A life with Lillian had been full of affection, though it hadn't always set her up well for conventional life. Maggie had found that where most of her school friends talked of pop groups and PlayStations, she had been more au fait with bridge and Bach. It hadn't seemed to matter, though. Not to Will or Gus – not to those she cared about the most. Maggie smiles at the memory and sighs. How can she deny her grandmother this one, small outing? 'Of course I'll take you,' she says. 'Though only for a little bit, mind you. We mustn't wear you out.'

'Good,' says Lillian. 'Now, up there on the top shelf, can you reach? I want to look through those boxes.'

It's the hats that Lillian wants to look at. 'In my day, it wouldn't do to attend a social occasion without one.' She indicates the little stool in the corner of the room and Maggie spends the next half hour perched on top of it, fishing down dusty hatboxes. 'I think this is the one,' says Lillian, opening a large gold box and unwrapping from within layers of white tissue paper a beautiful teal beret with several peacock feathers jutting to one side. She places it on her head at a jaunty angle and peers out at Maggie, a whimsical, eccentric old lady playing dress-up. 'What do you think?' she asks, eyeing Maggie from beneath the feathers.

'It's fantastic.'

'Too much?'

'Never.'

'Good.' Lillian gives a satisfied nod. 'You must choose one,' she says, indicating the array of boxes now spilling from the cupboard. 'Hats aren't meant to spend their lives collecting dust in cardboard boxes. They should be worn. Try the yellow one.'

Maggie reaches for the one Lillian is pointing at, a wide-brimmed straw hat in pale lemon yellow, relatively simple but for the soft netting around the crown and the single yellow quill held in place with a brooch. She picks it up and studies it from different angles before placing it on her head and regarding herself in the mirror. 'It's really lovely.'

'One of my favourites. Come here.' Lillian reaches up to adjust it slightly, angling it so that the brim falls across her eyes. 'There. You look beautiful.' Lillian points back to her wardrobe. 'Look in there for the yellow dress. It goes perfectly.'

Maggie does as she's been asked, rummaging through the hangers until she finds the dress Lillian means, a pretty yellow cotton sundress with tiny white flowers dotted across the fabric. She slips out of her jeans and pulls it on, surprised to find it an almost perfect fit, the boat-neck collar scooping her shoulders, the zip at the back just about doing up with a deep inhalation.

Lillian looks at her for a long moment. 'You must be almost the exact same age I was when I wore this dress.'

'Twenty-six?'

Lillian nods. 'You have a lovely figure. You should show it off more, not hide it beneath those tatty jeans and T-shirts you're always wearing.'

Maggie turns in front of the mirror, pushing back her shoulders, feeling the soft fabric move about her bare legs. She doesn't feel like herself. 'It's not very me.'

'You look beautiful.'

'But probably a little much . . . you know, for what is essentially just standing around in a field with a lot of other people drinking tea and admiring vegetables?'

Lillian laughs. 'Why should you care what other people think? Worrying about them will only stifle your own life. Trust me, everyone is far too wrapped up in themselves to worry about you, Maggie Oberon. You'll see.' There is a force to her grandmother's words that surprises Maggie. 'You will never be as young or as beautiful as you are today. Be bold. Seize the life that was meant to be yours. Make it magnificent.'

Maggie is reminded of the inscription engraved on the lighter she'd taken from her grandfather's drawer all those years ago. 'Boldness be my friend,' she muses.

Lillian glances up at her. 'Where did you hear that?'

'Oh. I don't know.' She blushes, wondering if her grandmother might have guessed her secret. 'I read it somewhere.'

Lillian nods. 'Well, it's true. It's too late for me, but perhaps you can be bold for the both of us.'

Maggie wonders if she's imagining the tears in her grandmother's eyes. 'Let's not get ahead of ourselves,' she says gently. We'll see how you're feeling tomorrow, shall we?'

Maggie helps Lillian back down the stairs, gives her supper and settles her into bed before returning to the kitchen, where she makes tea and sits at the table, tying the last ribbons around the jam jars for her flower arrangements. She wishes she could take Lillian's advice and care a little less what people think, live with less fear; but deep down, she knows what she most hopes for is that Lillian, come the morning, will have given up on her madcap idea to attend the show so that she might hide at Cloudesley and avoid the rest of the village altogether.

CHAPTER 17

'It's another beautiful day,' says Sarah, moving about
Lillian's bedroom, folding discarded garments and tidying
the assorted brushes and combs on the dressing table.
'Perfect for the show.'

Lillian, threading a gold stud through her earlobe, catches
Sarah's eye in the mirror and shares a smile with her housemaid. 'Yes, aren't we lucky?'

'Not according to Mrs Hill. She's in a terrible state already,
convinced her Battenberg is a disaster. And don't get me
started on the lemon curd drama we had yesterday. It's this
heat, apparently . . . it's playing havoc with her baking.'
She rolls her eyes.

Lillian smiles. She likes Sarah and her cheerful, chatty
demeanour. Charles has complained that she's a little gauche,
a little too familiar with her mistress but, most days, Lillian
feels closer to her than anyone else in the house. At least,
she thinks, threading the other stud through her earlobe,
she did, until Jack arrived.

Sarah picks up the ashtray from beside the bed before
turning to Lillian. 'Is everything all right, Ma'am? I hope
you don't mind me saying, but you look a little peaky.'

'I'm fine, thank you,' says Lillian. 'I didn't sleep very
well last night. It's the heat.' She turns back to the mirror,
looking for traces of whatever Sarah has seen in her face.

If only she knew the real reason for Lillian's restless night. What would sweet Sarah think of her mistress then?

Sarah nods. 'It's none of my business. I was just . . . I was just worrying for you. What with Mr Oberon still away, it must get lonely.'

Lillian studies Sarah in the mirror as she continues to tidy her garments. Could she know about Jack? There is no way. They have been so careful. Sarah finishes her duties by straightening the bed covers. 'You'll be glad when he's back.'

'Yes. Just a few more days,' she says, careful to keep her voice even.

'We'll miss him in the tug-o-war today though. Mr Oberon's always on the winning team.'

'That's very true.'

'My Stan is running the tombola,' she adds, eagerly. 'Will you drop by and say hello?'

'Of course. I'd like to meet the man lucky enough to be stepping out with you, Sarah.'

Sarah blushes and gives a funny little curtsey before backing out of the room.

Lillian steps into the yellow cotton dress Sarah has laid out for her, then turns back to the mirror and scrutinises her reflection, wondering what people will see when they look at her today. She must wear some outward traces of her internal state – tired, yes, but somehow full of a pulsing energy too; as if aware of every tiny vibration in the atmosphere, alert with impossible aliveness. She brushes her hair, then takes up her straw hat and gloves.

Normally, she would dread these village functions, feeling like one of Charles's baubles paraded for display; but today she can't deny there is a part of her that is thrilled. Any opportunity to see Jack, even if it is in public where they will have to maintain a careful reserve, is welcome. Lillian has sat on enough village committees and boards to know that there is nothing a small English village likes more than the tantalising scent of a scandal.

Three white marquees stand proudly on the village green in horse-shoe formation, between which the rest of the fete stalls have been set up. Patriotic red, white and blue bunting flutters in the breeze welcoming a steady stream of villagers decked out in their Sunday best. The road is already clogged with cars. Bentham guides their vehicle once around the green then pulls up outside the Old Swan. 'It might be best, Ma'am, if I drop you here,' he says. 'I'll park in the field and wait for you.'

'Thank you,' says Lillian. 'But please don't wait for us. Come and enjoy the fete. I'm sure we'll find you if we need you.'

Bentham nods. 'As you wish.' He opens Lillian's door as Albie scrambles from the backseat, a scroll of paper tucked carefully under one arm.

Lillian straightens her straw hat, then tucks her arm companionably into Albie's. 'So,' she says, turning to survey the bustling village green, 'I'm needed in the exhibition tent but afterwards we can have some fun. Are you sure you won't show me your entry?' she asks, eyeing the rolled-up scroll in his arms. 'A little peek?'

'No, you have to wait.'

She smiles. Since Albie announced his decision to enter in the 8-10-year-olds group of the portrait competition, he's been very cagey. She assumes it's down to Jack Fincher having been invited to be guest judge this year, or perhaps he's taken a leaf out of the artist's book and decided to keep his work hidden until the grand unveiling. Either way, she's pleased that he's decided to involve himself with the show this year. 'Do you have enough pocket money?' Albie nods and jingles the change in his trouser pocket. 'Don't spend it all on candyfloss and toffee apples; you know how you made yourself sick that time.'

'That was two years ago,' he says, rolling his eyes at her. 'I'm not a little boy anymore.'

'Of course you're not,' she says, squeezing his arm. 'In that case, I suggest you stay away from the beer tent.'

He is still grinning as they cross the road and venture on past a couple of unsuspecting Shetland ponies tethered to a tree stump, waiting to carry boisterous children back and forth across the green for sixpence a turn. A man in a striped apron is setting up his lucky-dip barrel while nearer the tea tent, players from a local brass band adjust their jackets and arrange sheet music on stands. 'Well, this is me,' she says. 'Good luck.'

They part outside the exhibition tent, Albie slipping away to submit his painting, Lillian heading inside to join her fellow judges. 'Here she is,' exclaims Mrs Palfreyman, chair of the flower-show committee, pointedly checking her watch, an icy edge lurking at the corners of her smile. 'I was just suggesting we start with the savoury produce, then move on to jams and chutneys and finish with the cakes and biscuits. Are we all in agreement? Very good,' she nods, and makes for the table laden with pies and tarts before any of them can reply. Major Bramfield, Mrs Bingle and Lillian share rueful smiles and fall in obediently behind their self-appointed leader.

'At least we'll get a decent spread this year,' says the major, 'now rationing's finally over.'

Lillian sees Mrs Bingle glance at the straining buttons on the major's linen jacket and knows she is wondering exactly how much rationing he might have suffered over the last few years.

It is slow going and Mrs Palfreyman, a stickler for the rules, does not miss a single opportunity to display her impressive knowledge of home baking, insisting on debating everything from the appropriate thickness of the peel in the marmalade to the ideal quantity of dried fruit in the rock cakes. Lillian is happy to bow to her superior knowledge but the usually agreeable Mrs Bingle proves to be an eloquent and opinionated sparring partner. Lillian, beginning to feel increasingly warm and lightheaded in the airless tent, fans herself with the show programme and takes a backseat with the major, though she is pleased to note that Mrs Hill secures a unanimous first-prize placing for her lemon curd, and a highly commended ribbon for her Battenberg.

Just as Lillian is beginning to think she'd be happy never to see another cake in her life, Joan sidles up to her, looking fetching in a blue tea dress. 'Hello, darling. Enjoying your power as our resident Mrs Beeton?' She scans the array of entries and prizes. 'Tsk tsk,' she tuts, 'poor Mrs Lacey. She'll be positively crushed. Only *third* prize for her coffee and walnut cake?'

'I shouldn't be too much longer,' she whispers. 'Assuming Mrs Palfreyman and Mrs Bingle can ever agree on the appropriate spread of jam in a Victoria sponge cake.'

Joan grins. 'Hang in there, old girl. I've seen just the thing for a little fun.'

'Mrs Oberon,' calls Mrs Palfreyman, pointedly.

'Sorry,' says Lillian, rolling her eyes discreetly at Joan. 'Coming.'

Lillian traipses back to her post and finishes off the judging by awarding the last ribbon to a wonderful treacle flapjack. Then, at last, she is back at Joan's side and making for the bright square at the far end of the tent. They pass trestle tables loaded with groupings of runner beans, carrots and potatoes. Joan points out a large, inappropriately shaped marrow with a snort and Lillian has to hide her smile as she swats her with the show programme. 'You are incorrigible.'

'Come with me,' says Joan, ignoring her. 'I've had the most splendid idea.'

Outside, they weave their way through the crowd, past a group of enthusiastic Morris dancers clashing sticks and waving hankies with impressive effort for such a hot day. 'Keep it up, boys,' yells Joan, storming by. The heady scent of spun sugar, sawdust, warm trampled grass and anticipation hangs in the air. 'Where are we going?' asks Lillian, but Joan doesn't answer, marching on until they are standing in front of a small, jewel-coloured caravan sheltering in the shade of a tree at the edge of the green.

'Palm reading,' she says, turning to Lillian with a wicked glint in her eye. 'I thought it would be a bit of a hoot.'

Before Lillian can protest, Joan has already disappeared through the beaded curtain covering the entrance to the caravan, the emerald-coloured glass clinking behind her. There is nothing for it but to follow.

The caravan interior is small and cramped and a heavy scent, something like cedarwood and cinnamon, hangs in the air. A young, curly-haired woman with green eyes and an armful of silver bangles sits behind a card table. 'It's two shillings a reading,' she says. Joan slips eagerly into the empty seat opposite the fortune-teller, placing her money on the table. 'For both of us,' she says pointedly, 'so you can't chicken out,' she adds, turning back to Lillian.

The young woman slides the coins into her dress, then takes Joan's palm in her own hand and studies it silently.

'You have a long life line,' the woman says. 'Strongly governed by your heart. Lucky in love and money.'

Joan smiles. 'What every girl wants to hear.'

'There are two men in your life.'

Joan nods. 'That'll be Gerald and Georgie.'

'And I see a girl, too . . . with blue eyes, like her mother.'

Joan smiles. 'I'd like another child.'

Lillian looks around the interior of the caravan, noting the colourful fabric draped from the ceiling to create a tent-like atmosphere, the small bed in the corner, the smoking incense burning over the hearth. She wishes she were outside, sitting under a tree.

'There will be a choice to make soon,' the fortune-teller continues. 'I see travel in your future. Perhaps with your husband's job?'

Joan nods eagerly. 'Yes, yes, we've talked about it.'

'Your heart line is very deep. It dominates. Your marriage is strong but you need to learn to control your temper. It's a good hand. You'll live a long and fruitful life.'

Joan beams up at Lillian and she smiles back, thinking what a waste of money it all is.

'Your turn,' says Joan, vacating the chair for Lillian.

Lillian settles at the table and holds out her hand. The young woman takes it in her own, her touch surprisingly soft. She stares intently down at Lillian's palm, then frowns and clears her throat. 'You have experienced great sadness. You've lost something very precious. You feel it, deeply.'

Lillian swallows hard but doesn't move. She doesn't want to sway the woman's reading with her own reactions. It's all a load of rubbish, she knows; a clever mix of body language and mumbo-jumbo.

'Someone has come into your life,' she continues. 'Someone important. They have something to teach you. You must listen to them, but ultimately you must find your own way.'

Lillian can't help but think of Jack. Does *he* have something to teach her?

'You are strong.' The woman looks up at Lillian, her almond eyes staring into Lillian's, a soft smile on her face. 'Stronger than you know. This is good. You will need to be strong for what is coming.'

Lillian blinks and then averts her gaze slightly to the left of the woman, settling on the small painting of a white horse hanging on the wall behind. 'There is a branch here,' the woman adds, stroking a line on her palm, sending a tingling sensation through Lillian's arm. 'It indicates change. A moment, or perhaps an event. But I can see something else. It's a warning. You need to take care.'

The woman's bangles jangle on her arm as she grips Lillian's hand a little tighter. Lillian feels strange, a little giddy, her head swimming with the close atmosphere and cloying scent of the incense as the fortune-teller leans in and lowers her voice. 'I see danger.'

Lillian shudders, but she lifts her gaze to meet the fortune-teller's clear green eyes. The young woman leans in closer still, her voice no more than a whisper. 'Be very careful. Someone is watching.'

Lillian snatches her hand away, as if scalded. 'Sorry. I . . . I think I need some fresh air.' She pushes her way out of the airless caravan, through the clinking beaded curtain and bursts, blinking, back out into the bright daylight. Joan joins her a moment later. 'What a fraud,' she snorts. 'She can't have been more than sixteen years old.'

Lillian nods and tries to smile. 'I knew it would be a waste of money.'

'What was she whispering about at the end there?'

'Nothing. Silly nonsense. I think she was trying to scare me.'

'It's all a lot of rot. What would a girl like her know about life and love?'

Lillian tries to smile but the muscles in her face are fixed rigid.

'Come on,' says Joan, threading her arm through Lillian's, 'let's get a cup of tea and calm our nerves with the soothing racket of the brass band.'

The tea tent is crowded with people taking respite from the afternoon sun. Joan guides Lillian through the crowd. The air is hot and close, the scent of well-trodden grass trapped under the canvas. Lillian stands in the queue and watches children weaving in and out of the tables and chairs. Standing there in the brightness of the tent, surrounded by the crowds, it's easier to push the fortune-teller's words from her mind. Just a load of mumbo-jumbo. *I see danger.* How ridiculous.

'So where's that scrummy husband of yours today?' Joan asks.

'He's still in London.'

'Why didn't you tell me? I would have had you over for a game of tennis or dinner. You must be going out of your mind with boredom. Although,' she adds, 'perhaps you haven't been so lonely after all?'

Lillian follows her friend's gaze and sees Jack, for the first time that day, standing near the tea urns, looking handsome in a pale-blue shirt, caught up in conversation with a couple of elderly ladies from the village. Her stomach lurches at the sight of him, but she bats Joan on the arm with her flower-show programme, feigning shock. 'Really! I'm a married woman.'

'Oh I know. It must be simply awful having to look at that face all day,' she adds with a lascivious twinkle in her eye.

'I never see him,' she protests, a little too quickly. 'He's always locked away in the room, working on his murals.'

'Well, I'd say that was a missed opportunity, wouldn't you?' says Joan. 'Maybe *I'll* invite him over for dinner,' she continues, seemingly unaware of Lillian's furious blushes. 'A few martinis and a game of rummy with some of the local ladies and I'm sure we'll knock that conscientious streak out of him. Look at them all fawning around him, like bees glued to the honeypot.'

Lillian sees that Jack and his companions have been joined by three younger women from the village, all glossy hair and swishing skirts, laughing and teasing.

'He's quite the introvert,' she says softly. 'I don't think he much likes these social gatherings.'

'I'm not sure you know Mr Fincher as well as you think,' retorts Joan and, as if to prove her point, peals of laughter erupt from the group surrounding Jack.

At last Joan and Lillian reach the front of the queue. They order their teas then head to wait near the urn, closer to where Jack stands. Susan Cartwright's shrill voice carries towards them. 'Oh go on, be a sport. It's for a jolly good cause.'

Lillian watches Jack throw his arms up in defeat.

'Yes,' murmurs Joan, her gaze scanning Jack from top to toe. 'Quite a dish.'

They sit themselves at the far end of a trestle table and after a moment, as she'd hoped he would, Jack appears beside them. 'May I join you?'

'Be our guest,' says Joan.

Jack pulls out the chair next to Lillian and as he sits, she feels his foot settle beside her own, a light but insistent pressure brushing against her heel. Joan teases him briefly on his newfound status as village heartthrob and engages him in a conversation about his art, but as soon as her attention is diverted by the arrival of others from the village, Jack slides his own hand beneath the table and strokes the soft part of Lillian's wrist where it rises out of her glove. 'You look beautiful,' he murmurs.

She jumps at his touch, the words of the fortune-teller echoing in her mind. *Someone is watching.* 'Don't,' she says. 'Not here.'

He has an intense way of looking at her, the undercurrent of a smile hidden in his dark grey eyes, the slightly predatory way his gaze sweeps over her that brings a flush to her skin as she remembers the intimate things he did to her the night before; her hands gripping the bedhead, the way she had bitten down on the back of her hand to prevent herself from crying out. It's agony not to be able to touch him. To hell with virtue and propriety; all she wants to do is seize his hand and drag him away from prying eyes and idle gossip and those pretty girls, back to Cloudesley, back to the privacy of her bedroom.

'I've been bullied into sitting for the sponge throw,' he says at a normal volume. Then, lowering his voice so that only she can hear, he adds, 'Perhaps we could escape afterwards? The whole village is here. Who will miss us?'

Before she can answer, Susan Cartwright is standing over them again, tugging at Jack's shirtsleeve. 'Come on, Jack. You're up next.' She turns to Lillian, smiling sweetly. 'You don't mind if I steal him away, do you?'

Lillian returns her smile. 'Be my guest.'

Lillian would be happy to stay where she is, but Joan is already up and out of her seat. 'Now this I have to see,' she says. 'Come on.'

They stand squinting in the sunshine as Jack is locked into the old village stocks and a gaggle of giggling girls take it in turns to hurl wet sponges at him. It is Susan who has the best aim, her last sponge hitting him square on the forehead. He emerges slick and wet, his damp linen shirt clinging to his body. Susan rushes across and poses for the photographer from the local newspaper, her lips pressed to Jack's cheek. Joan lets out a wolf whistle but Lillian turns away, a horrible blaze of desire and jealousy flaring inside her.

'Lillian, Lillian, come with me.' Albie is at her side, tugging her hand. 'I won! Come and see.'

It takes Lillian a moment to realise what Albie is talking about. 'You won? How wonderful.' Casting a last glance back at Jack, she takes the boy's hand in her own. 'Show me.'

They enter the craft tent and Albie leads her proudly to the makeshift gallery where the children's paintings have been tacked to display boards.

'Oh my,' she says, seeing the colourful watercolour marked with a red ribbon. 'It's . . . it's . . .'

'It's you,' says Albie, turning to her with a delighted smile. 'Do you like it?'

'Yes,' says Lillian. 'I do. I really do. It's lovely.'

Albie has captured her with beautiful, childish innocence: a round pink face, her blonde hair a yellow sweep on her head, eyes the colour of a clear lake, spidery black eyelashes and a pearl choker around her throat.

'This calls for a celebration,' says Lillian.

They leave the exhibition tent and make for the long queue waiting for ices. The line snakes beside a red-and-gold striped puppet booth with a show in full swing, rows of children sitting on the grass and a large crowd of parents standing behind. The audience is laughing uproariously as the grotesque form of Mr Punch, with his hook nose and curved chin, turns to the crowd and crows 'that's the way to do it' in a high falsetto. Judy pops up from below, holding a puppet baby. She asks Mr Punch to babysit the infant and the audience falls about laughing as Judy disappears and Punch proceeds to sit on the baby. Moments later Judy is back and the two puppets begin to fight, Punch hitting Judy repeatedly with a large wooden stick.

Lillian feels her stomach twist. She looks down and finds Albie watching the performance, his eyes wide and his face as white as a sheet, his hand gripping her own more tightly as the puppets tussle and fight.

'Lilli,' he asks, looking up to her, 'why are they all laughing?'

She stares down at the boy. 'I don't know, Albie. I really don't know.'

CHAPTER 18

The white tents billow on the village green like sailing ships straining to be free of their moorings. Maggie feels surprisingly good in the yellow dress Lillian has loaned her, but she is glad she has tempered the look with her Converse trainers and thought to fix the straw hat firmly to her hair with a few extra pins. The warm wind tugs at it playfully like a young boy attempting to pull it from her head and toss it away. The air carries with it the sweet scent of candyfloss and trampled grass as well as the rising squeals of children being entertained by an old-fashioned puppet show. 'That's the way to do it!' screams a hook-nosed puppet. Lillian tuts. 'Dreadful show,' she mutters under her breath as they pass by. 'Can't believe they wheel it out, year after year.'

Maggie pushes her grandmother in the rickety wheelchair around the fete stalls, where they peruse the tables of plants and cushions, candles and cakes. They've already taken a turn around the exhibition tent, admiring the displays of local produce, the prize-winning entries of flowers, fruits and vegetables, both pleased to see that Jane has taken the red ribbon for her green tomato chutney. They stop briefly at the tombola where Maggie wins a pink plastic heart-shaped picture frame, then watch as a heavily tattooed man knocks three shells off the coconut shy. As she turns, she spots Will standing a short distance away, chatting to an older couple beside the hoopla stall. Away from Cloudesley, he looks different, somehow. Less familiar – taller and tanned – and very handsome. He says something to the couple that makes them laugh, and as he glances round he spots her watching him across the crowds. Maggie waves and Will holds her gaze for a moment, then nods and turns back to his companions. Maggie blushes, unsure why she should suddenly feel so hot and unsettled. It is a very warm day. She should get Lillian into the shade.

Nearby, the vicar is shouting over the PA system, trying to drum up entries for the egg and spoon race, his voice having to compete with the raucous dance music blaring from a nearby fairground ride. Beside him, an inflatable bouncy castle bends and lurches under the pressure of the children leaping on it.

Maggie is looking around for the tea tent when the vicar's voice bellows out over the PA again. 'Roll up, roll up. Over at the stocks it's just one pound for three sponges. Now's your chance to hit Gregory where it hurts.'

She sees Gregory Wells, the florid-faced publican at the Old Swan being locked into the stocks for the sponge-throwing competition. He is hamming it up for the growing audience in fantastic, pantomime fashion.

'I'm sure there are many of you out there who'd like to hurl things at this man and I know I don't need to remind you that it's all for a good cause. All proceeds go to helping us fix the church roof.'

Maggie isn't planning on going anywhere near the stocks and is pushing Lillian resolutely past with her head down when she hears Gregory call loudly; 'Well, well . . . if it isn't Maggie Oberon. Surely we can tempt you to step up and have a go? You always used to like a lock-in.'

Maggie stops dead in her tracks, her hands clenching the grips on her grandmother's chair, aware of the curious glances of the crowd. She glowers at Gregory, willing him to shut up.

'Oh, if looks could kill.' He chuckles. 'I see you're here with your grandmother, the lovely Lillian Oberon. How are you, deary? Feeling better?' he calls loudly and slowly, as if to a very senile person.

Maggie looks down at Lillian in desperation.

'Come on, ladies,' goads Gregory. 'Don't be shy. It's for a good cause.'

Her grandmother gives her an imperceptible nod, reaches into her handbag and pulls out a five-pound note. 'I'll pay. You throw.'

Maggie hesitates, already feeling far too conspicuous for her liking.

'You heard the vicar,' says Lillian. 'Hit him where it hurts.'

Maggie sighs. 'I'll try.'

Gregory is still grinning and goading her as she takes up the first sponge from the bucket of water and hurls the dripping mass at the wooden frame. It hits Gregory on the corner of his chin, sending water spraying across his face and generating a low rumble of appreciation from the crowd. Her second sponge hits his left temple while the third brings a rousing cheer as she scores a direct hit to the bridge of his nose. Gregory rolls his eyes in a mock swoon, making the crowd laugh even louder. As she turns back to Lillian her grandmother gives her a satisfied nod. 'Now, how about a cup of tea?'

Mrs Lovell has clearly had her way with the fifties-style theming for the event, but Maggie has to admit that the tea tent looks lovely, decked out in pastel bunting, floral tablecloths and her own flower arrangements sitting on the tables. In the far corner a string quartet plays a sedate waltz. The marquee is awash with blue-rinses and walking sticks. Maggie parks Lillian at a table then queues for tea and cucumber sandwiches. The lady serving gives Maggie a long, hard stare as she takes her money and Maggie can still feel the heat rising in her cheeks as she carries their refreshments back to Lillian.

'Hello there, dear,' says a grey-haired woman who has appeared at Lillian's side. 'I was just telling your grandmother how lovely it is to see her out and about. I can't remember the last time we saw her at a village event.'

'I couldn't keep her away,' says Maggie, giving Lillian a wink.

'We heard you were in hospital,' says the woman. 'Nothing serious, I hope?'

'Oh no, still very much alive, I'm afraid.'

'Oh,' says the woman, startled, 'I didn't mean . . . yes, well . . . I'm sure we're all delighted to see you up and about. There were rumours you might be thinking of selling Cloudesley now. Unless of course Albert is back to take the place on?' the woman asks slyly.

'Albie's away on business.'

'Of course he is,' says the woman in an overly understanding tone that makes even Maggie bristle.

'Well, I'm sure I'm not the only one in the village would love to see the house returned to her former splendour,' continues the woman. 'It's been years since you opened up the gardens or hosted an event. It used to be de rigueur.'

'Yes, and didn't it also used to be de rigueur that you'd throw yourself at any new man who arrived in Cloud Green?'

Maggie stares at her grandmother, unsure whether to laugh or reprimand her.

The woman seems to take the insult on the chin. She turns to Maggie. 'And how are you getting on, dear? It's good to see you back in Cloud Green, holding your head high. I know there are some round here who didn't think you'd have the gall to show your face after that sad business with the Mortimers, but I knew you'd return. Nerves of steel, you Oberon women.' The elderly lady smiles sweetly, as if she has just delivered a generous compliment.

'Oh, be off with you, Susan,' says Lillian impatiently. 'Go and bother someone else with your sly gossip and nasty digs.' She waits for the woman to huff away across the tent before she turns to Maggie. 'Always was a terrible busybody, that Susan Cartwright.'

They drink their tea in silence, Maggie feeling a dreadful anxiety well up. This is exactly what she'd been afraid of, everybody knowing her business. Glancing about the tent, she's certain she can see furtive looks and stares, nudges in her direction. Then she realises why. Mary and David Mortimer stand across the tent, deep in conversation with friends. Sweat trickles between Maggie's breasts and she wants to reach up and remove the hat that had felt stylish earlier but now makes her feel like a try-hard, drawing attention in a way that she'd rather it didn't. 'Are you still hungry?' she asks Lillian.

'A little slice of cake wouldn't go amiss.'

'I'm on it,' says Maggie, grateful for the opportunity to move, even if it does mean circulating through the crowds again.

She skirts her way around the edge of the marquee, head down, taking a circuitous route to avoid the Mortimers, then waits in the cake-stall queue to order two slices of chocolate cake. As she turns to leave, she crashes into someone crossing her path. 'I'm so sorry,' she says, realising she has smeared chocolate icing on their white shirt, then lets out a long breath. 'Oh God,' she says, pulling back. 'It's you.'

Gus stares at her, equally confounded. 'Hi,' he says, after what feels like a very long time.

'You're here.'

'Yes. So are you.'

She shrugs, the flimsy paper plates wobbling dangerously in her hands. 'How are you?'

'Fine.' He looks fine. Very fine, with his tanned skin and his brown hair shaved close to his scalp. She'd forgotten how blue his eyes are, piercingly clear like a calm sea on a summer's day. 'You?' he asks, though she can tell from his darting eyes that he'd rather be anywhere but standing there with her.

'Yes, fine. I'm here with Lillian,' she adds, gesturing towards the corner of the tent.

He nods but his gaze still can't quite seem to settle on her face. 'Nice hat,' he says after another moment. 'Suits you.'

'Thanks.' She clears her throat. 'I saw your mum.'

'She said.'

Maggie chews her lip. 'Listen, do you think we could perhaps sit down sometime and talk about everything? I'd like to try and expl—' She stops, suddenly aware of the petite woman in a pretty lace dress sidling up behind Gus and sliding an arm about his waist.

'Look what I just bought,' she says, holding up a crocheted dream-catcher dangling brightly coloured feathers. 'There's a truly ancient gypsy woman selling them at a little caravan over there. She offered to read my palm but I'm not sure I'm up for that.' She turns to Maggie with a bright smile, awaiting an introduction. 'Hello.'

Gus clears his throat. 'This is Camilla. Cam,' he says, gesturing towards Maggie, 'this is Maggie.'

It takes a moment, but Camilla's eyes widen so suddenly it's like the aperture of a camera adjusting. Yes, Maggie wants to say: *that* Maggie. 'I'd shake your hand but . . .' She gestures unnecessarily towards the two paper plates. 'Nice to meet you.' She wishes the ground would open and swallow her whole.

'Oh, yes . . . *Maggie*. Hello.' Camilla turns to Gus. 'Gosh,' she stutters, 'you two must have a lot . . . would you . . . I can go—'

'No,' interjects Gus. 'Maggie was just leaving.'

'Yes,' she says, shrinking even further into herself. 'That's right. I should get back to Lillian.' She begins to back away. 'I'm so sorry – about your shirt,' she adds, though they both know the apology she owes him is for things far greater than a little icing smeared on a shirt.

Maggie turns and darts away through the crowd, her cheeks burning, hoping that the sudden burst of laughter erupting from a nearby group isn't at her expense. She finds her grandmother exactly where she'd left her, slumped in her chair wearing a pained expression. Maggie dumps the cake on a nearby table and reaches up to pull the hat from her head, barely feeling the hairpins as they wrench through her hair.

'Oh good,' says Lillian. 'You're just in time to save me from a slow and painful death by school choir.' Lillian is smiling, but her eyes narrow when she sees Maggie's face. 'What's wrong?'

'Gus is here . . . with his girlfriend.' She grips the back of the chair beside Lillian and lets out a long breath.

Lillian purses her lips. 'I see.'

'I shouldn't have come.'

Lillian shakes her head. 'Nonsense. You can't stay shut away at Cloudesley for the entire summer.'

'It might be for the best.'

Lillian eyes her sternly. 'How long are you going to punish yourself?'

Maggie doesn't answer.

Lillian sighs. 'If there's one thing I've learned in my eighty-six years, it's that there's a time for tea and cake, but this, my dear, is most certainly not it. Come on.'

'What? Where are we going?'

'Stop talking and start pushing.'

Maggie studies Lillian. 'If I'd known getting out of the house would *revitalise* you like this, I'd have insisted we did this weeks ago.'

They take a haphazard route through the various fete stalls, Maggie muttering and cursing and bumping the wheelchair over the rutted grass, until they come to a halt outside a smaller tent. 'In here,' says Lillian.

'The beer tent?'

'Yes. I happen to know they sell some of the very best elderflower wine. We'll consider it medicinal.'

Maggie queues up at the trestle table masquerading as bar for two glasses of elderflower wine. She hands them to Lillian, intending to push the wheelchair over into the shade where they will be partially hidden from the crowds, but Lillian has other ideas, pointing to a row of striped deck chairs lined up along the main thoroughfare. 'Just there.'

'I don't think—' begins Maggie.

'We're going to sit here and hold our heads high. Take a sip,' she orders. 'You'll feel better.'

Maggie puts the plastic cup to her lips and drinks. The wine is cold and sweet, fizzing slightly on her tongue.

'Good.' Lillian nods approvingly. 'We'll sit here, where we can see everything. We're not going to hide.'

'But I feel like the most loathed person in the village,' says Maggie in a small, self-pitying voice. 'You heard Susan Cartwright. No one thought I'd have the "gall" to return.'

'Oh, don't talk rubbish. I doubt most people know or care what happened between you and that young man last year. And even if you do provide a flutter of interest today, my dear, come tomorrow they'll have moved on to the next titbit. You think all these people here don't have their own messy lives to worry about? Besides, you'll find people are a little less quick to judge when they have to look you in the eye.' As if to make her point, a small child with his face painted in tiger stripes wanders past with a helium balloon. He stares at Lillian and her extraordinary feathered hat and she stares back; eventually the little boy smiles and gives her a pretend roar before being dragged off into the crowds by his mother.

'You've had that look on your face ever since you returned home.'

'What look?'

'That frown. It's that same look you got as a child when you knew Albie was about to leave.'

Maggie pulls herself up. 'I'm not frowning.'

'My eyesight may not be the best, but I can still tell a frown when I see one.' Lillian pats Maggie's hand, softening slightly. 'Tell me, what was the worst thing that could have happened today?'

'Bumping into Gus was probably right up there.'

'And did you survive it?'

Maggie nods. 'I guess so.'

'Well there you go. Most anxiety is the fear of something that hasn't even happened yet, and it's usually over something we can't control. The older I've grown, the more I've realised what a waste of energy it is. We're sitting here, on this beautiful day, the sun overhead and the grass under our feet, drinks in hand. Let's enjoy this moment, shall we?'

Maggie looks at Lillian and smiles. 'I hardly recognise you today. Are you feeling all right?'

Lillian shrugs. 'You get to my age and you realise all the more keenly how precious are our days. I don't want you to waste a single one.'

They sit together in the sunshine and sip their wine, Maggie trying to relax. She understands Lillian's point, but it isn't that simple. Gus. Will. Her stalled career. Lillian's health. Saving Cloudesley. There is *so much* to worry about. She closes her eyes and tries to do what Lillian has suggested; she tries to concentrate on the plastic cup in her hands, her feet resting on the grassy earth, the sound of children laughing and shrieking, the far away strains of the band. She opens her eyes and sees children with painted faces running squealing towards the bouncy castle. A red helium balloon floats away into the blue sky.

They take another quick turn around the fete before Maggie drives them home, the sun a golden orb flickering behind the trees as it sinks towards the horizon. Beyond the church, a swallow swoops from the trees and soars ahead of the car, as if pulling them in its wake. Maggie smiles at the sight of it and turns to point their escort out to Lillian, but Lillian isn't looking at the road. Her face is tilted towards the open window, the afternoon sun playing on her face, her arm resting upon the window ledge and her fingers splayed as if to catch the passing breeze. Maggie smiles at the sight of her grandmother's neon-pink fingernails, aware that wherever Lillian is at that moment, she isn't in the car beside her. She is like that red balloon, cut adrift, floating somewhere far away, lost in a memory.

Maggie thinks of this place – the village, the hills, the house and grounds. She thinks how they echo for her with the ghosts of her own memories. All the places she has lived and loved. The dell where she sledged with Will and Gus as teenagers in winter; the woods where she walked and talked with Gus after their first kiss and they decided to give it a proper go; the village hall where they had offi-cially 'outed' themselves as a couple at a Christmas Fair. Each passing place connects with a moment from her past, bringing it into the light.

It must be the same for Lillian, she realises, but tenfold. Perhaps one day Maggie will take a car ride beside a grandchild and find herself transported back to a memory of this day with Lillian. And for the briefest time, Maggie sees her life clearly: all the moments, large and small that have been, and all the ones yet to come, connected by some long, silvery thread, strong yet invisible, like a spider's web. She feels this singular moment joining to all the rest and finds the thought strangely comforting.

CHAPTER 19

'I wonder where he went,' says Lillian, gazing around at the flower-show crowds, searching for Albie. She can feel Jack standing behind her, a warm presence at her back. Somehow, amid the jostling crowds, it feels safe to press closer. They are hidden in plain sight.

'He'll be off with friends. Getting up to mischief. Doing whatever boys his age should be doing. Albie doesn't need his step-mother fussing over him.'

'I'm not fussing. I just feel awful leaving without letting him know.'

'Bentham can take him home. And if not, it's only a mile or so to walk back to Cloudesley.' The heat of his breath on the back of her neck sends a pulse of desire through her body. 'Let's go. Now, before anyone notices.'

'Where?' she asks, still refusing to turn around, but suddenly breathless at the idea.

'I have an idea . . . My car's in the next field.' His hand lightly skims the curve of her hip.

'You go. I'll follow in a few minutes.'

He slips away into the crowd and Lillian counts to one hundred, resisting the urge to turn and watch him go.

A husband and wife walk past, both dressed in their Sunday best, the man's hat cocked on his head and two well-turned-out children trailing behind looking pleased as punch with their sticks of candyfloss. She smiles at them as they pass. The scene is so wholesome, so respectable. What would they think if they knew what she was doing? Mrs Charles Oberon up to no good.

She finds him perched on the hood of his car smoking a cigarette, one foot resting on the bumper. His hair is slicked back off his face, still a little damp from the sponge throw.

Neither of them says a word as Jack throws his cigarette into the grass before opening the passenger door for her and sliding into the driver's seat.

He bumps the car out of the field and onto the lane that will take them away from Cloud Green and deeper into the Chiltern Hills, leaving the flower show and the milling crowds, the wilted bunting and the litter-strewn grass far behind. Lillian removes her straw hat and gloves and places them on her lap, unwinding her window to allow the warm, summer-scented air to rush into the vehicle, trailing the ribbon from her hat over and over through her fingers.

The further they get from Cloud Green, the more she feels her shoulders relax and her jaw unclench. Away from the flower show, she can feel the mantel of her public self being cast off like a scarf tossed to the wind. It is a relief to be free from the intense scrutiny of the village. Here in this car, with its torn leather seats and its faint scent of tobacco and leather and mints, the glove compartment spilling papers and maps and Jack at the wheel, the road stretching endlessly before them, it's as though Charles, Cloudesley and her duties as a wife and step-mother no longer exist. It's as if she has woken from a dream. This is reality, she thinks, not the other. *This* is what it means to be alive.

When they are some way from the village, Jack pulls up onto the grass verge and turns off the engine. He pulls her into his arms and kisses her. Lillian feels something like sunshine spreading in the pit of her stomach. She pulls back and studies him for a moment; there are a few freckles emerging across the bridge of his nose and flecks of sapphire-blue paint caught in his hair. 'I've been wanting to do that all afternoon,' he says, turning the key in the engine. 'Now, about this idea of mine,' he adds, turning to her with a smile.

Lillian is expecting him to suggest a secluded picnic spot, or perhaps an early return to Cloudesley so that they might be alone together in the house; so it comes as some surprise when he says, 'I thought we could visit Helena.' He watches her carefully, as if trying to gauge her reaction. 'Of course, only if it feels right to you,' he adds. 'I bought some flowers from a stall.' He indicates that she look in the back seat with a gesture of his head. 'We could take them to her?'

Lillian looks round and sees the bunch of roses, lavender and ox-eye daisies tied with twine lying on the leather seat. Jack has bought flowers for Helena.

'Is that a yes?'

She swallows and turns back to Jack, feeling terribly torn. 'She . . . she can be quite . . . difficult.'

He places his hand on hers. 'I'd like to meet her.'

Lillian bites her lip, then nods. 'All right then. Yes, I'd like you to meet her too. Very much.'

She leads Jack into The Cedars and signs them both into the visitors' book. 'Hello, Mrs Oberon. Lovely day out there,' says one of the nurses as she passes them in the entrance hall, a bundle of white, folded sheets in her arms. 'I think Miss Helena's in the conservatory. They've got the turntable out.'

'Thank you, Diane.'

The high operatic sound of a woman's voice pulls them down a corridor until eventually they reach a bright, sun-drenched conservatory. Lillian spots Helena right away, sitting in the far corner, her face turned to the window, eyes closed. There are two other residents in the room, an older man nodding in appreciation at the music and a sleeping lady, snoring softly, mouth slack, beads of drool falling onto her chest. Another nurse Lillian recognises, sits beside the record player, sliding a disc back into its sleeve. 'Hello, Mabel,' says Lillian, greeting the nurse. 'What a beautiful song.'

The nurse smiles. 'Your sister likes this one, too. "Depuis le Jour" by Charpentier. I didn't think we'd see you today. Isn't it the flower show?'

Lillian nods. 'Yes, but I wanted to introduce my friend to Helena. He's brought her some flowers. This is Mr Fincher,' she adds.

'Well now,' says the nurse, casting an admiring eye over Jack who stands a little behind, clutching the posy, 'aren't they lovely? I'll find you a vase.'

'Thank you.' Lillian moves across to Helena and perches on the empty seat beside her sister. 'Helena,' she says softly. 'Helena, it's me.'

Helena stirs at the sound of Lillian's voice. She turns slowly and regards Lillian with a blank expression. Lillian reaches out and strokes the right side of her sister's face – the side that still resembles the girl she once knew. The bright sunlight flooding through the conservatory windows catches in her fair hair and illuminates the left side of Helena's face, revealing its full devastation. Lillian forces herself to look at Helena's empty eye socket, the twisted corner of her mouth and the deep concave crater running from her temple to her chin where the shrapnel struck and the bones have collapsed in on themselves. Her disfigurement is neither new nor shocking to Lillian, but she wants to see again what Jack is seeing for the very first time. She wants to see it as if through his eyes and understand how difficult he might find it.

Lillian reaches for Helena's hand. 'I've brought someone to meet you. This is Jack. He's a friend of mine.'

She turns to find Jack has moved closer. He smiles down at Helena then crouches so that she can look at him properly with her one good eye. 'Hello, Helena. It's lovely to meet you.'

The record player crackles in the corner and the soaring aria comes to an end. Helena doesn't say anything.

'Shall we go for a walk?' Lillian asks her sister. 'Would you like some fresh air?'

A noise leaves Helena's mouth and her free hand – the one Lillian isn't holding – jerks up to touch Jack's cheek. Lillian holds her breath, ready to intervene, but Jack remains still as Helena clumsily caresses his face. 'I think she likes you.'

They take Helena out into the grounds, Jack pushing the wheelchair as Lillian points out the summer flowers that have blossomed since her last visit and the birds flittering through the tall cedar trees. They settle for a while beside the banks of the stream meandering through the grounds, Lillian chatting to Helena about the flower show while Jack reclines on the grass, sketching a picture onto a white paper napkin retrieved from his pocket. It is peaceful out in the grounds and Lillian is relieved that Helena is so calm. She had been silly to worry about bringing Jack. The gentle and considerate way he has moved her sister about the gardens and included her, always, in their conversation has put Helena at ease and speaks volumes for Jack's aptitude for compassion and kindness.

On the walk back up to The Cedars, Helena begins to shift in the wheelchair. Lillian, sensing her agitation, reaches for her hand. 'It's all right,' she says. 'It'll be supper time soon.'

But Helena lets out a low moan and throws off Lillian's hand. Lillian bends down to face Helena as she starts to thrash and strain against the chair. 'Helena,' she says. 'Helena, look at me.' But Helena lets out a loud howl and lurches forward, her hand striking Lillian's face, the force of her movement pushing her backwards onto the ground. Helena kicks out, spit flying from her contorted mouth as her howl turns into a piercing shriek.

'Lillian!' Jack shouts in alarm.

'I'm all right,' she says, standing quickly and brushing herself off, though her cheek is agony where her sister's nails have raked her face and when she reaches up to rub it, beads of blood come away on her fingers. 'Will you help me? We should get her back to the house. I need you to hold her in the chair. She'll only get hurt if she throws herself out of it.'

Helena's cries grow increasingly distraught as Jack helps to hold her in place and Lillian pushes the wheelchair back to the house. A nurse, hearing the commotion, appears and guides them into the conservatory. 'Now, now, Miss Helena,' the woman says, 'there's no need for this fuss. I'm sure you've had a lovely afternoon.'

She turns to Lillian. 'Let us handle this, Mrs Oberon. I think it's best if you go.'

Lillian nods. 'Goodbye, Helena,' she calls, struggling to hold back her tears. 'I'll visit next week. I promise.'

Back in Jack's car, Lillian pulls a clean tissue from her handbag and presses it to her cheek. 'I'm sorry,' she says, gazing unseeing out of the windscreen. 'I hoped you wouldn't see her like that.'

'Don't be sorry. Don't *ever* be sorry. At least, not on my account.'

'Sometimes she gets upset when I leave; other times it's just a bad day and I know the moment I arrive that the visit won't go well.'

'Are you all right?' Jack is looking at her with concern.

'Yes, it's just a scratch.'

They both fall silent. 'It can't be easy.'

'I just wish we knew how much of her remains. Sometimes, when I'm with her, I think I see flashes of something – recognition, life – passing over her eyes; but it always fades as quickly as it arrived. Charles thinks I'm seeing what I want to see, hoping she knows who I am still. But I'm not sure.'

'You're a good sister.'

Lillian shrugs. 'I do what I can, but it never feels enough.'

'You're quite alike, you know.'

'We are?'

'Yes.' He reaches into his pocket and hands her the white napkin. Lillian's eyes widen at the sketch: the two sisters seated together beside the stream, cast in dappled sunlight. 'It's . . . beautiful,' she says, gazing at the image. She stares at her sister's face. He has captured her good side, the side untouched by the shrapnel. In the picture they do look alike. Lillian can see it, too. 'She reminds me more and more of my mother, the older she gets.'

'Your mother must have been a very beautiful woman.'

'She was.' Lillian smiles up at Jack, only just managing to contain her tears. 'Thank you. I will treasure this.'

They follow the road into secluded green valleys, before climbing back up into the chalk hills. She looks across at Jack and finds him smiling at her. 'Eyes on the road,' she warns, but she takes up his hand and places it on her warm thigh, gradually directing it under the edge of her skirt and petticoat. He glances across at her again, his smile broadening. Lillian shifts a little in her seat, parting her legs slightly, releasing a soft sigh as his fingertips graze her inner thigh. After the distressing visit to Helena, she craves life and warmth and love.

They drive on, taking roads at a whim, until Lillian recognises where they are. 'Can you pull over?' she asks. 'There's somewhere else I'd like to show you, before we head back.'

They park in a small roadside clearing then set off on foot, taking a trail leading through woodland until they emerge out onto the near-summit of a hill. Jack breaks his stride and stops to take in the view of the vale stretching far below, a green and yellow patchwork of fields and farmland, villages and market towns dotted as far as the eye can see. Ahead of them, on the very crest of the hill stands a tall monument, an impressive stone pillar jutting up into the sky. Lillian is already halfway to it when she turns back to him. 'Come on,' she says. 'You get the best views from up here.'

'What is this place?' he asks, approaching the monument, before turning to look out over the vista. 'It's breathtaking.'

'Coombe Hill. You can see for miles. Chequers is down there somewhere. Aylesbury to the north, the Thames valley to the south,' she says, pointing it all out. 'You can see all the way to Salisbury Plain on a day like today.'

'It's wonderful,' he says, gazing out at the view. 'I should like to come back with my paints.'

Lillian smiles, pleased at his reaction. In no hurry to leave, she sits on one of the stone steps leading up to the Boer War monument. Jack settles beside her, his arm brushing hers. She marvels at how the merest touch of his skin can make every inch of her body long to be closer, a sort of alchemical reaction, a physical, cellular longing.

They have the place to themselves and for a while they simply sit and look out at the view, her body relaxing into his. The cloudless sky is a spectacular wash of graduated colours – navy highest above them, fading to lighter cyan closer to the earth, under-lit by the rosy blush of the sun hovering upon the horizon. There is a peace to the place, a certain stillness, nothing but the setting sun and the occasional silhouette of a soaring bird to distract from the awe-inspiring view.

Jack wraps an arm around her shoulders. She turns to meet him and they kiss and kiss until she is overwhelmed once more with desire.

'I love you,' he says.

She pulls away, and studies him carefully, but the words rise up in her too, undeniable, irrepressible. 'I love you.'

He smiles. *'L'amour étend sur moi ses ailes!'*

'What is that?'

'A line from the song your sister was listening to.'

'What does it mean?'

'Love spreads its wings over me.'

'How beautiful.' She looks out over the horizon and sighs. 'What are we going to do?'

'Shhh,' he says, pulling her closer, his eyes reflecting the rose-gold fire of the fading sun. 'Enjoy this moment with me.'

'But we should talk about—'

He shakes his head and silences her with another kiss.

On the drive back to Cloudesley, Lillian feels her mood shifting with every passing mile. All the gaiety and freedom she'd felt just an hour or so ago is fading with the setting sun. She loves Jack's ability to be so present – to focus only on the here and now – but with it comes a sense of unease. Does he realise how impossible a dream they are?

Jack too seems more solemn now, his brow furrowed and his eyes fixed on the road ahead. It's as if the shadows of their old selves – who they must be under the roof of Cloudesley – snap at their heels like dogs chasing them back to the house. She would reach out to him but something holds her back, and this time his hands remain fixed upon the steering wheel.

She begins to rehearse excuses to Albie in her head. He might be cross to have been deserted at the show. The cooler night air wraps itself around her, making her shiver. She longs for a warm bath and her bed. She longs for Jack's arms around her. 'Come to me tonight, won't you?'

Jack nods and reaches out to squeeze her hand.

The first stars are beginning to emerge in the darkening sky as they turn through the wrought iron gates, the car headlights sweeping the gravel drive and illuminating the overhanging branches of the trees. As they round the final corner to the house, Jack takes a sharp intake of breath and slams on the brakes. 'Christ,' he says, the car skidding to a sudden halt, throwing Lillian against her seatbelt. He switches off the car headlights and sits staring straight ahead.

She follows his line of sight, looking for whatever creature has run across their path. But caught in the lights blazing at the windows of the house is no animal but the distinct outline of Charles's navy blue Aston Martin, parked across the drive. Dread unfurls in the pit of her stomach. Jack, still hunched over the steering wheel, shakes his head. 'Damn. I thought we had more time.'

Lillian stares at the car. She is having trouble formulating words. He turns to her. 'Are you all right? You've gone as white as a sheet.'

She nods, but inside her guts twist with fear. 'He must know.'

'He doesn't know,' says Jack firmly. 'There's no way he could know. We've been careful.'

She wants to agree that of course Charles doesn't know and that everything is and will be fine, but the words stick in her throat, and what she says instead blurts from her mouth in a strange, shrill tone: 'But he *will* know. As soon as he sees me, he will know.'

Jack shakes his head. 'No. He won't.'

'He isn't a fool.'

'Lillian, please, there's no need to panic.'

'I'm afraid,' she says, her voice barely a whisper. 'Turn the car around. Let's go, right now.'

'No!' says Jack. 'Don't be afraid. We just need a little time, that's all. I have to finish the room.'

'But why?'

'It's . . . it's important.' He frowns. 'I can't explain. It's just a feeling. I can't leave it half-done.'

Lillian sighs. 'Of course you must finish it.' She stares out at the dark blue car and the huge house towering at the end of the drive. Charles. Cloudesley. Jack will be gone by the end of the summer but here she will remain, caught in its grip like an insect stuck in a web.

'Lillian,' Jack says suddenly. 'Lillian, look at me?'

She meets his gaze, his grey eyes shining black in the darkness. 'Lillian. I'm not a rich man. I can't offer you a fancy house or sports cars straight off the production line or expensive jewellery. I rent a couple of rooms in London. I own a modest house in Somerset. The life you are accustomed to . . .'

Lillian feels something hot rise within her. 'If you think any of those things are important to me then you don't know me at all.'

'What I'm trying to say is that you'd be giving up a lot to be with me.'

'Please,' she says, resigned, 'you don't need to explain. I understand.'

'No, Lillian. I don't think you do.' He reaches for her hand. 'I love you. I *want* you to come away with me, just as soon as I've finished the room. I'll complete Charles's commission and then we'll sit down and talk to him. We'll explain everything.'

'Explain?' She can't help her small, sharp laugh.

'Yes. He won't like it, of course, but what choice does he have if you want to leave?'

Lillian shakes her head, baffled at his naivety. 'I can't leave him.'

Jack frowns again. 'Why not? Things have changed since the war. It's not so shocking to divorce in this day and age.'

'You don't understand. It doesn't matter if Charles wants me or not, he will never let me go. I belong to him. Like one of his fancy cars or his fine paintings.'

'But you're not his *property*. You're a woman, with her own free will.'

Lillian doesn't know how to explain it to Jack. She changes tack. 'He'd ruin you.'

'I'm not afraid of him. And nor should you be. I understand, he'll be angry. His ego will be bruised. But what choice does he have if *you* choose to leave? He'd have to let you go.'

Lillian shakes her head and lets out a low moan. 'What about Helena? You've seen her. You've seen what she needs. I couldn't afford to keep her at The Cedars, not without Charles's help. And there's Albie, too. I *promised* him.'

Jack leans back in his seat, the first signs of defeat dragging at his shoulders. But then he turns to her. 'I know it will be hard, but we can find a way.'

She shakes her head. 'You make it sound so simple.'

'It is simple.' Jack reaches out and gently tilts her chin, angling her face so that she is looking up at him. 'I love you, Lillian. I want to spend the rest of my life with you. Isn't that as simple as it gets?'

Lillian shakes her head. Jack doesn't understand. He lives in a different world; a world of freedom, colour and sensation; of beautiful moments and optimism; a world where love is enough. She wants to believe in this world, but she knows it doesn't exist. Not for her. It is a beautiful picture he paints, but like his work, it isn't fully rooted in reality. It is a fantasy . . . a dream.

He reaches across and squeezes her hand. 'There's no need to be afraid. Let me finish the room. It will give us time to make arrangements. I won't slink away into the night with you.'

Lillian nods, even though every particle of her being wants to insist Jack turn the car round and drive away from Cloudesley.

'Do you trust me?' he asks.

Lillian nods.

'Good. Then go inside,' he says. 'Play the dutiful wife, for now.'

She would give a hollow laugh if she weren't so frightened. *Play the dutiful wife.* Jack, in that moment, strikes her as so simplistic, so naive, so unaware of all that her life entails that she could almost strike him. All her rage, her passion, her simmering desire for this man at her side, her anger and frustration at her impossible situation – at how little he understands it – threatens to burst out of her right there in the car and tear her in two.

'We will make a plan and find a way to be together,' he continues, oblivious to her rising emotion. 'Everything is going to be all right.'

She nods but she's only half-listening. A plan? Jack is dreaming. She is Charles Oberon's wife and he will never allow her to bring shame or scandal upon his family name. He will never let her go.

The weight of her panic is overwhelming, like a wave threatening to pull her under but Jack, seemingly unaware of her distress, squeezes her hand one last time then turns on the car headlights and puts the car into gear, beginning the slow creep up to the house and parking his battered Morris Minor next to the sleek Aston Martin. Lillian's breath is constricted in her chest. She has to put her hands in the folds of her dress to hide their shaking. Jack is wrong. Nothing will be right. There is no way that anything can be right again.

CHAPTER 20

The flower show seems to have taken it out of Lillian. Maggie's not sure what has happened on the drive home, but returning to the house has seen a cloud descend over her grandmother. She declines Maggie's offer of supper and retires to bed with a cup of tea and her medication. Maggie tucks her in, straightening the blankets.

'We lived in separate worlds,' says Lillian.

Maggie looks up from the end of her bed, puzzled. 'Who did?'

'All the things he loved about me were the things that kept me from him. He could never see that.' Lillian gazes into the empty hearth. 'But he was so wonderful with Helena that day.'

Maggie frowns. She hasn't heard Lillian mention her late sister in years.

'I wish I had known then to be braver — to at least try.'

'You are brave, Gran. One of the bravest people I know.' It's true, Maggie thinks. The only time she has ever seen her grandmother cry was on learning of Helena's death. Lillian had always been the very definition of stoic.

Lillian shakes her head. 'We should have left that day. Left and never looked back.'

Maggie doesn't know what to say to this. She senses Lillian has wandered again into distant memories, so she waits with her a while longer, quietly tidying the room, lighting lamps and pulling the curtains shut. By the time she has finished, Lillian is close to sleep. 'Good night,' she says, leaning over to kiss her forehead. 'Thank you for making me go to the show today.'

Upstairs in her own room, the silence of the house settles around her. Maggie sits on the bed and looks around at the mess of her youth scattered about the room: the tangle of scarves draped over the dressing table, her favourite leather jacket hanging on the back of the door, a cluster of discarded boots and shoes spilling from the wardrobe, a basket of old lipsticks and eyeshadows on the windowsill, the photo montage tacked to a gilt-framed mirror over the fireplace.

One image in particular draws her eye. Bonfire Night a few years ago. She and Gus stand together at the village tennis court, their faces pressed close, smiling into the camera lens. Maggie wears a red bobble hat, her russet-coloured hair long and loose around her shoulders with Gus beside her, his arm around her, their noses and cheeks glowing in the cold air. It had been taken the autumn after she'd finished art college when she'd returned to Cloud Green for Lillian's birthday – a quiet November day, with the two of them playing cards and sharing a slightly disastrous cake Maggie had baked herself. As the evening had drawn in, they'd switched on the television and Lillian had sat nodding off in her chair until Maggie's phone had beeped.

Why aren't you at the fireworks? Get yourself down here. There's free booze!

Lillian hadn't seemed to mind at all. 'I do like those boys. Go and enjoy yourself.'

Maggie had cycled to the tennis courts where the milling crowds awaited the display. She'd seen Gus almost straight away. 'Hello, stranger,' she'd said, pushing through the throng to get to him.

Gus had wrapped her in a hug. 'I knew the free booze would get you down here.'

'No Will?' she'd asked, looking around.

'Not tonight. He's got some big legal project on that's keeping him in London.'

She'd tried not to mind that she only had one of the Mortimer boys for the night, focusing instead on Gus and how lovely it was to see him again.

'Are you cold?' he'd asked. 'You're shivering.' Before she could answer, he was pulling off his woollen scarf and tying it around her neck.

'You'll freeze,' she'd protested.

'I'll be fine.'

She'd buried her face in the scarf, breathing in the indefinable scent of Gus. 'It's nice. I might have to pinch it off you.'

'It looks good on you,' he'd said, and although he was smiling, there was a look in his eyes that had made her glance away.

They'd stayed together for the fireworks, drinking warm cider and mingling with friends and neighbours. She'd insisted on giving the scarf back, but a little later, when he'd noticed her shivering again, he'd stood behind her, and wrapped her in his arms, drawing her close as they watched the fireworks explode across the night sky, Maggie acutely aware of him at her back, the pressure of him drawing her into him. It had felt good and safe.

As the fireworks had built towards a final crescendo, as small children had laughed and squealed around them, writing their names with sparklers in the air, he'd spun her around, and though his face was cast in darkness, she'd seen his eyes fixed intently on hers. Her smile had faltered. Did this mean what she thought it did? Gus . . . and her? But then there was no more time for thinking because his face was leaning in towards hers, so close his features blurred and then his lips touched hers – warm and firm – their first kiss: soft and tentative, the taste of spiced cider mingling with the scent of smoke and autumn leaves.

She'd pulled away, her eyes asking him the question she couldn't quite say out loud and he'd shrugged and let out a soft laugh. 'What can I say? I fancy the pants off you, Maggie Oberon. Have done for ages.'

Beneath his smile there had been uncertainty. She could read it on his face. They both knew that with that one kiss everything was on the line: their friendship and their future hanging in the balance.

She had wanted to stop the clocks, or better still, rewind them a minute or two. She'd wanted to pause everything and take a moment to think about the cliff's edge they stood upon. With one kiss they would move their relationship into new territory. Their friendship of three could become a pairing of two. The comfortable dynamic they'd spent years building and nurturing would be destabilised, propelled onto new and uncertain ground. Surely there was too much to risk?

But time hadn't stopped. The clocks had kept ticking. Somewhere overhead a last firework had exploded and, faced with a split-second decision, Maggie had done what she did best in moments of uncertainty: she hadn't thought at all but had leapt, both feet first, pulling him towards her by his lapels and kissing him back. Gus – sweet, funny Gus. The one who had been there for her over the years, when her mother had not been. The one who had picked her up every time her father had let her down. Gus who had been constant and present and dependable – unlike the family she was supposed to be able to rely upon. How could it not be right?

The cardboard boxes stacked against the bedroom wall loom at her from the shadows. She could swear they are growing in size, the longer she ignores them. 'Well all right then,' she says to herself. Perhaps her present mood is exactly right for a little self-flagellation. With a heavy sigh, she stands and lifts the first box down.

Gus has taped it well and it takes several attempts to wrestle it open. Inside, she finds the items a haphazard jumble, as if he couldn't throw them into the carton fast enough. She pulls out books and jewellery, photos and ornaments, a favourite velvet cushion that had once sat on their sofa and the quirky collection of antique eggcups she'd taken from the kitchen at Cloudesley and displayed on a windowsill of their north London flat. He's thrown in a couple of half-filled sketch pads and her box of charcoals. She feels a little stung at the inclusion of a framed water-colour of Primrose Hill, a gift she had painted and given him one birthday, the return of which only seems to emphasise his need to scour every trace of her from his life. At the very bottom, below a couple of her crumpled sweaters, lies a single red rose, a wooden stem and its petals glued pieces of shiny, red fabric. She pulls the artificial flower up into the light and stares at it.

She can trace the moment she knew their relationship was doomed, to that one red rose and the night they'd gone to meet Gus's best friend from school. She'd been fighting a headache and mild nausea all day and the last thing she'd felt like was a night of tacos and margaritas, but Gus had coaxed and cajoled her, telling her the night had been arranged specially so that they might meet his friend's new girlfriend. In the end she'd rallied.

The four had met at a noisy Mexican in Covent Garden and from the moment she and Gus had slid into their side of the padded booth, Maggie had known it was going to be a disaster. Her nausea had only grown as they'd listened to the happy new couple narrate, through irritating fits of giggles, how they'd met on a dating app, watching their overzealous displays of affection, their snuggling and whispers, their endless touching and kissing, seemingly oblivious to the discomfort of their dinner companions sitting opposite. They might as well have not bothered to come for all the attention they were paying them, Maggie had thought, turning to Gus and rolling her eyes at him. He'd smiled back at her and reached for her hand, before pulling her in for a kiss. Instinctively she'd leaned back, not wanting to play that charade and as he'd frowned, the hurt evident in his eyes, she had known: it wasn't right. *They* weren't right.

They had only been together a couple of years, but she didn't feel giddy with butterflies every time he reached for her. She didn't look forward to the moment he walked through the door in the evening. She didn't even feel that bothered when he went away on his business trips. The truth was staring her right there in the face, cast in stark relief by the overbearing romance playing out opposite them: she and Gus were best mates. Best mates who found themselves living together and who once in a while shagged each other. It wasn't breath-stealing, heart-pounding, passionate love. It was a mistake.

An elderly woman had approached the booth with a basket of red fabric roses. 'Don't waste your money,' she'd warned Gus under her breath, but seeming to have some-thing to prove in the face of his friends' amorous display, Gus had reached into his wallet and given the grateful woman ten pounds.

'It's not a waste,' he'd said, presenting her with the tacky rose. 'Not for you.'

Later that night, she'd turned away from him in bed. 'Sorry. I'm not in the mood. I still don't feel well.' In the morning, she'd called in sick from her waitressing shift at the restaurant.

'A day at home won't hurt,' Gus had said, regarding her with concern from the bedroom door as he'd adjusted his tie. 'You don't seem yourself and they won't thank you for dragging yourself in and making their customers ill.'

He'd left for work and Maggie had remained in bed all morning, nagging doubts about her relationship with Gus merging confusingly with the low-lying nausea gripping her. At one point she'd raced to the bathroom and hung her head over the toilet bowl and it was only as she'd stood again, her gaze fixing on an unopened box of tampons in the medicine cupboard, that a worrying thought had come to her: when exactly had her last period been?

She'd dragged herself to the pharmacy round the corner from the flat and half an hour later she was staring at two thin blue lines on the white plastic stick. Half an hour after that, she was throwing a hastily packed bag into the boot of her car and driving, in a state of blind panic, to the only person she knew she could turn to.

Lillian had been exactly as she had hoped she would be: calm, clear-headed and compassionate. 'This is not the end of the world, my dear girl. It's not how it was back in my day. You have choices.'

'I'm not ready for this, Lillian. I can't do it.'

Lillian had sat at the kitchen table with Maggie, pushing a cup of tea into her hands and offering her the box of tissues. 'And what about Gus? What does he want?'

'He doesn't know yet. I can't tell him. I'm not even sure we're right for each other. To keep this baby would tie us together for the rest of our lives.'

'The baby . . . Gus. Perhaps they are two separate issues?' Lillian had suggested gently.

Maggie had sat for a moment, thinking. 'I'm terrified by the idea of motherhood. It's not something I think I know how to do . . . not something I think I'm capable of.'

'And why would you say that?'

Maggie had looked out of the kitchen window, watching a single magpie flittering through the branches of a tall beech tree. When she had turned back to Lillian, she had said something she'd never thought she'd say out loud. 'I think I need to see her. I think I need to find my mum.'

Lillian had given Maggie a steady look, before reaching out and patting her hand. 'I imagine it's very hard to know who you are or what you want to be when you've never had the full picture of where you've come from.'

Downstairs, the sound of the bell ringing outside the oak front door pulls Maggie from her thoughts. She sits very still on the edge of the bed. It is late for unexpected visitors. She is tempted to ignore it, but the bell chimes again and, worried that it will wake Lillian, she heads downstairs and opens the door a crack.

Gus stands on the top step, half-turned away from her as he stares up into the night sky. 'There's a huge bat out here,' he says. 'Over there above the trees.' He points. 'Can you see it?'

Maggie peers out into the darkness but the only thing she can see is the pale crescent moon filtering its milky light behind the swaying beech trees. 'What are you doing here?'

'I've been thinking,' he says, turning back to her. 'We *should* talk.'

'Now?'

He shrugs. 'Fancy a pint?'

She casts a glance back into the house. 'Let me check on Lillian first. Do you want to come in?'

'No,' he says. 'I'll wait here.'

She stands at the door to Lillian's darkened room listening to her grandmother's slow breathing, then heads upstairs to retrieve a cardigan. By the time she has returned to the front door she half-expects Gus to have disappeared.

'There's only an hour or so before last orders,' he says. 'Do you mind if we go to the Swan?'

'Sure,' she says lightly, 'whatever you want.'

It's a relief to find the pub surprisingly quiet, the sunburned crowds from the flower show having died away, just a few stalwarts propping up the bar. 'Well, well, if it isn't Cloud Green's champion sponge-thrower,' says Gregory, greeting them from behind the bar. 'You've got quite an arm on you, young lady. We'll have to get you to try out for the cricket team.'

Maggie manages a weak smile, grateful to see that if anyone is surprised to see her and Gus having a drink together, they are keeping it to themselves. 'Sorry about that.'

'Why don't you find us a seat back there,' Gus suggests.

She nods and heads for one of the more discreet tables tucked into a nook beside the unlit fire. It is all disconcertingly familiar – the low-beamed ceiling, the wide stone fireplace, the horseshoes hanging on the walls, the sweet scent of beer and fermented apples in the air. She reaches for a beer mat and rips shreds off its corners until Gus returns with two pints. They clink glasses out of habit. Just like old times, she thinks, except neither one of them can quite meet the other's eye.

'What made you change your mind?' she asks, placing her drink back onto the table, picking up the torn beer mat again and flipping it over in her hands.

'Camilla. She thinks we have unfinished business. She thinks I need to "work through my resentment" if I'm going to move on with her.'

'Right.' Maggie swallows. Of course he does. It all sounds perfectly logical. 'She seems nice,' she says lightly.

'She is.'

'How long have you two been dating?'

'A few months.' There's a defensive note in his voice, a slight tilt to his chin.

'Great.' It sounds insincere and Maggie wishes she could just shut up and let him speak.

'Are you with anyone?' he asks, studying her over his glass.

'No. No, I'm not.'

The silence opens up between them again. Maggie shifts on her chair. 'I owe you an apology,' she begins. 'I'm so sorry about what happened. I'm sorry that I hurt you. I'm sorry for the way I left. You deserved so much better. I'm so ashamed of the way I handled things.' Gus stares down into his pint. 'Running away like that . . . I can see how that must have been for you and I'm sorry.'

Gus has been listening quietly, but at this he lifts his head and stares at her, the incredulity written on his face. 'You know, Maggie, I don't think you do know how it was for me.' He glowers at her over his pint and Maggie braces herself.

'I wasn't a total idiot, you know. I knew something was wrong. I'd felt you withdrawing from me for weeks, before you took off like that. But when I came home from work and found you gone – not even a note . . .' He shakes his head. 'I couldn't understand it. I phoned Cloudesley and Lillian told me – thank God – that you were there, that you were safe. I wanted to hear your voice. I just needed to know you were OK, but she said you couldn't speak to me. She told me that you "needed some time".' He shakes his head. 'She was exasperatingly stubborn.'

Maggie nods. 'I asked her to tell you that. It wasn't her fault.'

'Well, I couldn't understand it. None of it made any sense . . . not until I found the empty pregnancy-test box in the rubbish bin at home.' Gus is looking at her keenly

233

across the table but Maggie looks away, suddenly unable to hold his eye.

'As soon as I saw it, I knew I had to return to Cloud Green to fight for you. I rearranged all my work for the week and headed back as soon as I could. I chatted things through with Mum and I asked her for my grandmother's engagement ring. Everything was so clear in my head.'

Maggie nods, remembering Gus's surprise arrival at Cloudesley, opening the door to him standing there, hope and expectation written all over his face, a small black jewellery box in his hands.

'I thought you'd be pleased to see me. I thought my reassurances, my promise to love you *and* the baby, would be all you'd need to see that we could make it work – that it wasn't an accident but actually something wonderful – something that would bring us closer together. Instead . . . your face when you saw me . . . I should have known then. You treated my proposal like . . . like . . .'

'Like an ambush,' she finishes for him.

Gus stares at her. 'An ambush? Was that how it felt?'

She nods.

Gus looks at her, aghast. 'It wasn't a throwaway gesture. It wasn't me knee-jerking at the sight of the positive pregnancy test, thinking I should make an honest woman of you. I *wanted* to marry you. I *wanted* to start a family.'

Gus slumps into his chair. 'Jesus, Maggie! It tore me up. You said you'd think about it – sleep on it. You said you'd give me your answer the next morning.' He gives a bitter laugh. 'And I suppose you did. Leaving the ring in the porch like that, and just taking off? I guess that was one way to give me your answer.'

'I'm sorry.' It comes back to her so clearly, standing outside Damson House in the early-morning sun. She'd held the ring box tightly, staring at the doorbell, unable to press it and face the moment she knew she would break Gus's heart.

She had sat up late the night before, discussing her fears with Lillian, explaining how trapped she felt at the thought of the baby and Gus's marriage proposal. 'What would you do, Gran?' she'd implored. 'You had a successful marriage. What advice would you give me?'

She'd been surprised by the look that had flashed across Lillian's face. 'No relationship is perfect, Maggie. No love – no matter how great – can be the source of your life's happiness.'

'But forty-seven years together . . . the way you cared for Grandfather after his stroke . . . If that isn't love I don't know what is.'

'Love. Duty. There is a marked difference between the two,' Lillian had said, her voice surprisingly soft.

Maggie had thought for a moment. 'If I kept the baby . . . if I stayed with Gus . . . do you think that would be love or duty?'

Lillian had studied Maggie carefully. 'Only you can answer that. But it's your choice. You have a choice.'

'Do I?' She had gazed down at the single glittering diamond set into the platinum band. 'Now Gus knows, I'm not sure I do.' She'd sighed. 'I haven't even made a dent in my art career – I'm still waitressing at that poxy restaurant. I've achieved nothing of what I hoped I would have by now. I've been feeling so stalled – so off track. And now this. A baby is sure to keep me from everything I'd hoped for. I can't help but feel trapped.'

Lillian had reached forward and taken Maggie's hand. 'I have some savings. A little rainy-day fund. Call it what you will. I want you to have it. Whatever you decide, it will help you.'

'I can't accept it.'

'You can and you will. I insist,' she'd added, with surprising ferocity. 'No woman in this family will feel trapped in a life she doesn't want. Not if I can help it. Use the money however you wish. Spend it on baby clothes, or a ticket to Timbuktu . . . or simply leave it in your bank account for a rainy day. I won't judge you. Just know it's there, should you need it. Your safety net.'

You have a choice. Lillian's words had run through her head all night and at first light, she'd risen from her bed and dressed hurriedly, her intention being to talk to Gus face to face. But standing there at the front door, remembering all the moments she had shared with the Mortimer family, knowing what she was about to do, she hadn't been able to face him – to face any of them. She'd opened the door and left the ring on the shelf above the boot rack, slipping away down the drive and leaving Cloud Green far behind her.

She's imagined what she put him through a hundred times over, but it's never been quite as painful as hearing him recount it in his own words. She also knows it will never be as bad as actually living it. 'I'm sorry,' she says again, barely a whisper.

'It wasn't just me you hurt. I had to tell Mum and Dad what was going on. I'd asked for my grandmother's ring. I'd told Mum about the baby. *Her* first grandchild. I had to explain where you were . . . what you'd said . . . why I was such a mess. I had to try and answer their questions when I didn't even understand myself why you wouldn't want to keep it. "Why isn't she here?" they kept asking me. "You must know something?" But I didn't. I knew nothing, Maggie. Only that I thought you'd loved me.'

'It must have been terrible.'

Gus nods. 'So tell me. What happened? What made you walk away? I think you owe me that much of an explanation, at the very least.'

Maggie takes a deep breath. She leans back in her chair and meets his gaze. 'I went to find my mum.'

Gus does a visible double-take. 'You what?'

'I went to see her. I had to talk to her — to know why she left all those years ago. I had to understand why she couldn't be a mother to me. I had to know if I was like her . . . if I had the same weakness inside me.'

'And did you find her?' Gus has gone very still, watching her intently across the table. 'Did you get the answers you were looking for?'

Maggie sighs. 'She wasn't that hard to find. Her name's been there in black and white on my birth certificate all these years. A little searching on the internet was all it took to track her down to a small village just outside York.'

'Go on.'

'I honestly didn't know what she'd do when I knocked at her front door, unannounced. I suppose, from the little I knew of her from Albie's stories, and the little I remembered, I'd been expecting a glamorous free-spirit of a woman. Someone beautiful, bohemian and bold. I was prepared to forgive a woman who had left us for a bigger, better life. I was ready to accept her decisions, when I saw the wonderful life she had escaped to. And I suppose I hoped that she would find me delightful and surprising and infinitely lovable, and perhaps we would find a way to connect after all these years apart.'

'But it didn't play out like that?'

'No,' says Maggie flatly. 'It didn't play out like that.'

Maggie remembers with a burning shame the look on her mother's face as she'd opened the front door of a townhouse on the outskirts of the village she had tracked her down to, her expression slowly changing from polite suspicion to undeniable horror as Maggie had shakily introduced herself. 'Not here,' she'd hissed, looking back into the house. 'I can't talk to you here.'

'I've waited a long time to meet you again,' Maggie had said, holding her nerve. The woman standing across the threshold in her drab brown sweater and pleated skirt had looked smaller, greyer, somehow so much *less* than Maggie had ever imagined.

'There's a cafe in the village, next to the shop. I'll meet you there in half an hour,' and with that she had shut the door in Maggie's face.

Maggie had ordered a pot of tea and waited at a small, slightly sticky pine table, half-expecting her not to show, but Amanda had scurried in, glancing about the cafe, before sliding into the chair opposite. 'I'm sorry,' she'd said. 'I couldn't have you at the house.'

'Right,' Maggie had said, holding the woman's eye, suddenly somehow more confident in the face of her obvious discomfort.

'What do you want?' Amanda had asked, glancing around the cafe again.

'Oh, I don't know. I thought it might be nice to catch up on the last . . . hmmm . . . what is it, twenty-one years? Shoot the breeze. Exchange our news.'

Her mother had had the good grace to look shame-faced, staring down at her lap. 'How's your father?'

Maggie shrugs. 'I wouldn't know. I haven't seen him in a while.'

'Oh. But . . . but you look well?' Amanda had tried again, hopefully.

Maggie had laughed, aware that if this woman thought she looked well with her green-tinged face and the dark circles around her eyes then she truly didn't know her at all. 'Thanks. So, you're married?'

Amanda had nodded. 'John. He's a good man. We live our lives under the watchful eye of Our Lord. Faith is everything to him – to us,' she'd corrected herself. 'So you see,' she adds quickly, twisting a spare napkin round and round in her hands, 'I really can't have you turning up at the house like that. He doesn't know.'

'He doesn't know about your illegitimate child? The one you abandoned years ago?'

She'd winced again. 'No.'

'He wouldn't like it?'

'I haven't told him about . . . about that time of my life.'

'Isn't that a little . . . hypocritical? You know, under the *watchful eye of Our Lord*?'

Amanda had sighed. '"We must all appear before the judgement seat of Christ",' she'd quoted at her. 'I put my trust in God. He will be my Judge, when the time comes.'

Maggie had studied her mother, the picture of the woman before her growing a little clearer and a little more disappointing with every passing minute. Amanda had cleared her throat. 'So . . . was there something you needed?'

'Just answers.'

'Answers?'

'Yes. I can't help but wonder what makes a mother abandon her own child and never look back. Not once.'

She'd sighed. 'I know it seems cruel, Maggie, but it was for the best. I met Albie while travelling through Europe. I was a bit of a lost soul, I suppose. He had that old truck he was driving through Spain and he let me hitch along with him.'

Maggie had nodded. 'I remember that truck. It's one of the few things I do remember from that time – the rainbow stripes.'

Amanda had nodded, the first glimmer of a smile appearing on her face, before fading just as fast. 'We grew close and then I fell pregnant – with you. For a while, it seemed as if we might make a go of things.'

'Only for a while?'

Amanda had shifted in her seat, reaching for a serviette lying on the table in front of her, scrunching it tightly between her fingers. 'I wasn't a very . . . stable person. I'd had a difficult upbringing myself. Albie and I were two lost souls. We were dragging each other down. I could see that we were going to fail each other – fail you. I thought it best that I leave. I knew your father came from a wealthy family. I knew he had the resources to look after you properly.'

'You thought it best a young girl – your own daughter – grow up without her mother? You thought money and a fancy house might make your absence bearable?' Maggie had studied her, incredulous.

Amanda had eyed her warily. 'I hoped the sacrifice I made would be in your best interests.'

'The *sacrifice* you made?' Maggie had fought to control her angry laugh. 'I see.'

'It was for the best,' Amanda had said suddenly and vehemently. 'I returned to England. I found God . . . and John, my husband. He is a pillar of the Church here. He has brought me peace and salvation.'

Maggie had to fight the urge to roll her eyes. 'Well I'm glad you found *your* peace.' She'd thought for a moment. 'Do you have any other children?'

Amanda had dropped her gaze, still fidgeting with the napkin. 'Yes. We have three.'

'Three! I have three half-siblings?' Maggie had shaken her head in bewilderment. 'For fuck's sake.'

Amanda had eyed her nervously. 'You won't cause any trouble, will you?'

Maggie had kept her waiting, letting the anger settle like bile in the pit of her stomach. 'No, *Mum*,' she'd added pointedly, saying it just the once, allowing the word to roll off her tongue, 'don't worry. I won't cause any trouble. I won't be bothering you again.'

She'd stood and left the cafe without a backwards glance at the small, hunched woman sitting at the table, still wringing the ripped serviette in her hands.

'She wasn't who I imagined she would be,' she tells Gus, her voice flat and empty of emotion. 'She wasn't the strong, independent woman I'd been imagining all these years, travelling the world, living a life of adventure. It turns out she was simply weak and selfish . . . and afraid. Seems she ran from one kind of life, fearing entrapment, and just exchanged it for another kind of stifled existence: a small, hum-drum life of fear and self-righteousness.'

'I'm sorry,' says Gus, softening slightly.

'Thanks.' Maggie takes a moment to gather her thoughts. She draws a circular pattern with her fingertip in the condensation on the outside of her pint glass. 'Seeing her did help, though. It told me that I didn't *ever* want to be like her. I didn't want to bring a child into the world, unprepared and afraid. I didn't want to inflict that damage on another human being. I didn't want to repeat the pattern.'

'So you left your mum in York and . . .'

Maggie nods but can't look at Gus. 'I scheduled the abortion the very next day.'

Gus goes still.

'I'm sorry. I know it wasn't what you hoped for, but it *was* the right decision for me. I wasn't ready. There is still so much I want to do — with my art, with my life. I had the procedure a couple of days later and then I booked a flight, as far away as I could get. I ran away. I thought it would be easier if I just disappeared.'

Gus can't seem to help his hollow laugh. 'Easier for me, or easier for you? There was nothing *easy* for me about what you did, Maggie. Did you even stop to consider the torturous days that came afterwards? Going to bed every night wondering where you were . . . who you were with . . . wondering if that had been the day you'd aborted our baby. And of course, as it always seems to round here, word got out. There was all the whispering and gossip to contend with. All the excruciating sympathy. The whole of Cloud Green seemed to be talking about it. *About us*. Do you know how that felt?'

She nods but he thumps his fist angrily on the table. Maggie looks around, but no one has noticed. 'Actually, I don't think you do. Because you weren't here. You weren't the one left to face it all because you had conveniently done a runner, hadn't you? You were off God knows where, living it up on the other side of the world while I returned to the flat in London and went about slowly and methodically unpicking our life together, trying to ignore your clothes still hanging in my wardrobe, your make-up in my bath-room, all your sketchbooks piled up on the kitchen table, the half-finished paintings in the spare room.'

Maggie's head droops even lower.

'I still don't understand why we couldn't work through it together. You shut me out. It was cruel. I could only assume there was someone else.'

She hesitates. A face flashes before her eyes but she pushes it away. 'No. There was no one else.'

'Well why then, Maggie? Why did you leave me? Were we not worth more than that?'

'I . . . I . . . it wasn't right.'

'What wasn't right? You and me?'

Maggie nods. 'We'd been friends since, well, forever. But . . . marriage . . . babies . . .'

'Yes, Maggie. Marriage. That thing two people do when they love each other.'

'I did love you, Gus. Just not in the right way. I didn't realise until it was too late.'

'What the fuck does that mean?'

'We fell into a relationship. We got swept up onto a tread-mill of expectation – everyone else's expectation – and we let it lead us. Before we knew it, we'd moved in together. It felt as if we were sleepwalking. We went down a path we probably never should have, and the further we went, the harder it was to turn back. It was so comfortable. So easy. I *knew* you.'

Gus is staring at her. 'You *never* wanted to be with me? It was a mistake, right from the very beginning?'

'No. Yes. No.' She sighs with exasperation. She's imagined trying to explain this to Gus a thousand times, but nothing seems to be coming out right. 'There was a letter . . .'

'What letter? I didn't get a letter. There was nothing from you – no note, no explanation. Just silence.'

'No, nothing I wrote. Something else.' She shakes her head in frustration. 'Look, it docsn't matter. I realised, too late, that the way I loved you was more . . .' She hesitates.

'More what?'

'More like . . .'

'Go on.'

'More like a friend. A brother. Not a lover . . . not a husband.'

Gus's shoulders sag. He looks down into his beer. 'Oh.'

'I'm sorry.' She stretches out her hand, reaching for the sleeve of his shirt. 'I never wanted to hurt you.'

'Don't.' He shrugs her off. 'You could have talked to me. Instead of running off and making the decision on your own; we could have talked about it like adults. Found a way. Even if you didn't want to be with *me*, even if you didn't want to get married, perhaps we could have raised the child, separately but amicably. Did you ever think of that?'

She shakes her head. 'You arriving with that ring, so elated at the news of the pregnancy,' she looks down into her pint, 'it scared the living daylights out of me. You had it all mapped out. You were so certain of everything. But I was terrified of what becoming a mother meant. I couldn't go through with it. You weren't supposed to know. No one was supposed to know.'

'So you were never going to tell me about the pregnancy? You were just going to *deal* with it yourself, and pretend our baby never existed?'

'It was my body.' She looks at him, imploring him to understand.

'But it was *our* baby.' He shakes his head, the anguish evident in his eyes. 'You took everything away from me – not just our future – but the chance for me to be a father to that child.'

Maggie swallows, shame burning in the pit of her stomach.

'I really thought you loved me.'

'I did. I do,' she corrects. 'You're my best friend.'

Gus looks out over the half-empty pub and sighs. '*Was* your best friend. Looking at you now, Maggie, I'm not sure I ever really knew you.' He drains the last of his beer from his glass. 'Tell me, how is your glittering career as an artist coming along?' He eyes her coldly. 'Have you finished any of the paintings for that exhibition you talked about?'

Maggie hangs her head.

'Just as I thought. You're all talk, Maggie. Talk and empty promises. You can't see a single damn thing through, can you?'

She can't answer him. She is too ashamed.

'Come on,' he says, standing so fast his chair scrapes horribly across the flagstone floor. 'I've heard enough. I'll take you home.'

They drive back to Cloudesley in silence, Maggie wilting in the passenger seat with her hands thrust deep into her cardigan pockets. Now that they've spoken, it seems clear that it is far too late for bridges to be built and Maggie longs to be free of the oppressive atmosphere of the car, certain Gus can't wait for her to be gone either. But as they round the final corner, Gus slows the car and leans forward over the steering wheel. 'Hello,' he says. 'What's going on here?'

Maggie looks up, startled to see the house lit up, lights blazing at every ground-floor window. Her gaze falls upon the dusty Land Rover parked at an angle in front of the house. 'Albie,' she says.

Gus pulls up alongside the car. 'Wow. So now *he's* back. Quite the family reunion.' He keeps the engine running but she can feel his glance sliding in her direction. 'What does he want?'

'I don't know.'

'Can't be anything good.'

Maggie feels a flicker of resentment ignite in her belly. She knows Gus is right, but she can't help feeling defensive of her father. It's a default setting she has when it comes to Albie. She hesitates, one hand on the door catch. 'Goodbye, Gus,' she says.

'Bye, Maggie. Take care,' he adds, indicating Albie's car with a jerk of his head.

She nods. 'I will.'

It feels like a long walk up to the front door, the car engine idling and Gus's gaze following her, waiting – ever the gentleman – to ensure her safe return home. Entering through the front door, the sound of the car turning on the drive, she drops her keys onto the tarnished silver plate sitting on the console and calls out, 'Hello?'

The only response is her greeting echoing back at her. She walks from room to room, noting that doors that were shut now stand thrown open, lights blazing in each room as she passes, dust sheets glowing white under the glare. Further along the corridor, she can see light slanting onto the parquet floor from the library. She pushes on the door and finds Albie standing across the room, his back to her, his feet bare and a brandy glass in one hand as he rifles through the drawers of a walnut bureau.

'Hello, Dad. Looking for something?'

Albie spins round, his lined face weathered brown and framed by a mop of shaggy, white hair, quickly morphing from surprise to delight at the sight of her. 'Maggie, my love. I didn't hear you return.' He smiles and opens his arms, inviting her into his embrace.

She hesitates, battling the sudden flurry of emotion: relief and excitement mixing with anger and rejection too. She hates herself for wanting to run over and throw herself into his outstretched arms. He can't just walk in here and make everything all right with a smile and a hug.

Albie doesn't appear to notice her turmoil. He walks towards her, arms still held wide and draws her into his embrace.

Maggie holds herself rigid and closes her eyes, willing herself to resist; but the scent of him – aftershave, the faintest tang of tobacco, the sweet brandy on his breath – brings a rush of weakness. After her confrontation with Gus, it's all she can do not to burst into tears there in her father's arms.

'My darling girl,' he says. 'I'm glad to see you.'

She opens her eyes, blinking back tears, and fixes on the faded pattern woven into the carpet beneath her trainers; a blood-red flower motif repeated over and over, petals splaying in ever-increasing circles. 'I'm glad to see you, too,' she says, the words leaving her mouth before she's even realised it's the truth. There are questions burning on the tip of her tongue: where has he been? Why hasn't he been here for Lillian? And what is he looking for? But she resists, stoppering her questions and recriminations. Not now, she thinks. There is time.

'Are you all right?' he asks, eyeing her carefully. 'You look like hell.'

'Thanks,' she says. 'I've had a bit on my plate.'

Albie ruffles her hair. 'Well your old dad's back now. How about you pour us another one of these,' he suggests, waving his almost empty glass at her, 'and you can tell me everything that's been going on.'

She eyes him for a moment. Is she really going to let him do this? Is she really going to let him through her defences again?

She sighs. 'Come on,' she says, turning for the kitchen. She's sick of feeling so lonely. She's sick of facing this fight on her own. Besides, Lillian said it herself, didn't she? *Just like Albie.* Why fight biology?

'There's a bottle of very expensive Scotch in the other room,' she says over her shoulder. 'Want to help me sink it?'

PART THREE

'I must go walk the wood so wild,
And wander here and there
In dread and deadly fear;
For where I trusted I am beguiled,
And all for one.'

Anonymous, 15th century

They say that beauty is in the eye of the beholder. Certainly, in a house such as this, there is much beauty to behold. Gilt. Glass. Gold. Everywhere you look, precious treasures beckon. Only nothing seems to shine as brightly as she does. She is a flower – a natural treasure – unfolding in the light.

Her transformation is so obvious: the candlelight catching in her hair; the colour rising on her cheeks; the flames of desire burning in her eyes. She is lit up – her allure irresistible. A flame, enticing the moth ever closer. How does he not see her blossoming, right here under his nose?

For this is the trouble with beauty: it can never be enough simply to revere or admire it. With beauty comes desire – a yearning to touch – a need to possess. The coveter's grasp moves ever closer, reaching out to seize and steal, to hold too tightly that which must not be taken.

But while others remain oblivious, the watchman sees the threat. The watchman sees everything. He stands in the shadows, watching and waiting . . . waiting for the moment he must act.

CHAPTER 21

Charles mentions the dinner party three days after his return from London. 'Just a couple of chaps from the bank and their wives,' he says, folding *The Times* and laying it on the table beside his plate of half-eaten kedgeree. 'I thought a clay-pigeon shoot on Friday, followed by dinner might make them more agreeable to my proposal. You'll make the necessary arrangements with the staff?'

'Yes.'

'Good.'

She waits, tensed, sensing something; an atmosphere hanging over the table. 'Is that all?'

Charles narrows his eyes. 'I think so. Were you expecting anything else?'

Lillian shakes her head.

For all her shock at returning from the flower show to find Charles's car on the drive, and her fear that he would somehow be able to read her betrayal, she had escaped lightly. She'd found him settled in his study, head bowed over a mountain of paperwork, a glass of whisky at his side and Monty stretched luxuriously at his feet. 'Hello,' she'd said, hovering at the open door.

He'd spun in his chair. 'Darling, you're so late. Had a good day?'

'Yes. Joan insisted I return for sundowners after the

flower show.' She'd held her breath, her lie hanging in the air between them.

'I'm sorry to have missed it this year. Was it good?'

'Yes. Very well attended.'

He'd smiled and opened his arms to her, beckoning her to come to him. Lillian, with a feeling akin to dread, had forced herself across the room and stepped into his waiting embrace and Charles had drawn her close, pressing his face against her stomach, breathing her in. 'I missed you. It's been hellish in London.'

Lillian, holding herself stiff in his embrace, had hesitated, before lowering her hands onto his head. Her complicated, damaged husband. Sometimes he could be so hard to hate.

'Have you seen Albie?' she'd asked with a sudden flash of guilt and fear. Would Charles be cross that she had left him to his own devices?

'Yes, safely tucked up in bed. He said he lost you in the crowds. Bentham drove him home.'

Lillian had swallowed down her relief and offered up silent prayers of gratitude for the always reliable Bentham.

'I brought him a little gift,' Charles had added, pulling back a little and looking up at her. 'A record player of his own. He seemed to like it.'

Lillian had nodded. The pattern was repeating to the letter: violence followed by tenderness and lavish bribes. 'Yes, of course. Lucky boy,' she'd added, the words sounding hollow.

'What happened to your face?' He'd frowned, peering more closely at her cheek. 'You've scratched it.'

'Helena,' she'd said simply, no other explanation required.

Charles had tutted, before leaning back in his chair. 'I'm afraid I'll be a while yet,' he'd said, indicating the desk of papers in front of him.

'In that case, if you don't mind, I'll retire,' she'd said, jumping at the chance to leave him. She'd bent to kiss the top of his head before he'd waved her away, already returned to his paperwork.

Lillian looks at Charles now, seated across the dining-room table. She assumes he will return to his breakfast and the newspaper, but he is still staring at her, a frown on his face. 'I need Friday to go well, Lillian. It's important.'

'I understand.'

Charles's frown deepens. 'Perhaps Albie should join us for the shoot,' he adds. 'Some sport would be good for the boy.'

Lillian studies her husband, noticing how tired he looks, how drawn. The stress he wears seems caused by something more than a couple of late nights in his study or a little too much whisky. *I need Friday to go well*. She has never thought of Charles as a man of needs; more one of wants and desires. Need has always been a little too close to weakness for Charles Oberon.

'I received another bill from Cole & Osborne this morning,' he continues. 'Fincher is certainly racking up quite the expense sheet.'

'He's been very busy since you've been away.'

Charles tuts. 'He must think me as rich as Croesus.'

Lillian stares at Charles. 'You told him yourself that no expense was to be spared.'

Charles sighs. 'Yes. I did. You're quite right.' He reaches for the sugar bowl and drops a lump into his tea. 'Bentham says he never dines with the staff. Keeps to himself. I can't help wondering if he might have found a lady friend.' Charles stirs his tea slowly, the silver spoon moving round and round, clinking against the edge of the china cup. 'Can't blame a chap, I suppose. As long as she's not distracting him from his work.'

Lillian looks up from the table.

'Probably someone from the village,' Charles continues. 'Any guesses who she might be?' he asks, eyeing her over his own cup.

Lillian's thudding heart takes flight in her chest. There is no way he could know.

'My money's on that rather eager blonde down in the village,' Charles continues. 'The bubbly one with the irritating giggle.'

'Susan Cartwright?'

'Yes. That's the one.' Charles looks thoughtful. 'I'll ask Fincher to dine with us on Friday night. I'm sure my city friends would be interested to meet him. I'll press him for a finish date . . . perhaps a few details about his after-hours activities, too.' Charles's lips curve in a smile for the first time that morning.

Lillian tries to return his smile but fails. It's not the end of the world if Charles thinks Jack is having an affair with someone in the village. But she will have to warn him about the dinner party and Charles's intentions.

'You know it did occur to me that it might all be some clever ruse,' he continues.

Lillian's knife hovers over her toast. 'A ruse? Whatever do you mean?'

'The room. No one has seen a jot of what he's been working on. What if it's the greatest Emperor's New Clothes trick ever performed?' He lets out a gruff laugh. 'I suppose that would make me the prize fool.'

Lillian lays her knife on the tablecloth. 'No one could make a fool out of you, Charles.'

'Perhaps not, but it doesn't seem to stop people from trying.' He eyes her again, then snatches up the newspaper, obscuring his face and signalling the end of their conversation.

Lillian looks out through the French doors across the terrace, her appetite completely gone. He can't know, she tells herself. There is no way he can know.

Lillian agonises all morning about how to warn Jack. She doesn't dare visit him in the west wing, but neither does she trust the house staff to carry a message for her; though in the end, it is he who finds her, on her way to talk to Mrs Hill about the menus for the dinner party. Her attention is fixed on the list in her hand, when a figure steps out from the kitchen at the far end of the panelled corridor. She glances up, expecting Bentham or Sarah, but finds Jack instead, striding towards her.

He doesn't stop until he is standing right in front of her, taking her face in his hands and pressing his lips to her own.

It is a perilous situation yet she can't help but respond, moving against him until they are pressed against the panelled wall, his weight against hers, the fear of discovery somehow adding to her desire. His lips are on her lips, her face, her neck. His hands are in her hair. 'My dearest heart,' he murmurs into her ear.

Somewhere, far away, she registers the sound of pans crashing in the kitchen, the distant murmur of voices, but she can't stop herself, until, as quickly as their embrace has begun, it is over, Jack moving away, putting a respectful but unbearable distance between them. They stand staring at each other, breathing hard.

'Did Bentham tell you? There's a dinner,' she says, her voice wavering. 'Tomorrow night.'

'Yes. But I need to see you. Alone.'

'It's too risky. Charles seems . . . he seems suspicious. He thinks you're carrying on with someone from the village.'

Jack shrugs. 'Good. Let him think that. Meet me in the woods. Saturday,' he says, his voice low. 'You know the place?'

She nods, an image of the leafy clearing where they first kissed clear in her head.

'Midday. I'll wait for you. If you can't make it, I'll try again the next day. I'll be there . . . until you can come.'

He waits for her to nod and then he is gone, striding away down the corridor. She runs a finger over her mouth, tracing where he has kissed her. Saturday. Just two days to wait until they can be alone again.

There is a sudden burst of noise from the kitchen. A loud shout followed by a peal of laughter. Sarah appears in the doorway with a tray of silver. 'Mrs Oberon,' she says, nodding and smiling as she passes.

Charles's guests arrive the following morning, two private bankers from London by the names of Edwin Parker and David Molesworth, with their wives Catherine and Miriam. The morning passes quickly with greetings and coffee and organising lunch with a flustered Mrs Hill before the men and a reluctant Albie troop off with Bentham for the shoot. Lillian sits in the parlour with the ladies, exchanging news while listening to the slow tick of the carriage clock. At three they take a walk about the gardens, Lillian pointing out interesting features and plants as they go.

The day creeps on. Charles and the men return from the clay-pigeon shoot mud-spattered and elated and after tea and scones, they all retire to change for dinner. Lillian opts for a simple black dress and a single string of pearls but when Charles arrives in her dressing room he frowns. 'You're looking a little funereal, my dear.' He throws open the doors to her wardrobe and rummages through it, pulling out a long, low-cut gold dress covered in elaborate beading. 'Wear this. I need you to be at your most appealing. I want the chaps to understand that we're . . . a solid investment.'

'We?' She laughs lightly. 'Surely *you're* the one they're investing in? I doubt any dress I wear will have an impact on the business deals you're cooking up.'

'For God's sake, Lillian,' snaps Charles, 'just do as you're told. Wear the damn dress.'

She flinches as he throws the garment at her. 'As you wish,' she says. She waits, braced, breath held tightly in her chest, but Charles is already heading towards the door.

By seven o'clock, Charles's facade is back in place. Lillian joins him and the guests in the drawing room. As she enters, the other wives coo and swoon over her flamboyant gown and Lillian accepts their compliments while trying not to feel like an out-of-season festive cracker next to their more conservative attire. Charles hands out cocktails. 'To fruitful business ventures,' he toasts, and Lillian takes a sip of the martini and watches her husband, noting the gleam in his eye and the high colour on his cheeks, wondering how much he has had to drink already. Something is off. She can't put her finger on it but if there were a barometer measuring the atmosphere in the room, she knows the dial would be pointing towards change.

'I simply adore your peacocks,' says Catherine Parker, gazing out at the birds strutting across the terrace. 'They're divine. But tell me, I always thought they were supposed to bring bad luck?'

'Only if you believe in superstitious nonsense,' laughs Charles. 'Why fear something so beautiful? I consider it a privilege to gaze upon such a creature.'

'And you just let them roam freely around the place?'

'Of course.'

'Why don't they fly away?'

'Fly away?' Charles laughs again. 'Where would they go that could offer them better than a life at Cloudesley?' He turns to the other lady at his side. 'David tells me you have four boys, Miriam, the eldest at university?' Charles shakes his head in admiration. 'You look far too young!'

Miriam Molesworth flushes pink and lets out a high-pitched giggle. Lillian turns her back on the room and gazes out across the grounds, bathed in evening sunshine, to where the dark line of trees sits upon the horizon. Just a few more hours to get through and she will be with Jack again.

'Ah, here are the stragglers.'

She turns to see Jack and Albie being welcomed into the gathering. 'May I introduce another of our house guests: the artist, Mr Jack Fincher.'

Jack greets each of them in turn. When it comes to Lillian, he takes her outstretched hand and she feels the tip of his index finger momentarily brush the underside of her palm. 'Mrs Oberon. How are you?'

'Very well, thank you.' Albie has sidled across the room to stand at her side. She smiles down at the boy. 'Did you have a good day?'

He nods and holds out his hand, uncurling his fist to reveal a small, crumpled green leaf. Lillian peers more closely. 'A four-leafed clover? How clever you are. Wherever did you find it?'

'Over in the shooting field. It's for you. Something beautiful,' he adds, with a shy smile.

'Oh no, this is yours. You must keep it,' Lillian insists. 'It's lucky.'

'Albie was quite the sharp shooter today, weren't you, boy?' says David Molesworth.

'He could have hit even more targets if he'd spent more time practising his shot and less time drifting about in the clover.' Charles turns to Jack. 'How about you, Fincher? A successful day in the west wing?' he asks, clapping Jack on the shoulder before handing him a martini.

'Yes, very good.'

'Glad to hear it.'

Charles takes a moment to introduce Jack and explain his extravagant commission as they move into the dining room and take their places at the long table, Lillian and Charles seated at either end with the guests scattered between them. She is relieved to have David Molesworth on her left and Edwin Parker to her right, with Jack a little further down the table, just out of direct eye-line. The wine is poured and over a smoked trout starter the conversation glides into a discussion of the recent execution of Ruth Ellis.

'But don't you think it is rather barbaric, in this day and age?' asks Miriam, turning to Charles.

'Justice is justice,' says Charles. 'She shot the man in cold blood. The jury convicted her in twenty minutes. Of course the woman should have hanged.'

'Though it does seem rather medieval. What about redemption? If she really were a danger to others couldn't they have simply kept her locked up?'

'Ah yes, locked away, a perpetual drain on the state. That's the trouble with caged birds. They cost a fortune in upkeep.' Charles turns to Lillian. 'We know another young lady like that, don't we, darling?' She knows, instantly, that he's referring to Helena, but is too shocked to reply. Charles carries on, regardless. 'You only feel sorry for her because Ruth Ellis is young and attractive,' he continues, addressing Miriam again. 'If it were a man who'd shot a woman I'm sure you'd feel differently.'

'It's the child I feel most sorry for,' says Lillian, through gritted teeth. 'Just ten years old and left without a mother.'

'Better off without her, I say,' says Charles, ripping into his bread roll.

'Oh gosh, we have turned rather gloomy, haven't we?' says Miriam. 'Tell everyone about that new play we saw at the Arts Theatre, David.' She nudges her husband. 'You know the one . . . *Waiting for Godot*. Oh it was quite unfathomable. Two men sitting by a tree waiting for someone who never arrives. I ask you?'

'Sounds dreadful,' says Edwin Parker.

'It was,' agrees Molesworth. 'Coarse and dull.'

'Why it's getting such raves is quite beyond me,' says Miriam.

'Do you get to the theatre much?' asks Catherine, turning to Lillian.

'No, not often,' says Lillian.

'Oh Lillian's far too busy running this place to go gallivanting up to London, aren't you, darling?'

She looks across at her husband and smiles. 'That's right.'

'So, Jack,' Charles begins, turning his spotlight on the artist as the plates are cleared, 'the question I really want to ask is when you think you'll have finished my room?' He leans forward in his chair, elbows propped on the table.

Lillian is as interested as Charles in the answer, but she keeps her attention fixed on her wine glass as she twirls its stem in her fingers, watching how the candlelight catches the blackberry-coloured liquid, turning it blood-red.

'Two weeks,' Jack says, with surprising conviction.

'Two weeks?' Charles leans back in his chair, looking pleased. 'Why, that's excellent news.'

It takes every ounce of Lillian's willpower to keep her gaze fixed on her glass; then realising her mouth has gone horribly dry, she takes a sip.

'That is assuming you approve of what I have done,' adds Jack. 'It's such a grand space, I've had to go with a rather ambitious design.'

'I'm certain I will. I'm in a state of high anticipation.' Charles turns to his other guests. 'Mr Fincher has been most mysterious all summer long. I have no idea what he's painting in there. I'm not usually one for surprises, but there's something rather marvellous about the thought of having a room unveiled in its entirety.'

'Bravo, Charles,' says Edwin Parker. 'Very bold. Life can be such a dull affair. It's good to take a few risks.'

'That's exactly how I like to run my business, Parker. Calculated risk and return.' Charles turns back to Jack. 'I do hope you have enjoyed your summer with us? That you have found enough to occupy you in this quiet corner of the countryside?'

Lillian senses Jack's eyes drifting in her direction, senses his discomfort from the way he shifts in his chair. Gripping the napkin in her lap, she wills him to keep his composure. 'Indeed. I've found my time here to be very . . . inspiring.'

Charles smiles. 'Excellent. I wonder if it's vanity on my part to hope we might see a little of the Chilterns or perhaps even ourselves in some of your future works?' Charles chuckles.

'I wouldn't be at all surprised,' Jack agrees quietly. 'My time here in your home is certain to leave quite the impression.'

'And perhaps a little of the time you have spent out of the home too. Enjoying some of our local . . . sights?' The innuendo hangs on Charles's last word.

Jack merely raises his glass at Charles and to Lillian's relief, the conversation is halted by the arrival of a large silver platter rolled in on a trolley, the domed lid lifted to reveal a show-stopping triple crown roast of lamb sporting tiny white paper hats.

Before dessert is served, Lillian excuses herself and slips outside onto the terrace to smoke a cigarette. She stands by the balustrade, blowing smoke across the lawn, watching it evaporate into the warm night. Her heart is a clenched fist in her chest. Two weeks, he'd said.

She turns at the sound of footsteps approaching, expecting Bentham, summoning her in for dessert; but is surprised instead to find Jack. He stands at a polite distance, leaning against the balustrade as he lights his own cigarette.

'He's watching us,' she says quietly, glancing back through the French doors to where Charles and the other guests remain conversing.

'I know.' Jack seems calm. 'But it would be far more suspicious if we didn't talk, don't you think?'

She nods and looks back out across the dark lawn. 'It doesn't seem so long ago that we stood here that very first time, you and I.'

Jack smiles. 'When you played that cruel trick on me? Pretending to be someone else.'

'That was no trick. That was your own foolish assumption.' Her smile fades as she looks out to the velvet blackness hanging over the gardens. 'Two weeks?'

He nods. 'I can't stay here forever, Lillian. Charles is getting impatient.'

She nods. 'I don't know how I will bear it here without you.'

'You'll come to the clearing tomorrow?'

'Yes.' Through the French windows she can see Charles peering out at them. 'I should go.' She stubs out her cigarette on the balustrade then slips from the terrace and returns to her seat.

Sarah serves generous slices of Mrs Hill's summer pudding onto their best bone china and Charles, his tongue loosened by wine, moves the conversation into the more contentious sphere of politics and business, discussing his hopes for Prime Minister Eden and the trade potential with America.

Lillian, no longer hungry, but somewhat bolstered to have stolen a moment with Jack, turns to Edwin Parker on her right. 'Have you enjoyed your day in the Chilterns, Mr Parker?'

'How could I not? Beautiful countryside. This wonderful house.' He lowers his voice. 'And *such* attractive company.'

Lillian smiles in what she hopes is a bland, un-encouraging way.

'One might ask why Charles would keep a sophisticated young lady like you tucked away,' he continues, patting her arm. 'But perhaps he likes to keep you all to himself. He'd be wise.'

The man takes a sip of his wine then licks his lips. She knows he is flirting with her. She can sense Charles watching from the far end of the table and smiles again, hoping that he is, at least, pleased to see her putting in a little effort with his guests. 'Catherine,' she says, trying to draw the man's wife into the conversation, 'how about you? Are you a town or a country person at heart?'

'Oh town. Most definitely town. I can't imagine looking out and seeing only green every day. It would drive me mad.'

Miriam Molesworth has caught wind of their conversation. 'Yes, what exactly do you *do* around here?' she asks Lillian, looking utterly bewildered. 'No shops, no restaurants, no society events? Of course the countryside is perfectly charming, but—'

'Oh, you'd be surprised. We have our social calendar, the parish council, the WI, fetes and charity functions, the same as everywhere. We find ways to amuse ourselves.' She can't help glancing quickly at Jack.

'But is that enough for you, my dear? Times are changing. Since the war, there are so many more opportunities.'

Charles gives a snort from the other end of the table. 'Lillian's a homebody through and through, aren't you, darling? No personal ambition whatsoever.'

'Except of course to support you, I'm sure,' says Miriam with a small, ingratiating smile. 'You know what they say, behind every great man . . .'

'Perhaps Charles is just worried you will show him up,' teases Parker, patting her on the arm again. 'Maybe that's where you're going wrong, Charles? Involve her in the business,' he suggests, turning to Charles. 'A woman like Lillian – brains and beauty – she might be just what you need to pull Oberon & Son out of the doldrums.'

Charles goes very still and Lillian holds her breath. She knows he won't like any reference to his business struggles being mentioned at the table. But after a beat, he smiles. 'You're all quite right,' chimes Charles. 'Times have changed. It's almost impossible to find good staff these days, which is why I need Lillian here. A house like this doesn't run itself. Besides,' he adds, knocking back another slug of wine, his eyes glinting dangerously in the candlelight, 'if she had just done her wifely duty and sired me a few more sons, she'd have plenty to keep her busy.'

A silence falls over the table. Lillian folds her napkin and lays it carefully on the table. She reaches for a glass of water and takes a sip. Out of the corner of her eye she can see Jack's knuckles blanching white on his wine glass.

'Cover your ears, Albie,' says Edwin Parker, who then turns to the assembled adults. 'As a father of three, I think I speak with some authority when I say that I've always found the act of siring children to be far more pleasurable than the actual children themselves.'

The man winks crudely at Lillian. Catherine Parker blushes pink and slaps her husband on the arm with her napkin. 'Really, Edwin!'

But Charles, after a short moment, lets out a loud bellow of a laugh. 'Well said, Parker. Well said.'

Jack is the first to excuse himself after a last round of digestifs in the drawing room, citing another early start as his reason for retiring. Lillian waits dutifully for the other guests to head to bed, first the Molesworths, then finally the Parkers, both couples having grown surprisingly animated as the night progressed. With the sound of the Parkers' goodnight calls still echoing on the staircase, Bentham appears in the room and begins to clear the glasses and ashtrays. Charles pointedly holds on to his tumbler. 'Thank you, Bentham. That will be all.'

'Very good, Sir.'

Lillian is hoping she might slip away herself, but Charles is already pouring himself another large brandy from the drinks cabinet. 'Well, darling, how do you think that went?'

'Oh,' she says, watching Bentham disappear through the open doorway, a little startled that Charles should consider her opinion in any way important. 'I think everyone enjoyed themselves. Don't you?'

Charles smiles grimly and takes a large swig of his drink. 'Tedious bores, the lot of them.'

'Excuse me?' She notices the slight slurring of his words, the sway in his stance.

'Pandering to those bland moneymen all day, charming their dull little wives, having them poke and prod and paw at the house. Nobody knows the things I have to do to keep the business . . . this house . . . our family afloat. Nobody understands the hoops I have to jump through.'

Lillian, wishing she had retired with the guests, has one eye on the door. 'You work very hard,' she says in a soothing voice.

Charles takes another large slug of brandy. 'Did you enjoy yourself this evening?'

'Yes,' she lies. 'It was very pleasant, though I am rather weary now. Forgive me, darling,' she says, rising from her seat, 'but I think I'll go up too.'

Charles's eyes narrow slightly. 'It's no wonder you're exhausted . . . after that little display.'

She stops halfway across the room, uncertain to what he is referring. Was he pleased with the way she responded to his guests? Or was he, she wonders, cold ice now gripping her insides, hinting at something more sinister . . . something to do with Jack?

Charles takes a last gulp from his tumbler then returns it unsteadily to the mantel beside him. 'That was quite a performance.'

'I'm not sure what you mean?'

'Your friendly little tête-à-tête.'

'You asked me to be friendly.'

'Friendly . . . yes.' Charles's eyes flash. 'Flagrantly whoring yourself in front of our guests is another matter entirely.'

'Charles,' says Lillian, her heart squeezing tight in her chest as she realises that to reach the open door she will need to pass her husband, 'perhaps we should discuss this in the morning, when things might seem a little clearer.' She takes the first few steps across the room but doesn't make it any further.

It is the shock, initially, more than the pain that takes her breath away. One minute she is making for the door, the next she is on the rug in front of the hearth, lying in a pile of broken glass, her head ringing. The force of his fist crashing into her temple has sent her sprawling against the drinks cabinet, glasses and the brandy decanter toppling as if in slow motion and smashing onto the tiled hearth, her left leg twisted beneath her at an awkward angle.

With the sound of shattering glass still ringing in her ears, she looks up at Charles, one hand to her temple, trying to clear her blurred vision. 'Please, Charles,' she says, her voice sounding strangely far away. 'Don't.'

His shadow falls over her, an ugly sneer coming into focus. 'You think I'm a fool?'

Before she can reply, he has dragged her up by an arm and pinned it behind her back until she is cowed before him, whimpering with pain. She can feel the spilled brandy seeping through her dress, cold and wet against her skin.

'Please,' she cries, wincing in fear, 'not my face. Think of the guests . . .'

Charles's eyes flash dangerously but she sees her words register and his raised fist drop to his side. 'I don't know why you're angry,' she implores.

'You don't know why I'm angry?' he hisses. 'You're *my* wife! You're mine. The only reason people look at you is because of me. You were nothing before you met me. Nothing.'

'You're right,' she says, knowing that to appease him now might be her only chance to bring this to a swift conclusion. 'I was nothing,' she agrees through her tears.

'And after all I've done for you, and for your *vegetable* of a sister.' He shakes his head and gives a bitter laugh. 'You think I'm a fool. But I saw you with him . . . twirling your wine glass . . . smiling and batting your lashes.'

Lillian's heart sinks. He knows. Somehow he knows.

He wrenches her arm more forcefully and she whimpers in pain, defeated, her head still ringing. 'We – we didn't mean – it was so unexpected.' At that moment she knows she will spill every secret – tell him everything there is to know about her and Jack. 'We . . . we . . .'

But through her fog she hears Charles shouting, apoplectic in his rage. 'I told you this was important. I told you to be charming. Not to act like some wanton strumpet. You were an embarrassment. A bitch on heat.'

Lillian swallows. 'I'm so sorry . . .'

'And with his poor wife sitting right there.'

It takes Lillian a moment to process Charles's words. 'His wife? I don't understand.' The cogs in her brain are struggling to turn. He isn't talking about Jack. He is talking about that man. The banker. Edwin Parker.

It is so ridiculous she could almost laugh. 'You're right,' she says, putting a hand to her lip, bringing it away and seeing blood on her fingers, seeing it trickling onto the beaded bodice of her dress, garish red and gold mingling. 'Catherine was right there. The three of us were sharing a joke. I did nothing but what you asked of me. The dress. The conversation. Only what you asked.'

'Only what I asked?' He punches her hard in the stomach, dropping her arm so that she collapses onto the ground, gasping for air. She lies very still, hoping that if she remains passive she won't incite any further violence, but the ordeal isn't over yet. He kicks out at her, catching her painfully between her ribs with his dress shoe.

Lillian moans and curls in on herself as he kicks her twice more then bends and pulls her up by the hair so that she sits slumped against the marble hearth, a grotesque parody of a rag doll as Charles stands before her, a monstrous blur, hissing vile words in her face.

'Let's go upstairs, shall we?' he suggests. 'Let's wake Albie and show him what a disgusting whore he has for a step-mother.'

'No,' she cries. 'Please, don't.'

'*Please don't*,' he mimics in a high whine.

'Please, not Albie.'

'He's *my* son,' he hisses, then slaps her so hard her head knocks back into the marble fireplace with a sickening thud. 'My son, you hear? He's nothing to do with you. You useless, barren whore. You couldn't even keep our baby alive, could you?'

It seems to Lillian as though his voice is coming from the end of a long tunnel, fading away. 'I'm sorry,' she murmurs.

'Get up,' he is telling her, but she cannot move.

'You disgust me,' he says and with one last, half-hearted kick, he turns away from her, breathing heavily. She hears him wrestling with the door on the overturned drinks trolley. There is a clinking sound as he takes up one of the unbroken bottles of spirits, then the crunching of his shoes on broken glass as he leaves the drawing room, closing the door behind him. Lillian leans back against the mantelpiece and allows the darkness to take her.

'Lillian? Can you hear me?'

It feels like being dragged up from the murkiest depths, like being hauled from the bottom of a deep well. Coming round, every bone in her body aches, every muscle protests as she fights against the reality of consciousness. She doesn't want to wake up but someone's desperate voice is bringing her round. 'Lillian. You have to wake up. Please! I can't get you upstairs on my own.'

'Jack?' she says, her voice little more than a croak.

'No, it's me. Albie. You have to get up. Before anyone sees you.'

Lillian feels Albie tugging at her arm, but she slumps back against the hearth.

'Lillian?' Albie's hands shake her gently, until she moans in pain. 'Can you hear me?' The boy sounds close to tears, but still she can't rouse herself.

'Go back to bed,' she mumbles. 'Leave me. If he finds you here—'

'Shhhh . . . it's all right. He's in his study. He's already passed out. I checked.'

'I can manage,' she says, but only half-heartedly. She knows there is no way she can make it up the stairs by herself; and if she stays where she is, come morning she will be discovered by the servants, or worse, one of their guests.

'Wait here. I'll be back,' says Albie.

She doesn't know how long she lies there, but after a while she becomes aware of another presence in the room. Strong hands grasp her underneath her arms and lift her gently. She feels strangely disconnected, airborne, floating weightless like a feather. 'This way,' she hears Albie say. 'Hurry.'

A series of familiar faces float in and out of focus as she is carried up the stairs, painted eyes leering at her out of the dimly lit stairwell. When they reach her room, she is laid upon the covers of her bed. She hears Albie speak again. 'Thank you. You may go. And please, don't tell anyone.' The tall, dark figure, little more than a blur, leaves the bedroom.

'Jack?' she croaks.

'No, I told you. It's me. Albie.'

The boy carefully removes her shoes and places a pillow behind her throbbing head, then she feels him gently wipe a trickle of blood from her nose with a damp towel. He pulls the sheets back from underneath her. 'Can you get under the covers?' he asks.

She nods, and somehow stands and shrugs off her dress, but even the soft mattress and the brush of the sheets against her skin as she lies back down make her gasp in pain.

'Will you be all right?' he asks.

Lillian reaches out to stroke his cheek. 'Please don't cry. I'll be fine.'

Albie burrows his head in his arms, and sits for a moment, overcome. 'I hate him,' he mutters into the bedcovers. 'I hate him so much.' When he looks up, he grips her hand tightly. 'I know Father can be beastly, but I couldn't bear it here without you.'

She nods. 'I know. Go to bed. It's late.'

She waits for him to leave, waiting for the sound of the door clicking shut behind him before she allows herself to slip away once more into a mercifully deep sleep.

She dreams of peacock screams, fists and smashing glass and when she wakes, a triangle of daylight has hit the centre of the ceiling rose above her bed. A fly that has been buzzing agitatedly at the windowpane, pulling her every now and then from sleep, falls silent at last. Lillian's head throbs and her ribs ache every time she moves but she wriggles herself up from under the covers and props herself into a sitting position. She squints around at the room, noting the ruined gold dress strewn across the chair, her shoes lying discarded on the floor. Slowly, she reaches up and touches her face, tenderly assessing the damage. Her lip feels cracked and dry and there is a nasty, throbbing lump at the back of her skull, a crust of dried blood around her nostrils. But her face, thank goodness, seems relatively unmarked.

She lies there for a very long time. Listening to the fly. Watching the sunlight moving across the ceiling of the room, drifting in and out of full consciousness until the door to her room opens and she sees him standing framed in the doorway, a tray in his hands. She looks at him for a long moment before turning her face away.

Charles clears his throat then crosses the room, laying the tray on the stool at the end of her bed. 'Mrs Hill was sorry to hear you're under the weather. She's made you a little porridge.'

Lillian doesn't say a word. It's always the same. Pretence followed by remorse, apologies and pleading promises that it will never happen again. That he never meant to hurt her. She knows the pattern well.

He moves across to the window and lifts the catch, propping it open to let a little air into the room. When he turns back to her, she feels him inspecting her with a tentative, sideways look. She lifts her face to him and he has the good grace, at least, to wince before looking away. 'About last night . . . I was . . . I was very upset. I'm sorry.'

He waits but Lillian doesn't say anything.

'I've been under a lot of pressure. I've lost a lot of money. It's been difficult.'

He approaches the bed and reaches for her hand. She withdraws it.

She doesn't want his excuses. 'What's the time?' she asks, the words thick on her tongue.

He glances at his watch. 'A quarter to twelve. You've slept most of the morning; but you don't need to worry about that. The guests have been well looked after. They left after breakfast. I'm here for you; me . . . Albie . . . the staff. You don't need to leave this room, not until you're feeling stronger. We all just want you well again.'

Not until I'm feeling stronger, she thinks. She turns away from Charles and looks out of the window.

'Would you like me to call Doctor May?'

She shudders at the man's name, remembering the last time he inspected her. Remembering his cool hands roaming over her stomach, pressing and prodding. His stern face as he turned to her and told her that she had lost the baby. In his cold manner had been the suggestion she had been nothing more than careless, when really it was plain to both of them that the wounds and bruises on her body that had caused the miscarriage could in no way have been self-inflicted. 'There's no need,' she says, coldly.

That's the miracle in all of this, she thinks. Her body and its amazing process of renewal; each cell and bone and strip of flesh regenerating, closing up, healing, making her physically well. It's a betrayal, her body perfecting itself again and again – on the outside at least – hiding the truth

274

of their marriage to the outside world, readying her to take Charles's brutality again and again.

'You should eat something,' Charles says.

'I'm not hungry.'

Somewhere down on the terrace she hears a door open and close. She imagines Jack, stepping out into the bright day, making his way across the terrace and onto the lawn, heading into the woods to wait for her in the clearing.

'There, there,' says Charles, moving back to the bed and patting her leg over the covers. 'Don't cry. Everything is going to be fine. I saw Parker and Molesworth before they left. They were most impressed by dinner last night. They were sorry not to be able to thank you in person . . .' Charles clears his throat. 'It's good news, actually. They've offered to lend me the money I need for the business. As I'm sure you can imagine, it's quite a weight off my mind.'

The steady beat in her temple increases in intensity. If she could reach the tray she would tip it up and send its contents crashing to the floor, but instead she turns her face back to the wall.

'I haven't been myself of late,' Charles continues. 'The disappointment of losing the child, the pressures of the business. But with a little investment, I really think this could be a turning point for Oberon & Son . . . for us.'

Charles continues with his self-pitying monologue but Lillian isn't listening. She is imagining Jack, striding through the wildflower meadow, tiny insects fluttering up from the grass all around him. She wonders how long he will wait for her in the clearing. How long will he give her before he assumes she isn't coming and returns to the house? Will he think she doesn't care enough to come? That she has changed her mind?

And then, despair truly rises; for even if she had made it, what good would it have done them? A few snatched moments here and there, until the room is finished and he leaves Cloudesley forever. In two weeks she will be nothing but a memory, perhaps a figment in his dreams, a shadow on one of his canvases. She thinks of Jack out in the world living his life while she remains trapped at Cloudesley, entombed like the fading butterflies encased in glass boxes, or the hunting trophies hanging upon the walls.

Another tear slides down her cheek. She used to think she could stomach this life. When the fairy-tale had turned to nightmare, she'd told herself that a life with Charles could be tolerated. For Albie. For Helena. Besides, she had nothing but what Charles had given her and knew nothing of love but what he had taught her. Where else could she go?

But one summer has changed her. She knows now about love and desire. Jack has opened her eyes to a different kind of love. He has brought dreams of a different kind of life and the knowledge that he will now leave her makes the thought of remaining in this one unbearable.

'So you see,' continues Charles, his voice cutting through her thoughts, 'nothing at all has changed. Not really.' He reaches down and tentatively strokes her hair. 'Everything is going to be fine. We will get you better and everything will carry on as normal.'

Nothing has changed. Carry on as normal.

How little Charles understands.

Externally, perhaps, nothing has changed. The cuts and bruises will heal, in time. But her heart is another matter. Her heart is rearranged, alive, beating, wide open. Her heart is a bird, ready to soar. Yet here it must remain, locked away at Cloudesley, just another curiosity in Charles's collection of dead things, trapped and gathering dust.

CHAPTER 22

Maggie slams her laptop closed and lays her head on her grandfather's desk. Even with her eyes closed, scarily large numbers dance before her eyes. Whichever way she arranges her budget, the bottom line remains a depressing reality. They simply cannot afford for Lillian to live at Cloudesley. And in the meantime, the house continues to fall into disrepair just as fast as they are able to patch it up. Only that morning she'd put her foot through a step on the back staircase, the wood crumbling perilously beneath her, the tiny holes visible in the timber a sure sign that they might have the added problem of woodworm to contend with.

With a sigh, Maggie opens her eyes and stares out across the surface of the desk. This close, she can see in infinite detail the furry layer of dust clinging to the wood. It can't be good for any of them, least of all Lillian. Lillian is still adamant that Cloudesley is the only place she wants to be, but Maggie can't help wondering if a nursing home, with clean carpets and warm radiators and caring staff mightn't be a better place for her grandmother's ailing health. But how to tell Lillian? It would break her heart.

Giving up on her sums, Maggie leaves the study and enters the kitchen. She makes up a lunch tray for Lillian and carries it through to the drawing room where her grandmother lies dozing in bed. She places the tray on a side table, only noticing Albie seated in the shadows, his head in his hands, as he shifts in the chair. 'Hello,' she murmurs, resting a hand on his shoulder. 'How is she doing?' Albie glances up and Maggie is surprised to see that he looks as if he has been crying.

'Oh fine. Fine.' He rubs his face and straightens his shoulders. 'She's been sleeping.'

'And you?'

'Me? I'm all right.'

She eyes him carefully. 'Sure?'

He nods. 'Just taking a trip down memory lane. You know how it is. This old place hums with ghosts. You can't avoid them for long.'

Maggie doesn't know what to say. She feels as if she's intruded on a private moment.

'Well,' says Albie, straightening up and fixing a smile onto his face, 'I said I'd give Will a hand. Best get on.'

Maggie waits for Albie to leave, then pulls up a chair beside Lillian. As her grandmother begins to stir, she reaches for her hand. Lillian frowns then turns to stare out of the window.

'How are you feeling?'

'Weary.'

Maggie gives her a moment, tidying a newspaper that has spilled onto the floor and straightening the bedcovers.

'What's the time?' Lillian asks, still gazing out of the window.

Maggie checks her watch. 'It's just gone twelve.'

'He'll be waiting for me.'

Maggie frowns. 'Who'll be waiting?' When Lillian doesn't answer she tries again. 'Gran, who's waiting?'

Silence. Maggie, realising how stuffy the room has grown, opens a window before fetching a cushion from the settee and placing it behind her grandmother's back. 'Let's make you a bit more comfortable, shall we?'

Lillian allows Maggie to adjust her sitting position, but still gazes vacantly at the garden. 'Gran, I've brought you lunch. Are you hungry?'

Maggie reaches for the lunch tray and fusses with the cutlery and napkin. 'It's Jane's watercress soup,' she says encouragingly. She dips the spoon into the thin green liquid.

'I'm not hungry,' Lillian murmurs.

'Won't you try a little, for me?'

But Lillian shakes her head. 'Leave me be.'

Maggie sighs and returns the spoon to the bowl. She looks out to the gardens. It's going to be one of *those* days.

After a while, Lillian closes her eyes and begins to doze again. Maggie, realising there is little more she can do, leaves the room and steps out onto the terrace. Down on the lawn, Will is attempting to revive the browning grass with a hose and sprinkler. Albie is standing beside him, his crumpled linen shirt now unbuttoned to his navel revealing a paunch covered in grey hair, a roll-up dangling from his lips. As Maggie approaches, he shares a joke with Will, flexing his muscles in a pastiche of a strong man, making Will laugh. The intensity of her father's mood just moments earlier seems to have lifted. 'Ah good,' says Albie, as she draws closer, 'come and join us. You know what they say, all work and no play . . .'

'Some of us *are* still working,' says Will, pointedly, but if Albie hears him he doesn't respond.

'Why the frown?' Albie asks, settling himself on the edge of the ha-ha.

'I'm worried about Lillian. She seems a little off, a little vacant. I was wondering if perhaps I should call the GP. Get her checked out.'

'She's doing remarkably well for eighty-six, if you ask me.'

Maggie isn't convinced, but Albie is already moving on. 'Is there anything else bothering you?'

She sighs and lowers herself beside him. 'Where do I start? I'm getting nowhere with plans for the house.'

Albie reaches out and stubs his roll-up on the stone wall before flicking it into the meadow below. 'You worry too much, Mags. The house is choc-full of valuable antiques. Sell some.'

Maggie notices Will's eyebrows shoot skywards before he tactfully turns and busies himself with coiling the hose and moving the sprinkler a short distance away.

'It seems you've done a pretty good job of selling a lot of them already,' she says.

Albie shrugs, nonplussed. 'No point them just sitting here collecting dust.'

'So you'd have us sell all the furniture and let Lillian rattle around in an empty house?' She shakes her head. 'I don't want to run the place into the ground. I had hoped to protect Lillian's home, so that she could stay here as long as she wants to – as long as she needs to.'

Albie frowns. 'I don't know why she's so insistent. I'd have thought she'd have got shot of the place as soon as Father died.'

'She's lived here almost all her life. Surely you can see how emotionally attached she is to Cloudesley. It's her home.'

Albie gives a bitter laugh. 'It's certainly an unusual phenomenon: the caged bird so conditioned to a life behind bars that when the door is finally unlocked, the poor creature won't fly away.'

Maggie frowns. 'A cage? I'm not sure Lillian sees Cloudesley the same way you do. This is our history. This house is our home. Everything that Charles and Lillian worked so hard for, we're just going to throw it away?'

Albie shrugs. 'It might be easier than the alternative.'

Maggie shakes her head with frustration. Always the *easy* way for Albie. 'Perhaps you know some investors who might be able to help us?'

Albie lies back and smiles benignly up at the sky. 'I doubt I know an investor alive who would think me worth a punt. I'm afraid I've burned too many bridges over the years.'

Silence falls over them. From somewhere down in the wildflower meadow a skylark sings. Maggie feels the sun beating onto her shoulders. She gazes across at the browning lawn and imagines Todd Hamilton strutting around the gardens, ushering his bulldozers up the drive. There's got to be another way.

'What are you doing here, Mags?'

Albie's question cuts clean through her thoughts.

'What do you mean? You know why I'm here. For Lillian.'

'You're young. You should be off meeting people, having fun, building your career. Not nursing an old lady and watching this place disintegrate around you. Why aren't you painting? Why aren't you off living your life? You're as bad as Lillian, trapped in this cage. Fly away.' He flaps his hands at her. 'Go on, fly!'

She fixes him with a serious stare. 'You'd like me to be more like you?'

'I had my reasons for leaving.'

Maggie can feel the frustration building inside her. 'Even if that were true, don't you feel *any* sense of responsibility now, to help her, to protect the home she is so attached to?'

'There's a wonderful freedom to be found in letting go of the things from your past that weigh you down.'

Maggie feels her anger surging. It's so Albie, she thinks, to see it that way. To suggest she seek pleasure over responsibility, convenience over hard work. He sounds like a bad self-help book and can't help wondering, is *she* on his list of 'things' that weigh him down? She can't bring herself to ask, too afraid of his answer. All she knows is that if he *had* been here, if he had been a better father, a more present son, then perhaps they wouldn't be in this mess in the first place. Or at least she wouldn't feel as though she were bearing the brunt of the worry on her own. She glances across at Will, noticing he has moved even further away, giving them the space to talk.

It's a confusing legacy, her need for her father: her love for him – versus the constant sense of having been abandoned or let down. Never really knowing when he might show up, but certainly never being there for her, for all those important firsts a daughter might experience: her first triumphant bike ride, wobbling down the gravel drive on two wheels; her first day at boarding school, sitting on the end of a narrow bed gazing out of the window at a retreating car; her sixteenth birthday; her school exam results; her first hangover; her first broken heart. While her mother had never been an option – always an absent ghost, an idea that she couldn't really miss for never having known her – Albie was different. Albie was somehow more real, moving tantalisingly in and out of her life, raising her hopes then dashing them time and again with his unpredictable departures. It's hard to know which is worse.

No. There is only one person who has remained a constant in her life. Lillian. She's been there for her in all the moments – big and small – that she's ever needed someone. There, most importantly, when she hit crisis point last year. No judgement, just careful advice and comfort.

How can she explain to this impossible man that it is Lillian who has made her feel like she has one place in the world that she can call home. This woman, who is not even her blood relation, but a grandmother through marriage, has been more family to her – more like a parent – than any other person in her life. How can she explain this to a man who has spent his life running from Cloudesley, only ever returning when it offers some benefit to him: money, shelter, a place to dump his child. How can she explain this to a man who has been absent for most of her life? Is there even any point trying after all these years, if he still can't see that Lillian *is* her family – her home?

'I have to do this,' she says after a moment, swallowing back all her anger and her arguments, knowing that at sixty-eight, her father is never going to change. 'For Lillian. I owe it to her.'

Albie shrugs. 'Well I think you're wrong. I think Lillian would want you to go and live your life.'

Go and live her life. How easy he makes it sound when she doesn't even know what shape her life is anymore. Her once-promising career has stalled in the most awful creative block. Her life with Gus has fallen over. She certainly can't spend her days backpacking around the world, avoiding real life and responsibility. Maggie shakes her head in frustration. 'Let me ask you the same question then.' He turns his head to look at her blankly. 'What are *you* doing here?'

'Me?'

'Yes.'

'I'm here catching up with my darling daughter.' He stretches his arms wide. 'Enjoying this beautiful sunshine. Living in the moment.'

Maggie sighs and slumps back upon the grass. She closes her eyes and tries to stem her irritation.

Albie seems to think for a moment, and then lets out a long sigh. 'Look, Maggie, I know I've been a terrible father – and hardly the ideal son to Lillian. But I'll make you a promise. I won't leave you alone with this. Not when I can see how much you care about Lillian and the old house. I'll stay, until you don't need me anymore.'

Maggie turns her head to eye Albie with suspicion. 'It might take months.'

Albie shrugs.

'And it's not going to be easy.'

'I know, but I think I owe you this. I'd like to stay and help . . . if that's what you want?'

Maggie lets out a sharp laugh. 'I can't think of anything I'd like more.'

Albie smiles. 'Good.'

She eyes him. 'We have to shake on it, though. No more broken promises.'

He nods and reaches out his hand. She takes it firmly in her own and shakes.

'No more broken promises,' agrees Albie. 'Here,' he adds, plunging his hand deep into his trouser pocket and pulling out a small, smooth, heart-shaped stone, grey-purple in colour. 'A token of my intention. I found it in the woods. Something beautiful – for you.'

Maggie takes the stone and holds it up against the sky. She runs her finger over its smooth, warm surface. 'Thank you.' Silence falls over them again.

'So are you going to tell me what's going on between you two?' Albie asks, after a while, jerking his head in the direction of Will.

'Between me and Will? There's absolutely nothing going on between us. I don't think he can bear to be within twenty paces of me, look.' She nods across to where Will unloads a wheelbarrow of mulch into the herbaceous border.

'You wouldn't be the first person in the world to make a mistake in love. And I'm sure you won't be the last. Better to leave, than to marry the wrong man.'

'Like Mum?'

Albie winces.

'I went to see her, you know.'

'Amanda?'

Maggie nods.

Albie looks at her with obvious interest. 'How was that?'

'Disappointing.'

'I'm sorry.'

Maggie shrugs. 'It helped to clarify some things. It helped me to close that door once and for all. But I'm still ashamed of how I handled things with Gus. I was a coward. I ran away, and I hurt a lot of people in the process.'

'Did you hurt anyone intentionally?'

Maggie shakes her head. 'Of course not. I was trying to do the right thing, admittedly in a very roundabout way.'

Albie nods. 'Have you considered that perhaps you *did* do the right thing? Perhaps you did the bravest thing you could do at the time, by choosing to leave. Sometimes running away *is* the answer because you know the people you are leaving behind will be better off without you.' He is studying her intently and Maggie realises that they aren't talking about Gus anymore. Albie is trying to offer some kind of convoluted, half-arsed explanation for his absence over the years.

'When your mother ran out on us . . . left me holding the baby . . . I tried my best but I was a terrible father. It was far better that I brought you here and that Lillian brought you up and gave you a life of love and stability. She was exactly what you needed . . . and in a funny way, I think you might have been what she needed, too.'

How convenient, she thinks. Of course he would spin it that way. 'I'm very grateful to Lillian. But I still wish *you* hadn't left. I was lonely,' she says.

'I understand, believe me. But I wouldn't have left you here if I hadn't thought it the safest place for you. I didn't have the kind of life that could,' he pauses, as if trying to find the right word, 'accommodate a child. I had some issues that I needed to address. Drink. Drugs.' He picks at the grass at his side. 'I didn't want you to have the same kind of childhood I had, but I knew things had changed at Cloudesley. Things were more . . . stable. You must believe me that I wouldn't have left you if I didn't feel that this weren't the very best place for you.'

Safe. Stable. They seem like such strange words for Albie to use. 'I suppose we all have our reasons for the painful things we do to others, don't we?' she says carefully.

Albie looks off to the horizon, where the beech trees rustle in the woods beyond the meadow. 'Indeed we do.' He glances at her sideways. 'And none of us ever has the full picture or the whole truth, even if we think we do.'

Maggie sighs. 'I just wish I hadn't had to lose my two closest friends in the process.'

'Will can't hate you that much.'

'What makes you say that?'

'He's here, isn't he? You know, I'd always assumed if you were going to marry anyone it would have been the older brother.' He jerks his head to where Will stands loading a wheelbarrow. 'But then,' he throws his hands up, 'what would I know?'

Maggie swallows, feeling a dull ache beneath her ribs. 'Right,' she says, 'what would you know? A: you were hardly ever here and . . . B: you're not exactly a roaring success in the romance department yourself, are you?'

Albie grins at her. 'Touché!' he says and then, before she has even realised what he is doing, he has tugged on the hose lying nearby and dragged the sprinkler towards them, directing its spray over her, showering her with ice-cold water. Maggie shrieks and leaps up, running for the house, laughing all the way up to the terrace with the shock.

*

Upstairs in her bedroom, she stands in her underwear towelling her hair dry, trying to put what Albie has said out of her mind. *I'd always assumed if you were going to marry anyone it would have been the older brother.*

Lying out in the garden, she had felt a piece of her heart crack wide open at her father's words, for how could he – her absent, errant father – have ever glimpsed the truth of her feelings when they had been so jumbled and confused in Maggie's own heart?

Will and Gus. Gus and Will. There had never been any question of anything romantic between either of them until one summer, when the three of them had been lying sprawled on a picnic blanket under the old damson tree after a late summer BBQ at the Mortimers'. Gus had drunk too much cider and fallen asleep while she and Will had lain there a while longer beneath the tree, watching the sun moving through the twisted branches laden with purple fruit.

'Don't you ever wonder where she is?' Will had asked her, his voice soft and low. 'Aren't you curious about her?'

He hadn't had to spell out who he had been referring to. Maggie had shrugged, her eyes fixed on the shimmering leaves overhead. 'Why should I? She left us. I have Lillian now. She's all I need.'

'Your grandmother is pretty amazing,' agrees Will. 'But I don't buy that for a second. You must think about her.'

Maggie had shrugged. 'So what if I do? I can't make her come back. I've learned that lesson the hard way.'

'But what if your mum came to find you . . . what if she tracked you down? Wouldn't you want to get to know her?'

Maggie had shaken her head vehemently. 'She made her choice. The way I see it, she gave up any right to know about my life the day she left us.'

Will looks at her appraisingly. 'I think you might be one of the strongest people I know.'

Maggie shrugs. 'Lillian has always taught me to think of it as *her* loss.'

'Yes,' Will had said, turning to look at her, reaching for the hand lying at her side and squeezing it tightly in his own, 'Lillian's right. It is your mum's loss.'

She had turned to face him then and Will had reached out and stroked the curve of her face. Maggie had leaned in a little closer, staring into his achingly familiar blue eyes, holding her breath, wondering if she was imagining the sudden stillness between them. Will's face had moved a little closer and just as she had found herself silently willing him, with all of her being, to kiss her, Gus had stirred beside them.

'Sun's gone in,' he'd murmured. 'We should go inside.'

The spell had been broken. They'd picked themselves up, dusted off the grass clinging to their clothes, and retreated to the kitchen where the echoes of their shared moment had vanished with the familiarity of old routines. Will had returned to London that evening and a year later, it had been Gus who had kissed her at the village fireworks display. It was Gus she had fallen into a relationship with – a relationship that had felt familiar, comfortable and easy and whenever she had seen Will after that, he had seemed cooler, somehow more distant, until Maggie had been convinced she'd imagined the strange moment of connection beneath the damson tree; that perhaps it had been nothing but an instance of naive, hormonal longing on her part.

And perhaps Gus would have been enough for her – perhaps she could have been content with their laid-back, matey relationship and the chance he had offered her to be a proper part of his warm, wonderful family – if it hadn't been for the letter.

She had found it in Charles's desk, the night she'd left Gus in London and returned to Cloudesley, shaken from the results of the pregnancy test. Jittery, terrified and hell-bent on destruction, she had gone to her grandfather's study, seeking forgotten cigarettes or brandy, something to calm her nerves. And there, at the back of a drawer, not the box of cigarettes she'd been hoping for, but a folded piece of paper caught on the runners, preventing her from closing the drawer. She'd reached right in and hooked it out, and when she'd folded it flat on the surface of the desk, she'd been surprised to see a scrawl of words written in Lillian's distinctive, spidery handwriting.

Maggie goes across to her own dressing table and rummages through a jewellery box, pulling the sheet of paper from beneath a tangle of necklaces and bangles. She knows it almost off by heart now, but she reads the words anyway.

My dearest heart,
I once told you that the spark between us was so
powerful it could steal the oxygen from the air around us.
Today, you leave Cloudesley and that is exactly how
I feel, as though you take with you the very air I need
to breathe. You have shown me what it is to love and be
loved – what it means to be seen and understood. It is a
torture I can hardly bear to be apart from you, but from
breath to breath, heartbeat to heartbeat, know that there
will be no other while my love for you burns bright.
I am forever yours.
Lillian

Maggie holds the letter in her hand as she moves across to the bedroom window and watches Will in the distance, dragging the sprinkler across the lawn to water a new patch of brown grass. He adjusts the hose then stands and watches the spray, water droplets forming falling rainbows in the sunlight. Will watches the water. Maggie watches Will. After a long while, he reaches out and catches some of the spray from the sprinkler in his cupped hands, throwing it on his face and hair, shaking off the excess, before repeating the act. Then, drenched, he peels off his T-shirt and tucks it into the waistband of his shorts before he lifts the wheelbarrow at his side and pushes it towards the walled garden.

There will be no other while my love for you burns bright.

Maggie sighs and turns away from the window.

CHAPTER 23

Albie sits perched on the end of her bed, a leather-bound book balanced carefully in his small hands as he reads to Lillian in a boyish, singsong voice. "'I withdrew the bolt and opened the door with a trembling hand. There was a candle burning just outside, and on the matting in the gallery. I was surprised at this cir – cir . . .'"

Albie stumbles over the word then corrects himself, "' . . . circumstance: but still more was I amazed to perceive the air quite dim, as if filled with smoke; and, while looking to the right hand and left, to find whence these blue wreaths issued, I became further aware of a strong smell of burning.'"

The words from *Jane Eyre* drift over her. She isn't really listening to the story. It is one of her favourite books and Albie has visited her daily since Charles's brutal attack to read to her, stumbling over some of the harder words, but resolutely reading on, as if by this one act of devotion he might single-handedly heal her.

It is a sweet torture to look upon his face as he reads to her, this boy she loves. This boy she would give anything for, to protect and nurture. But in choosing Albie and in promising her devotion, she hadn't known what she might be giving up. How *could* she have known? She had never expected someone like Jack to unbalance her life, to test everything she thought she knew and understood.

On her dressing table she can just make out the small square of paper propped among her perfume bottles – a pencil sketch of a jug of sweet peas with 'Get well soon' written in Jack's cursive handwriting in one corner. It had been pushed under her door one night – their only communication in ten days. Her attention slides to the clock on the mantelpiece. Eleven. As if sensing her shift in focus, Albie stops reading and looks up from the book. 'You look a little better.'

'I do?'

He nods. 'Much brighter.'

Lillian smiles. 'Thank you for reading to me. You should go outside and play now. It looks like a lovely day.'

'But I want to stay with you.'

Lillian shakes her head. 'Go and explore. Find me something beautiful?'

Albie smiles and places the book on the footstool at the end of Lillian's bed, kisses her carefully on the cheek, then leaves the room. Lillian waits for him to shut the door before sliding out of bed and moving over to the dressing table. Albie is right. She does look less wan, and she can walk now, without doubling over. When she inspects her body beneath her nightdress, however, she can see that it's a different story. The large bruises on her ribs have bloomed the full rainbow spectrum but are still there, a sickly blue-green colour, yellowing at the edges like dying flowers. Still, they can be concealed beneath clothing and she knows her strength is returning; she has healed enough for what she knows she has to do.

She slips down the shadowed corridor and descends the back staircase, sliding unseen past the open door to the kitchen. As she steps through the back door into the service courtyard, she walks straight into Bentham, coming the other way, holding a large, dusty trunk in his arms. 'Oh, gosh,' she says, putting a hand to her beating heart. 'You startled me.'

'Ma'am. I'm sorry, I wasn't expecting you.'

'It's my fault,' she says. 'I was rushing. I fancied a walk around the garden. A little fresh air . . .' She trails off.

'Very good.'

She hesitates. 'I've been wanting to thank you,' she says, 'for your help . . . when I was . . . when I was . . .' she sticks with Charles's pretence, 'taken ill.'

Bentham, who usually can't look anyone in the eye, lifts his head and stares at her. His lips part, as if he is about to say something, but then they close again and he gives her one of his curt nods and stands aside, allowing her to pass through the door and out into the bright day.

Concerned that she has been observed leaving the house, she delays for a few minutes, hovering near the walled garden, as if in appreciation of the roses flowering spectacularly along the border. When she considers it safe, she hurries down the lawn and drops down into the wildflower meadow. She is at the stile when she hears the church clock ringing out twelve chimes. She quickens her pace, pushing on through the shaded woods.

All these days she has been stuck in her room, her injuries too painful to hide, too excruciating for her to make the walk into the woods, she has listened for the sound of Jack leaving the house at a quarter to twelve. Every day he has committed to their plan like clockwork and every day she has suffered the torture of knowing that as he makes for the woods, putting his faith once more in her, she remains trapped in bed, absent and unreachable, a bird with her wings brutally clipped, as their final days together slip away – too fast – like sand through a timer. As she retraces the steps they took together all those weeks ago with the sparrowhawk in the hatbox, she can't help fearing that today will be the day he has given up on her.

She tells herself that if this is the case, if the clearing is deserted, it will be for the best. For truly, what can be gained by this final encounter? What can they possibly bring each other but pain at the knowledge they cannot be together? She cannot abandon Albie and leave him motherless once more. And she cannot leave Helena and risk her sister losing the stability of The Cedars and the care she so desperately needs. But even knowing this, Lillian can't stop herself. Every moment she thinks she has convinced herself to turn back, her feet tread resolutely on, carrying her deeper into the woods.

Stepping out from the trees into the open space, a wave of relief rushes over her to see him sitting there on the wooden log, his back to her and a forlorn pile of cigarette ends stacked up beside him. Jack is here and her heart momentarily sings at the sight of him.

She hesitates on the edge of the clearing, wanting to capture the moment and lock it away somewhere safe. Jack Fincher, waiting for her. One last time. She watches as he picks at the bark on the trunk, the light filtering through the branches and playing on his skin, catching in his hair. She takes another step forward and a twig cracks beneath her foot.

'You came,' he says, turning at the sound, standing so suddenly that his cigarettes and lighter fall to the ground. He seems to be afraid to move; afraid to startle her; afraid, perhaps, that if he does she will vanish as suddenly as she appeared.

She nods and glances around the clearing before her gaze comes to rest on his face again. 'Hello.'

'Are you feeling better?' he asks.

'Yes, thank you.'

'I was worried. They said you had a summer flu.'

The days they have spent apart – not speaking, not touching – have created a new reserve between them. Lillian feels uncertainty hovering where once there was only desire. 'Yes,' she says, hating herself for lying to him.

'You look pale.'

She nods. She wants to go to him but she holds herself back, unsure of him and how he will respond; unsure whether she will be able to keep her nerve if she draws too close. 'I wasn't sure you'd still be here.'

'I came every day.'

They stand motionless for a moment; then Jack is closing the distance between them, reaching for her, pulling her into his arms. She tries to resist, holding herself stiff and unyielding; but the scent of him, the familiarity of his skin, is intoxicating.

'This is agony, Lillian. You have to come away with me. I've never been so certain of anything. I want to spend the rest of my life with you.'

She can't help herself. At his words, she softens and, feeling her respond, he pulls her to him more forcefully, wrapping her in his arms, embracing her tightly until she gasps at the pressure against her bruised ribs.

'What is it?' He holds her at arm's length, studying her face. 'What's wrong?'

She shakes her head and a single tear runs down her cheek. The pain of her bruised ribs is nothing compared to the tight ache in her chest. 'I can't leave him, Jack.'

Jack stares at her, disbelief written on his face. 'You're choosing him?'

'He's my husband. For better or worse. I don't have a choice.'

'Of course you have a choice. You can tell him the truth. Tell him that you've fallen in love with someone else.'

He reaches out to caress her cheek but she flinches and steps back. 'Don't.'

'What? What is it, Lillian? Don't you love me?'

He looks so confused, so hurt, but she cannot open up to him. If she lets him through her defences she will never be able to say goodbye. She shakes her head.

He looks dumbfounded. 'I love you. You told me you loved me, too.'

'It's not that simple.'

'Yes it is. I've told Charles that I'll open the room for him tomorrow. We're out of time. Pack a bag – take only what you need. Write a note for Albie. Tell him that we'll be in touch when we're settled. He can come and visit. But we have to leave . . . as soon as Charles has seen the room.'

Jack softens, seeing the look in her eyes. 'I know you're scared. I know what it is I'm asking of you,' says Jack, not unkindly. 'But he'll survive. In these modern times people *do* divorce. The scandal will blow over.'

'And what about you?' she asks softly. 'What kind of a future will you have with me by your side? What kind of damage will I do to your reputation? Charles won't roll over and let us go. He's a proud man. He'll try to ruin you.'

'I'm not Charles, Lillian. I don't care about reputation or scandal. I only care about you.' Jack shakes his head. 'I don't understand. There's more to this than Charles and my career, isn't there? What is it?'

'It's Albie,' she says. 'I love him as if he were my own. You know that I will never have another child and I can't abandon him. I can't leave him here with Charles, mother-less. Not again. I made him a promise.'

'Albie's hardly a baby. He's away at school in term time and he'll leave home himself at some point.'

'Not for years. And in the meantime, if I'm not here he'll be . . . he'll be . . .'

'He'll be what?'

A swirl of fear and shame stops her from telling him. She bites her lip and seeing her distress, he tries to draw her into his arms again, but she pulls away.

'I know better than most what it feels like to lose your family. I can't do that to him again.'

'Will he be more upset than you? Than me?' Jack runs his hands through his hair in frustration.

'There's Helena, too.' Lillian looks up at Jack, holding his gaze for the first time. 'You've seen her. You know I can't leave her.'

'She's well cared for at The Cedars.'

'Yes, she is. Thanks to Charles.' She gives a bitter laugh. 'Do you think he would continue to pay her bills if I left him and ran away into the night with you?'

'All these people to care for . . . but what about you? Don't you deserve a little happiness?'

'You are my happiness,' she says, quietly. 'This summer with you has been my greatest joy. But I cannot leave. Surely you understand.'

'I don't understand, Lillian. I can't. We could have a good life together. I would paint and you would be my Muse. You'd be free to do whatever you choose. Don't you see, you owe it to yourself to leave with me?'

'This life you're imagining . . . these pictures you create,' she shakes her head in frustration, '. . . they aren't real, Jack. They're a fantasy – an illusion – so far removed from my reality and responsibilities.'

Jack swallows hard. The fight seems to leave him. 'So what are you saying, Lillian? That *we* are the illusion? That you want me to leave without you? That it's over?'

She hangs her head, unable to look him, a catalogue of faces flashing before her – all the faces that she loves: Albie. Helena. Jack. She thinks of Evelyn Oberon, the painted woman in the portrait, and the promise she made to her as much as to Albie to love and protect her boy. She thinks of her sister and her own caged existence, trapped in her poor, damaged body. Why does she have to choose like this? The pain is unbearable. Her heart feels as if it might split in two. 'Yes. It's over,' she says at last, the words barely a whisper.

Jack reels backwards. 'So that's it?'

She takes a breath, then nods.

'You realise I'll be gone the day after tomorrow?'

She nods again, another tear sliding down her cheek.

Jack looks about the clearing, bewildered. 'I don't understand. I thought this meant something to you. I thought *I* meant something to you.'

'You did.'

'Did? Past tense.' Jack folds his arms across his chest. 'So what was this to you, Lillian? A summer fling? A little light relief from your dull life?' He shakes his head. 'I thought this was . . . special.'

'It was,' she says, unable to bear his anger. 'It is.'

'Though not special enough for you to give up all of *this*?' He indicates the estate with an airy wave of his hands. 'I can't offer you the *lifestyle* you're accustomed to? I was just a fun distraction?' His words are loaded with bitter disappointment.

'No! You were never just that.'

'Then what? I wish you would explain because I'm having a very hard job reconciling the woman I spent the summer making love to, to this cold . . . ghost standing before me.'

Lillian bites her tongue, holding back the words she wishes she could say to him.

Jack throws up his hands. 'What can I say to convince you to put yourself – to put *us* – first. What can I do? Tell me,' he implores.

Lillian stares at Jack, her heart thudding in her chest, but no words will come. There is nothing she can tell him.

Jack waits a beat then, in the face of her silence, he turns and begins to walk away across the clearing, towards the well-beaten path through the woods.

Lillian watches him leave. From somewhere high above her head a single yellow beech leaf falls from the canopy, drifting to the forest floor. She watches it settle at her feet, sees Jack walking away through the trees, and knows that it is too much to see him go. It is too much to know that their summer together is over; that he will leave believing she has chosen Charles and a lavish existence at Cloudesley over an honest, loving life with him. She can feel her heart throwing out its invisible lifeline, trying to reel him back in. 'Jack,' she calls. 'Jack, wait.'

He is moving with such determination that she isn't sure he will stop, but after a moment's hesitation, he does, halting at the edge of the clearing, his figure caught in a splinter of yellow light. She runs towards him, closer and closer and when he turns she hurls herself into his arms. 'I'm sorry,' she murmurs, over and over again, her body pressed up against his.

He reaches down and takes her face in his hands, kisses her full on the mouth, tastes her tears.

She is shaking. 'I'm so sorry.'

A sound of cracking wood comes from the undergrowth behind them. They spin around just in time to see a grey squirrel darting up the trunk of a beech tree. Lillian puts her hand to her thudding heart.

'God. I'm so sick of all this hiding and pretence. Just come with me.' He pulls her closer, murmuring in her ear. 'Just say yes. I depend on you too, you know.' He runs his hands down her body and circles her waist, pulling her close, his body pressing up against her own. She tries to supress it, but she can't help wincing again at the pressure, a low moan escaping her lips.

'What is it?' he asks, looking at her in concern. 'Are you hurt?'

She shakes her head, but Jack, sensing her lie, reaches out and tugs the edge of her blouse from the waistband of her skirt.

She pulls back, ripping the fabric from his fingers, but not quickly enough.

'What on earth?'

She knows what he has seen and feels a terrible shame rising up within her. Lillian retreats another step and begins to hurriedly tuck her blouse back into her skirt. 'It's – it's nothing.'

'Lillian, that is *not* nothing.' He stares at her, uncomprehending then pulls her towards him. 'Let me see.'

Gently, Jack unfastens the lower buttons on her blouse and peels the fabric back to reveal the mottled yellow-green bruises spread across her ribs. She averts her gaze, unable to bear the look on his face. 'What is this?' he asks. 'How did this happen?'

She can't meet his eye.

'Is this why you've been hiding in your room? It wasn't flu, was it?'

She doesn't say anything.

'How did this happen?' Jack swallows. 'Was it Charles? Did he find out about us?'

She shakes her head. 'No, he doesn't know.'

'But it *was* Charles?'

Her silence tells him everything he needs to know.

'Why?'

Lillian can't look at him. 'The dinner party. I embarrassed him . . . He gets angry sometimes.'

'Angry enough to hurt you?' Jack studies her with disbelief. 'My God, Lillian. Why didn't you tell me?'

'What could you do?'

'How often does this happen?'

Lillian bites her lip but doesn't answer.

Jack runs his hands through his hair. 'You can't stay here. You *have* to leave him. Even if you won't come with me, you cannot stay here.'

'I can't leave Albie. I can't leave him alone with Charles.'

Jack stares at her. 'He hurts the boy, too?'

'If I'm here I can protect him. That's why I must stay.'

Jack shakes his head. 'How can I have lived here all summer and not seen the truth staring me in the face? Lillian, your husband is a monster. You must leave with me. I won't let you stay and suffer here a moment longer.'

'It's not your decision, Jack. I've thought long and hard about this, but I know I have to stay. I made promises . . . promises I must keep.'

'No.' Jack is insistent. He is pacing around her, thinking it through. 'You leave with me the day after tomorrow. We get ourselves settled and then we send for the boy. He can stay with us.'

'You make it sound so simple.'

'It is.'

She shakes her head. 'Charles would never allow it. Albie is his son. No court would allow it. You know how he has the police and the politicians in his pocket. Doctor May covered up the loss of our baby.'

'Charles did that to you, too?'

When Lillian doesn't answer Jack wrings his hands and glances furiously back in the direction of the house. 'I should march up there and . . . and . . .'

Lillian sighs. 'Please don't talk like that.' She can't bear to hear such anger from Jack – kind, gentle, loving Jack. 'You cannot do or say anything about this,' she says. 'You will only make things worse for Albie and me. Helena's

301

care . . . he could take everything away. It all hangs in the balance. Promise me.'

'I can't leave you here with him. He's dangerous.'

'He's complicated, damaged . . . but I can take care of myself.'

Jack throws her a look. 'It doesn't appear that way to me.'

'Please,' she implores, grabbing both his hands, 'before you do anything in haste, think of Albie and Helena.'

'So you'd sacrifice yourself, for them?'

Lillian holds Jack's gaze. 'I love them.'

He looks as though he is going to say something else, and then shakes his head. 'I don't understand you, Lillian. I'm offering you a way out. The door is open. Why won't you step through?'

'I can't.'

'What if I made you? What if I went to Charles now and told him everything? What if I gave you no choice?'

She eyes him warily. 'Then you'd be no better than my bully of a husband.'

Jack's shoulders slump. He looks down at the ground. When he eventually looks up again, she can see the sadness and resignation written on his face, but something else too – the spark of a fire – anger burning like an ember in the dark circles of his eyes. 'These poor, damaged souls you are staying to protect. Don't you see that if you remain here, you'll end up as damaged as them?'

'I'm all they have,' she says, her voice pure anguish. 'Don't make me choose.'

'I love you, Lillian. How can I let you go?'

She is the first to look away. 'All the things you love about me – that make me who I am – are the reasons why I must stay.' She swallows. 'You have to let me go.'

'I can't bear this,' he says, wringing his hands, the anguish written all over his face. He moves towards her, as if he will embrace her, then turns away with a groan. 'I can't stay here. I have to go.' He storms away through the trees and Lillian stands at the edge of the clearing, waiting until she can no longer hear his footsteps.

CHAPTER 24

Lillian sits in her armchair in the drawing room, a crocheted blanket laid over her knees as she looks out onto the overgrown garden and listens to the distant wheeze of Maggie's car engine turning over on the drive. It coughs and splutters like an old man. She stares at the unruly hydrangeas and the unclipped hedgerows; she tries to concentrate on the flowers, their pale pink overblown heads as soft and puffy as marshmallows; but the sound of the car plunges in and hooks round a fragment lodged deep in her memory, drawing it up to the surface.

It brings her back to this very room, daylight flooding through the same arched windows, glancing off the familiar mahogany furniture. Only in this memory she is her younger self and she is standing, not sitting, watching from the edge of the rug as her husband lies twitching and convulsing like a fish drowning in air, gasping his last breaths.

'We should fetch help,' she says.

Charles's legs kick out, his black brogues knocking repetitively into the leg of a side table, spilling a stack of coasters to the floor. One of his laces has come undone. She bends to help him but a hand reaches for her arm.

'Wait,' says Bentham. He watches Charles over her shoulder, his presence solid and reassuring. Lillian doesn't move and neither does he.

Charles thrashes again, his arms flailing wildly as if reaching out for her, even though she knows he cannot see her, not with his eyes rolled back to the whites. They stand and wait until at last he falls still, his face mottled, an unappealing red and white, like Mrs Hill's corned beef, a strange blue colour ringing his mouth. His lips glisten with drool.

Only then does Bentham leave the room. She hears his steady footsteps walking across the checked floor tiles. She hears him pick up the telephone receiver in the entrance hall and dial three numbers. 'This is Cloudesley,' he says, his deep voice calm and composed. 'We have a medical emergency. Yes, an ambulance, please. Thank you.' The sound of his footsteps indicates his return.

'Is he dead?' she asks.

He steps forward and bends over the body, feeling for a pulse. 'No,' he says, turning back to her, not quite meeting her gaze. 'Not dead.'

Lillian stares at Charles and sees the shallow rise and fall of his chest. It takes her a moment to identify the feeling rising up in her: disappointment.

When she looks back at Bentham, she nods, half thank you, half acknowledgement of the strange moment they have shared, complicit in another's suffering.

The car engine splutters once more out on the drive. Lillian casts the memory back into the wash of her mind, though the taste of it lingers like sour milk on her tongue. Her reflection stares back at her from the window pane. No longer that unmoved woman watching her husband suffer a stroke, but an old lady, sitting hunched and useless in an armchair. Is it any wonder, she thinks, that the past often feels more real to her than the present? The sharpness of the life she lived, the emotion and the memories that come to her – the pleasure and the pain – somehow always more

305

vivid than the soft, blunt present, trapped in this slow, traitorous body?

All those versions of herself she has lived; so many different Lillians, all in this one body. If she could reach back through the years and warn the person she once was, what would she say? What would she tell that sorrowful girl standing in a London graveyard scattering earth onto the lid of her mother's coffin? Or the young woman with grazed knees and a twisted bike lying at her feet? The woman staring down at a solitaire diamond ring, marvelling at its dazzling promise? Would she have a warning for the wife walking away into the woods carrying a crumpled bird in a cardboard box? Or wisdom for the cold-hearted woman standing in this very room watching a man thrash and convulse in front of her? Life, she thinks, is strange and mysterious. Not linear, but a jumbled mess of moments: elation, sadness, pain and excruciating boredom.

All those versions of herself she has lived. So many moments when life veered on a startling new trajectory, splitting her from the old life like a knife falling and separating her forever from what once was – from those she once loved. What would she say to the girl – the woman – who experienced those moments, who made her decisions and had to live by them? What would she say to the ghosts who now inhabit her days? So many of those she has known and loved are now nothing but dust and memory. Oh, the tyranny of old age. The loneliness of living.

So many times it's felt as though she has taken a wrong turn; that she's been living a life that was not meant to be hers; the one she wanted always tantalisingly out of reach. Though perhaps, she wonders, gazing at her slumped reflection in the window, the time has come to accept that all these moments and all these versions of herself are what make up her life. For it all brings her to where she sits now, an old lady with a lined face and jewelled rings on her fat, wrinkled fingers. This is the life she lived. Perhaps it's even the life she chose.

The car engine outside gives one final loud splutter then revs loudly. Life in the old dog yet, she thinks. She feels as though she has been given a last-minute reprieve. There is something she holds. Something she must pass on . . . to Maggie. But whether it is medication or memory clouding her brain, she cannot for the life of her think what it could be.

CHAPTER 25

Maggie knows there is something different about the house as soon as she steps through the back door. She dumps the bags of groceries on the kitchen table and makes her way through the ground floor, trying to work out what it might be. Everything seems to be in order. Lillian is dozing in her armchair in the drawing room, the radio playing softly. The doors to the unused ground-floor rooms are all closed. No sign of disturbance or alteration. It's only as she arrives in the entrance hall that she begins to have an inkling what it might be.

On the dusty console, a ring on the wooden surface marks where a tall porcelain vase once stood, and beside the empty space lies a sheet of paper. Maggie picks it up and reads the words scrawled across it. When she has finished, she screws the paper up into a tight ball and hurls it across the hall. 'Fucking bastard,' she says to the empty room.

Later that night, Maggie forgoes dinner and opens the bottle of whisky in the cupboard beneath her grandfather's desk, sniffing its contents. Probably years old, but it smells OK. Does whisky even go off? She puts the bottle to her lips and swigs, feeling the burn as it slides down the back of her throat. It tastes OK, so she settles herself in the leather chair and props her feet on the desk. 'Cheers,' she says to the photograph of her grandfather and takes another swig.

It takes about a third of the bottle and an almost constant internal dialogue before she is convinced that it is a good idea to go and see Will. She gathers her car keys and heads out into the night, only narrowly missing one of the gateposts as she turns out of the drive. The lanes are dark and she has to lean right over the steering wheel to anticipate their twists and turns. Halfway there she stops dead in the middle of the lane. She reaches into her pocket and pulls out a purple-grey heart-shaped stone. 'Something beautiful, my arse,' she says and sends the rock flying out of the open window and skittering into the dark woodland beyond.

When she reaches Will's parents' place, she turns off the car headlights and parks outside their garage, heading for the entrance to the studio annexe.

'I just came to tell you that you,' she says, pointing one finger at Will's chest as he opens the door to her, 'that you were right.'

'Hello,' he says, clearly surprised to see her standing at his door. 'Are you OK?'

'I'm fine.' She leans against the open doorframe and tries to focus on his face.

'How did you get here?' He looks past her into the darkness. 'You drove?'

'It's fine,' she says, only slightly slurring. 'I was very, very careful.'

'How much have you had to drink?'

'Just a little whisky.'

Will takes her by the arm. 'Come inside. I'll make you some tea.'

She groans. 'Tea and sympathy. Just what I need. Haven't you got anything a little stronger?'

'Coffee?'

She rolls her eyes at him.

'Come in and we'll negotiate.'

He takes her by the arm and steers her into the studio. It's a modest space, just big enough for a small kitchen area, a couch and a large iron bed, but nicely done. There are simple white curtains at the windows, velvet cushions plumped on the sofa and pale grey carpet laid across the floor. All very tasteful – all very Mary Mortimer – but now with touches of Will here and there in the guitar propped in a corner, the muddy boots at the door and the family photos across the hearth.

'You've made it nice,' she says, looking about.

'Thanks.'

Will fills the kettle and spoons coffee grounds into a cafetière. 'We'll start with coffee and see how we go.'

Maggie flops onto the sofa with a sigh. 'So aren't you curious what you were right about?'

'Tell me.'

'Albie. He's fucked off. He's taken one of Charles's most precious porcelain vases and he's pissed off and left us again. So much for his big promises: "I'll stay, until you don't need me anymore,"' she mimics.

Will turns around from the cupboard where he is retrieving mugs. 'I'm sorry. That's rubbish.'

She nods. Will's feet are bare. There is a rip in the arm of his T-shirt, exposing the tanned skin of his bicep. Maggie's eyes skim over his body as he opens the fridge door.

'You know, I came across him rifling through some drawers in the house,' he continues, pulling milk from the fridge. 'I couldn't think he was up to any good.'

Maggie nods, dragging her mind from Will's strong brown arms, as the shadow of a memory forms of Albie's return, when she had found him rummaging through the mahogany dresser in the library. 'I think the only reason he came back was to see what he could fleece off Lillian.'

Will joins her on the sofa, placing two mugs of coffee on the table in front of them.

She sighs. 'It's the same pattern every time. The big, emotional return. The lavish promises. It's as if he's convinced himself that it's going to be different and then . . .' she shakes her head, 'something shifts. He starts to clam up. He goes all moody and quiet. I see him walking around as if the weight of the world is on his shoulders, until . . . bam! The sudden departure.' She groans. 'Why do I fall for it, every single time?'

'Don't be too hard on yourself. Some people can do that to us,' says Will. 'They know how to press the right buttons. We want to believe they can be different. So we let them in and they hurt us, time and time again.'

'Well I'm sick of it.'

'Yes,' says Will carefully, not quite meeting her eye. 'I'm sure you are.'

She glances around again at Will's scattered possessions in the studio. Her eye catches on a framed photo, one of Will and Gus standing on top of a snow-capped mountain, bundled up in ski-gear, both of them grinning the same wide smile at the camera, arms slung around each other's shoulders. She remembers the holiday. She remembers fumbling to remove her thick ski gloves so that she could catch the moment on her phone. She'd taken the snap four or five years ago, before she and Gus had got together. Before anything had gone wrong between the three of them.

'Why are you here?' she asks, turning back to Will.

'Excuse me?'

'Well, you had it all going on in London, didn't you? A nice girlfriend. A good career at that law firm. Why did you throw it all away to come back to this tin-pot village? Living above your parents' garage. Working for Lillian. It doesn't make any sense.'

'Really? It doesn't make any sense?'

'No.'

Will is staring at her. She is struggling to focus on his face and read his expression. It's either exasperation or annoyance. She's not sure which.

'Well, if you really want to know, Georgia and I hadn't been right for a while. When we split up it just made sense to come back here to sort myself out. Then Lillian offered me the job and I thought "what the hell". I like her and it feels good to be helping out. It's been good for me, I think, to leave the city behind for a while – to decompress – to work outside.'

Encouraged by his openness, and perhaps by the fact that this is the first time he seems to have dropped his angry guard since the bathroom tap incident, she pushes a little harder. 'I thought you'd want to stay as far away from my family . . . from *me* as possible.'

Will holds her gaze. 'What happened between you and Gus was bad, Maggie. He's my brother and I care about him. But I'm guessing you must have had your reasons to do what you did. Mum might not be able to see it that way, but then Mum's always been more black and white about stuff. In her eyes things are either good or bad, right or wrong. Besides, she doesn't know you like I do.'

Will holds her gaze – perhaps a little longer than is strictly necessary – but then Maggie is drunk and she's not sure if she's reading the situation too well. What is he trying to tell her? 'So you don't hate me?' she fishes.

Will sighs. 'No, Maggie, I don't hate you.'

Encouraged, she reaches out and takes hold of his hand. 'I'm sorry. I fucked everything up, didn't I?'

He stares down at his hand in hers. 'You're drunk, Maggie. I should take you home.'

She leans in a little closer, looking up at him through her lowered eyelashes. 'Do you remember how we used to stay up late, watching those horror movies, the three of us huddled on your parents' sofa? A duvet and a bottle of wine shared between us.'

'I remember.'

'I think those nights with you guys might be some of my happiest ever.'

Will returns his mug to the coffee table, then leans further back into the sofa. 'Yes, Maggie, they were fun times.'

'It was more than fun.'

Will raises an eyebrow.

'I miss the closeness we shared.' She leans forward a little and puts a hand on the front of his shirt, trying to focus on his face. 'I miss you.' She waits, breath held in her chest. He doesn't say anything but he doesn't pull away either.

Feeling encouraged, staring into his blue eyes and feeling the hot twist of something building inside her, she continues, suddenly reckless with desire, not caring what his answer might be but knowing that she needs to understand how he feels about her, once and for all. 'What if I told you that I want to stay the night with you?'

Will hesitates. 'You want to stay here and watch horror movies with me?'

'No. I want to stay here with you. In your bed,' she adds, just in case he really hasn't understood what she is asking of him.

Will studies her for what feels like the longest time. 'Even if I felt the same way, Maggie, don't you think that ship has sailed? We could never be together. You chose Gus.'

The effort of holding his eye and keeping him in focus is immense, but she tries her hardest. 'I didn't know I had a choice.'

Will sighs.

'I made a mistake.'

Will doesn't look away. 'Yes, you did.'

Maggie swallows. 'I couldn't tell him. I didn't know how to.'

'Couldn't tell him what?'

'Something I only realised far too late.'

'What's that?'

'That I was with the wrong brother. That it's you I'm in love with. Not Gus. It was always you.'

Will doesn't say anything and in the face of his silence, Maggie blunders on. 'I've spent the past year running away from so much, burying myself in anything that will stop me thinking about what I did to Gus, about how much I hurt him . . . but also hiding from this other huge thing, a fact that the last few weeks here with you have made clear . . . and that's just how much I am in love with you. Head over heels in love with you.'

Maggie holds her breath. Will remains silent, but he doesn't look away and somewhere, in her whisky-addled brain, she takes his silence as a good sign. 'Gus is with someone else now,' she says. 'We're both single. Why can't we be together?' She leans in a little closer, close enough to feel his breath on her cheek. 'I feel something between us . . . you feel it too, don't you?'

Will opens his mouth but no words come out.

'What is it? Say something. Please.'

Will finally finds his voice. 'So you think we should forget the mistakes of the past?'

She nods.

'You think we should hop into bed together?'

She gives him what she hopes is a winning smile. 'Well . . .'

'You think we should act on reckless impulse? To hell with everyone else and their feelings?'

'No, I'm not say—'

But he cuts her off, pulling back so that her hand slips from his chest. 'Because that would be just like you, Maggie, wouldn't it? Acting on impulse with no regard for anyone else. And that would make you just like Albie, don't you think? Arriving back at Cloudesley with your high emotion and your lavish promises. Tell me, how long would you give it with *me* before you took off again? How long before *you* cut and run?'

Maggie stares at him, trying to catch up with the sudden shift in mood.

'I can't do it, Maggie. I'm sorry.'

'Fine,' she says, feeling the snub of his rejection like a physical blow. 'I'm sorry. I'm sorry I misread the situation between us. I'm sorry I told you how I feel. I'm sorry I came here tonight!' She stands and sways slightly, feeling a sudden rush of nausea.

'Where are you going?'

'Cloudesley.'

'You can't drive. You've had too much to drink.'

'I'm fine,' she says, but even as she starts to move towards the door, she knows she won't make it. Instead, she turns and runs for the bathroom, only just making it before a stream of hot bile and whisky splatters into the toilet bowl.

Maggie wakes in the double bed, alone and fully dressed, the first glimmer of dawn just visible through the white curtains. She closes her eyes and lies very still, trying to remember the events of the night before. She recalls Albie's departure. The whisky. Careening round the dark lanes of Cloud Green in her car. Washing up at Will's door. Her hand on his chest. And then . . . oh God . . .

In the half-light, she can just make out Will lying on the sofa, curled under a blanket. Outside the studio the dawn chorus has begun. Her head is pounding and her mouth is dry and dusty, as if she's spent the night eating dirt. Worst of all is the shame. It unfurls inside of her, a huge, black mass.

Sliding out of bed, she tiptoes past Will and scrawls a brief apology on the back of an envelope. She leaves it propped against the kettle, then lets herself out of the studio, closing the door and scurrying shame-faced to her car, where she sits in the driver's seat for the longest time, with her head resting on the steering wheel and her eyes closed. She hadn't thought it possible to make the situation with the Mortimers any worse, but as flashes of her conversation with Will return unbidden, she can't help a low groan. What on earth has she done?

CHAPTER 26

What on earth has she done?

Lillian paces the floor of her bedroom, gripped by a terrible panic. How foolish, to think that she could meet Jack in the woods and somehow conceal the evidence of Charles's brutality. Of course he would know something was wrong. And now he knows, she can't help feeling afraid about what he might do with the knowledge. He seemed so angry. Will he keep the revelations to himself, or might he confront Charles in some misguided sense of chivalry and ignite a whole new nightmare? Upstairs, in her room, she torments herself with a hundred violent visions.

Yet somehow, more painful to face than her fears about what an enraged Charles might be capable of, is the knowledge that in just a few hours, Jack will leave Cloudesley forever. Even though she herself has seen to it that he will leave – without her – this is, perhaps, the greatest torture of all. The irony that after the punches and blows she has been dealt, after the cruelty and abuse she has endured, that it should be Jack's tenderness that should split her wide open is not lost on her.

Lillian's hands won't stop shaking. She drinks a little brandy, then lies on her bed and tries to sleep. But sleep won't come. At some point in the night, she finds herself tiptoeing through the corridors of the west wing and standing outside the old nursery. The door is closed but she senses sound and movement behind it. There is the scrape of the ladder being dragged across the wooden floorboards, the clatter of a paint tin lid. Jack sounds furiously busy. She stands with one hand poised to knock before letting it fall, turning and heading back to her bedroom. What could she tell him that she hasn't already said in the woods? There is only one way this can play out now. Jack must leave.

The night hours creep by until at last Lillian opens her eyes and sees the rosy blush of dawn caressing the tops of the beech trees. She would normally welcome the arrival of the sunrise, but today it marks the day that the room will be opened and Jack will leave Cloudesley. And with the sun comes one last dawning realisation.

In holding herself so tightly in the woods, in trying to hide the violent truth of her marriage to Charles, she lost her way, for she failed to tell Jack what he truly meant to her. Lillian knows she can't bear the thought of leaving Albie, but likewise she cannot bear the thought of Jack leaving her and never understanding that her love for him was real. Not a summertime dalliance but perhaps the most important and meaningful encounter she has ever had. She has to find a way to explain.

Her eyes are gritty with tiredness and her hands are still shaking as she takes up a pen and paper from her dressing table and begins to write.

My dearest heart,
I once told you that the spark between us could steal
the oxygen from the air around us . . .

She writes freely, allowing the emotion to rush through her pen onto the page, and when she has finished, she stares at the letter, re-reading the words that have flowed so easily.

There will be no more meetings in the woods. She will have to find another way to get the letter to him. And then she remembers: the one place in Cloudesley that still belongs to him, if only for one more day.

Her intention had been to slide the envelope beneath the door and leave it there for Jack to discover, but as she arrives at the end of the west-wing corridor, she is startled to find the door to the room ajar, the key she gave him all those weeks ago sitting in the lock and a splinter of green-gold light escaping into the hallway. The air is thick with the scent of paint and turpentine but there is stillness, too. A heavy silence. She listens for a moment, wondering if he could still be inside, then knocks lightly and pushes the door open a little further.

After the gloom of the corridor, the light-filled room requires a sudden adjustment. Lillian blinks rapidly, but even after her tired eyes have refocused she still isn't convinced she is seeing properly. She stands fixed to the spot, staring about, not quite trusting what she sees. Perhaps she is sleepwalking.

She finds herself, by some miraculous feat, no longer standing in the old nursery but returned to the clearing in the woods. It is the 'green cathedral', the place she first kissed Jack all those weeks ago. The place where they laid out the stunned sparrowhawk, then watched it spring miraculously back to life.

All around, the smooth, grey trunks of ancient beech trees rise up from the walls of the room to tower over her, spreading their branches across the ceiling in a fan of tangled branches and leaves, paint and gold-leaf cleverly combined to create the shimmering effect of a leafy canopy at its most dense and opulent. And yet it is not the clearing, not in any real or grounded sense, because instead of leaves, the trees taper up to a canopy of extraordinary feathers shimmering and spreading out like a peacock's tail across the ceiling, a hundred green, gold and sapphire eyes gazing down upon her. Jack's startling embellishments twist an otherwise literal interpretation of their woodland glade into a fantastical, dreamlike version of itself. Their green cathedral, more spectacular and beautiful than she could have ever imagined.

She moves closer to one of the trees and stretches out a hand, feeling instead of rough bark, the smooth, cool surface of a wall. She can't help but smile. The trompe-l'oeil effect is dazzling and disorientating in equal measure. Even the window shutters and cornicing have been painted to maintain the illusion of the trees, while high above her head the glass dome set into the roof spills light as if it were the sun itself, pouring through the canopy of eyes. The only other light falls from the glass window panes above the window seat, still flanked by the old green velvet curtains, which somehow appear to blend seamlessly with the painted scene. The whole effect is eerie and unsettling. Lillian feels unbalanced, no longer sure what is real and what is not. It is like that book she read to Albie once – the one where the boy walks through the wardrobe into another world. That's what it feels like, she realises: as if she has stepped into another realm, a place both fantastical and otherworldly.

It's not just the peacock-feather eyes that are staring at her. Her gaze finds other details: a shy muntjac deer peering out from the undergrowth, a squirrel, sitting high up in a tree holding a green nut between its paws, small birds flitting here and there. The tiniest details have been captured by Jack's brush: a silver spider's web, a creeping ladybird, a puffy white toadstool. The only thing missing is the sound of the leaf canopy rustling and the soft scuttle of insects moving across the forest floor.

As she spins in the space, she glimpses even more details between the tree trunks, rural vignettes painted in the distance, adding a greater sense of depth to the already dazzling illusion of the mural. Through the trees, Lillian spies a far-off scene of a village green, men dressed in cricket whites scattered across the lush grass. Another shows two fair-haired women sitting beneath a cedar tree, a winding stream at their feet. Further away she sees the stone monument at Coombe Hill rising up in the distance. A fourth cameo depicts a manicured lawn sloping up to meet a grand old house: Cloudesley, standing proudly, several peacocks strutting the grounds, a small boy throwing a ball to a grey wolfhound while the figure of a man lies on the lawn with a red sketchbook in his lap, drawing them. She smiles at Jack's self-portrait, woven into the mural as an incidental detail.

The most poignant image of all is one she only notices as she takes another turn and gazes at the ceiling. In a single patch of blue sky, a solitary gap in the dense canopy, she sees the outline of a familiar bird: a sparrowhawk flying free. She smiles to see it, remembering that first day with Jack in their woodland cathedral.

It's then that she realises, finally, what the room represents. It isn't just a playful depiction of their woodland place, a triumph of the mastery of illusion. This painted room is something else entirely. It is a declaration of love. It is a veiled tribute to their love affair – a depiction of the most precious moments they have shared, laid out in a secret code only she will understand. Lillian spins around, astounded, drinking it all in.

But turning again, she notices a section of the mural, painted low on the curved wall, near a propped ladder and a tangle of dust sheets. How did she not see the fox lurking there in the darkest shadows? It stands over its prey, dark russet fur, flashing amber eyes, an odd shock of white marking its crown and its white muzzle dripping and stained with fresh blood. And there on the ground before it, a second sparrowhawk, lying limply, bloody and torn, feathers scattered all around it.

It's a savage moment in an otherwise idyllic scene. She reaches out to touch the section of the wall where the blood glistens, impressed at the realistic effect, but when she pulls her finger away she finds her skin wet and stained red. Not trompe l'oeil — not this time — but fresh paint that is yet to dry. It dawns on her that this is what Jack has been doing all night. He has been altering his creation with this final, brutal detail.

She stares at the limp bird and the blood and beads of shining saliva on the fox's pointed teeth, studies the savage look in its slanting eyes and understands. It is Charles. Right down to the white tuft of hair on its russet crown and the amber eyes. Jack has revealed the truth about her husband to anyone who is prepared to look into the shadows. He has revealed the true, savage nature of Charles; and in this final vignette he is offering her a final warning: if she stays, she will be like the sparrowhawk: caught and crushed.

Lillian sways a little, losing her footing as though the ground beneath her feet were moving. She is already dizzy with exhaustion, but the room is too much to take in. She places the letter to Jack on the table next to his paints and brushes — her words striking her as horribly inadequate in the face of his creation — then moves to the window seat, where she collapses on the velvet cushion.

She stares at the fox, transfixed by the gore dripping from its mouth.

She gazes around at the trees and the feathers, the shimmering eyes watching from above.

She looks at the sparrowhawk flying free against the patch of blue sky. Freedom.

The room is a declaration of love.

She faces a man who will crush her if she stays.

But if she goes, an innocent boy will suffer, and so might her sister.

She feels the judgement of the thousand peacock eyes painted on the ceiling gazing down at her, waiting for her decision; but contemplating the awful truth of her predicament, she feels something give in her heart, as if a tightly curled bud has finally let go and allowed the first petal to unfurl.

The longer she sits there on the seat, looking around at the dazzling painting, the truth of Jack's love spread out all around her, the more keenly she understands that there is only one thing she can do. She *must* leave with Jack. Even though it will break her heart to abandon Albie, even though she risks Helena's continued care at Cedar House, she knows she must leave Charles before he can destroy her. She will find another way to protect those she loves and she will do it with Jack by her side.

The room feels stifling and airless. Dizzy with the decision, her head heavy with exhaustion, she tries to open the window behind her. The catch is stiff and after a half-hearted attempt, she gives up, leaning back behind the curtain, curling her legs up under her on the cushioned seat. The sun is warm on her back. She will wait for Jack. She will tell him her decision as soon as he returns. For she knows this is the one place he will come. His roll of brushes remains on the table in the centre of the room, his case of oil paints is still open. It feels as if she hasn't slept properly for days but, having finally settled on her decision, she cannot leave until she has seen him. She closes her eyes, finally at peace. They will leave today. It is the only way.

When she wakes the room has performed another trick: the trees have disappeared, as if hidden by a thick mist. She

323

wonders if she is still asleep, but then she smells the smoke, sees it rolling towards her, and she knows that it is no trick. This is no illusion. Something real and fearsome crackles and fizzes inside the room. An orange blaze moves towards her through the thick, grey air. Outside, a dog begins to bark.

A trail of flames, hot and red, creeps towards the window seat. Somewhere further away she hears furious banging and a voice rising up over the din. 'Open up! Unlock the door.'

That's odd, she thinks, remembering the key she saw in the lock, I didn't lock it. The long velvet curtain beside her shifts in a hot current of air and she sees the first orange flame creep along its hem and start to curl up in licking flames. She pushes the fabric away and turns back to the window pane, banging on the glass, but the catch is still jammed shut and there is no way she can force it open. The smoke thickens and the light from the glass dome above disappears. She begins to cough and for the first time fear hits her, a silent scream building in her throat. She is trapped in a burning room. 'Help,' she cries. 'Help me.'

The pounding on the other side of the door increases and through the window she can just make out something or someone moving across the grass. 'Help,' she shouts again, banging on the window pane. 'I'm in here.'

She coughs again and cannot stop, every breath hurts, smoke hot and thick in her lungs. Instinctively she crouches on the ground and begins to crawl towards where she knows the door should be, but the heat in the room is building quickly and the smoke is so disorientating she loses any sense of direction. Something heavy and dark falls from above, landing on her legs. She sees the shower of orange cinders raining down on her, feels the searing pain on her skin. She closes her eyes and tries not to breathe. Behind her comes the sound of smashing glass. Please, she thinks, the darkness rising up to meet her, please help me.

CHAPTER 27

Everything is a jumble in Lillian's mind, fragments of memory splintering and fusing. She is running through a London garden, hearing the fast patter of her sister's feet behind. The high-pitched scream of an air-raid siren pierces the sky as she dives into the black interior of a shelter. The next moment she is trapped, lying in an airless room, a terrible pain in her legs and her lungs filling with acrid smoke as someone bangs on a wooden door. There is a loud explosion. The crackle of flames. Her sister's cry. Shifting peacock eyes moving like a kaleidoscope all around her. She is pinned to the past – a butterfly trapped in a glass case – a caged bird fluttering at bars. She can't breathe.

'Lillian,' says an urgent voice. 'Lillian, it's Maggie. You're dreaming. Wake up.'

Lillian can't wake up. The blackness is all consuming.

'Lillian?'

She feels a cool hand being laid against her forehead before the sound of footsteps once more, this time running away.

'How did she seem to you?' asks Maggie, more nervous than she cares to admit.

The doctor snaps open her briefcase and pulls out a prescription pad. 'Her blood pressure is elevated and she does have a high temperature. I'm going to prescribe an antibiotic and a new medication to stabilise her blood pressure. I'd like to check on your grandmother again in a few days; but if you have any concerns before then, please call the surgery immediately.' She writes the new prescription and hands it to Maggie.

'Thank you. What about her breathing? She said she couldn't breathe. She kept talking about smoke.' Maggie looks at the doctor, baffled. 'It was so odd.'

The doctor nods. 'Everything seems normal now. It might have been a hallucination brought on by the fever . . . perhaps a bad dream or a panic attack? The most important thing is to keep her well rested and hydrated. I don't think it's anything serious to worry about, but after the kidney infection earlier this year, I don't want to take any chances. In the meantime, anything you can think of to lift her spirits – sunshine, conversation, old photographs, favourite pieces of music – it's all beneficial. We like to take a more holistic approach with our elderly patients these days.'

Maggie sees the doctor out to her car and stands for a long time in the sunshine, thinking. Something to raise Lillian's spirits.

Maggie hands her the piece of paper in the drawing room. She feels a little sheepish. 'I'm sorry. I've held on to this for far too long. I should have given it to you the moment I found it.'

Lillian, lying pale and wan against her pillows, takes the folded page from Maggie's outstretched hand. 'What is this?' she asks, unfolding it, her eyes scanning over the first words. '*My dearest heart* . . .' she murmurs. She reads a couple more lines silently before looking up at Maggie, astonishment on her face. 'Where did you get this?'

'I found it in a drawer.'

'Which drawer?'

'In Charles's study. His desk. It was jammed right at the back.'

Lillian stares down at the page in her hand, running her finger over the words, her lips moving silently. It's as if she can't quite believe her eyes. 'All this time . . .'

'I don't know why I held on to it for so long. I'm sorry. It belongs to you.'

'I never thought I'd see this again.'

Maggie hangs her head. 'I knew it was private – something special that should have been shared between just the two of you.'

Lillian nods but doesn't look up, still transfixed by the letter in her hand.

'But I'd like you to know that in many ways it gave me great comfort,' continues Maggie. 'It was important for me to know that such a passionate love could exist. You and Granddad had the longest and happiest marriage out of anyone I've known. And the devotion you showed him, caring for him as you did after his stroke . . .' Maggie shakes her head, 'well, it told me everything I needed to know about my own feelings for Gus.'

Lillian finally looks up and Maggie sees the tears in her eyes. 'Oh my dear girl,' she says softly.

'I don't want to upset you. I'm sorry. I thought it might remind you of Charles, and of happier times. Something to lift your spirits,' she adds helplessly, parroting back the doctor's own words.

'Oh, Maggie,' says Lillian, reaching for Maggie's hand. 'You left Gus because of this?'

Maggie shrugs. 'Not because of it, no. But it helped to bring my feelings for him into focus.'

Lillian looks at the paper in her lap and shakes her head. 'Things aren't always what they seem. We humans can create wonderful illusions for each other.'

'What I saw was no illusion,' says Maggie firmly. 'The way you looked after Charles after his stroke. The way you ran this house. You're an inspiration.'

Lillian shakes her head sadly. 'I let him suffer, Maggie. I stood by and watched as he suffered. I had no compassion for him left in my heart.'

'No,' says Maggie. 'That's not true. I saw you, day in, day out, caring for him. That was true love.'

This isn't going the way she had imagined it. She'd thought Lillian would be thrilled to be reunited with her love letter, but she seems more sad and confused than ever. 'It might have felt that way to you. I'm sure it was exhausting looking after him, and so hard to see him trapped in that wheelchair. I know he wasn't always the most . . . grateful. But you stuck around. You were there for him, always. For better or worse.'

Lillian's head snaps up. She looks at Maggie, suddenly clear-eyed and intent. 'Listen to me, Maggie. You're right to wait for a love that feels passionate and true − a love that you can't live without − but in the meantime, take the reins.' She sounds urgent. 'Don't let life just happen *to* you. Go out there and make it wonderful. Paint your pictures. Make them beautiful. Love. Laugh. Live.'

Maggie grips Lillian's hand and squeezes it back. 'I will. I promise.'

Lillian nods and turns her face to the window. 'This house should have been filled with love and life. There should have been children running through its corridors and climbing the trees. Instead, it was a house of dust and dead things, beauty trapped behind glass, pinned to boards, caught in frames. Life fluttering at the bars of an invisible cage. It wasn't how it was meant to be.'

'Gran, don't upset yourself. I'm sorry. I thought seeing the letter again would cheer you up.'

'Death and decay,' murmurs Lillian, her face still turned to the window. 'It was all death and decay. Perhaps it would have been better if it had all gone up in smoke.'

Maggie watches Lillian. She looks so tired and drawn and Maggie can't help the terrible feeling that her grandmother is somehow slipping from her, like the leaves that have started to turn on the trees across the estate, the first of them falling on the breeze, drifting and spiralling to the ground.

CHAPTER 28

When she opens her eyes, she is in the hospital. Charles sits in a chair beside her, slumped forward with his head resting in his hands. Lillian finds her gaze drawn to the startling white of his scalp, the skin visible where his once thick hair has begun to thin at the crown. She has never noticed this before about him. A small, physical sign of Charles's advancing age, his fallibility.

Her legs throb with a dull pain. She moves, trying to rid herself of it, and Charles lifts his head at the sound of her shifting on the mattress. 'You're awake.'

She nods and tries to pull the mask from her face.

'Here,' he says, 'let me.' Gently, he removes it and lays it on the pillow beside her. 'How are you feeling?'

She swallows. 'Tired. My legs hurt.' She looks down and sees for the first time that both her legs are dressed in white bandages, from the ankle to just above her knees.

He nods. 'I'm so sorry, my darling. I feel wholly responsible.' His eyes shine, filled with remorse and tears. 'It's all my fault.' He reaches for her hand.

'What happened?' Her voice is a dry rasp.

'I was the one that invited him to the house. I was the one that persuaded him to stay and work on the room.' Charles gives a little shudder. 'To think, I could have lost everything – you – Cloudesley . . . it doesn't bear thinking about.'

Lillian gazes at him, uncomprehending. 'Where's Jack?'

'I don't want you to worry about a thing. I've had a word with my friends at the police station and they're taking care of it all. The most important thing is that you are safe.'

'I don't understand . . .'

'The fire, in the painted room. It was started deliberately.'

'The fire?' She closes her eyes and it comes back to her. The smoke. The flames. The terrible, burning heat. She glances down at the bandages on her legs. 'What happened?'

'It seems our friend decided to punish us for our generosity and hospitality.'

'Who?' asks Lillian, struggling to keep up; but suddenly she knows the name that will leave his lips before he speaks it out loud. 'No,' she says vehemently. 'Not Jack.'

'I know. I felt the same as you but I'm afraid the evidence is clear. Someone lit the fire and locked the door, trapping you inside the room.'

Lillian swallows. 'That doesn't make any sense.'

Charles stares at her evenly. 'It doesn't?'

'No. I was there. I went in to . . . to see the murals.'

Charles studies her carefully. 'So did *you* lock the door, Lillian? Did you lock yourself in the room and set the fire?'

She shakes her head. 'No.'

'Only it seems,' he adds carefully, 'that there were only two people who went into the room that morning: Jack Fincher . . . and you.' He holds her gaze. 'Just the two of you,' he repeats.

And it's then that she realises he knows. He knows about the affair.

He shakes his head sadly. 'I won't say I'm not disappointed, Lillian. I know I haven't been the perfect husband. I know my temper leaves a lot to be desired. But to run into another man's arms like that . . .'

331

Lillian looks at the blank ceiling overhead. How does he know? And suddenly, a more chilling thought: where *is* Jack?

Charles continues, oblivious to her growing panic. 'What I'm struggling to understand is why he would have wanted to destroy the room, and possibly you in the process.' Charles shakes his head, sadly. 'It suggests a very unhinged mind. Someone who would be a great danger to themselves and others. If the fire had really had a chance to take hold, the whole house could have gone up.' He gives a shudder. 'It simply doesn't bear thinking about.'

She wants to laugh at Charles's ridiculous suggestion, but the sound catches in her throat and turns into a great, racking cough.

'Careful, my love,' says Charles, reaching for the mask and placing it tenderly over her nose and mouth. 'You inhaled a great deal of smoke. You've suffered some nasty burns on your legs. It's going to take time for you to heal.'

She sucks in the oxygen, waiting for her heart to stop thudding in her chest, then removes the mask from her face again. 'Where is Jack?'

'Please, you mustn't concern yourself with him.'

'Is he . . . is he all right?'

'The police are interviewing him.'

The rush of relief she feels is enormous. He's alive.

'I'm afraid they've found clear evidence that points to Jack. His lighter was found at the scene.'

Lillian's relief that he is still alive disintegrates again at the knowledge of what he is suspected of. She shakes her head. 'Jack wouldn't have done it.'

Charles eyes her. 'Yes,' he says firmly. 'Jack started the fire.'

Lillian stares at him. 'No.'

'He was the only person with the key to the room. And . . .' he adds pointedly, 'he had a motive.'

'What motive?' Lillian can't believe what she is hearing.

332

'The spurned lover. If he couldn't have you, no one would.' Charles is watching her face closely. 'Your beautiful, heartfelt letter of farewell. It might have been just the red flag to set him off. These temperamental artist types . . . they feel things *so* deeply. A jealous rage . . . who knows what he was capable of?'

'How do you know about the letter?'

Charles pats her hand. 'Don't worry yourself about the details. Your only job is to get better.'

Lillian eyes him coldly. Jack would never have destroyed that room. He would never have hurt her. He was angry, of course. He'd spent that final night in a rage, painting the last piece of the mural, adding the fox with the savaged hawk at its feet. He was jealous and angry, but he never would have gone to such violent lengths.

'I want to see Jack.'

'I hardly think that's a good idea, do you?'

'I need to see him.'

'You don't seem to understand. Mr Fincher is in serious trouble.' He tuts. 'Sad really, to throw it all away now, at the height of his career . . . and for what? A woman?' He shakes his head again pityingly. 'This job could have made him. It could have set him up for life. Instead he faces charges of arson, possibly attempted murder. He could be locked away for years.'

Lillian sinks back against the pillows. The morphine is beginning to wear off and the dull ache she has felt in her legs is sharpening now, like a blade scoring her skin. 'You're wrong. Jack would never destroy that room.'

Charles shakes his head, sadly. 'The terrible irony is not lost on me. A man so skilled at creating trompe l'oeil; well, he certainly deceived my eye.'

'It's all an illusion, Charles.' Lillian says, her voice rising in frustration and pain. 'Don't you see? You, me. The business. Cloudesley. You work so hard to present the perfect

333

image, with your parties and your peacocks, but it's you, Charles. You are the master of trompe l'oeil. It's all false. Jack has lifted a mirror to your own deception.'

Charles stares at her. 'Well, well, I do believe you might love him after all.'

Lillian glares at him. 'Jack would never hurt me.'

'Tell me this then,' says Charles, his tone suddenly shifting to ice-cold, 'if it wasn't Jack, that only leaves one other person.' He eyes her. 'Locking yourself into a room, setting fire to it. They're hardly the actions of a sane woman. Perhaps we should ask for a psychologist to come and visit you? Dr May, I'm sure, would provide some interesting background . . . a woman who so recently suffered the loss of her own child. It might be enough to weaken an already distressed mind.'

'The loss of our baby is your fault, Charles, yours alone,' she spits. 'It was your rage, your fists, that robbed us of that child.'

Charles's eyes flash. 'The secrets you keep, Lillian. If I had known you were carrying my child, if I had known how delicate you were, do you really think I would have . . . have hurt you?'

'I was going to tell you, but it was too early. I wanted to wait. I wanted it to be a surprise,' she says, the words leaving her throat with a sob.

Charles narrows his eyes. 'A wife shouldn't keep secrets from her husband. Who knows what the repercussions could be. The loss of our baby was on you, my dear. Just as anything that happens to Jack now is on you.'

Lillian leans back against the pillows and blinks back the hot tears of anger and frustration threatening to spill from her eyes.

Charles carries on, regardless. 'Perhaps a medical evaluation of your mental state might help us get to the bottom of this terrible mystery. I hear they have some very sophisticated facilities these days for . . . damaged women.'

She hears the unspoken threat in his voice and stares at him, horrified. 'You can't do this.'

'I can't do what, Lillian? *I* haven't done anything wrong. I haven't betrayed my spouse. I haven't destroyed another man's property.'

'But you're punishing Jack for something he didn't do.'

'You seem so very sure he is innocent. Perhaps you know of another motive?'

'I didn't set the fire,' says Lillian weakly, her legs burning with pain. 'And neither did Jack.' And it's then that she knows. The fox. The hawk. There is only one person she's ever known to be full of uncontrollable violence and rage. And the letter? How did Charles know about her letter to Jack? She had taken it to the room. She can picture it clearly, lying there on the desk where she left it, waiting for Jack's return. How would Charles know about her letter – how would it have survived a fire, a flimsy piece of paper – unless Charles too had been in the room that morning to take it?

'It was you,' she says through gritted teeth. 'You did it.'

'Don't be ridiculous.' Charles stares at her, coldly. 'You think I'd set fire to my own house? My pride and joy?'

'We both know what you're capable of in a moment of rage.'

Charles leans back in his chair. 'You're beside yourself, Lillian dear. It's the morphine playing with your mind. You don't know what you're talking about. Let's leave all of this detective work to my friends at the police station, shall we?'

Lillian shudders. She well knows what sort of treatment Jack might receive in the hands of Charles's 'friends'.

'Frankly,' Charles adds, after a moment's silence, eyeing her carefully, 'I'd be happy for this whole mess to disappear. If only we could wave some sort of magic wand . . .'

Lillian studies her husband's face, reading the expression in his eyes. 'What do you want, Charles?'

He holds up his hands. 'I'm sure I speak for all of us, Lillian, when I say it might be better for this family to avoid a full-blown scandal. It's a precarious time for the business, as you know. I'm on a knife edge with investors. I for one can't bear to think of the police and the press raking through our personal business, uncovering your sordid little affair, printing their terrible muck.' Charles gives a little shudder. 'I suppose it's fortunate that Chief Inspector Timbrell is such a close personal friend of the family. I'm sure if I were to have a little word in his ear, reassure him that I'm keen to avoid any unnecessary drama and not interested in pressing criminal charges . . . well, perhaps there is a way we can *all* avoid the scandal.'

Lillian eyes him carefully, starting to understand.

'It's not just your reputation at stake, you see. Imagine poor Albie, returning to school to face the whispers and gossip. Children can be so cruel.'

Lillian swallows. 'And any scandal that rocks the business right now might have a terrible knock-on effect. I'd hate to think what would happen to Helena should I not be able to meet the high cost of her care at The Cedars.' He stares at her pointedly. 'And of course, there is Mr Fincher himself, facing a prison sentence and the certain end of what was once such a promising career. So many lives affected by your betrayal. But of course,' he continues in a smooth, reassuring voice, 'if you could *promise* me that the affair was over, that Mr Fincher was out of your life for good . . . if you could promise me that you would never see him again . . .' Charles shakes his head sorrowfully, 'well, perhaps it would be best for us all if I were to drop the charges and let him be on his way.'

336

Lillian understands. Jack's freedom rests in her hands. If she promises never to see him again, Charles will allow him to walk free.

'He didn't do it,' she says, almost a whisper.

'One of you will be charged,' hisses Charles. 'If I don't intervene, the police will arrest one of you. Is that what you want? They have the evidence. They can lock him up like that.' He snaps his fingers to make his point.

She closes her eyes. She will never see him again. She will never feel his lips on hers or his arms around her. And her letter – he will never read it. He will never truly understand how she felt about him.

She can't bear to think of him never knowing that she was prepared to give it all up; understanding that she would have put everything on the line for him. But the alternative is Jack behind bars and his career cut off in its prime. She will not let Charles ruin both of their lives. She will not be the cause of Jack losing everything. She loves him too much for that. She closes her eyes. 'Drop the charges,' she says.

'And you will never see him again?'

Lillian nods.

Charles sits back in his chair. 'I'm glad you've come to your senses. I really think it's for the best. You will feel so much better when you are home again.'

'How did I . . . who got me out?'

'Bentham,' says Charles firmly. 'Monty was barking, going crazy. Bentham and Albie saw the smoke from outside. They raised the alarm and smashed the windows. Bentham dragged the pump up from the ornamental fountain and got the hoses in there and he and Blackmore put the flames out before the fire could spread too far. It was a remarkable rescue. You owe them your life.'

'Yes,' she says. 'Remarkable.' She turns to study the flowers in the vase behind Charles. 'The room? Is it . . . ?'

337

She can't bear to think of Jack's labour of love, a fleeting, beautiful thing, lost forever.

'Destroyed. But don't you worry about that,' he says, patting her hand again. 'It's a small sacrifice to make for your safe return. All that matters is that this nasty business is finally over. We'll have you home again and everything back to normal in no time.'

Normal. The word sends a chill down her spine. The pain in her legs rears up, bad enough to make her gasp. 'I think I need a little more morphine.'

'Of course,' says Charles, rising from the creaking chair, reaching over to smooth a lock of hair from her face. 'I'll call the nurse. Oh, and Joan's outside. She's most insistent about seeing you. Shall I send her in?'

'Oh, my darling,' says Joan, rushing in, hovering by the bed, seemingly uncertain whether to throw herself at Lillian or take up the chair just vacated by Charles. In the end she opts for the more sensible choice and seats herself at Lillian's bedside. 'You poor thing. I can't believe what has happened. I had to come, as soon as I heard. I couldn't leave without seeing you. What a frightening ordeal.'

Lillian nods and tries to smile. 'Thank you for coming.'

'How are you feeling?'

'Bloody awful.'

'Of course you are. Your poor legs,' adds Joan, glancing down at the bandages. 'Does it hurt terribly?'

'Yes.'

Joan's words suddenly chime in Lillian's foggy head. 'You're leaving?' she asks, trying to adjust herself on the mattress, trying to ease the growing pain in her legs.

Joan nods, looking a little sheepish. 'Gerald's been offered a posting to America. I wasn't keen at first but when he said it was California . . . well . . .' She smiles. 'Imagine the mischief I can get up to in LA! I'll write to you with *all* the gossip. But I'm sorry, darling. It's just the most awful timing.'

Lillian tries to smile but all she can see is another void opening up in her already barren life. 'Of course you must go. It will be a wonderful adventure.'

'You had such a lucky escape,' continues Joan, gazing back down at Lillian's legs. 'They say it could have been so much worse. That poor, poor man.'

'Who?'

'That lovely artist.' Joan nods, her eyes brimming with tears.

Lillian stares at her friend, uncomprehending. 'Jack?'

Joan bites her lip and nods.

'But Charles said—'

'He helped to pull you out, did you know? What a brave thing to do.'

Lillian stares at her, cold fingers wrapping tightly round her heart. 'He was in the room?'

Joan nods slowly and Lillian senses something dreadful in her friend's eyes. 'What is it? What happened to him?'

Joan presses a hand to her mouth. 'Didn't Charles say?'

Lillian shakes her head.

'Oh, my dear. It's his hands. I overheard a nurse saying they're completely ruined. He suffered terrible burns when he pulled you out of the room. The poor man will likely never paint again.'

Lillian stares at Joan. 'His hands?'

Joan nods, a tear spilling from her eye and landing on the bag in her lap.

She sniffs. 'Oh, perhaps I shouldn't have said anything?'

Lillian rests her head back on the pillows, her eyes gazing up at the blank white ceiling overhead. The pain in her legs rising through her body like fire.

Joan squeezes her hand. 'Don't cry, darling. Shall I call the nurse? You look like you're in terrible pain. Oh, thank goodness. Nurse! I say. Nurse!'

Lillian tunes out all sound and motion around her bed as a nurse stands beside her bed, tapping a needle before bending to inject the clear liquid into a vein on her arm. Jack – her lovely, talented Jack – will never paint again and it is all her fault. The morphine flows through her vein and Lillian allows it to do its work, welcoming the numb abyss that swallows her up.

CHAPTER 29

The wheelchair has been parked at an angle in the shade of a tall plane tree. Lillian sits slumped in it, a blanket spread across her lap. Maggie spots her from up on the terrace and feels a flicker of annoyance. Will has taken her right down to the edge of the ha-ha. What if she gets tired or cold? What if she wants to come back up to the house? And where is he, anyway?

She looks around, growing increasingly worried, until she sees his head pop up over the edge of the wall, like a rabbit emerging from a burrow, just a few metres from where Lillian sits. A spade is thrown up over the ledge, followed by several large pieces of stone. He says something to Lillian and she watches her grandmother acknowledge him with a raise of her hand, before he is gone again, ducking down behind the wall. Maggie lets out a long sigh. She knows she needs to talk to him. She can't let what happened at his studio the other night hang over them forever.

She joins them a little later, rolling out a picnic blanket beside Lillian's chair and pulling a Thermos of tea and some of Jane's walnut cake from a Tupperware box. She is careful not to disturb Lillian, who is now dozing, her chin resting on her chest, hands folded loosely in her lap. In the shade of the tree, Lillian's face looks as translucent as a sheet of crumpled tracing paper. Maggie studies her for a moment, then picks up the stick of charcoal she has brought with her and begins to sketch the outline of Lillian onto a page in her sketchpad. While she draws, the leaves overhead move and rustle in the breeze, accompanying the rhythmic sound of Will hammering stones into the wall.

She tries to push her tasks for the afternoon out of her thoughts. She tries not to think of the pile of marketing brochures for drab-looking care homes lying on her grandfather's desk awaiting her attention. Or what Harry will say when she calls him to ask if the Hamilton Consortium might still be interested in negotiating on the house and land. She concentrates instead on the smooth path of her charcoal moving over white paper.

'We saved one once.'

Lillian's voice breaks through Maggie's reverie. She puts down the pencil. 'Hello. I thought you were asleep.'

'Just resting.'

'What did you save?'

'Up there,' Lillian says, nodding towards the sky.

Maggie shields her eyes with her hands and sees a dark shadow hovering against the blue. 'What is it?'

'A sparrowhawk.'

'It's beautiful.'

'We saved one once,' she says again. 'It crashed into a window. We carried it into the woods, convinced it was dead, but moments later it was up, hopping about; then it just took off through the trees.' Lillian smiles. 'A tiny miracle.'

Maggie looks across to her grandmother and notices how her face is transformed by the memory; a sudden burst of animation, as if the echoes of the young woman she once was hover over her again.

'Maybe this is a descendant, returned to say "thank you"?'

Lillian smiles again. 'Far more likely he has his beady eyes trained on a field mouse in the meadow.'

342

They watch the bird for a while, gliding in the thermals. 'It's funny. Granddad never struck me as much of a conservationist,' says Maggie. 'You know, what with his shooting and hunting and all those stuffed animals everywhere.'

'Oh. Not Charles,' says Lillian with a small sigh, as if Maggie were a very foolish girl indeed. 'Jack.'

'Jack?' Maggie frowns. 'Who's Jack?'

Lillian smiles and looks out towards the woods. 'I went to find him. Just the once, a few years after Charles's stroke. He was feeding the ducks with his wife and daughters.' Her smile falters a little. 'Sweet little things they were. All rosy cheeks and curls.'

Maggie is still puzzled. 'I'm not following.'

'I couldn't face him in the end, knowing what I'd done to him. But I was glad to see that life had been kind to him in other ways.'

'Gran, who is Jack?'

But Lillian either hasn't heard or doesn't want to answer. She turns her face towards the sun and closes her eyes once more. 'Life was kind to me, too,' she murmurs, her eyes still closed. 'It brought me you.'

Maggie doesn't know if she is still talking of the mysterious 'Jack'. Another one of Lillian's addled moments. Maggie pats Lillian's hand and adjusts the blanket over her legs.

'I'm glad to see you're drawing again,' Lillian says, her eyes still closed.

'It's early days,' says Maggie, studying her rough sketch of Lillian through critical eyes.

'He's a hard worker, your Will,' Lillian says quietly, after another long silence.

'He's not *my* Will,' says Maggie, and she waits for her grandmother's response, before realising that her breathing has slowed and she has fallen asleep once more.

343

She sits cross-legged on the grass beside Lillian, running her fingers through the soft green blades, picking the last of the daisies and threading them into a chain on her lap. *Not her Will.* Saying the words out loud is painful, but it's the truth. She has to let him go. She can't keep up the fantasy that one day they will be together. She blew that chance a long time ago and it will be far easier on all of them if she can accept it.

He appears again, hoisting himself up over the edge of the dry stone wall and seeing her sitting beneath the tree, nods at her in greeting. She pours him a cup of tea from the Thermos and carries it over to him. 'A peace offering?'

'Thanks,' he says, lifting his T-shirt to wipe the sweat from his face before taking the cup from her hands.

Maggie shrugs. 'Thank you for repairing the wall.'

'If I hadn't done it, you'd have had some of the farmer's more friendly livestock marauding through your grand-mother's gardens.' They share a smile at the thought of a herd of cattle grazing the lawns of Cloudesley.

'I suppose that would be one way to keep the grass under control.' Maggie feels the moment of levity fall away. It doesn't matter how many stones they put back into place, she isn't going to be able to save this place for Lillian.

'How was your head the other morning?' he asks, not quite meeting her eye.

'Dreadful. I'm sorry for bringing my drama to your door-step. I won't let it happen again. I promise.'

His gaze settles on her face and he seems to study her for a long moment before nodding. 'OK.'

'Do you want some help?' she asks, eyeing the pile of rocks at his feet.

'Sure,' he says, throwing back the last of his tea. 'I'm almost done but you can help me with the last stones.'

She takes the hand he offers and jumps down into the meadow where she spends the next half an hour in surprisingly satisfying activity, passing the stones to Will for him to fit into the wall.

'Great,' he says, standing back to survey their work when the last rock is in place. 'Now I just have to fix the gate down by the lane and we're good to go.'

Maggie nods. She hasn't yet broken the news to Will that all his hard work could be in vain, if Todd Hamilton gets his hands on the estate. She turns to look out over the meadow. 'The trees are just starting to turn,' she says, noticing the copper colour creeping across the green foliage. A gust of wind moves across the meadow, combing the long grass like fingers moving through hair. 'I should take Gran back to the house. I don't want her to catch a chill.' She looks across to where Lillian is seated beneath the tree, still asleep but slumped forward again, her chin resting at an awkward angle on her chest.

'I'd be happy to speak to Joe about moving his livestock next week?' Will is making the offer as the first flutter of unease comes over her. Without replying, she turns and pulls herself up over the ha-ha, heading for the tree.

'Maggie? What is it?'

But she doesn't stop, not until she is kneeling at Lillian's feet, reaching for her hand.

'Gran?' she says. 'Can you hear me?'

A gust of wind catches the pages of Maggie's sketchbook where it lies forgotten on the rug, making them flutter and stir; but Lillian doesn't move. Her grandmother's hand, resting in her own, feels stiff and her skin strangely cold. 'Gran?' she says again, even though as she does, she understands that Lillian can't answer.

Will moves alongside her and crouches down. He reaches for Lillian's other hand and feels for a pulse in her wrist.

Maggie tries to take a breath but finds her lungs have turned to stone. She already knows what Will is going to say when he turns to her.

'I'm so sorry.'

A terrible, empty ache opens up inside her. A hard lump rises in her throat. Not yet, she wants to cry. Not now.

Will stands and opens his arms to Maggie. She leans in, resting her head against his shoulder, gazing out across the meadow where the wind still moves across the grass and plays in the trees beyond. Higher up, above the treetops, she sees the sparrowhawk still wheeling on the breeze. It soars on the thermals, performing several slow turns, before heading away towards the distant spire of the church. She watches it, a distant speck of black against the blue, until it vanishes completely from view.

CHAPTER 30

The fine weather breaks on the day of Lillian's funeral, the late Indian summer departing in a rush of grey storm clouds and cold drizzle. Maggie sits on a hard pew at the front of the village church, Lillian's casket resting on a plinth before her. It's hard to imagine her grandmother lying stiff and cold inside the wooden box. It's hard to believe that the woman she has loved all these years – the woman who helped to raise her, the mother she never had – has gone. Maggie knows she hasn't resolved in her head or her heart that she will never see her again. She is too numb.

Seated somewhere behind her are Will and Gus, Harry Granger, and a handful of stalwarts from the village. There is no sign of Albie, though she has turned to check several times throughout the service, hopeful he is just running late. She's done all she can to try to track him down and pass on the news of Lillian's death, leaving messages at various hostels and with odd friends he has collected over the years. But she's had no word since Lillian's passing and sitting there at the front of the chapel, she has never felt so alone. What would Lillian tell her? What words of advice would she have for her in this moment? She can't seem to conjure her – not even her voice.

After the service, Maggie stands outside under an umbrella and accepts handshakes and condolences from the few who have attended. Gus gives her a stiff hug. 'I wanted to come, but I'm afraid I have to run straight back for a meeting.'

She nods. 'She would have appreciated you being here. Thank you.'

Will studies Maggie. 'How are you holding up?'

She nods. 'OK.' She clears her throat. 'I'm sorry to ask, but could you come back to the house with me after this?'

Will looks a little uncomfortable, glancing at Gus, who turns away, his jaw clenched. 'I'm not sure that's—'

'It's Gran's lawyer,' she says, cutting through the awkward moment. 'He's going to read the will and he's specifically asked that you be there.'

'Oh,' he says, looking surprised. 'Yes, OK.'

'Thank you.' She glances across the graveyard at Gus retreating, hunch-shouldered through the rain. 'It was good of him to come.'

Back at the house, Jane makes a large pot of tea and unwraps the plates of sandwiches she made earlier that morning. Maggie, needing something stronger, opens a bottle of wine before they all gather in Charles's study, sitting cramped around her grandfather's desk.

Harry reads the will. The last few shares Lillian held in the business, which Maggie knows are all but worthless, are bequeathed to Albie, along with several of Charles's most valuable pieces of Chinese porcelain. Maggie isn't sure she knows the pieces. Perhaps Albie has taken them already, sold them off. Serve him right, she thinks.

Jane is given a large silver platter and a pearl choker that Maggie knows is worth a small fortune. There is a small bequest for Mr Blackmore, the former gardener of the estate, and a rather strange note for Will: 'Look in the hay barn on the edge of the estate. You'll find Charles's last remaining sports car hidden under a tarpaulin – an Aston

348

Martin he couldn't bear to sell. If you can get it going again it's yours to enjoy.'

Harry had looked up from the will with a raised eyebrow. 'It's a little unconventional, I know, but Lillian thought you might appreciate the gesture.'

Will is smiling. 'God love her.'

Finally, Harry tells Maggie that she is to inherit the house and the estate with instructions to do whatever she thinks is best – and apologies for the mess she finds it in. Maggie glances across and sees Will nodding in approval. She feels numb. Cloudesley is hers – for now.

'Oh, and there's this one last thing.' Harry reaches for a wooden box next to his papers. 'In Lillian's own words, Maggie, she says, "I can't give you the house without also giving you the key".' He pushes the box towards her. 'Your grandmother says,' he looks back down at the papers in his hands, finding his place, '"I hope you'll understand why I kept it to myself all this time."' He looks up from the paper again and gives her a look that shows he is as baffled as she is.

Maggie reaches for the box and lifts the lid. Inside is a large brass key tied to a piece of green silk. Maggie stares at it for a moment, confused. 'The west wing,' she says suddenly, understanding coming in a rush. She turns to look at Will again, a sense of trepidation rising.

He shrugs. 'There's only one way to find out.'

'Come with me?'

Will holds the tapestry in the entrance hall to one side as Maggie tries the key in the locked door. It turns smoothly. Maggie shares a quick glance with Will before turning the handle and pushing open the door. A corridor looms ahead of her, cloaked in darkness, a musty scent of dust and ash drifting towards her on a draught.

They walk the corridor, heading for the faintest splinter of light falling from an open door at the far end, grit crunching underfoot. 'In here?' Maggie asks.

'I guess so,' says Will.

She pushes on the door and steps into the room.

The interior is cast almost in darkness, only a glimmer of daylight filtering through a grime-streaked glass dome high above their heads. Will tries the light switch but it doesn't work, yet as Maggie looks up, tracing the source of daylight, she sees a faded map of something intriguing fanning out across the ceiling. Here and there, through the gloom, traces of gold and blue and green shimmer seductively.

'Do you smell that?' asks Will.

'Yes. Fire.'

She puts a finger to the nearest wall and it comes away dirt-streaked and sooty, but where she has touched, a burst of emerald green appears.

'Look,' says Will, pointing to the blackened shell of a bay window. 'This part's been completely destroyed.' His shoes crunch on broken glass and fragments of blackened timber.

He moves across to the furthest window and opens a bolted shutter. The glass here is still boarded up from the outside, but a little more light filters through the gaps in the wood.

Maggie turns and surveys the room, her eyes beginning to trace the outline of something quite extraordinary.

'What is it?' asks Will.

'It's incredible,' murmurs Maggie, spinning around in a slow circle, unable to tear her eyes from the scene laid out before her.

After a long pause, she hears Will's footsteps moving to the far side of the room. 'Come and look at this,' he says.

She joins him by the fireplace and they stand looking over a pile of familiar items: vases, paintings and ornaments, all taken from the main house. 'More treasure.' Maggie shakes her head.

'What's it all doing here?'

'Lillian,' she says. 'She must have hidden it here.'

'To keep them safe?'

Maggie thinks of Albie's ad hoc removals from the house. She thinks of Lillian's night-time wanderings. Her soot-stained feet. 'Perhaps.'

The hoard holds their attention for a short time, but it is the room itself that really captivates. Maggie and Will spend a long time studying the walls around them, trying to identify elements of the extraordinary painting hidden behind the layers of soot and dust. 'Look, there are trees . . . and feathers everywhere.'

'Yes. And a bird up there, see it?'

'Something happened in here,' says Maggie, staring around at the devastated scene.

'Here's something else.' Will is pointing to a cleaner section of paintwork, low to the skirting board to the right of the door.

'It looks like a name,' says Maggie, bending to peer more closely. 'John . . . Jack . . . Jack . . . Fincher.' She turns to Will and smiles. 'The artist has signed his work.'

Maggie spends all of the next day researching Jack Fincher, though it proves to be a frustrating trail. She uncovers images of some of his earliest work, completed as a war artist during the Second World War, and a couple of newspaper clippings reviewing exhibitions in the late 1940s and early 1950s. There is a black-and-white photograph of the artist as a young man, seated on the bonnet of an army vehicle, smiling and holding his hand up to shield his eyes from the sun. And another, more interestingly, from an online archive of a 1955 edition of the Cloud Green parish magazine, showing a man standing in front of wooden stocks being kissed on the cheek by a fair-haired girl. The photo is a little grainy, but she can see enough to know the man is very handsome.

With a little more digging she finds an old dissertation lodged online by a former Slade student, whose thesis had attempted to chart the rise and fall of Jack Fincher and the mystery of his disappearance. The student had gone so far as to trace the artist to a small town in the West Country, but when he had arrived at the given address hoping for an interview, the student had been sent packing by the wild-eyed drunk who had opened the door. The student had concluded that Jack Fincher was a man crushed by his early success and the weight of expectation. He was a man in ruins, but for the legacy of two paintings still housed at the Tate Britain gallery.

Maggie opens the home page for the Tate galleries website. She types the name 'Jack Fincher' into their search engine and is immediately redirected to a page showing two oil paintings. She stares at the images on her screen for a long while before reaching for her phone.

'Hello. Is this the National Trust? Could I please speak to someone in your acquisitions department? I've found something that I think you might be interested to look at.'

After a long but promising conversation, Maggie hangs up and returns to her laptop. She focuses on the second clue in the student's dissertation: a small town in the West Country. She types in various search threads and suddenly finds herself staring at the home page of a small gallery in Frome, Somerset: Fincher Fine Art. The website describes the gallery as a small, family-run business, founded in the late 1960s.

Maggie clicks through to the 'contact us' page. A young woman answers the phone on the third ring. 'Hello, Fincher Fine Art; can I help you?'

PART FOUR

'In the depth of winter, I finally learned that within me there lay an invincible summer.'

Albert Camus

For all my vigilance, it turned out that I was looking the wrong way. I was focused on the wrong threat. Diversions and distractions are the watchman's enemy and I had my eye turned. I waited too long. I waited to step from the shadows; and in my delay I risked it all: the house and all its dazzling treasures. But most distressing of all . . . I risked her.

It pains me now, to look back on those days, to know that the damage could have been avoided, that those flames might never have been lit and that the scars she now bears — both the visible ones marking her skin and those that remain only as a glimmer in the darkness of her eyes — will be there for all time. Regret weighs heavy on my shoulders.

But I am changed too and while she will never know of my devotion, I will not let her down again. I will remain here, for as long as she needs me. She may be strong — stronger than she knows — but while I am here, I shall see to it that neither flames nor fists will ever hurt her again. For I am the eyes of the house . . . and I am always watching.

CHAPTER 31

It's madness, really. There is far too much work to be done to justify a day trip to London and lying in bed thinking through the excuses she will have to make to Will and Jane, she can almost hear their sighs and grumbles: *leaving us to slave over the to-do lists while you get a head start on your Christmas shopping? Well, that's just lovely, that is.* But it's not a trip to the shops that Maggie has planned. She's hoping that the day ahead might help her piece together the final puzzling segments of her grandmother's life, or at least bring a new understanding to the legacy she has been left to caretake.

The hills are all winter browns and greys as she drives to the local station, catching a train to London before switching onto the Underground and eventually stepping out onto a smart Pimlico street. It's raining in the city and she jumps the puddles and turns her coat collar up against the late November breeze.

The Tate Britain stands like a solid white monument facing the slow-moving waters of the Thames. She checks the time as she climbs the entrance steps – she's early – and then spreads the gallery map out on the nearest bench. She's been here many times before, but somehow, today's prize has always passed her by. Orienting herself, she sets off with determination, a nervous excitement growing in the pit of her stomach.

She makes her way through the rooms dedicated to the 1930s and 40s, admiring a Graham Sutherland painting and a bronze of a Madonna and Child by Henry Moore, but unwilling to stop until she finds the room dedicated to the artists of the 50s. The room is pleasingly quiet, just two grey-haired women in matching brown raincoats standing in front of a Lowry and a young man in a battered leather jacket listening to the gallery tour on headphones. In the far corner a young woman dressed head-to-toe in black hovers discreetly, watching over proceedings. She acknowledges Maggie with a slight nod of the head then averts her gaze to the empty space in the centre of the room.

Maggie scans the walls. Francis Bacon. John Bratby. Patrick Heron. She has already seen images of what she is seeking on the internet, but it is still a thrill to recognise them: two small oil paintings in simple gilt frames hung side by side in the far corner of the room. She moves closer, hungry to view them up close.

The first is a still life. A wooden box spilling paints and brushes. A simple painting but for the extraordinary trompe l'oeil effect the artist has created, using skilful perspective and depth to create the illusion that the viewer might simply stretch out a hand and reach right inside the box to grasp any of the twisted tubes of paint or one of the well-used brushes. In the corner she notes the artist's signature, her eyes tracing the now-familiar looped 'J' and the flourish on the tail of the 'F'.

The second painting is more reminiscent of the work in the painted room at Cloudesley. It shows a rural landscape of a field at harvest time, hay bales dotting a distant vale of fields, the scene glowing golden in an orange-fire sunset. Once more, it is a simple painting, a rural idyll, but for the quirky perspective added by the farm labourer lying in the foreground, a discarded jar of cider in the grass beside him.

The small white card beside the second painting reveals it to be titled *Somerset Glory* and tells her that it was painted in 1953, as part of a collection of rural studies by the artist. The card gives a short précis of the artist's training, details Maggie already knows from her internet research, and goes on to mention that while the artist would go on to enjoy success with several more celebrated collections, being regarded by *The Times* in 1954 as one of Britain's most promising young artists, he had all but dropped out of the art scene by the late 1950s, in what was widely reported as a crisis of confidence. The final point notes that despite his sudden decline, Jack Fincher is widely recognised as an important counter to the rise of abstract expressionism, and as having an influence on the superrealism movement of later decades.

She turns back to the painting of the Somerset landscape and scrutinises it so closely she begins to lose all sense of the image as a whole, distilling it down to individual brush-strokes. While executed on a fraction of the scale, there's no denying it shares a similar style to the painted room at Cloudesley. She is moving between the two paintings, hoping to glean further secrets, when she glimpses the small print at the bottom of the information card she missed in her first hurried reading: *Generously donated to Tate galleries from the private collection of Charles Oberon, 1956.*

Seeing her grandfather's name printed there in black and white next to the landscape is startling. Charles once owned this painting? She looks again at the date: 1956. From what she's pieced together, that would have been just a year after the completion of the room. It doesn't make sense. Why would Charles go to the trouble of commissioning an elaborate painted room by someone she assumes was a favoured artist, only to lock it up, forbid anyone to go inside and then give away a valuable original work by the same man? It's baffling.

She hears the subtle clearing of a throat. Maggie glances round and finds the gallery assistant has moved a little closer, perhaps agitated at Maggie's proximity to the painting. Reluctantly, she steps back. She checks her watch. She still has twenty minutes to wait, so she continues with a cursory tour around the rest of the gallery, then rifles fruitlessly in the gift shop, hoping to find a print or postcard of one of the Fincher paintings to take back with her, for posterity. At five to three she makes her way back to the room.

The original guard has left and been replaced with a slim man, again dressed in black, who stands on the other side of the room discussing one of the paintings with a shrill Italian lady. The only other visitors are an elderly man seated on a bench in the centre of the room, a walking stick resting beside him, and a young woman with blonde curly hair seated to his right. They talk in low voices. Maggie, feeling her butterflies take flight, inhales deeply and approaches them. 'Mister Fincher?' she asks, addressing the seated man.

The man looks up at her. His face is an extraordinary map of lines and crags but his eyes are dark and clear. 'Miss Oberon. It's a pleasure to meet you.' She smiles, unsure whether to offer her hand to the seated man, not wanting him to have to stand on her account, but he is already indicating the woman at his side with a tilt of his head. 'This is Lucy,' he says, introducing her. 'She very kindly drove me here today.'

'Thank you,' says Maggie quickly, taking the woman's outstretched hand in her own, noting her dark eyes, her fair, curly hair and the straight aquiline nose. The family resemblance is striking. His granddaughter, she presumes. 'This really does mean so much to me. Will you join us for afternoon tea?'

Lucy shakes her head. 'I'm sure you two would like some time to talk. How about I meet you out in the entrance hall, when you're done? There's no rush; I'll be perfectly happy amusing myself round here.' Lucy leans down and kisses the old man's cheek tenderly, then leaves them with a small wave.

Maggie notices that the old man's eyes have tracked back to the two paintings hung on the opposite wall. 'Is it strange seeing them again?' she asks, taking a seat beside him.

'Yes.' Jack Fincher smiles. 'They certainly stir my emotions.'

She nods. 'I love them.'

'You do?'

'Yes. I love the light you've captured in both of them. They're so playful. It feels as though you're testing us. As if you're asking us to think about what's real, and what's not real.'

He looks at her with interest. 'Are you an artist?'

'Do you know,' she says with a sigh, 'I've been asking myself that very question for some time now.'

The man nods, as if in understanding.

'I've certainly enjoyed researching your career.' She smiles as she turns to him. 'Though I have to say, it's been a frustrating trail. I couldn't find any information about your other works. They're all held in private collections. Do you still paint?'

Jack Fincher shakes his head. 'Oh no. I haven't lifted a paint brush in years.'

'That's a shame. What made you stop?'

He hesitates, just for a fraction, then pulls his hands from deep within his coat pockets and lays them in his lap. 'An accident.'

Maggie has been preparing encouraging platitudes about how it's never too late to try again, about how all he has to do is pick up the brush and give it a go, about how age is irrelevant, but when she sees his hands, all words fail her.

She knows it's rude to stare but she can't help it because they're not really hands at all, but twisted claws, rivers of deep scar tissue and pink gristle spreading up into his shirt sleeves.

'The nerve damage made it virtually impossible for me to hold or control anything that required fine motor skills or a certain level of dexterity.'

'Like a paintbrush,' says Maggie softly.

'Yes. Like a paintbrush.'

'I'm so sorry.' She looks at him, then back to the painting.

Something is fluttering at the edges of her mind, like a moth seen from the corner of an eye. She looks at the man's hands. She thinks of the locked room, its soot-streaked walls and the lingering scent of smoke and ash. Gradually, all the pieces of a story fluttering wildly in her head drop into place. She stares from the man's hands to the paintings on the wall, and then back to Jack Fincher.

'You were there, weren't you? At Cloudesley. On the day of the fire.'

'Yes,' he says, his voice so soft she has to crane to hear him. 'I was there.'

Maggie lets out a long breath. This man is more valuable than the key she'd been given to open the door. Questions leap into her head, but she forces herself to wait. 'Shall we go and get a cup of tea? I have so many questions . . . and, while I don't want to upset you or bring up any painful memories,' she glances away from his hands and concentrates on his dark, grey eyes, 'it would mean so much for me to be able to ask you about your work, and the room . . . and about my grandparents.'

The man nods.

'Thank you,' she says. 'I think there's a cafe, right this way.'

In her excitement, she takes a wrong turn and instead of leading him to the gallery cafe, they find themselves heading down an art deco staircase and arriving at the entrance to the Rex Whistler Restaurant. 'Two for afternoon tea?' asks a small man with an imperious French accent. Maggie looks behind him to the genteel scene of well-heeled ladies drinking tea and selecting cakes and sandwiches from elegant silver cake stands. It's far more formal than she had intended, but she is afraid she has already dragged the elderly man further than perhaps he wanted to go. 'Yes please,' she says quickly. She will think of it as research for the tea room they plan to open at Cloudesley next year; and then, just in case her companion should be worried about the expense, she adds, 'My treat.'

The waiter seats them at a table near the back of the low-ceilinged room. All around them stretches a colourful, fantastical painted mural. Maggie gazes at it for a moment, her eye caught by a white unicorn kicking up its heels before she turns back to Jack with a smile. 'It's rather appropriate, don't you think, Mr Fincher?' says Maggie with a smile. 'A painted room.'

'Yes,' he nods. 'Rex Whistler was a master. It was a tragedy he died in the war.'

She waits until the waiter has taken their order before launching into her questions. 'My grandfather commissioned you to paint the room in the west wing at Cloudesley?'

Jack Fincher nods his head. 'He did. I have no idea why he chose me. I think he liked my work. He held an earlier painting of mine in his collection.'

'The one hanging in the gallery upstairs?'

Jack nods.

'The card said Charles donated it to the gallery the year after you finished work at the house.'

'Yes, he did.'

'That was very generous,' she says carefully.

'Yes, it was.'

Maggie sits back in her chair. She senses an undercurrent hovering below the surface of their conversation, something she can't quite pin down. Had the two men fallen out over the room? Was that why Charles offloaded a once-cherished piece of art to the gallery?

Before she can dwell further on the matter, their tea arrives. The waiter makes a great performance of placing china cups and saucers, silver teapots, milk jugs and sugar on the table in front of them. They pour the tea and Maggie watches silently as Jack wrestles with a small pair of silver tongs and the sugar bowl, holding them awkwardly in his damaged hands. She has to fight the urge to reach across and help. Eventually he drops a lump into his cup of milky tea. 'The effort it takes, you'd think I'd have given it up by now,' he says with a wry smile.

Maggie waits a moment before she asks her next question. 'Do you mind if I ask . . .' she stares at his hands, wondering how best to approach the event, 'if I ask how it happened? The fire.'

The heavy furrows deepen in the man's brow. 'I wish I could tell you, but even after all these years, it's not something I understand.' He sighs and Maggie can see him trying to cast his mind back.

'I'm sorry. I don't want to cause any upset.'

He doesn't seem to hear her. He is staring across the room, unseeing, returning to a place of memory. 'The room was finished,' he says. 'I'd stayed up all the previous night working on the . . .' he hesitates, 'the final touches.'

Maggie nods encouragingly but knows not to interrupt.

'I knew it was time for me to leave Cloudesley. I had retired upstairs to my room to pack when I heard a commotion. The dog – Monty – was barking outside. And there were

364

shouts out in the grounds. Something about those sounds, the urgency . . . I just knew something was terribly wrong.'

'I ran down the back staircase to the west wing and it was there in the corridor that I saw the smoke rolling out from beneath the door to the painted room. When I went to open it, I found it was locked. There was no key. I had to kick it open with brute force. I was only thinking of trying to save the room. I had no idea she was in there.'

'Who? Lillian?'

The man nods. 'All I could see was smoke. There were flames creeping up the curtains beside the window seat and then I heard the coughing. She was on the floor, down on her hands and knees. Just as I saw her, the curtains over the window seat fell onto her. There was the sound of glass smashing. I knew I had to get her out.'

Maggie stares at the man, horrified. She remembers the sight of the twisted scars on her grandmother's legs and winces.

'She was unconscious by the time I reached her. Her legs were caught in the burning curtains, all tangled up. I didn't think. I just reached for them and dragged them off her, then pulled her from the room.

'It was a very confused situation. Lillian was badly hurt. She was taken away in the first ambulance and it was only after she'd left, when someone came to check on me, that they saw what had happened.' He looks down at his hands. 'It must sound strange, but I hadn't felt a thing.'

Maggie shudders. She can't imagine. She busies herself with pouring more tea, allowing Jack Fincher a moment to compose himself.

'How was the fire put out?'

'Whoever was outside must have activated the pump system. They smashed the window and fed the hoses through, taking water from the fountain. I believe that's how they saved the house. Extraordinary, really; Cloudesley could have been razed to the ground.'

'What about you?'

'I was taken to the same hospital as your grandmother – though they wouldn't let me see her. It was only when the police came to question me – when they told me they were treating it as an act of arson – that I realised they believed someone had deliberately started the fire. I was told they had found my cigarette lighter at the scene and that I was the prime suspect.'

Maggie stares at the man, fascinated and horrified in equal measure. 'They thought *you'd* set the fire? Why would they think you'd destroy your own work? Something you'd spent all summer creating?'

'Why indeed?'

'Were you charged?'

'No.' Jack sighs. 'It didn't look good for me for several days; but then, out of the blue, Charles had a change of heart. He had the police drop the charges.'

'Because he knew you were innocent?'

The artist shrugs. 'I have no idea. It's as baffling to me now as it was then. All these years and I haven't been able to understand the events of that day. All I know is that I had lost my lighter – in the woods, the house, or somewhere in the grounds of the estate. Whoever found it must have set the fire and left the lighter behind, to frame me, perhaps.'

'Who could it have been?'

'My suspicion was Charles. Though I have no proof.'

'Why?' Maggie is struggling to follow Jack's explanation. 'Why would he destroy the room he had commissioned, a room in his own house?' Maggie studies Jack Fincher. She remembers her grandmother's final moments, sitting beneath the tree beside the ha-ha. *We saved one once.* Understanding rings like a bell. 'She loved you.'

'I believe she did,' he says softly. 'And I loved her. Very much.'

Maggie nods, but doesn't interrupt.

'I fell for her over the course of that one summer. You may be shocked to learn this, but I wanted her to leave Charles and come away with me. The day before the fire, we met in the woods behind the house. We argued. I didn't feel she would be . . . safe . . . remaining at Cloudesley; but she refused to come with me. After we'd parted, I was in a terrible fury. I went back to the painted room and, in my rage, I added a final scene.'

'What scene?'

'I made a small addition. A fox, painted in one corner, a sparrowhawk lying dead at its feet. The fox, I rather foolishly, gave some . . . identifying characteristics. Anyone who knew the man would have seen quite clearly I had meant it to represent Charles. It was crudely done, but a message I wanted Lillian to see.'

'Oh.' Maggie is taken aback.

'It was very foolish. You see, in doing so, I believe I either incited Charles's rage and gave him a motive to destroy the murals, or I created a strong reason for Lillian to want to hide the evidence, before he found out about our affair. She must have felt so exposed . . . so afraid. I didn't think, you see, what it might mean for her.'

Maggie is still trying to assemble the jumbled pieces of the puzzle in her head. 'But you said Lillian was trapped inside the room at the time of the fire. It was locked?'

Jack nods.

'So if it were Charles who started the fire, was he trying to kill her? Or if it were Lillian, trying to hide evidence of your affair, was she . . .' Maggie can't quite believe what she is about to ask, 'was she trying to kill herself?'

'No. She wouldn't have left Albie, or her sister, Helena.

She was devoted to them. In my mind, everything points to Charles. I think he set the fire in a rage – to punish me. I'm not even sure he knew Lillian was in the room at the time. I found her over by the window seat. Perhaps she had been resting there. Hidden, somehow, behind the long drapes. It must have been a dreadful accident.'

Maggie thinks of the dark marks climbing the walls near the destroyed window seat, evidence of the curtains that once hung there. She shudders to imagine them, thick velvet cloth catching alight, going up like tinder.

He shakes his head. 'Charles could be . . . aggressive.' He glances across at Maggie. 'And he was certainly impulsive. But I don't think he would have deliberately tried to kill her. He did set me up to take the fall, though. I can only imagine he backed away from the charges when he realised what sort of a scandal it might bring to the Oberon name.'

'Did you see Lillian again? After the fire?'

Jack Fincher shakes his head. 'No.'

'Why not? You loved her. Why didn't you try to find her again? To find out the truth?'

'I thought about it. But she'd told me herself the day before the fire that she wouldn't come away with me . . . and afterwards,' he looks down at his hands, 'everything had changed. I no longer had any kind of future to offer her. I wasn't the man she'd fallen in love with. I would never paint again. I couldn't even hold her hand, stroke her face. I didn't want her to see me like that. I thought she'd be better off without me.'

'Wasn't that her decision to make?'

Jack shrugs. 'Perhaps.' He glances up at Maggie. 'Though after Cloudesley, I was damaged in more ways than this,' he says, lifting his gnarled hands, dropping them back into his lap. 'I was never paid for the work I completed that summer and I grew very poor. But worse than that, my heart was broken. I couldn't work. I went through . . . a very dark time. Too much drink. Not enough hope.'

Maggie nods.

'I've never forgotten her. I've thought of her every day since the fire. I saw her . . . in my dreams, many times, but elsewhere too. Sometimes just a flash of blonde hair or a certain laugh could evoke her. Once, I even chased after a woman. I was on a bridge in Frome, with Gertie and the girls, feeding the ducks. I saw a woman in the distance in a red coat and for a moment I really thought it was her. I set off in pursuit but lost her in the crowds. It took me a while to come to my senses . . . but for just that moment, I was convinced it was her, come to find me after all those years.'

The echo of something is rattling in Maggie's mind. A man with his little girls feeding the ducks. But she has a head full of questions for this man and doesn't want to waste a moment. 'So you did eventually marry? You had children? Girls, you say? Lucy is your granddaughter?'

Jack shakes his head sadly. 'Oh no. Gertie was my sister. She had three delightful daughters. I eventually pulled myself together enough to be their uncle. A good one, I hope. Lucy is my great niece,' he adds proudly. He is smiling, but Maggie can see the pain and regret in his eyes. 'After many lost years, I cleaned up my act and opened the gallery in Frome. I turned my attention to supporting other artists and made a modest income – enough to get by. Though whenever I thought of contacting your grandmother – and there were many occasions when I thought of her – I felt a terrible shame. I never wanted her to see me this way. The failed artist.'

'I'm sure she wouldn't—'

But he is already waving away her words, deflecting with a new question. 'So you're Albie's daughter?' he says. 'How is the boy?'

Maggie can't help the laugh that escapes her. 'Boy? He's sixty-eight! But yes, I suppose in many respects he is still a boy. The boy who refused to grow up and settle down.' She smiles. 'He's a terrible father. I've learned the hard way not to expect anything from him. It's easier that way. But I'd be lying if I said it didn't hurt still. He's my dad. Probably the best thing he ever did for me was to leave me at Cloudesley with Lillian and ask her to raise me; although I didn't know it for a long time.'

'Did your father ever talk to you about his childhood?'

Maggie shakes her head.

'Try not to judge him too harshly. We all carry our own scars, our own pain.'

Maggie narrows her eyes. She wants to ask more but Jack is clearing his throat.

'And so you grew up at Cloudesley too, like Albie?'

'Yes, I rattled around that huge house with my grand-parents. Lillian was my saving grace.'

'And Charles?' The man is eyeing her keenly.

Maggie shrugs. 'I wasn't as close to him. He was an invalid for most of my childhood. Stuck in a wheelchair.' She eyes Jack Fincher again. 'I'm told he was a force to be reckoned with, back in the day, before the business went under and he suffered his stroke. But I only ever really knew him as an old man diminished by poor health. It's sad, really. You probably knew a very different Charles?'

'I certainly did.' Jack clears his throat. 'What happened to him?'

'He collapsed in the drawing room one day. Poor Charles. To spend the rest of his life like that, trapped in his own failing body.'

'Life is strange,' Jack murmurs.

'If I'm honest, I preferred to keep out of his way. It was Lillian who ran the show. Cloudesley was so obviously her

370

domain. She made all the decisions, kept the place going, with Bentham's help.'

'Ah, Bentham. Whatever happened to the fellow?'

'I believe he stayed on at Cloudesley for years, though eventually he retired in the late 80s, I think. He became something of a friend to Gran, after Charles's death. He'd call in on her. I'd see them together, drinking tea out on the terrace, or taking a walk around the house and grounds. I used to tease Gran that he had a crush on her. I don't think it was ever romantic, but she was very sad when he died. She told me then that she'd come to see him as a sort of protector.' Maggie shrugs. 'I never quite understood it, but I suppose she meant she saw him as a custodian to Cloudesley, someone who helped to watch over the old place.'

Maggie notices Jack's watering eyes and turns away to pour a second cup of tea for them both.

'She was a good woman,' he says after a while. 'Devoted to Albie and her sister, Helena.'

Maggie sighs. 'Well, I'm not sure my father deserved her devotion. He hasn't been very good to her over the years.'

'Perhaps you made up for that?'

Maggie smiles. 'God, do you think so? Poor Lillian.'

'Your grandmother was driven by a wonderful instinct to care for others – a strong maternal streak. I imagine you must have brought her great joy.'

'And great strife too, I'm afraid. I'm no angel.'

'Are any of us? I've found great joy from the closeness I share with my sister's family. Perhaps it was the same for Lillian? Besides, it sounds to me as if you were there when it mattered most. At the end, by her side. That's what counts.'

Maggie thinks for a moment. 'You were there too, in a way.'

The man looks up from his cup, startled. 'Excuse me?'

'What I mean is that she spoke about you at the end. On the day she died, she told me about a hawk you rescued together.'

A gentle smile breaks over Jack's face, drawing a light into his dark eyes. 'Did she now? Well, well.'

The waiter is back at their table. He offers them fresh hot water for their tea, but they both decline. Maggie checks the time on her watch. 'I'm so sorry. I've kept you rather a long time. Would you mind if I asked you one last question?'

'By all means.'

'What was your inspiration for the room?'

Jack Fincher sighs and a small smile comes over his face. 'It was your grandfather who commissioned the painted room, but from the very first brushstroke, it was hers. Not that anyone else could have known, but I was creating a tribute.

'I had intended for the room to be the story of our summer together, full of signs and symbols only she would recognise, moments we had shared. My hope was that it would stand as a secret legacy.' Jack looks around at the Whistler murals on the wall beside them. 'So much that is beautiful about life is fleeting, impermanent. I think that's why I felt compelled to try to capture it. I wanted my paintings to remain as reassurance of my devotion, permanent evidence of what we had shared, to remain long after I had left Cloudesley and our moment together had faded.' He clears his throat. 'It's been one of my greatest regrets that it was destroyed by the fire – that she only ever saw it the once.'

Maggie has been fiddling with the silver tea strainer as she listens, but when she hears these words, she places it carefully back in its tray and turns to him. 'She only saw it the once?' She shakes her head. 'You don't *know*?'

'Know what?'

'About the room?'

He looks at her, puzzled.

'It's still there,' she says, watching as his dark eyes slowly widen. 'I unlocked it just a few weeks ago. There's some significant fire damage, of course, to the walls near the window seat. There's some damp here and there too, a few worrying cracks along the curved, outer wall; but the majority of your work remains. Soot-stained, of course, but surprisingly intact. It seems that by shutting up the room, boarding up the windows, protecting it all these years from sunlight, Charles unwittingly helped to preserve the integrity of your work.'

The old man looks stunned. 'I don't believe it.'

'It's true. The National Trust sent a specialist to survey the room. They were very excited to see it. They've reassured me that most of it is salvageable. It's really quite remarkable.'

It is Jack Fincher's turn to look astonished. 'But Charles – he told me . . .' Maggie notices the man's hands trembling. 'When he came to the hospital that day, he told me the room had been lost. He said it had been completely destroyed.'

Maggie shakes her head. 'It's not true. I don't know why he lied to you, but he did. Your murals survived.'

'Well I never.' Jack Fincher shakes his head, clearly confounded. 'All this time . . .'

'He must have hated that Lillian loved you. Perhaps that's why he told you it was destroyed? A form of revenge. He boarded the windows and locked the entire wing, but Lillian must have taken the key, after Charles's stroke. Presumably he couldn't keep her from the room any longer. I believe she spent many secret hours in there over the years.' Maggie thinks of Lillian's night time wanderings, her sooty feet, the way Jane had found her collapsed outside the locked door in the hall, her grandmother's unwavering insistence that she remain at Cloudesley. 'I think she was going in and out, right up until her death. It was a private sanctuary for her. Her personal treasure. The reason she couldn't bear to leave.'

Jack shakes his head. 'So she saw it again, after the day of the fire?'

'Yes. Again and again.'

'After all this time . . . it seems like a miracle.'

'Yes,' agrees Maggie, 'it *is* a miracle; because it's your room that has given Cloudesley a future. Thanks to your murals, the National Trust has determined that the house has special cultural significance. They're sending in a team of specialists to work on its restoration in the New Year. I'm going to stay on in one part of the house in a residential capacity, but we'll open most of the interior and the grounds to the public for the first time next spring, with a special exhibition of your room. There's a great deal of excitement building already. You must come and see it,' she adds. 'We will have a grand unveiling – a party. You must be our guest of honour.'

Jack still looks dazed. It's as he reaches for a napkin and presses discreetly at the corner of his eyes that she remembers something else.

'Besides,' she adds, thinking of the letter she'd found in Charles's desk drawer, 'I have something else that I think might belong to you – something from Lillian that you should have received years ago. Promise me that you'll come? Bring your sister, your nieces, Lucy. You're all welcome.'

Jack doesn't say anything and Maggie waits, fearful that he will say no. She has no idea what even the thought of returning to Cloudesley might stir up for this man; but she knows that she is asking a lot of him.

'I always felt that I left part of myself in that house,' he says, softly.

Maggie holds her breath and after another long moment he nods and wipes his eyes. 'It would be an honour.'

CHAPTER 32

Maggie approaches the room along the west-wing corridor, the sound of clinking glasses, conversation and laughter bouncing off the wood panelling and drawing her on. She is wearing one of Lillian's dresses, a simple cream silk shift that she pulled from her wardrobe. It seems fitting somehow, and fitting too that they should be opening the house to the public for the first time on May Day, given the history of Charles's infamous annual ball.

Frankly, she's relieved they are ready. A team of fine-art specialists has been working long hours over the last four months to clean, stabilise and retouch the murals. She had silently wondered if they would pull it off, but they had performed a miracle. The room is a phoenix, risen from ashes, dazzlingly beautiful.

She'd walked Jack Fincher privately through the room earlier in the day, aware that it might be an overwhelming and emotional experience for him after all these years. She knows that the look on his face as she opened the door for him that morning is something she will never forget. 'What do you think?' she'd asked. 'Is it how you remember?'

He'd nodded, a single tear on his cheek catching in the sunlight falling through the restored glass dome in the ceiling and refracting off the painted peacock eyes. 'It always did get the best light in the morning.'

She'd given him a little time to wander the room and reacquaint himself with his work, before joining him over by the restored window seat.

'We thought we'd keep that one section of fire damage on the wall there. Just for now. It feels important, like part of the story of the room, somehow. But if you prefer, we could replicate the original. We have the sketchbook you left here all those years ago, with all your ideas drawn out, so we think we can accurately recreate it, if you didn't mind another artist working on the room at some point in the future?'

Jack had looked out of the window. 'You still have peacocks,' he'd said.

Maggie had followed his gaze to where two males strutted through the arboretum, their extravagant tail feathers trailing through the recently mown grass. 'Actually, no. We had a couple brought in especially for the launch. It seemed only right. But they look quite at home, don't they? Look at them preening and posing. Perhaps we'll have to get some of our own.'

'I wonder what Charles would make of all this?' Jack had mused, looking back around the room.

'I hope he'd be pleased. After all, wasn't it his original intention to create something for the public? A "jewellery box of a room", you said when we last met. I get the impression he was a bit of a show-off himself.'

Jack had smiled. 'Has there been much interest? Do you expect many people to attend this afternoon?'

Maggie couldn't help her laugh. 'Mr Fincher, we've been turning them away in droves. Today's launch is the hottest ticket in town.'

'The hottest ticket in Cloud Green? You do surprise me,' he'd said, a little drily.

Maggie had given him a sideways look. 'Talented and feisty. I can see why Lillian liked you.'

She hadn't been exaggerating. Since they had announced their find in the west wing, the interest from the art world had been overwhelming. The National Trust had invited both the local and national press to the launch and Maggie had opened up the invitations to the village as well, wanting to keep as many locals as possible on side and invested in the changes at Cloudesley. So far, she's been thrilled that the response has been overwhelmingly positive. The room has been billed by many as an exquisite lost treasure, brought back to life.

It isn't just the room, either. The whole west wing has been restored and reopened, now the site of an exhibition about the house and Jack Fincher's hidden commission. The Tate gallery had very kindly agreed to loan their Fincher paintings, which now make up an extra-special part of the display. In addition, glass cabinets dotted throughout the room reveal Jack's original box of paints and brushes found in the barn, the techniques he adopted to paint on such a grand scale, as well as some of his original sketches – everything from his pencil drawings of feathers and leaves, right down to a simple image of a jug of sweet peas Maggie had found while clearing out Lillian's dressing-table drawers, the words 'Get well soon' written in one corner.

When he'd seen enough, she had taken Jack into the drawing room to rest, helping him to Lillian's armchair. 'I'm sorry. It must be overwhelming.'

'A little, but I'm glad to be here.'

'I mentioned when we met at the Tate that I had something for you.' She had moved across to Lillian's writing desk in the window and reached inside for the envelope she'd placed there earlier that morning. 'I've had this for a while now. I found it in my grandfather's desk, though I believe it belongs to you.' She'd held out Lillian's letter and Jack had reached up and clasped it in his damaged hands. 'Would you like me to give you a moment?'

Jack had looked down at the folded paper. 'Thank you.'

'I'll bring you some tea.' And she had left him on his own, sitting in a pale square of sunshine.

Stepping into the painted room now, scanning the throng of guests milling in the space, champagne flutes in hand, many of them gazing up at the ceiling, admiring the extraordinary painted murals, she can't help smiling. She wonders if this is how Cloudesley used to feel, back in the day, when her grandfather would open the house for one of his infamous parties. Through a gap in the crowd she spots Jack sitting on the restored window seat, a plate of cucumber sandwiches resting on his lap and Will beside him, the two men chatting intently.

The house is filled with noise and laughter. There are so many admirers – many of whom want to congratulate her on the opening's success. She accepts their greetings and praise while steadily making her way across to the window.

'What are you two talking about?' she asks, finally reaching Will and Jack.

Jack smiles up at her. 'Nothing too serious. Life. Love.'

'I see, just a little small talk, then.'

'This nice young man was asking if I had any wisdom to share. He seems to think my advanced years might give me some sort of advantage over the rest of you.' Jack laughs, a warm, natural laugh, and Will looks down at his lap, a small smile playing on his face.

'And do you?' asks Maggie.

'All I can tell you both is that life passes in the blink of an eye. It's a cliché – but it's true. I think we owe it to ourselves, and each other, to go after what we want – what we love. *Who* we love. We won't always get it right, but I believe it's better to live a life of passion and make a few mistakes along the way than to suffer a lifetime of regret.'

Maggie studies Jack for a moment. She thinks of the love letter she passed to him earlier that morning. She glances across to Will again, but he is still staring down at his hands.

'But what if loving someone means hurting others?' he asks quietly.

Jack shrugs. 'True, passionate, life-altering love is rare. When you find it, you must fight for it. If this tired old heart of mine has anything of any value to share, it's probably that,' he says, with a matter-of-fact smack of his lips.

Will looks up at Maggie and throws her a sheepish smile, but before she can reply, Jane is at her side, gently touching her arm. 'Maggie, love,' she says, looking worried, 'I'm afraid we need you.'

Albie is sitting at the kitchen table, his head in his hands. Two employees from the catering company stand at the sink, rinsing and drying champagne flutes, eyeing her father awkwardly. 'Would you mind giving us a few minutes?' she asks, waiting as they nod and discreetly disappear.

Albie looks up at her voice. She notices for the first time what a terrible state he is in, his clothes rumpled and his eyes bloodshot. He looks like hell. 'I didn't know about Lillian,' he says, tears welling in his eyes. 'I didn't know.'

She joins him at the table. 'I'm so sorry, Albie. I tried to get in touch with you but I had no idea where you were.' She covers his hand with her own.

'I can't believe she's gone.' He slumps further down in the chair. 'I thought we had more time. All these years when I could have been there for her . . . but I couldn't do it.'

Maggie sighs. She doesn't know how to console him.

'I tried, but it was always too hard to face her, to stay close, knowing what I had done. It was the guilt. It festered inside me.'

'I don't understand,' says Maggie. 'What had you done?'

Albie rubs his face with his hands. He looks even worse close up. Maggie wonders where he's been all these months. Something tells her it's nowhere good.

'She asked me to find her something beautiful.'

'Who did?'

'Lillian.'

'Right.' Maggie isn't following. She decides it might be best just to let him ramble.

'And I did. I found a flint. Arrow-shaped with a flame of orange at its core. It was perfect.'

She is still completely lost, but she nods encouragingly.

'I was going to take it to her in her room, but then I saw her in the gardens, admiring the roses. She turned and began to walk towards the meadow. I followed. I was so excited to show it to her. I called out, but she didn't hear. She didn't stop. She just kept going, through the meadow and on into the woods, walking so fast, I thought I'd lost her.'

Maggie frowns. She doesn't know what Albie is talking about, but she senses she shouldn't interrupt.

'And then I came upon them. They were standing among the trees.' Albie swallows. 'At first I thought they were fighting. I thought he was hurting her and I was about to step forward and tell him to get his hands off her . . . but then I saw that I was wrong. They weren't fighting. They were kissing.' Albie wrings his hands. 'I sat there for ages after they'd gone. I sat on a tree trunk in a daze. I saw a pile of cigarette butts – too many for just one day – and I realised that it couldn't have been the first time they had met in the woods like that. It must have been going on for ages, perhaps all summer. And I knew then that he was going to take Lillian away. I knew he was going to steal the one good thing in my life.'

'You mean Jack?'

Albie can't look at her, but he nods. 'It was only as I stood to leave that I saw it. It was lying on the ground near the tree trunk: his lighter, staring up at me. *Boldness be my friend*, it said.' He lets out a bitter laugh. 'It seemed like a sign.'

Maggie stares at her father, sitting at the kitchen table so shrunken in on himself, and understanding finally dawns. '*You* had the lighter. You set the fire.'

'I couldn't let him take her away from us.' Albie leans back in the chair, defeat written on his face. 'It was all there in the room. A few paint-covered rags. A little turpentine. There was a sheet of paper on the table. I was going to use that too but then I saw Lillian's handwriting. It was a love letter – to him. I stuffed it in my pocket – I wanted to make sure that he would never have it – and I put a flame to the rags and threw them into a corner.' Albie rubs his hand over his face. 'The fire took so quickly – too quickly. I panicked. I left the room, locking it from the outside, I think just on sheer instinct, so no one would see what I had done, and then I ran into the garden.'

Maggie doesn't interrupt. She is both spellbound and horrified by Albie's confession.

'I was going to run away. I knew the whole house would go up if the fire wasn't put out.'

'What happened?'

'Bentham was outside, with the dog. Monty was going crazy, trying to pull him on his lead round towards the arboretum. Bentham saw me and he must have known from my face that something was terribly wrong.

'He came and shook me out of my panic and I told him – I told him I thought there was a fire in the nursery. I dragged him round to the outside window of the turret room and the dog was still going crazy as we peered through.' Albie's face is ashen with the memory. 'But it was then that we heard her. Calling for help, from inside the painted room.

And it was then that I knew I had done the most terrible thing of all.'

Albie puts his head in his hands. 'I didn't know she was in there. I never saw her.'

Maggie reaches out and squeezes Albie's arm. She can see from his tortured look that he is spilling long-held secrets he has never told a soul before.

'It was Jack who saved her. He broke down the door and pulled her out of that burning room with his own bare hands. And it was Bentham who saved the house. He smashed the window and put out the fire with the pump – him and then Blackmore the gardener, who had heard the racket and came to help. Everyone in the house, Mrs Hill, Sarah, my father. They all came and helped, using anything they could to carry water from the fountain. And I just stood there, useless . . . doing nothing. Watching. Paralysed by fear and guilt.'

Maggie squeezes Albie's hand again. She tries to think of something comforting to say. 'You were just a child.'

Albie shakes his head, miserably. 'I got my wish. The artist left and Lillian stayed.'

Maggie's mind has caught on a detail from Albie's story. 'Lillian's letter. What did you do with it?'

Albie's eyes are bloodshot when he looks up at her. 'I left it on your grandfather's desk. I wanted him to know. I thought he might . . . he might change if he understood how close he had come to losing her.'

Maggie nods. It makes sense: the letter she'd found jammed at the back of Charles's desk, thrust there by her angry grandfather. It must have remained there, forgotten, for all those years, until she'd come upon it by chance.

'But father didn't change. He held Lillian like a prisoner, dangling Helena's care like a prize she had to earn, right up until the day of his stroke.'

'And you never told Lillian the truth?'

Albie shakes his head. 'She never knew. She thought it was Charles.' He looks up at Maggie, the anguish clear on his face. 'I tried so hard to be a good son to her, but I couldn't bear to see her sadness – to know what I had stolen from her. I'd come to visit with the very best intentions, but the guilt always got the better of me. It always drove me away, eventually. Over the years, it became easier to stay away than face what I had done to her. I couldn't bear to think about the happiness I had stolen from her.'

Maggie stares at Albie and understands, for the first time, how tortured her father is. What she had thought of as careless indifference to Lillian and the problems of Cloudesley, she now sees as something altogether different. Her father has a channel of guilt and pain running like a rich seam through his veins. 'Oh, Dad,' she says, squeezing his hand. Maggie is at a loss for words. 'What a terrible thing to live with.'

Albie looks up at her, his eyes swimming with tears. 'Do you think she would have forgiven me, if I'd ever had the courage to tell her?'

Maggie sighs. 'I don't know. I'd like to think so. You were just a kid.' But then she thinks about the painted room. And she thinks about Jack's thwarted career. She thinks of an intense love affair cut short and she knows she can't be certain what Lillian would have felt and thought, had she known the truth. 'It's done now,' she says. 'Lillian isn't here to forgive you. But I think it's probably time that you tried to forgive yourself.'

Albie doesn't say anything else and they sit in silence, the far-off sounds of the party echoing down the long corridor towards them.

'I read about the room,' Albie says after a long time. 'It's amazing what you're doing here.'

'Thank you.' She thinks for a moment. 'Would you like to see it?' Albie looks at her, a little boy's fear written on his face. 'I don't know if you could face it, but Jack Fincher is here, too. He came for the opening.'

Albie looks away from her, down into his lap.

'You're right that you can't apologise to Lillian,' she adds gently, 'but perhaps you could find some peace in talking to Jack?'

Albie looks up at her and then nods. 'You're very like her, you know.'

Maggie gives a small smile. 'Thank you.'

Maggie watches nervously from the door as Albie approaches Jack. She sees the way her father walks across the room, slowly, cautiously, his eyes scanning the painted walls, his gaze taking in the extravagant, jewelled feathers spread across the ceiling. As he reaches the window seat, he hesitates. She sees Jack glance up, then double-take at the sight of Albie. Albie says something, then holds out his hand. A soft smile breaks across Jack's face. Albie clasps the older man's ruined hand in his own, then settles on the window seat beside Jack. Albie turns to the older man and bows his head as he begins to speak.

Turning away from the scene, she finds Will waiting for her. 'Do you have a minute?'

'Yes, of course.'

He leads her out onto the terrace where they move to the far end, away from the milling crowds of guests. Maggie leans against the balustrade and looks up at the house towering before her. 'It's gone all right, hasn't it?'

'It's gone brilliantly.'

'I don't think I could have done any of this without you.'

'Yes, you could.'

She shakes her head.

Will shifts his weight from foot to foot, looking suddenly uncomfortable. 'That's what I want to talk to you about. The job I accepted off Lillian, well, it doesn't really exist anymore, does it?'

'No,' says Maggie, a feeling of foreboding coming over her. 'But we still need you.'

'No, you don't. You've got the professionals on your side now, and more than enough workers and volunteers ready and willing to get stuck in around here. I think half the village has signed up to help in the gardens alone. It feels like it's the right time for me to leave.'

Maggie stares at him, lost for words. 'But . . . but what if I don't want you to go?'

'You've done it, Maggie. You've pulled it off. You've saved Cloudesley.'

'Yes, but not without your help.'

'Well, it was my pleasure . . . mostly,' he teases with a small smile. 'What will you do?'

Maggie shrugs. 'I don't know. I haven't had time to think much beyond handling Lillian's probate and the restoration of the room.'

'You've done your duty. More than.' Will holds her gaze. 'You don't have to stay here, not if you don't want to. Haven't you wondered,' he adds gently, 'if it isn't time for you to stop caretaking someone else's legacy and start creating your own?'

She shrugs. 'Perhaps.' She thinks of the piles of sketches and the tentative paintings she has started over the last few weeks, working late into the night, the first feverish seeds of creativity building inside her again.

Will nods encouragingly. 'There's a big world out there waiting for you. The door is open.'

'I think I'm a little afraid to leave. I seem to have an uncanny ability to make a wonderful mess of things. Maybe

I should stay here in this bubble and carry on Lillian's work.'

Will nods. 'I understand, but I think that would be a shame.' He clears his throat. 'If you do decide to re-join the rest of us, perhaps you'd give me a call sometime? We could go for a drink?'

Maggie nods, not trusting herself to speak.

Will hesitates a moment before adding, 'I was wrong, you know. You're nothing like Albie.'

Maggie leans against the stone balustrade and listens to his retreating footsteps. She looks out across the gardens, all the way to the woods beyond. There is nothing she can do to stop the tears falling, blurring the meadow and the trees into a hazy wash of yellows and greens.

CHAPTER 33

Maggie can hear the trees calling to her. Not the painted ones in the room that has so consumed her these past months, but the tall grey beeches standing in the woodland across the meadow.

She'd woken early, to heavy summer downpours, but after a quick breakfast and an hour or two spent sorting out the final odds and ends in her room and stuffing the last of her clothes into a large black suitcase, she feels a restlessness building to be outside.

Dragging the case down the giant curved staircase, she notices that the rain has stopped and the sun now glints through the cracks of the thinning clouds. And there, in the distance, is the sound of the wind moving through the trees, calling her. She's sure of it.

Maggie leaves the suitcase at the back door and pulls on her boots and a raincoat. Out on the terrace, a group of visitors stand near one of the volunteer guides, listening to the man's patter as he takes them through the history of the house. She smiles in greeting, then carries on down the stone steps and across the lawn.

The grass in the meadow is wet and the ground gives a little beneath her feet. The herd of alpacas that have taken up residence in the meadow graze in the far distance. Maggie cuts a path towards the distant stile, watching as a flock of starlings takes flight, swooping up from the earth and across the bone-coloured sky until they come to settle in the treetops.

Stepping into the woods, Maggie senses the shift in atmosphere; here the air is a little cleaner, the light a little softer, glancing off the smooth, silver-grey trunks and dancing in the green canopy. She breathes the trees' exhalation, takes it in and makes it her own, inhales the moist-earth scent rising up from beneath her boots and fills her lungs. The leaves rustle in the breeze, dripping the last of the raindrops in a steady beat.

She treads carefully, stepping over thick tree roots, cast out like coiled ropes, anchoring the trees. For once her mind is clear. She's not thinking of contractors and bills or plans and progress. Among the trees, Maggie loses herself, allowing her feet to lead her in whichever direction they please. This place, she knows, is her home; as familiar to her as the embrace of an old friend, and all around, her own invisible roots snaking out, anchoring her to the soil, the house, the hills around. In this moment, there is no place in the world she knows so well or loves as deeply.

Eventually she leaves the trees and joins up with the lane, walking the asphalt for a short distance before turning through the creaking wooden gate into the churchyard. It's a Monday morning and the place is empty – just rows of ancient grey headstones, floral tributes dotted here and there. The path among the graves is well trodden. Maggie follows it behind the church to a simple headstone that marks the place where Lillian has been buried.

She brushes spots of rain from a nearby bench and sits for a while, thinking about her grandmother. She wishes she could talk to Lillian about the painted room. She wishes she could understand, fully, what it meant to her, and reassure her that the legacy will be preserved.

She remembers talking with Jack all those months ago, when he had reminded her about life being fleeting, how its most beautiful moments are impermanent and hard to hold on to. But what Jack has achieved through his painting is something both astonishing and comforting. He has achieved the impossible: he has captured a host of bygone moments and ensured their longevity, long after the sun has set, or a tide turned, or a life passed. It is thanks to this legacy that the house remains and will continue to stand in these hills for many more years to come. The peacock-carved front doors will continue to open. Visitors will arrive and walk the rooms. The gardens will fill with children and laughter. She wishes she could tell Lillian how Cloudesley will thrive once more.

Sitting on the bench, she wonders what else she would tell Lillian, if she had the chance. Perhaps, she'd tell her that she's going to be OK; that she's no longer afraid of who she is or the mistakes she has made. That she's stronger now, thanks to her grandmother and everything she has left her – not just the painted room, but all the lessons she has taught her. Perhaps she would tell Lillian about the inspiration she's found for her own paintings, a new collection built from her experiences of life and loss over the past months. *Seize the life that was meant to be yours. Make it magnificent. No half measures.* She hears the echoes of Lillian's words and smiles.

Maggie stretches her arms up towards the sky. High above she sees a flock of birds soaring against a patch of blue. She stands and presses a hand to the cool headstone. *Thank you*, she says; the only words she knows she really needs to say.

It's as she turns to leave that she notices the object lying at the foot of her grandmother's headstone. A glint of silver-orange lying among the green grass. She bends down and picks it up, turning the stone over in her hand, her finger running over the smooth curves of an arrow-shaped flint with a perfect orange flame nestled at its core. Something beautiful. For Lillian.

Carefully, she returns the stone to the grave before making her way back to Cloudesley, and to the life awaiting her beyond the peacock-crested gates.

ACKNOWLEDGEMENTS

Heartfelt thanks to my agent, Sarah Lutyens, and my publishers Clare Hey and Vanessa Radnidge, who all helped to make this book far better than the one I initially gave them. Thank you to Rabab Adams, Olivia Barber, Jennifer Breslin, Jo Carpenter, Andrew Cattanach, Ella Chapman, Francesca Davies, Katie Espiner, Rebecca Gray, Sophie Hutton-Squire, Juliet Mahony, Christa Moffitt, Brigid Mullane, Daniel Pilkington, Justin Ractliffe, Louise Sherwin-Stark, Chris Sims, Isabel Staas, Lydia Tasker, Jennifer Wilson, Mel Winder and the talented teams at Orion and Hachette Australia who have worked their magic on *The Peacock Summer*. Thank you to all the booksellers out there who spend their days matching the right book to the right reader. Thank you to David Andrews at the National Trust for answering my various queries regarding the acquisition of old properties. And thank you to the Arvon Foundation, for the time and space to finish this novel at The Hurst in Shropshire.

Every book is a challenge to write, but this one hit a wall after a personal tragedy. For their guidance and counsel I thank the extraordinary Wendy Liu and Louise Adams. I owe love and gratitude to Gill Norman, John Norman, Will Norman, Jude Richell, Gracie Richell, Adam Simpson, Auriol Bishop, Alexis Kenny, Marthe le Prevost, Toni Byrne, Clare

Young, Emily Biesbroek, Steph Lees, Ilde Naismith-Beeley, Stephanie Goodwin, Sara Hutton-Potts, Saul Wordsworth, Fraser Tant, Karl Wilson and the "Hodder Girls". Thank you for your support, and for helping me to pick up the pieces.

I first talked to my husband, Matt, about this novel on one of our long drives to Melbourne, the kids in the back of the car and the open road ahead of us. While we no longer travel roads together, Matt continues to inspire me every day. I hope he would be proud of how we strive to live with his immense light and love in our hearts.

Finally, this book is dedicated to my sister, Jess. Everyone needs a 'Jess' in their lives; someone to make you laugh till you cry, and hold your hand on the darkest days. You are still the only person I feel brave enough to share my first drafts with. Thank you – for everything.